EVERYMAN, I will go with thee,

and be thy guide,

In thy most need to go by thy side

Great Tales of Detection

NINETEEN STORIES
CHOSEN BY
DOROTHY L. SAYERS

DENT: LONDON
EVERYMAN'S LIBRARY

This book if bound as a paperback is
subject to the condition that it may
not be issued on loan or otherwise
except in its original binding

No. 928   Hardback ISBN 0 460 00928 1
No. 1928   Paperback ISBN 0 460 01928 7

INTRODUCTION

THE expression 'Detective Story,' though still loosely used to describe any tale dealing with crime and detectives, has acquired of late years a narrower, specialized meaning. Careful writers now reserve it for those stories of crime and detection in which the interest lies in the setting of a problem and its solution by logical means. Psychological studies of the criminal mind are more properly called 'crime stories'; while criminological problems whose solutions are arbitrarily revealed by coincidence or accident, or by straightforward explanations by the author, are styled 'mysteries' or 'thrillers.' Although, theoretically, there is no very good reason why a problem story should not be written about some subject other than crime, yet the detective story is, historically, an offshoot of the story of crime and sensation, and retains the marks of its origin: its intellectual structure is embellished by the emotional elements of horror, moral indignation, and excitement common to all types of crime literature.

It took some time for the detective story, as we know it, to establish itself as a specialized branch of crime fiction. We find sporadic examples of it in Oriental folk-tales, in the Apocryphal Books of the Old Testament, in the play-scene in *Hamlet*; while Aristotle in his *Poetics* puts forward observations about dramatic plot-construction which are applicable to-day to the construction of a detective mystery. But the story in which the logical problem is recognized as the main source of interest is, for practical purposes, the invention of the last ninety years. Even within this period it was only by slow degrees that the most important principle of the modern detective story was isolated and generally accepted: the principle which we know as the 'Fair-Play Rule.'

I say 'isolated and generally accepted,' because the fair-play rule was, on two occasions, discovered and applied quite early in the period. In three at least of Edgar Allan Poe's stories, published in the 'forties, the essential clues are all collected and set before the reader *before* the detective makes any deductions from them. Again, and apparently quite independently, Wilkie Collins hit upon the same method of narration in *The Moonstone* (1868). But neither critics nor imitators seem to have grasped at the time the essential difference between these stories and other stories dealing with the exploits of detectives. Not until the present century did readers, helped by such able critics as G. K. Chesterton and Father Ronald Knox, learn to make the observance of the fair-play rule the test of quality in a detective story.

The brilliant experiments of Edgar Allan Poe have something Melchizedek-like about them; in a literary sense they are, to all intents and purposes, without beginning or descent, and it is difficult to show that they derive from anything but his own analytical mind, which he enjoyed exercising upon real or invented criminological problems. Nor do they appear to have exercised any great immediate literary influence. Poe's style, at once harsh and affected, was against him; and although he himself says that his object in writing these stories was 'to depict some very remarkable features in the character of' his detective, Dupin, his character-drawing was not sufficiently vivid or sympathetic to capture the fancy of the common reader. Yet he gave us the working model of the Holmes-Watson combination and of that opposition between the conventional policeman and the unconventional amateur which was later to become a commonplace of detective fiction. He also established the two great formulae for the 'surprise' solution, by way of the unexpected means (*Murders in the Rue Morgue*) and the most unlikely person (*Thou Art the Man*), and, in *The Purloined Letter*, pointed the way to the solution achieved by psychological, rather than material, clues.

During the following four decades, however, the main development of the detective story lay along the lines of the English 'sensational novel' of Dickens, Collins, and Le Fanu, and the French *roman policier* of Gaboriau.

Now the main difference between these writers and Poe is, put crudely and plainly, that he was a short-story writer and they were novelists. Recent improvements in police organization on both sides of the Channel had aroused a widespread general interest in detective problems, but both in England and in France this particular interest was grafted on to the main stock of the novel of adventure and the novel of contemporary bourgeois manners. The writers approach the subject in the spirit of the novelist: however complicated the problem, they never present the story as an isolated episode existing solely in virtue of its relation to the mechanics of detection. They are interested in the social background, in manners and morals, in the depiction and interplay of character; their works have a three-dimensional extension in time and space; they all, in their various ways, offer some kind of 'criticism of life.' Dickens, delighting in humour and humanity; Gaboriau, wittily depicting the life of the French provincial town and interrupting the progress of the detection in order to go back and retell the story from the emotional point of view of the murderer; Le Fanu, with his emphasis on the picturesque and romantic and his masterly evocation of an atmosphere of spiritual evil; Collins, solidly preoccupied with such important social questions as the inequalities of the marriage law and the legal position of illegitimate children; all conceive of the 'mystery' as a constructional element in a work of universal scope, and view their characters in relation to a life outside the limits of the plot. Even in *The Moonstone*, in which the human interest is most rigidly subordinated to the plot-structure, the handling is unmistakably that of a novelist; Poe might have constructed the impeccable 'fair-play' plot, but he could never have surrounded it with such suggestive and rounded studies of life and character as Rachel Verinder, Gabriel Betteredge, and Rosanna Spearman.

In this rich and complex structure which we know as the 'sensation novel' of the 'sixties, contemporaries naturally failed to single out the element which was new in European literature or to see the possibilities of special development inherent in the fair-play plot. Lesser exponents imitated, as usual, the worst qualities of the masters. They grasped the rough idea of a secret, a sensation, a surprise solution; what escaped them was the importance of the logical elements in the unravelling of the mystery. By piling secret on secret and shock on shock and leaving the solution to chance coincidence, they succeeded in debasing the sensation novel until it became as vulgar, trivial, and unwholesome as its worst enemies had ever thought it. Good novelists, now earnestly tackling religious, social, moral, and political questions, would have nothing to do with it, and it was left for hack writers to concoct, ever more thick and slab, the hotchpotch of murders, bigamies, lost wills, missing heirs, impersonations, thefts, frauds, and sensational coincidences, to tickle the undiscriminating palate in defiance of sense and decency.

When, towards the end of the century, Conan Doyle came to put new life into detective fiction and lift it once more to a plane where self-respecting readers could take notice of it, it is significant that his great success was achieved in short-story form. True, the first Sherlock Holmes tale was, in its material aspect, a brief novel, with its formal structure modelled upon Gaboriau (*Study in Scarlet*, 1887). But he is the spiritual heir, not of Gaboriau, and still less of Dickens, Collins, or Le Fanu, but of Poe. Holmes and Watson (whoever may have been their prototypes in real life) are Dupin and his friend made human and lovable. Brilliantly as they are conceived, they do not belong to the wide and complex world of the novel, but to the more restricted field of the short story. They are static figures; after forty years they have not aged or developed in any essential manner, and, despite all ingenious speculation about the number of Dr. Watson's marriages, they remain men with no private lives. Again, the social background and the minor characters are sketched in with no more elaboration than is strictly necessary to the plot. If we compare, for example, *No Name* with *The Hound of the Baskervilles* we realize at once that it is something more than a difference in wordage that makes the one a novel and the other an expanded short story.

On the other hand, Conan Doyle does not invariably follow Poe's stern example in laying *all* the clues before the reader: over and over again, Holmes presents his deductions first and his observations after.

> 'How do you know that he values it [the pipe] highly?' I asked.
> 'Well, I should put the original cost of the pipe at seven-and-six-pence. Now it has, you see, been twice mended: once in the wooden stem and once in the amber. Each of these mends, done, as you observe, with silver bands, must have cost more than the pipe did originally. The man must value the pipe highly when he prefers to patch it up rather than buy a new one with the same money.'
>
> *The Yellow Face.*

'Fair play' would have described the pipe and its repairs first and given the detective's conclusions only after the reader had had the opportunity of drawing them for himself. Poe sometimes allows Dupin to let off detective fireworks in this arbitrary manner, as in the famous 'thought-reading' passage in *The Rue Morgue*, but with him they are incidental decorations only, whereas Conan Doyle frequently allows them to intrude into the investigation of the central problem.

Thus, the Sherlock Holmes stories, in a sense, miss the great qualities both of Poe and of the great sensation novelists, having neither the analytical purity of the one nor the wide human range of the others. Yet Doyle's contribution to detective fiction is of enormous importance. His style is clear, witty, workmanlike, and persuasive, free from violent sensationalism on the one hand and from academic pomposity on the other; his characters, within their limitations, have the breath of life in them and command belief and enthusiastic affection; finally, he initiates the reader into the romantic adventure of the intellect, exciting him, not by a multiplication of shocks and horrors, but by contemplation of 'the great issues that may hang from a bootlace.' Poe had been too abstract, the sensation novelists too emotional; but now it became possible for the detective story to win the heart of the public in its own right as a problem.

The immediate result was a huge demand for more stories of this kind and a stimulation of the reader's intellectual powers. People began eagerly to observe phenomena for themselves and make their own deductions. They became more critical and demanded from detective writers an increased regard for technical accuracy. Doctors complained of sketchy medical detail; policemen of infractions of official etiquette; lawyers of impossible court scenes and indefensible tamperings with the rules of evidence. Writers, hastening to comply with these requirements, found huge stores of material ready and waiting to be used. The possibilities of science were explored: L. T. Meade, in collaboration first with Clifford Halifax and later with Robert Eustace, wrote the long series of tales beginning with *Stories from the Diary of a Doctor* (1893) and ending with *The Sorceress of the Strand* (1902), and this paved the way for R. Austin Freeman and the modern scientific detective story. In 1913, Frank Froest, an ex-superintendent of Scotland Yard, wrote *The Grell Mystery* along the lines of real-life detective methods; and after him came others—Freeman Wills Crofts, J. J. Connington, John Rhode, Henry Wade, E. R. Punshon— to make the policeman the hero, instead of the butt, of detective fiction. Legal technicalities were exploited: the laws of marriage and inheritance, the peculiar pleas of *autrefois acquit* and *autrefois convict*; the custom of gavelkind and the intricacies of the law of entail. Settings were chosen (such as railways, artists' studios, ancient universities) in which special local knowledge played its part in propounding and solving the problem. New discoveries in all spheres (wireless telephony, 'heavy air,' the new barbituric compounds, invisible rays, infra-red photography, Freudian psychology) were pressed into the service to bring about a murder or a discovery. As the public became familiar with the technique of detection by finger-prints, analysis of bloodstains, tests for poison, micro-scopic examination of bullets, and so forth, the fictional machinery was elaborated to keep pace with the intensive education of the reader's mind. The fair-play rule came to be established; and it was finally accepted that, while the clues must be shown and the solution reached by reasonable deduc-tion, yet the writer might assume the reader to be acquainted with *any* established and recorded fact, however obscure or recently discovered.

Though it was no doubt highly necessary to achieve this perfection of technique, the result was that the detective story became over-intellectualized. The human interest was lost in the mechanical ingenuities of the plot; and since any com-petent craftsman could hammer together a problem of this kind, the genre once again began to be neglected by the genuine literary artists. Though much of the best detective work was produced in novel form, the technique was still that of the short story 'with a twist in the tail,' and everything—more especially psychological probability—was sacrificed to the 'surprise ending.'

A few writers, such as E. C. Bentley and A. E. W. Mason, still remembered that they were novelists and strove hard to keep the detective story in touch with life; but these were rare exceptions. It became axiomatic that the great romantic emotions were out of place in detective fiction, so that we observed the extraordinary phenomenon of a whole literature based upon a hypothesis of crime and violence and yet abstain-ing from any serious treatment of the sins and passions—particularly the sexual passions—which commonly form the motives for violent crime. H. C. Bailey, indeed, founded his 'Mr. Fortune' stories on a genuine morbid psychology, while G. K. Chesterton—a voice crying in the wilderness—succeeded, almost alone, in bringing the name of God into a detective story without making it sound like a blasphemy. But the mass of writers shrank from any profound treatment of the larger emotions, and preferred to handle their characters as mere chess-pieces endowed with conventional attributes.

Now, no kind of fiction can survive for very long cut off from the great interests of humanity and from the main stream of contemporary literature. Many readers complained they 'couldn't read detective stories' because the characters were uninteresting and the writing was uninspired. It looked as though the time had come to revert—but this time with the improved fair-play technique—to the Victorian conception of a detective story that should at the same time be a novel of character and manners; and the modern tendency is towards this kind of development. We can now handle the mechanical elements of the plot with the ease of long practice; we have yet to discover the best way of combining these with a serious artistic treatment of the psychological elements, so that the intellectual and the common man can find common ground for enjoyment in the mystery novel as once they did in Greek or Elizabethan tragedy.

The present collection of examples, being necessarily confined to short stories, cannot altogether do justice to those writers whose best work has been produced in novel form; it does, however, illustrate certain tendencies in the development of the detective story. Poe's *Purloined Letter* shows his criminal using his knowledge of psychology to bamboozle the police, and outwitted by a detective expert in drawing psychological inferences. In *The Biter Bit*, Wilkie Collins makes use of his technical legal knowledge within the narrow frame of the short story. The excerpt from Stevenson's *Master of Ballantrae* is an excellent early example of the 'perfect murder' that seeks to baffle justice by escaping beyond the range of legal and material proof. *The Man in the Passage* displays G. K. Chesterton both in his strength and weakness—the material clues a little neglected (though fairly presented as far as they go); the psychological clues illuminating by their insight into human nature and leading up to a brilliant surprise ending. E. C. Bentley's *Clever Cockatoo* and Ernest Bramah's *Ghost at Massingham Mansions* achieve a delicate balance of the humane and the intellectual elements. The purely scientific detective story is represented by *The Tea-Leaf* (by Edgar Jepson and

Robert Eustace) and *The Contents of a Mare's Nest* (a typical Austin Freeman). Thomas Burke's sinister tale, *The Hands of Mr. Ottermole*, creates so fine an atmosphere of horror that only at a second reading do we observe how fairly the clues are laid. Father Ronald Knox in *Solved by Inspection* deals in plain inference from observation. Agatha Christie, though better known through her 'Hercule Poirot' detective stories, provides in *Philomel Cottage* a modern specimen of the 'perfect murder' by psychological means for comparison with the Stevenson tale. Anthony Berkeley's *Avenging Chance* is the 'short story with a twist in the tail'; he is a master of this method, and subsequently elaborated this same plot to novel-length, giving it an extra twist in the process (*Poisoned Chocolates Case*). In *The Sleeping-Car Express* and *The Elusive Bullet*, Freeman Wills Crofts and John Rhode make use of their expert technical knowledge of railways and ballistics, respectively. *The Image in the Mirror* is my own attempt to make fair use of a motif which has sometimes been used unfairly to spring a surprise which the reader could not have foreseen; here the clue is openly and even ostentatiously trailed for the reader who happens to have dabbled about among popular works on biology. Henry Wade's *A Matter of Luck* is the kind of story in which the reader is shown the crime first and the detection afterwards; it shows his realistic handling of police methods. In *Superfluous Murder*, Milward Kennedy uses the method first popularised by R. Austin Freeman of showing the method of the crime first and the method of detection after; adding a cynical twist in the modern manner. H. C. Bailey's *Yellow Slugs* is not only first-class detection but also a characteristic expression of his passionate hatred of spiritual cruelty. Finally, in *The Nail and The Requiem*, C. Daly King, the American psychologist who wrote the curiously Peacockian 'Obelist' novels, presents a short story; so that we end, where we began, in America.

DOROTHY L. SAYERS.

MAY 1936

CONTENTS

ACKNOWLEDGMENTS

The Editor is grateful to the following for permission to include copyright material:

Mr. Lloyd Osbourne and Charles Scribners Sons for the extract *Was it Murder?* from *The Master of Ballantrae* by R. L. Stevenson.

Mr. G. K. Chesterton and Cassell & Co. Ltd. for *The Man in the Passage* from *The Wisdom of Father Brown*.

Mr. E. C. Bentley for *The Clever Cockatoo*.

Mr. Ernest Bramah for *The Ghost at Massingham Mansions* from *The Eyes of Max Carrados*.

Mr. Edgar Jepson for *The Tea-Leaf*.

Dr. R. Austin Freeman and Hodder & Stoughton Ltd. for *The Contents of a Mare's Nest* from *Fifty Thorndyke Stories*.

Mr. Thomas Burke for *The Hands of Mr. Ottermole*.

The Rev. Father Ronald Knox for *Solved by Inspection*.

Mrs. Agatha Christie and William Collins Sons & Co. Ltd. for *Philomel Cottage* from *The Listerdale Mystery*.

Mr. A. B. Cox (Anthony Berkeley) for *The Avenging Chance*.

Mr. Freeman Wills Crofts for *The Mystery of the Sleeping-Car Express*.

Hughes Massie & Co. for *The Elusive Bullet* by John Rhode.

Miss Dorothy L. Sayers for *The Image in the Mirror* from *Hangman's Holiday*.

Mr. Henry Wade and Constable & Co. Ltd. for *A Matter of Luck* from *Policeman's Lot*.

Mr. Milward Kennedy for *Superfluous Murder*.

Mr. H. C. Bailey and Victor Gollancz Ltd. for *The Yellow Slugs* from *Mr. Fortune Objects*.

Mr. C. Daly King for *The Episode of the Nail and the Requiem* from *The Curious Mr. Tarrant*.

EDGAR ALLAN POE

THE PURLOINED LETTER

Nil sapientiae odiosius acumine nimio.—SENECA.

AT Paris, just after dark one gusty evening in the autumn of 18—, I was enjoying the twofold luxury of meditation and a meerschaum, in company with my friend, C. Auguste Dupin, in his little back library or book-closet, *au troisième*, No. 33 Rue Dunôt, Faubourg St. Germain. For one hour at least we had maintained a profound silence; while each, to any casual observer, might have seemed intently and exclusively occupied with the curling eddies of smoke that oppressed the atmosphere of the chamber. For myself, however, I was mentally discussing certain topics which had formed matter for conversation between us at an earlier period of the evening; I mean the affair of the Rue Morgue, and the mystery attending the murder of Marie Rogêt. I looked upon it, therefore, as something of a coincidence when the door of our apartment was thrown open and admitted our old acquaintance, Monsieur G——, the prefect of the Parisian police.

We gave him a hearty welcome; for there was nearly half as much of the entertaining as of the contemptible about the man, and we had not seen him for several years. We had been sitting in the dark, and Dupin now arose for the purpose of lighting a lamp, but sat down again, without doing so, upon G——'s saying that he had called to consult us, or rather to ask the opinion of my friend, about some official business which had occasioned a great deal of trouble.

'If it is any point requiring reflection,' observed Dupin, as he forbore to enkindle the wick, 'we shall examine it to better purpose in the dark.'

'That is another of your odd notions,' said the prefect, who had a fashion of calling everything 'odd' that was beyond his comprehension, and thus lived amid an absolute legion of 'oddities.'

'Very true,' said Dupin, as he supplied his visitor with a pipe, and rolled towards him a comfortable chair.

I

'And what is the difficulty now?' I asked. 'Nothing more in the assassination way, I hope?'

'Oh, no; nothing of that nature. The fact is, the business is *very* simple indeed, and I make no doubt that we can manage it sufficiently well ourselves; but then I thought Dupin would like to hear the details of it, because it is so excessively *odd*.'

'Simple and odd,' said Dupin.

'Why, yes; and not exactly that, either. The fact is, we have all been a good deal puzzled because the affair *is* so simple, and yet baffles us altogether.'

'Perhaps it is the very simplicity of the thing which puts you at fault,' said my friend.

'What nonsense you *do* talk!' replied the prefect, laughing heartily.

'Perhaps the mystery is a little *too* plain,' said Dupin.

'Oh, good heavens! who ever heard of such an idea?'

'A little *too* self-evident.'

'Ha! ha! ha!—ha! ha! ha!—ho! ho! ho!' roared our visitor, profoundly amused; 'oh, Dupin, you will be the death of me yet!'

'And what, after all, *is* the matter on hand?' I asked.

'Why, I will tell you,' replied the prefect as he gave a long, steady, and contemplative puff, and settled himself in his chair. 'I will tell you in a few words; but, before I begin, let me caution you that this is an affair demanding the greatest secrecy, and that I should most probably lose the position I now hold, were it known that I confided it to any one.'

'Proceed,' said I.

'Or not,' said Dupin.

'Well, then; I have received personal information, from a very high quarter, that a certain document of the last importance has been purloined from the royal apartments. The individual who purloined it is known; this beyond a doubt; he was seen to take it. It is known, also, that it still remains in his possession.'

'How is this known?' asked Dupin.

'It is clearly inferred,' replied the prefect, 'from the nature of the document, and from the non-appearance of certain results which would at once arise from its passing *out* of the robber's possession—that is to say, from his employing it as he must design in the end to employ it.'

'Be a little more explicit,' I said.

'Well, I may venture so far as to say that the paper gives its holder a certain power in a certain quarter where such power is immensely valuable.' The prefect was fond of the cant of diplomacy.

'Still I do not quite understand,' said Dupin.

'No? Well; the disclosure of the document to a third person, who shall be nameless, would bring in question the honour of a personage of most exalted station; and this fact gives the holder of the document an ascendancy over the illustrious personage whose honour and peace are so jeopardized.'

'But this ascendancy,' I interposed, 'would depend upon the robber's knowledge of the loser's knowledge of the robber. Who would dare——?'

'The thief,' said G——, 'is the minister D——, who dares all things, those unbecoming as well as those becoming a man. The method of the theft was not less ingenious than bold. The document in question—a letter, to be frank—had been received by the personage robbed while alone in the royal boudoir. During its perusal she was suddenly interrupted by the entrance of the other exalted personage from whom especially it was her wish to conceal it. After a hurried and vain endeavour to thrust it in a drawer, she was forced to place it, open as it was, upon a table. The address, however, was uppermost, and, the content thus unexposed, the letter escaped notice. At this juncture enters the minister D——. His lynx eye immediately perceives the paper, recognizes the handwriting of the address, observes the confusion of the personage addressed, and fathoms her secret. After some business transactions, hurried through in his ordinary manner, he produces a letter somewhat similar to the one in question, opens it, pretends to read it, and then places it in close juxtaposition to the other. Again he converses, for some fifteen minutes, upon the public affairs. At length, in taking leave, he takes also from the table the letter to which he had no claim. Its rightful owner saw, but, of course, dared not call attention to the act, in the presence of the third personage who stood at her elbow. The minister decamped, leaving his own letter—one of no importance—upon the table.'

'Here, then,' said Dupin to me, 'you have precisely what you demand to make the ascendancy complete—the robber's knowledge of the loser's knowledge of the robber.'

'Yes,' replied the prefect; 'and the power thus attained has, for some months past, been wielded for political purposes to a very dangerous extent. The personage robbed is more thoroughly convinced, every day, of the necessity of reclaiming her letter. But this, of course, cannot be done openly. In fine, driven to despair, she has committed the matter to me.'

'Than whom,' said Dupin, amid a perfect whirlwind of smoke, 'no more sagacious agent could, I suppose, be desired or even imagined.'

'You flatter me,' replied the prefect, 'but it is possible that some such opinion may have been entertained.'

'It is clear,' said I, 'as you observe, that the letter is still in the possession of the minister; since it is this possession, and not any employment of the letter, which bestows the power. With the employment the power departs.'

'True,' said G——; 'and upon this conviction I proceeded. My first care was to make thorough search of the minister's hôtel; and here my chief embarrassment lay in the necessity of searching without his knowledge. Beyond all things, I have been warned of the danger which would result from giving him reason to suspect our design.'

'But,' said I, 'you are quite *au fait* in these investigations. The Parisian police have done this thing often before.'

'Oh, yes; and for this reason I did not despair. The habits of the minister gave me, too, a great advantage. He is frequently absent from home all night. His servants are by no means numerous. They sleep at a distance from their master's apartment, and, being chiefly Neapolitans, are readily made drunk. I have keys, as you know, with which I can open any chamber or cabinet in Paris. For three months a night has not passed, during the greater part of which I have not been engaged, personally, in ransacking the D—— Hôtel. My honour is interested, and, to mention a great secret, the reward is enormous. So I did not abandon the search until I had become fully satisfied that the thief is a more astute man than myself. I fancy that I have investigated every nook and corner of the premises in which it is possible that the paper can be concealed.'

'But is it not possible,' I suggested, 'that although the letter may be in possession of the minister, as it unquestionably is, he may have concealed it elsewhere than upon his own premises?'

'This is barely possible,' said Dupin. 'The present peculiar condition of affairs at court, and especially of those intrigues in which D—— is known to be involved, would render the instant availability of the document—its susceptibility of being produced at a moment's notice — a point of nearly equal importance with its possession.'

'Its susceptibility of being produced?' said I.

'That is to say of being *destroyed*,' said Dupin.

'True,' I observed; 'the paper is clearly then upon the premises. As for its being upon the person of the minister, we may consider that as out of the question.'

'Entirely,' said the prefect. 'He has been twice waylaid, as if by footpads, and his person rigorously searched under my own inspection.'

'You might have spared yourself this trouble,' said Dupin. 'D——, I presume, is not altogether a fool, and, if not, must have anticipated these waylayings, as a matter of course.'

'Not *altogether* a fool,' said G——; 'but then he's a poet, which I take to be only one remove from a fool.'

'True,' said Dupin, after a long and thoughtful whiff from his meerschaum, 'although I have been guilty of certain doggerel myself.'

'Why, the fact is we took our time, and we searched *everywhere*. I have had long experience in these affairs. I took the entire building, room by room; devoting the nights of a whole week to each. We examined, first, the furniture of each apartment. We opened every possible drawer; and I presume you know that, to a properly trained police agent, such a thing as a *secret* drawer is impossible. Any man is a dolt who permits a "*secret*" drawer to escape him in a search of this kind. The thing is *so* plain. There is a certain amount of bulk—of space—to be accounted for in every cabinet. Then we have accurate rules. The fiftieth part of a line could not escape us. After the cabinets we took the chairs. The cushions we probed with the fine long needles you have seen me employ. From the tables we removed the tops.'

'Why so?'

'Sometimes the top of a table, or other similarly arranged piece of furniture, is removed by the person wishing to conceal an article; then the leg is excavated, the article deposited within the cavity, and the top replaced. The bottoms and tops of bedposts are employed in the same way.'

'But could not the cavity be detected by sounding?' I asked.

'By no means, if, when the article is deposited, a sufficient wadding of cotton be placed around it. Besides, in our case, we were obliged to proceed without noise.'

'But you could not have removed—you could not have taken to pieces *all* articles of furniture in which it would have been possible to make a deposit in the manner you mention. A letter may be compressed into a thin spiral roll, not differing much in shape or bulk from a large knitting-needle, and in this form it might be inserted into the rung of a chair, for example. You did not take to pieces all the chairs?'

'Certainly not; but we did better—we examined the rungs of every chair in the hôtel, and, indeed, the jointings of every description of furniture, by the aid of a most powerful microscope. Had there been any traces of recent disturbance we should not have failed to detect it instantly. A single grain of gimlet-dust, for example, would have been as obvious as an apple. Any disorder in the gluing—any unusual gaping in the joints—would have sufficed to ensure detection.'

'I presume you looked to the mirrors, between the boards and the plates, and you probed the beds and the bed-clothes, as well as the curtains and carpets.'

'That of course; and when we had absolutely completed every particle of the furniture in this way, then we examined the house itself. We divided its entire surface into compartments, which we numbered, so that none might be missed; then we scrutinized each individual square inch throughout the premises, including the two houses immediately adjoining, with the microscope, as before.'

'The two houses adjoining!' I exclaimed; 'you must have had a great deal of trouble.'

'We had; but the reward offered is prodigious.'

'You include the *grounds* about the houses?'

'All the grounds are paved with brick. They gave us comparatively little trouble. We examined the moss between the bricks, and found it undisturbed.'

'You looked among D——'s papers, of course, and into the books of the library?'

'Certainly; we opened every package and parcel; we not only opened every book, but we turned over every leaf in each volume, not contenting ourselves with a mere shake, according to the fashion of some of our police officers. We also measured the thickness of every book-*cover*, with the most accurate admeasurement, and applied to each the most jealous scrutiny of the microscope. Had any of the bindings been recently meddled with, it would have been utterly impossible that the fact should have escaped observation. Some five or six volumes, just from the hands of the binder, we carefully probed longitudinally, with the needles.'

'You explored the floors beneath the carpets?'

'Beyond doubt. We removed every carpet, and examined the boards with the microscope.'

'And the paper on the walls?'

'Yes.'

'You looked into the cellars?'

'We did.'

'Then,' I said, 'you have been making a miscalculation, and the letter is *not* upon the premises, as you suppose.'

'I fear you are right there,' said the prefect. 'And now, Dupin, what would you advise me to do?'

'To make a thorough search of the premises.'

'That is absolutely needless,' replied G——. 'I am not more sure that I breathe than I am that the letter is not at the hôtel.'

'I have no better advice to give you,' said Dupin. 'You have, of course, an accurate description of the letter?'

'Oh, yes!' And here the prefect, producing a memoran-

dum book, proceeded to read aloud a minute account of the
internal, and especially of the external appearance of the
missing document.   Soon after finishing the perusal of this
description, he took his departure, more entirely depressed
in spirits than I had ever known the good gentleman before.

In about a month afterwards he paid us another visit,
and found us occupied very nearly as before.   He took a
pipe and a chair and entered into some ordinary conversation.   At length I said:

'Well, but G——, what of the purloined letter?   I presume you have at last made up your mind that there is no
such thing as overreaching the minister?'

'Confound him, say I—yes; I made the re-examination,
however, as Dupin suggested—but it was all labour lost, as
I knew it would be.'

'How much was the reward offered, did you say?' asked
Dupin.

'Why, a very great deal—a *very* liberal reward—I don't
like to say how much, precisely; but I *will* say, that I
wouldn't mind giving my individual cheque for fifty thousand francs to any one who could obtain me   that
letter.   The fact is, it is becoming of more and more importance every day; and the reward has been lately doubled.
If it were trebled, however, I could do no more than I have
done.'

'Why, yes,' said Dupin, drawlingly, between the whiffs of
his meerschaum, 'I really—think, G——, you have not
exerted yourself—to the utmost—in this matter.   You
might—do a little more, I think, eh?'

'How?—in what way?'

'Why — puff, puff — you might — puff, puff — employ
counsel in the matter, eh?—puff, puff, puff.   Do you remember the story they tell of Abernethy?'

'No; hang Abernethy!'

'To be sure! hang him and welcome.   But once upon a
time, a certain rich miser conceived the design of sponging
upon this Abernethy for a medical opinion.   Getting up,
for this purpose, an ordinary conversation in a private
company, he insinuated his case to the physician, as that
of an imaginary individual.

'"We will suppose," said the miser, "that his symptoms

are such and such; now, doctor, what would *you* have directed him to take?"

'"Take!" said Abernethy, "why, take *advice*, to be sure."'

'But,' said the prefect, a little discomposed, 'I am *perfectly* willing to take advice, and to pay for it. I would *really* give fifty thousand francs to any one who would aid me in the matter.'

'In that case,' replied Dupin, opening a drawer, and producing a cheque-book, 'you may as well fill me up a cheque for the amount mentioned. When you have signed it, I will hand you the letter.'

I was astounded. The prefect appeared absolutely thunderstricken. For some minutes he remained speechless and motionless, looking incredulously at my friend with open mouth, and eyes that seemed starting from their sockets: then, apparently recovering himself in some measure, he seized a pen, and after several pauses and vacant stares, finally filled up and signed a cheque for fifty thousand francs, and handed it across the table to Dupin. The latter examined it carefully and deposited it in his pocket-book; then, unlocking an *escritoire*, took thence a letter and gave it to the prefect. This functionary grasped it in a perfect agony of joy, opened it with a trembling hand, cast a rapid glance at its contents, and then, scrambling and struggling to the door, rushed at length unceremoniously from the room and from the house without having uttered a syllable since Dupin had requested him to fill up the cheque.

When he had gone, my friend entered into some explanations.

'The Parisian police,' he said, 'are exceedingly able in their way. They are persevering, ingenious, cunning, and thoroughly versed in the knowledge which their duties seem chiefly to demand. Thus, when G—— detailed to us his mode of searching the premises at the Hôtel D——, I felt entire confidence in his having made a satisfactory investigation—so far as his labours extended.'

'So far as his labours extended?' said I.

'Yes,' said Dupin. 'The measures adopted were not only the best of their kind, but carried out to absolute perfection. Had the letter been deposited within the range of their search, these fellows would, beyond a question, have found it.'

I merely laughed—but he seemed quite serious in all that he said.

'The measures, then,' he continued, 'were good in their kind, and well executed; their defect lay in their being inapplicable to the case, and to the man. A certain set of highly ingenious resources are, with the prefect, a sort of Procrustean bed, to which he forcibly adapts his designs. But he perpetually errs by being too deep or too shallow for the matter in hand; and many a schoolboy is a better reasoner than he. I knew one about eight years of age, whose success at guessing in the game of "even and odd" attracted universal admiration. This game is simple, and is played with marbles. One player holds in his hand a number of these toys, and demands of another whether that number is even or odd. If the guess is right, the guesser wins one; if wrong, he loses one. The boy to whom I allude won all the marbles of the school. Of course he had some principle of guessing; and this lay in mere observation and admeasurement of the astuteness of his opponents. For example, an arrant simpleton is his opponent, and, holding up his closed hand, asks, "Are they even or odd?" Our schoolboy replies "Odd," and loses; but upon the second trial he wins, for he then says to himself, "The simpleton had them even upon the first trial, and his amount of cunning is just sufficient to make him have them odd upon the second; I will therefore guess odd"—he guesses odd, and wins. Now, with a simpleton a degree above the first, he would have reasoned thus: "This fellow finds that in the first instance I guessed odd, and in the second he will propose to himself, upon the first impulse, a simple variation from even to odd, as did the first simpleton; but then a second thought will suggest that this is too simple a variation, and finally he will decide upon putting it even as before. I will therefore guess even"—he guesses even, and wins. Now this mode of reasoning in the schoolboy, whom his fellows term "lucky"—what, in its last analysis, is it?'

'It is merely,' I said, 'an identification of the reasoner's intellect with that of his opponent.'

'It is,' said Dupin; 'and upon inquiring of the boy by what means he effected the *thorough* identification in which his success consisted, I received answer as follows: "When I wish to find out how wise, or how stupid, or how good, or how wicked is any one, or what are his thoughts at the moment, I fashion the expression of my face, as accurately as possible, in accordance with the expression of his, and then wait to see what thoughts or sentiments arise in my mind or heart, as if to match or correspond with the expression." This response of the schoolboy lies at the bottom of all the spurious profundity which has been attributed to Rochefoucauld, to La Bruyère, to Machiavelli, and to Campanella.'

'And the identification,' I said, 'of the reasoner's intellect with that of his opponent depends, if I understand you aright, upon the accuracy with which the opponent's intellect is admeasured.'

'For its practical value it depends upon this,' replied Dupin; 'and the prefect and his cohort fail so frequently, first, by default of this identification, and, secondly, by ill-admeasurement, or rather through non-admeasurement, of the intellect with which they are engaged. They consider only their *own* ideas of ingenuity; and, in searching for anything hidden, advert only to the modes in which *they* would have hidden it. They are right in this much— that their own ingenuity is a faithful representative of that of *the mass*; but when the cunning of the individual felon is diverse in character from their own, the felon foils them, of course. This always happens when it is above their own, and very usually when it is below. They have no variation of principle in their investigations; at best, when urged by some unusual emergency, by some extraordinary reward, they extend or exaggerate their old modes of *practice*, without touching their principles. What, for example, in this case of D——, has been done to vary the principle of action? What is all this boring, and probing, and sounding, and scrutinizing with the microscope, and dividing the surface of the building into registered square inches— what is it all but an exaggeration *of the application* of the one principle or set of principles of search, which are based upon the one set of notions regarding human ingenuity, to which the prefect, in the routine of his duty, has been accustomed? Do you not see he has taken it for granted that *all* men proceed to conceal a letter—not exactly in a gimlet-hole bored in a chair-leg—but, at least, in *some* out-of-the-way hole or corner suggested by the same tenor of thought which would urge a man to secrete a letter in a gimlet-hole bored in a chair-leg? And do you not see also, that such *recherchés* nooks for concealment are adapted only for ordinary occasions, and would be adopted only by ordinary intellects; for, in all cases of concealment, a disposal of the article concealed — a disposal of it in this *recherché* manner—is, in the very first instance, presumable and presumed; and thus its discovery depends, not at all upon the acumen, but altogether upon the mere care, patience, and determination of the seekers; and where the case is of importance, or what amounts to the same thing in the policial eyes, when the reward is of magnitude, the qualities in question have *never* been known to fail. You will now understand what I meant in suggesting that, had the purloined letter been hidden anywhere within the limits of the prefect's examination—in other words, had the principle of its concealment been comprehended within the principles of the prefect—its discovery would have been a matter altogether beyond question. This functionary, however, has been thoroughly mystified; and the remote source of his defeat lies in the supposition that the minister is a fool, because he has acquired renown as a poet. All fools are poets—this the prefect *feels*; and he is merely guilty of a *non distributio medii* in thence inferring that all poets are fools.'

'But is this really the poet?' I asked. 'There are two brothers, I know; and both have attained reputation in letters. The minister, I believe, has written learnedly on the differential calculus. He is a mathematician, and no poet.'

'You are mistaken; I know him well; he is both. As poet *and* mathematician, he would reason well; as mere mathematician, he could not have reasoned at all, and thus would have been at the mercy of the prefect.'

'You surprise me,' I said, 'by these opinions, which have been contradicted by the voice of the world. You do not mean to set at naught the well-digested idea of centuries.

The mathematical reason has long been regarded as *the* reason *par excellence*.'

'"*Il y a à parier*,"' replied Dupin, quoting from Chamfort, '"*que toute idée publique, toute convention reçue, est une sottise, car elle a convenu au plus grand nombre.*" The mathematicians, I grant you, have done their best to promulgate the popular error to which you allude, and which is none the less an error for its promulgation as truth. With an art worthy a better cause, for example, they have insinuated the term "analysis" into application to algebra. The French are the originators of the particular deception; but if a term is of any importance—if words derive any value from applicability — then "analysis" conveys "algebra" about as much as, in Latin, "*ambitus*" implies "ambition," "*religio*" "religion," or "*homines honesti*" a set of *honourable* men.'

'You have a quarrel on hand, I see,' said I, 'with some of the algebraists of Paris; but proceed.'

'I dispute the availability, and thus the value, of that reason which is cultivated in any special form other than the abstractly logical. I dispute in particular the reason educed by mathematical study. The mathematics are the science of form and quantity; mathematical reasoning is merely logic applied to observation upon form and quantity. The great error lies in supposing that even the truths of what is called *pure* algebra are abstract or general truths. And this error is so egregious that I am confounded at the universality with which it has been received. Mathematical axioms are *not* axioms of general truth. What is true of *relation*—of form and quantity—is often grossly false in regard to morals, for example. In this latter science it is very usually *un*true that the aggregated parts are equal to the whole. In chemistry also the axiom fails. In the consideration of motive it fails; for two motives, each of a given value, have not necessarily a value when united, equal to the sum of their values apart. There are numerous other mathematical truths which are only truths within the limits of *relation*. But the mathematician argues, from his *finite truths*, through habit, as if they were of an absolute general applicability—as the world indeed imagines them to be.

'Bryant, in his very learned *Mythology*, mentions an analogous source of error, when he says that "although the pagan fables are not believed, yet we forget ourselves continually, and make inferences from them as existing realities." With the algebraists, however, who are pagans themselves, the "pagan fables" *are* believed, and the inferences are made, not so much through lapse of memory, as through an unaccountable addling of the brains. In short, I never yet encountered the mere mathematician who could be trusted out of equal roots, or one who did not clandestinely hold it as a point of his faith that x^2+px was absolutely and unconditionally equal to q. Say to one of these gentlemen, by way of experiment, if you please, that you believe occasions may occur where x^2+px is *not* altogether equal to q, and, having made him understand what you mean, get out of his reach as speedily as convenient, for beyond doubt he will endeavour to knock you down.

'I mean to say,' continued Dupin, while I merely laughed at his last observations, 'that if the minister had been no more than a mathematician, the prefect would have been under no necessity of giving me this cheque. I knew him, however, as both mathematician and poet, and my measures were adapted to his capacity, with reference to the circumstances by which he was surrounded. I knew him as a courtier, too, and as a bold *intrigant*. Such a man, I considered, could not fail to be aware of the ordinary policial modes of action. He could not have failed to anticipate—and events have proved that he did not fail to anticipate—the waylaying to which he was subjected. He must have foreseen, I reflected, the secret investigations of his premises. His frequent absences from home at night, which were hailed by the prefect as certain aids to his success, I regarded only as ruses, to afford opportunity for thorough search to the police, and thus the sooner to impress them with the conviction at which G——, in fact, did finally arrive—the conviction that the letter was not upon the premises. I felt, also, that the whole train of thought, which I was at some pains in detailing to you just now, concerning the invariable principle of policial action in searches for articles concealed—I felt that this whole train of thought would necessarily pass through the mind of the minister. It would imperatively lead him to despise all the ordinary *nooks* of concealment. *He* could not, I reflected, be so weak as not to see that the most intricate and remote recess of this hotel would be as open as his commonest closets to the eyes, to the probes, to the gimlets, and to the microscopes of the prefect. I saw, in fine, that he would be driven, as a matter of course, to *simplicity*, if not deliberately induced to it as a matter of choice. You will remember, perhaps, how desperately the prefect laughed when I suggested, upon our first interview, that it was just possible this mystery troubled him so much on account of its being so *very* self-evident.'

'Yes,' said I, 'I remember his merriment well. I really thought he would have fallen into convulsions.'

'The material world,' continued Dupin, 'abounds with very strict analogies to the immaterial; and thus some colour of truth has been given to the rhetorical dogma, that metaphor, or simile, may be made to strengthen an argument, as well as to embellish a description. The principle of the *vis inertiae*, for example, seems to be identical in physics and metaphysics. It is not more true in the former, that a large body is with more difficulty set in motion than a smaller one, and that its subsequent momentum is commensurate with this difficulty, than it is, in the latter, that intellects of the vaster capacity, while more forcible, more constant, and more eventful in their movements than those of inferior grade, are yet the less readily moved, and more embarrassed and full of hesitation in the first few steps of their progress. Again, have you ever noticed which of the street signs over the shop-doors are the most attractive of attention?'

'I have never given the matter a thought,' I said.

'There is a game of puzzles,' he resumed, 'which is played upon a map. One party playing requires another to find a given word—the name of town, river, state or empire—any word, in short, upon the motley and perplexed surface of the chart. A novice in the game generally seeks to embarrass his opponents by giving them the most minutely lettered names; but the adept selects such words as stretch, in large characters, from one end of the chart to the other. These, like the over-largely lettered signs and placards of the street, escape observation by dint of being excessively obvious; and here the physical oversight is precisely analogous with the moral inapprehension by which the intellect suffers to pass unnoticed those considerations which are too obtrusively and too palpably self-evident. But this is a point, it appears, somewhat above or beneath the understanding of the prefect. He never once thought it probable, or possible, that the minister had deposited the letter immediately beneath the nose of the whole world, by way of best preventing any portion of that world from perceiving it.

'But the more I reflected upon the daring, dashing, and discriminating ingenuity of D——; upon the fact that the document must always have been *at hand*, if he intended to use it to good purpose; and upon the decisive evidence, obtained by the prefect, that it was hidden within the limits of that dignitary's ordinary search—the more satisfied I became that, to conceal this letter, the minister had resorted to the comprehensive and sagacious expedient of not attempting to conceal it at all.

'Full of these ideas, I prepared myself with a pair of green spectacles, and called one fine morning, quite by accident, at the ministerial hôtel. I found D—— at home, yawning, lounging, and dawdling, as usual, and pretending to be in the last extremity of *ennui*. He is, perhaps, the most really energetic human being now alive—but that is only when nobody sees him.

'To be even with him, I complained of my weak eyes, and lamented the necessity of the spectacles, under cover of which I cautiously and thoroughly surveyed the whole apartment, while seemingly intent only upon the conversation of my host.

'I paid especial attention to a large writing-table near which he sat, and upon which lay confusedly some miscellaneous letters and other papers, with one or two musical instruments and a few books. Here, however, after a long and deliberate scrutiny, I saw nothing to excite particular suspicion.

'At length my eyes, in going the circuit of the room, fell upon a trumpery filigree card-rack of pasteboard, that hung dangling by a dirty blue ribbon, from a little brass knob just beneath the middle of the mantelpiece. In this rack, which had three or four compartments, were five or six visiting cards and a solitary letter. This last was much soiled and crumpled. It was torn nearly in two, across the middle—as if a design, in the first instance, to tear it entirely up as worthless, had been altered, or stayed, in the second. It had a large black seal, bearing the D—— cipher *very* conspicuously, and was addressed, in a diminutive female hand, to D——, the minister, himself. It was thrust carelessly, and even, as it seemed, contemptuously, into one of the uppermost divisions of the rack.

'No sooner had I glanced at this letter, than I concluded it to be that of which I was in search. To be sure, it was, to all appearance, radically different from the one of which the prefect had read us so minute a description. Here the seal was large and black, with the D—— cipher; there it was small and red, with the ducal arms of the S—— family. Here the address, to the minister, was diminutive and feminine; there the superscription, to a certain royal personage, was markedly bold and decided; the size alone formed a point of correspondence. But then the *radicalness* of these differences, which was excessive; the dirt; the soiled and torn condition of the paper, so inconsistent with the *true* methodical habits of D——, and so suggestive of a design to delude the beholder into an idea of the worthlessness of the document; these things, together with the hyperobtrusive situation of this document, full in the view of every visitor, and thus exactly in accordance with the conclusions at which I had previously arrived; these things, I say, were strongly corroborative of suspicion, in one who came with the intention to suspect.

'I protracted my visit as long as possible, and, while I maintained a most animated discussion with the minister, upon a topic which I knew well had never failed to interest and excite him, I kept my attention really riveted upon the letter. In this examination, I committed to memory its external appearance and arrangement in the rack; and also fell, at length, upon a discovery, which set at rest whatever trivial doubt I might have entertained. In scrutinizing the edges of the paper, I observed them to be more *chafed* than seemed necessary. They presented the *broken* appearance which is manifested when a stiff paper, having been once

folded and pressed with a folder, is refolded in a reversed
direction, in the same creases or edges which had formed
the original fold. This discovery was sufficient. It was
clear to me that the letter had been turned, as a glove, inside
out, redirected and resealed. I bade the minister good
morning, and took my departure at once, leaving a gold
snuff-box upon the table.

'The next morning I called for the snuff-box, when we
resumed, quite eagerly, the conversation of the preceding
day. While thus engaged, however, a loud report, as if of a
pistol, was heard immediately beneath the windows of the
hotel, and was succeeded by a series of fearful screams,
and the shoutings of a terrified mob. D—— rushed to a
casement, threw it open, and looked out. In the meantime
I stepped to the card-rack, took the letter, put it in my
pocket, and replaced it by a facsimile (so far as regards
externals) which I had carefully prepared at my lodging—
imitating the D—— cipher, very readily, by means of a
seal formed of bread.

'The disturbance in the street had been occasioned by the
frantic behavior of a man with a musket. He had fired it
among a crowd of women and children. It proved, however,
to have been without ball, and the fellow was suffered to go
his way as a lunatic or a drunkard. When he had gone,
D—— came from the window, whither I had followed
him immediately upon securing the object in view. Soon
afterwards I bade him farewell. The pretended lunatic
was a man in my own pay.'

'But what purpose had you,' I asked, 'in replacing the
letter by a facsimile? Would it not have been better, at
the first visit, to have seized it openly, and departed?'

'D——,' replied Dupin, 'is a desperate man, and a man
of nerve. His hôtel, too, is not without attendants devoted
to his interests. Had I made the wild attempt you suggest,
I might never have left the ministerial presence alive.
The good people of Paris might have heard of me no more.
But I had an object apart from these considerations.
You know my political prepossessions. In this matter,
I act as a partisan of the lady concerned. For eighteen
months the minister has had her in his power. She has
now him in hers—since, being unaware that the letter is

not in his possession, he will proceed with his exactions as if it was. Thus will he inevitably commit himself, at once, to his political destruction. His downfall, too, will not be more precipitate than awkward. It is all very well to talk about the *facilis descensus Averni*; but in all kinds of climbing, as Catalani said of singing, it is far more easy to get up than to come down. In the present instance I have no sympathy—at least no pity—for him who descends. He is that *monstrum horrendum*, an unprincipled man of genius. I confess, however, that I should like very well to know the precise character of his thoughts, when, being defied by her whom the prefect terms "a certain personage," he is reduced to opening the letter which I left for him in the card-rack.'

'How? did you put anything particular in it?'

'Why—it did not seem altogether right to leave the interior blank—that would have been insulting. D——, at Vienna once, did me an evil turn, which I told him, quite good-humouredly, that I should remember. So, as I knew he would feel some curiosity in regard to the identity of the person who had outwitted him, I thought it a pity not to give him a clue. He is well acquainted with my MS., and I just copied into the middle of the blank sheet the words:

—*Un dessein si funeste,*
S'il n'est digne d'Atrée, est digne de Thyeste.

They are to be found in Crébillon's *Atrée*.'

WILKIE COLLINS

*From Chief Inspector Theakstone, of the Detective Police,
to Sergeant Bulmer of the same force*

LONDON, *4th July* 18—.

SERGEANT BULMER,—This is to inform you that you are
wanted to assist in looking up a case of importance, which
will require all the attention of an experienced member of
the force. The matter of the robbery on which you are
now engaged, you will please to shift over to the young
man who brings you this letter. You will tell him all the
circumstances of the case, just as they stand; you will put
him up to the progress you have made (if any) towards
detecting the person or persons by whom the money has
been stolen; and you will leave him to make the best he
can of the matter now in your hands. He is to have the
whole responsibility of the case, and the whole credit of his
success, if he brings it to a proper issue.

So much for the orders that I am desired to communicate
to you.

A word in your ear, next, about this new man who is to
take your place. His name is Matthew Sharpin; and he is
to have the chance given him of dashing into our office at
a jump—supposing he turns out strong enough to take it.
You will naturally ask me how he comes by this privilege.
I can only tell you that he has some uncommonly strong
interest to back him in certain high quarters which you and
I had better not mention except under our breaths. He
has been a lawyer's clerk; and he is wonderfully conceited
in his opinion of himself, as well as mean and underhand
to look at. According to his own account, he leaves his
old trade, and joins ours of his own free will and preference.
You will no more believe that than I do. My notion is,
that he has managed to ferret out some private information
in connection with the affairs of one of his master's clients,

which makes him rather an awkward customer to keep in the office for the future, and which, at the same time, gives him hold enough over his employer to make it dangerous to drive him into a corner by turning him away. I think the giving him this unheard-of chance among us, is, in plain words, pretty much like giving him hush-money to keep him quiet. However that may be, Mr. Matthew Sharpin is to have the case now in your hands; and if he succeeds with it, he pokes his ugly nose into our office, as sure as fate. I put you up to this, sergeant, so that you may not stand in your own light by giving the new man any cause to complain of you at headquarters, and remain yours,

FRANCIS THEAKSTONE.

From Mr. Matthew Sharpin to Chief Inspector Theakstone

LONDON, 5*th July* 18—.

DEAR SIR,—Having now been favoured with the necessary instructions from Sergeant Bulmer, I beg to remind you of certain directions which I have received, relating to the report of my future proceedings which I am to prepare for examination at headquarters.

The object of my writing, and of your examining what I have written, before you send it in to the higher authorities, is, I am informed, to give me, as an untried hand, the benefit of your advice, in case I want it (which I venture to think I shall not) at any stage of my proceedings. As the extraordinary circumstances of the case on which I am now engaged, make it impossible for me to absent myself from the place where the robbery was committed, until I have made some progress towards discovering the thief, I am necessarily precluded from consulting you personally. Hence the necessity of my writing down the various details, which might, perhaps, be better communicated by word of mouth. This, if I am not mistaken, is the position in which we are now placed. I state my own impressions on the subject, in writing, in order that we may clearly understand each other at the outset; and have the honour to remain, your obedient servant,

MATTHEW SHARPIN.

From Chief Inspector Theakstone to Mr. Matthew Sharpin

LONDON, 5th *July* 18—.

SIR,—You have begun by wasting time, ink, and paper. We both of us perfectly well knew the position we stood in towards each other, when I sent you with my letter to Sergeant Bulmer. There was not the least need to repeat it in writing. Be so good as to employ your pen, in future, on the business actually in hand.

You have now three separate matters on which to write to me. First, you have to draw up a statement of your instructions received from Sergeant Bulmer, in order to show us that nothing has escaped your memory, and that you are thoroughly acquainted with all the circumstances of the case which has been entrusted to you. Secondly, you are to inform me what it is you propose to do. Thirdly, you are to report every inch of your progress (if you make any) from day to day, and, if need be, from hour to hour as well. This is *your* duty. As to what *my* duty may be, when I want you to remind me of it, I will write and tell you so. In the meantime, I remain, yours,

FRANCIS THEAKSTONE.

From Mr. Matthew Sharpin to Chief Inspector Theakstone

LONDON, 6th *July* 18—.

SIR,—You are rather an elderly person, and, as such, naturally inclined to be a little jealous of men like me, who are in the prime of their lives and their faculties. Under these circumstances, it is my duty to be considerate towards you, and not to bear too hardly on your small failings. I decline, therefore, altogether, to take offence at the tone of your letter; I give you the full benefit of the natural generosity of my nature; I sponge the very existence of your surly communication out of my memory—in short, Chief Inspector Theakstone, I forgive you, and proceed to business.

My first duty is to draw up a full statement of the instructions I have received from Sergeant Bulmer. Here they are at your service, according to my version of them.

. . . . . .

At number 13 Rutherford Street, Soho, there is a stationer's shop. It is kept by one Mr. Yatman. He is a married man, but has no family. Besides Mr. and Mrs. Yatman, the other inmates in the house are a young single man named Jay, who lodges in the front room on the second floor—a shopman, who sleeps in one of the attics—and a servant-of-all-work, whose bed is in the back-kitchen. Once a week a charwoman comes for a few hours in the morning only, to help this servant. These are all the persons who, on ordinary occasions, have means of access to the interior of the house, placed, as a matter of course, at their disposal.

Mr. Yatman has been in business for many years, carrying on his affairs prosperously enough to realize a handsome independence for a person in his position. Unfortunately for himself, he endeavoured to increase the amount of his property by speculating. He ventured boldly in his investments, luck went against him, and rather less than two years ago he found himself a poor man again. All that was saved out of the wreck of his property was the sum of two hundred pounds.

Although Mr. Yatman did his best to meet his altered circumstances, by giving up many of the luxuries and comforts to which he and his wife had been accustomed, he found it impossible to retrench so far as to allow of putting by any money from the income produced by the shop. The business has been declining of late years—the cheap advertising stationers having done it injury with the public. Consequently, up to the last week the only surplus property possessed by Mr. Yatman consisted of the two hundred pounds which had been recovered from the wreck of his fortune. This sum was placed as a deposit in a joint-stock bank of the highest possible character.

Eight days ago, Mr. Yatman and his lodger, Mr. Jay, held a conversation on the subject of the commercial difficulties which are hampering trade in all directions at the present time. Mr. Jay (who lives by supplying the newspapers with short paragraphs relating to accidents, offences, and brief records of remarkable occurrences in general—who is, in short, what they call a penny-a-liner) told his landlord that he had been in the city that day, and had heard unfavourable rumours on the subject of the joint-stock banks. The rumours to which he alluded had already reached the ears of Mr. Yatman from other quarters; and the confirmation of them by his lodger had such an effect on his mind—predisposed as it was to alarm by the experience of his former losses—that he resolved to go at once to the bank and withdraw his deposit.

It was then getting on towards the end of the afternoon; and he arrived just in time to receive his money before the bank closed.

He received the deposit in bank-notes of the following amounts: one fifty-pound note, three twenty-pound notes, six ten-pound notes, and six five-pound notes. His object in drawing the money in this form was to have it ready to lay out immediately in trifling loans, on good security, among the small tradespeople of his district, some of whom are sorely pressed for the very means of existence at the present time. Investments of this kind seemed to Mr. Yatman to be the most safe and the most profitable on which he could now venture.

He brought the money back in an envelope placed in his breast-pocket; and asked his shopman, on getting home, to look for a small flat tin cash-box, which had not been used for years, and which, as Mr. Yatman remembered it, was exactly the right size to hold the bank-notes. For some time the cash-box was searched for in vain. Mr. Yatman called to his wife to know if she had any idea where it was. The question was overheard by the servant-of-all-work, who was taking up the tea-tray at the time, and by Mr. Jay, who was coming downstairs on his way out to the theatre. Ultimately the cash-box was found by the shopman. Mr. Yatman placed the bank-notes in it, secured them by a padlock, and put the box in his coat-pocket. It stuck out of the coat-pocket a very little, but enough to be seen. Mr. Yatman remained at home, upstairs, all the evening. No visitors called. At eleven o'clock he went to bed, and put the cash-box along with his clothes, on a chair by the bed-side.

When he and his wife woke the next morning, the box was gone. Payment of the notes was immediately stopped at the Bank of England; but no news of the money has been heard of since that time.

So far, the circumstances of the case are perfectly clear. They point unmistakably to the conclusion that the robbery must have been committed by some person living in the house. Suspicion falls, therefore, upon the servant-of-all-work, upon the shopman, and upon Mr. Jay. The two first knew that the cash-box was being inquired for by their master, but did not know what it was he wanted to put into it. They would assume, of course, that it was money. They both had opportunities (the servant, when she took away the tea—and the shopman, when he came, after shutting up, to give the keys of the till to his master) of seeing the cash-box in Mr. Yatman's pocket, and of inferring naturally, from its position there, that he intended to take it into his bedroom with him at night.

Mr. Jay, on the other hand, had been told, during the afternoon's conversation on the subject of joint-stock banks, that his landlord had a deposit of two hundred pounds in one of them. He also knew that Mr. Yatman left him with the intention of drawing that money out; and he heard the inquiry for the cash-box, afterwards, when he was coming downstairs. He must, therefore, have inferred that the money was in the house, and that the cash-box was the receptacle intended to contain it. That he could have had any idea, however, of the place in which Mr. Yatman intended to keep it for the night, is impossible, seeing that he went out before the box was found, and did not return till his landlord was in bed. Consequently, if he committed the robbery, he must have gone into the bedroom purely on speculation.

Speaking of the bedroom reminds me of the necessity of noticing the situation of it in the house, and the means that exist of gaining easy access to it at any hour of the night.

The room in question is the back room on the first floor. In consequence of Mrs. Yatman's constitutional nervousness on the subject of fire (which makes her apprehend being burnt alive in her room, in case of accident, by the hampering of the lock if the key is turned in it) her husband has never been accustomed to lock the bedroom door. Both he and his wife are, by their own admission, heavy sleepers. Consequently, the risk to be run by any evil-disposed persons wishing to plunder the bedroom, was of the most trifling kind. They could enter the room by merely turning the handle of the door; and if they moved with ordinary caution, there was no fear of their waking the sleepers inside. This fact is of importance. It strengthens our conviction that the money must have been taken by one of the inmates of the house, because it tends to show that the robbery, in this case, might have been committed by persons not possessed of the superior vigilance and cunning of the experienced thief.

Such are the circumstances, as they were related to Sergeant Bulmer, when he was first called in to discover the guilty parties, and, if possible, to recover the lost banknotes. The strictest inquiry which he could institute, failed of producing the smallest fragment of evidence against any of the persons on whom suspicion naturally fell. Their language and behaviour, on being informed of the robbery, was perfectly consistent with the language and behaviour of innocent people. Sergeant Bulmer felt from the first that this was a case for private inquiry and secret observation. He began by recommending Mr. and Mrs. Yatman to affect a feeling of perfect confidence in the innocence of the persons living under their roof; and he then opened the campaign by employing himself in following the goings and comings, and in discovering the friends, the habits, and the secrets of the maid-of-all-work.

Three days and nights of exertions on his own part, and on that of others who were competent to assist his investigations, were enough to satisfy him that there was no sound cause for suspicion against the girl.

He next practised the same precaution in relation to the shopman. There was more difficulty and uncertainty in privately clearing up this person's character without his knowledge, but the obstacles were at last smoothed away with tolerable success; and though there is not the same amount of certainty, in this case, which there was in that of the girl, there is still fair reason for supposing that the shopman has had nothing to do with the robbery of the cash-box.

As a necessary consequence of these proceedings, the range of suspicion now. becomes limited to the lodger, Mr. Jay.

When I presented your letter of introduction to Sergeant Bulmer, he had already made some inquiries on the subject of this young man. The result, so far, has not been at all favourable. Mr. Jay's habits are irregular; he frequents public-houses, and seems to be familiarly acquainted with a great many dissolute characters; he is in debt to most of the tradespeople whom he employs; he has not paid his rent to Mr. Yatman for the last month; yesterday evening he came home excited by liquor, and last week he was seen talking to a prize-fighter. In short, though Mr. Jay does call himself a journalist, in virtue of his penny-a-line contributions to the newspapers, he is a young man of low tastes, vulgar manners, and bad habits. Nothing has yet been discovered in relation to him, which redounds to his credit in the smallest degree.

I have now reported, down to the very last details, all the particulars communicated to me by Sergeant Bulmer. I believe you will not find an omission anywhere; and I think you will admit, though you are prejudiced against me, that a clearer statement of facts was never laid before you than the statement I have now made. My next duty is to tell you what I propose to do, now that the case is confided to my hands.

In the first place, it is clearly my business to take up the case at the point where Sergeant Bulmer has left it. On his authority, I am justified in assuming that I have no need to trouble myself about the maid-of-all-work and the shopman. Their characters are now to be considered as cleared up. What remains to be privately investigated is the question of the guilt or innocence of Mr. Jay. Before we give up the notes for lost, we must make sure, if we can, that he knows nothing about them.

This is the plan that I have adopted, with the full approval of Mr. and Mrs. Yatman, for discovering whether Mr. Jay is or is not the person who has stolen the cash-box:

I propose, to-day, to present myself at the house in the

character of a young man who is looking for lodgings. The back room on the second floor will be shown to me as the room to let; and I shall establish myself there to-night, as a person from the country who has come to London to look for a situation in a respectable shop or office.

By this means I shall be living next to the room occupied by Mr. Jay. The partition between us is mere lath and plaster. I shall make a small hole in it, near the cornice, through which I can see what Mr. Jay does in his room, and hear every word that is said when any friend happens to call on him. Whenever he is at home, I shall be at my post of observation. Whenever he goes out, I shall be after him. By employing these means of watching him, I believe I may look forward to the discovery of his secret —if he knows anything about the lost bank-notes—as to a dead certainty.

What you may think of my plan of observation I cannot undertake to say. It appears to me to unite the invaluable merits of boldness and simplicity. Fortified by this conviction, I close the present communication with feelings of the most sanguine description in regard to the future, and remain your obedient servant,

MATTHEW SHARPIN.

From the Same to the Same

7th July.

SIR,—As you have not honoured me with any answer to my last communication, I assume that, in spite of your prejudices against me, it has produced the favourable impression on your mind which I ventured to anticipate. Gratified beyond measure by the token of approval which your eloquent silence conveys to me, I proceed to report the progress that has been made in the course of the last twenty-four hours.

I am now comfortably established next door to Mr. Jay; and I am delighted to say that I have two holes in the partition, instead of one. My natural sense of humour has led me into the pardonable extravagance of giving them appropriate names. One I call my peep-hole, and the other my pipe-hole. The name of the first explains itself;

the name of the second refers to a small tin pipe, or tube, inserted in the hole, and twisted so that the mouth of it comes close to my ear, while I am standing at my post of observation. Thus, while I am looking at Mr. Jay through my peep-hole, I can hear every word that may be spoken in his room through my pipe-hole.

Perfect candour—a virtue which I have possessed from my childhood—compels me to acknowledge, before I go any further, that the ingenious notion of adding a pipe-hole to my proposed peep-hole originated with Mrs. Yatman. This lady—a most intelligent and accomplished person, simple, and yet distinguished, in her manners—has entered into all my little plans with an enthusiasm and intelligence which I cannot too highly praise. Mr. Yatman is so cast down by his loss, that he is quite incapable of affording me any assistance. Mrs. Yatman, who is evidently most tenderly attached to him, feels her husband's sad condition of mind even more acutely than she feels the loss of the money; and is mainly stimulated to exertion by her desire to assist in raising him from the miserable state of prostration into which he has now fallen.

'The money, Mr. Sharpin,' she said to me yesterday evening, with tears in her eyes, 'the money may be regained by rigid economy and strict attention to business. It is my husband's wretched state of mind that makes me so anxious for the discovery of the thief. I may be wrong, but I felt hopeful of success as soon as you entered the house; and I believe, if the wretch who has robbed us is to be found, you are the man to discover him.' I accepted this gratifying compliment in the spirit in which it was offered—firmly believing that I shall be found, sooner or later, to have thoroughly deserved it.

Let me now return to business; that is to say, to my peep-hole and my pipe-hole.

I have enjoyed some hours of calm observation of Mr. Jay. Though rarely at home, as I understand from Mrs. Yatman, on ordinary occasions, he has been indoors the whole of this day. That is suspicious, to begin with. I have to report, further, that he rose at a late hour this morning (always a bad sign in a young man), and that he lost a great deal of time, after he was up, in yawning and

complaining to himself of headache.   Like other debauched
characters, he ate little or nothing for breakfast.   His next
proceeding was to smoke a pipe—a dirty clay pipe, which
a gentleman would have been ashamed to put between his
lips.   When he had done smoking, he took out pen, ink,
and paper, and sat down to write with a groan—whether
of remorse for having taken the bank-notes, or of disgust
at the task before him, I am unable to say.   After writing
a few lines (too far away from my peep-hole to give me a
chance of reading over his shoulder), he leaned back in his
chair, and amused himself by humming the tunes of certain
popular songs.   Whether these do, or do not, represent
secret signals by which he communicates with his accom-
plices remains to be seen.   After he had amused himself
for some time by humming, he got up and began to walk
about the room, occasionally stopping to add a sentence to
the paper on his desk.   Before long, he went to a locked
cupboard and opened it.   I strained my eyes eagerly, in
expectation of making a discovery.   I saw him take something carefully out of the cupboard—he turned round—
and it was only a pint bottle of brandy!   Having drunk
some of the liquor, this extremely indolent reprobate lay
down on his bed again, and in five minutes was fast
asleep.

After hearing him snoring for at least two hours, I was
recalled to my peep-hole by a knock at his door.   He
jumped up and opened it with suspicious activity.

A very small boy, with a very dirty face, walked in, said:
'Please, sir, they 're waiting for you,' sat down on a chair,
with his legs a long way from the ground, and instantly
fell asleep!   Mr. Jay swore an oath, tied a wet towel round
his head, and going back to his paper, began to cover it
with writing as fast as his fingers could move the pen.
Occasionally getting up to dip the towel in water and tie
it on again, he continued at this employment for nearly
three hours; then folded up the leaves of writing, woke the
boy, and gave them to him, with this remarkable expression: 'Now, then, young sleepy-head, quick—march!   If
you see the governor, tell him to have the money ready
when I call for it.'   The boy grinned, and disappeared.   I
was sorely tempted to follow 'sleepy-head,' but, on reflec-

tion, considered it safest still to keep my eye on the
proceedings of Mr. Jay.

In half an hour's time, he put on his hat and walked out.
Of course, I put on my hat and walked out also. As I
went downstairs, I passed Mrs. Yatman going up. The
lady has been kind enough to undertake, by previous
arrangement between us, to search Mr. Jay's room, while
he is out of the way, and while I am necessarily engaged
in the pleasing duty of following him wherever he goes.
On the occasion to which I now refer, he walked straight
to the nearest tavern, and ordered a couple of mutton
chops for his dinner. I placed myself in the next box to
him, and ordered a couple of mutton chops for my dinner.
Before I had been in the room a minute, a young man of
highly suspicious manners and appearance, sitting at a
table opposite, took his glass of porter in his hand and
joined Mr. Jay. I pretended to be reading the newspaper,
and listened, as in duty bound, with all my might.

'Jack has been here inquiring after you,' says the young
man.

'Did he leave any message?' asks Mr. Jay.

'Yes,' says the other. 'He told me, if I met with you,
to say that he wished very particularly to see you to-night;
and that he would give you a look in, at Rutherford Street,
at seven o'clock.'

'All right,' says Mr. Jay. 'I'll get back in time to see him.'

Upon this, the suspicious-looking young man finished his
porter, and saying that he was rather in a hurry, took leave
of his friend (perhaps I should not be wrong if I said his
accomplice) and left the room.

At twenty-five minutes and a half past six—in these
serious cases it is important to be particular about time—
Mr. Jay finished his chops and paid his bill. At twenty-six
minutes and three-quarters I finished my chops and paid
mine. In ten minutes more I was inside the house in
Rutherford Street, and was received by Mrs. Yatman in
the passage. That charming woman's face exhibited an
expression of melancholy and disappointment which it
quite grieved me to see.

'I am afraid, ma'am,' says I, 'that you have not hit on
any little criminating discovery in the lodger's room?'

She shook her head and sighed. It was a soft, languid, fluttering sigh; and, upon my life, it quite upset me. For the moment I forgot business, and burned with envy of Mr. Yatman.

'Don't despair, ma'am,' I said, with an insinuating mildness which seemed to touch her. 'I have heard a mysterious conversation—I know of a guilty appointment —and I expect great things from my peep-hole and my pipe-hole to-night. Pray, don't be alarmed, but I think we are on the brink of a discovery.'

Here my enthusiastic devotion to business got the better of my tender feelings. I looked — winked — nodded — left her.

When I got back to my observatory, I found Mr. Jay digesting his mutton chops in an arm-chair, with his pipe in his mouth. On his table were two tumblers, a jug of water, and the pint bottle of brandy. It was then close upon seven o'clock. As the hour struck, the person described as 'Jack' walked in.

He looked agitated—I am happy to say he looked violently agitated. The cheerful glow of anticipated success diffused itself (to use a strong expression) all over me, from head to foot. With breathless interest I looked through my peep-hole, and saw the visitor— the 'Jack' of this delightful case—sit down, facing me, at the opposite side of the table to Mr. Jay. Making allowance for the difference in expression which their countenances just now happened to exhibit, these two abandoned villains were so much alike in other respects as to lead at once to the conclusion that they were brothers. Jack was the cleaner man and the better dressed of the two. I admit that, at the outset. It is, perhaps, one of my failings to push justice and impartiality to their utmost limits. I am no Pharisee; and where vice has its redeeming point, I say, let vice have its due—yes, yes, by all manner of means, let vice have its due.

'What's the matter now, Jack?' says Mr. Jay.

'Can't you see it in my face?' says Jack. 'My dear fellow, delays are dangerous. Let us have done with suspense, and risk it the day after to-morrow.'

'So soon as that?' cried Mr. Jay, looking very much

astonished. 'Well, I'm ready, if you are. But, I say, Jack, is Somebody Else ready too? Are you quite sure of that?'

He smiled as he spoke—a frightful smile—and laid a very strong emphasis on those two words, 'Somebody Else.' There is evidently a third ruffian, a nameless desperado, concerned in the business.

'Meet us to-morrow,' says Jack, 'and judge for yourself. Be in the Regent's Park at eleven in the morning, and look out for us at the turning that leads to the Avenue Road.'

'I'll be there,' says Mr. Jay. 'Have a drop of brandy and water? What are you getting up for? You're not going already?'

'Yes, I am,' says Jack. 'The fact is, I'm so excited and agitated that I can't sit still anywhere for five minutes together. Ridiculous as it may appear to you, I'm in a perpetual state of nervous flutter. I can't, for the life of me, help fearing that we shall be found out. I fancy that every man who looks twice at me in the street is a spy——'

At those words, I thought my legs would have given way under me. Nothing but strength of mind kept me at my peep-hole—nothing else, I give you my word of honour.

'Stuff and nonsense!' cried Mr. Jay, with all the effrontery of a veteran in crime. 'We have kept the secret up to this time, and we will manage cleverly to the end. Have a drop of brandy and water, and you will feel as certain about it as I do.'

Jack steadily refused the brandy and water, and steadily persisted in taking his leave.

'I must try if I can't walk it off,' he said. 'Remember to-morrow morning—eleven o'clock, Avenue Road side of the Regent's Park.'

With those words he went out. His hardened relative laughed desperately, and resumed the dirty clay pipe.

I sat down on the side of my bed, actually quivering with excitement.

It is clear to me that no attempt has yet been made to change the stolen bank-notes; and I may add that Sergeant Bulmer was of that opinion also, when he left the case in my hands. What is the natural conclusion to draw from the conversation which I have just set down? Evidently, that the confederates meet to-morrow to take their respective shares in the stolen money, and to decide on the safest means of getting the notes changed the day after. Mr. Jay is, beyond a doubt, the leading criminal in this business, and he will probably run the chief risk—that of changing the fifty-pound note. I shall, therefore, still make it my business to follow him—attending at the Regent's Park to-morrow, and doing my best to hear what is said there. If another appointment is made the day after, I shall, of course, go to it. In the meantime, I shall want the immediate assistance of two competent persons (supposing the rascals separate after their meeting) to follow the two minor criminals. It is only fair to add, that, if the rogues all retire together, I shall probably keep my subordinates in reserve. Being naturally ambitious, I desire, if possible, to have the whole credit of discovering this robbery to myself.

8th July.

I have to acknowledge, with thanks, the speedy arrival of my two subordinates—men of very average abilities, I am afraid; but, fortunately, I shall always be on the spot to direct them.

My first business this morning was, necessarily, to prevent mistakes by accounting to Mr. and Mrs. Yatman for the presence of two strangers on the scene. Mr. Yatman (between ourselves, a poor feeble man) only shook his head and groaned. Mrs. Yatman (that superior woman) favoured me with a charming look of intelligence.

'Oh, Mr. Sharpin!' she said, 'I am so sorry to see those two men! Your sending for their assistance looks as if you were beginning to be doubtful of success.'

I privately winked at her (she is very good in allowing me to do so without taking offence), and told her, in my facetious way, that she laboured under a slight mistake.

'It is because I am sure of success, ma'am, that I send for them. I am determined to recover the money, not for my own sake only, but for Mr. Yatman's sake—and for yours.'

I laid a considerable amount of stress on those last three words. She said: 'Oh, Mr. Sharpin!' again—and blushed

of a heavenly red—and looked down at her work. I could
go to the world's end with that woman, if Mr. Yatman
would only die.

I sent off the two subordinates to wait, until I wanted
them, at the Avenue Road gate of the Regent's Park.
Half an hour afterwards I was following in the same
direction myself, at the heels of Mr. Jay.

The two confederates were punctual to the appointed
time. I blush to record it, but it is nevertheless necessary
to state, that the third rogue—the nameless desperado of
my report, or if you prefer it, the mysterious 'Somebody
Else' of the conversation between the two brothers—is a
Woman! and, what is worse, a young woman! and what
is more lamentable still, a nice-looking woman! I have
long resisted a growing conviction, that, wherever there is
mischief in this world, an individual of the fair sex is
inevitably certain to be mixed up in it. After the experience of this morning, I can struggle against that sad
conclusion no longer. I give up the sex—excepting
Mrs. Yatman, I give up the sex.

The man named 'Jack' offered the woman his arm.
Mr. Jay placed himself on the other side of her. The three
then walked away slowly among the trees. I followed
them at a respectful distance. My two subordinates, at
a respectful distance also, followed me.

It was, I deeply regret to say, impossible to get near
enough to them to overhear their conversation, without
running too great a risk of being discovered. I could only
infer from their gestures and actions that they were all
three talking with extraordinary earnestness on some
subject which deeply interested them. After having been
engaged in this way a full quarter of an hour, they suddenly
turned round to retrace their steps. My presence of mind
did not forsake me in this emergency. I signed to the two
subordinates to walk on carelessly and pass them, while I
myself slipped dexterously behind a tree. As they came
by me, I heard 'Jack' address these words to Mr. Jay:

'Let us say half-past ten to-morrow morning. And mind
you come in a cab. We had better not risk taking one in
this neighbourhood.'

Mr. Jay made some brief reply, which I could not overhear. They walked back to the place at which they had met, shaking hands there with an audacious cordiality which it quite sickened me to see. They then separated. I followed Mr. Jay. My subordinates paid the same delicate attention to the other two.

Instead of taking me back to Rutherford Street, Mr. Jay led me to the Strand. He stopped at a dingy, disreputable-looking house, which, according to the inscription over the door, was a newspaper office, but which, in my judgment, had all the external appearance of a place devoted to the reception of stolen goods.

After remaining inside for a few minutes, he came out, whistling, with his fingers and thumb in his waistcoat pocket. A less discreet man than myself would have arrested him on the spot. I remembered the necessity of catching the two confederates, and the importance of not interfering with the appointment that had been made for the next morning. Such coolness as this, under trying circumstances, is rarely to be found, I should imagine, in a young beginner, whose reputation as a detective policeman is still to make.

From the house of suspicious appearance, Mr. Jay betook himself to a cigar-divan, and read the magazines over a cheroot. I sat at a table near him, and read the magazines likewise over a cheroot. From the divan he strolled to the tavern and had his chops. I strolled to the tavern and had my chops. When he had done, he went back to his lodging. When I had done, I went back to mine. He was overcome with drowsiness early in the evening, and went to bed. As soon as I heard him snoring, I was overcome with drowsiness, and went to bed also.

Early in the morning my two subordinates came to make their report.

They had seen the man named 'Jack' leave the woman near the gate of an apparently respectable villa-residence, not far from the Regent's Park. Left to himself, he took a turning to the right, which led to a sort of suburban street, principally inhabited by shopkeepers. He stopped at the private door of one of the houses, and let himself in with his own key—looking about him as he opened the door, and staring suspiciously at my men as they lounged along on the opposite side of the way. These were all the particulars which the subordinates had to communicate. I kept them in my room to attend on me, if needful, and mounted to my peep-hole to have a look at Mr. Jay.

He was occupied in dressing himself, and was taking extraordinary pains to destroy all traces of the natural slovenliness of his appearance. This was precisely what I expected. A vagabond like Mr. Jay knows the importance of giving himself a respectable look when he is going to run the risk of changing a stolen bank-note. At five minutes past ten o'clock, he had given the last brush to his shabby hat and the last scouring with bread-crumb to his dirty gloves. At ten minutes past ten he was in the street, on his way to the nearest cab-stand, and I and my subordinates were close on his heels.

He took a cab, and we took a cab. I had not overheard them appoint a place of meeting, when following them in the park on the previous day; but I soon found that we were proceeding in the old direction of the Avenue Road gate.

The cab in which Mr. Jay was riding turned into the park slowly. We stopped outside, to avoid exciting suspicion. I got out to follow the cab on foot. Just as I did so, I saw it stop, and detected the two confederates approaching it from among the trees. They got in, and the cab was turned about directly. I ran back to my own cab, and told the driver to let them pass him, and then to follow as before.

The man obeyed my directions, but so clumsily as to excite their suspicions. We had been driving after them about three minutes (returning along the road by which we had advanced) when I looked out of the window to see how far they might be ahead of us. As I did this, I saw two hats popped out of the windows of their cab, and two faces looking back at me. I sank into my place in a cold sweat; the expression is coarse, but no other form of words can describe my condition at that trying moment.

'We are found out!' I said faintly to my two subordinates. They stared at me in astonishment. My feelings changed instantly from the depth of despair to the height of indignation.

'It is the cabman's fault. Get out, one of you,' I said, with dignity—'get out and punch his head.'

Instead of following my directions (I should wish this act of disobedience to be reported at headquarters) they both looked out of the window. Before I could pull them back, they both sat down again. Before I could express my just indignation, they both grinned, and said to me: 'Please to look out, sir!'

I did look out. The thieves' cab had stopped.

Where?

At a church door!!!

What effect this discovery might have had upon the ordinary run of men, I don't know. Being of a strong religious turn myself, it filled me with horror. I have often read of the unprincipled cunning of criminal persons; but I never before heard of three thieves attempting to double on their pursuers by entering a church! The sacrilegious audacity of that proceeding is, I should think, unparalleled in the annals of crime.

I checked my grinning subordinates by a frown. It was easy to see what was passing in their superficial minds. If I had not been able to look below the surface, I might, on observing two nicely dressed men and one nicely dressed woman enter a church before eleven in the morning on a weekday, have come to the same hasty conclusion at which my inferiors had evidently arrived. As it was, appearances had no power to impose on *me*. I got out, and, followed by one of my men, entered the church. The other man I sent round to watch the vestry door. You may catch a weasel asleep—but not your humble servant, Matthew Sharpin!

We stole up the gallery stairs, diverged to the organ loft, and peered through the curtains in front. There they were all three, sitting in a pew below—yes, incredible as it may appear, sitting in a pew below!

Before I could determine what to do, a clergyman made his appearance in full canonicals, from the vestry door, followed by a clerk. My brain whirled, and my eyesight grew dim. Dark remembrances of robberies committed in vestries floated through my mind. I trembled for the excellent man in full canonicals—I even trembled for the clerk.

The clergyman placed himself inside the altar rails. The three desperadoes approached him. He opened his book, and began to read. What?—you will ask.

I answer, without the slightest hesitation, the first lines of the Marriage Service.

My subordinate had the audacity to look at me, and then to stuff his pocket-handkerchief into his mouth. I scorned to pay any attention to him. After I had discovered that the man 'Jack' was the bridegroom, and that the man Jay acted the part of father, and gave away the bride, I left the church, followed by my man, and joined the other subordinate outside the vestry door. Some people in my position would now have felt rather crestfallen, and would have begun to think that they had made a very foolish mistake. Not the faintest misgiving of any kind troubled me. I did not feel in the slightest degree depreciated in my own estimation. And even now, after a lapse of three hours, my mind remains, I am happy to say, in the same calm and hopeful condition.

As soon as I and my subordinates were assembled together outside the church, I intimated my intention of still following the other cab, in spite of what had occurred. My reason for deciding on this course will appear presently. The two subordinates were astonished at my resolution. One of them had the impertinence to say to me:

'If you please, sir, who is it that we are after? A man who has stolen money, or a man who has stolen a wife?'

The other low person encouraged him by laughing. Both have deserved an official reprimand; and both, I sincerely trust, will be sure to get it.

When the marriage ceremony was over, the three got into their cab; and once more our vehicle (neatly hidden round the corner of the church, so that they could not suspect it to be near them) started to follow theirs.

We traced them to the terminus of the South-Western Railway. The newly married couple took tickets for Richmond—paying their fare with a half-sovereign, and so depriving me of the pleasure of arresting them, which I should certainly have done, if they had offered a bank-note. They parted from Mr. Jay, saying: 'Remember the address—14 Babylon Terrace. You dine with us to-morrow week.' Mr. Jay accepted the invitation, and added, jocosely, that he was going home at once to get off his clean clothes, and to be comfortable and dirty again for the rest of the day. I have to report that I saw him home safely, and that he is comfortable and dirty again (to use his own disgraceful language) at the present moment.

Here the affair rests, having by this time reached what I may call its first stage.

I know very well what persons of hasty judgment will be inclined to say of my proceedings thus far. They will assert that I have been deceiving myself all through, in the most absurd way; they will declare that the suspicious conversations which I have reported, referred solely to the difficulties and dangers of successfully carrying out a runaway match; and they will appeal to the scene in the church, as offering undeniable proof of the correctness of their assertions. So let it be. I dispute nothing up to this point. But I ask a question, out of the depths of my own sagacity as a man of the world, which the bitterest of my enemies will not, I think, find it particularly easy to answer.

Granted the fact of the marriage, what proof does it afford me of the innocence of the three persons concerned in that clandestine transaction? It gives me none. On the contrary, it strengthens my suspicions against Mr. Jay and his confederates, because it suggests a distinct motive for their stealing the money. A gentleman who is going to spend his honeymoon at Richmond wants money; and a gentleman who is in debt to all his tradespeople wants money. Is this an unjustifiable imputation of bad motives? In the name of outraged morality, I deny it. These men have combined together, and have stolen a woman. Why should they not combine together, and steal a cash-box? I take my stand on the logic of rigid virtue; and I defy all the sophistry of vice to move me an inch out of my position.

Speaking of virtue, I may add that I have put this view of the case to Mr. and Mrs. Yatman. That accomplished and charming woman found it difficult, at first, to follow the close chain of my reasoning. I am free to confess that she shook her head, and shed tears, and joined her husband in premature lamentation over the loss of the two hundred pounds. But a little careful explanation on my part, and a little attentive listening on hers, ultimately changed her opinion. She now agrees with me, that there is nothing in this unexpected circumstance of the clandestine marriage which absolutely tends to divert suspicion from Mr. Jay, or Mr. 'Jack,' or the runaway lady. 'Audacious hussy' was the term my fair friend used in speaking of her, but let that pass. It is more to the purpose to record that Mrs. Yatman has not lost confidence in me and that Mr. Yatman promises to follow her example, and do his best to look hopefully for future results.

I have now, in the new turn that circumstances have taken, to await advice from your office. I pause for fresh orders with all the composure of a man who had got two strings to his bow. When I traced the three confederates from the church door to the railway terminus, I had two motives for doing so. First, I followed them as a matter of official business, believing them still to have been guilty of the robbery. Secondly, I followed them as a matter of private speculation, with a view of discovering the place of refuge to which the runaway couple intended to retreat, and of making my information a marketable commodity to offer to the young lady's family and friends. Thus, whatever happens, I may congratulate myself beforehand on not having wasted my time. If the office approves of my conduct, I have my plan ready for further proceedings. If the office blames me, I shall take myself off, with my marketable information, to the genteel villa-residence in the neighbourhood of the Regent's Park. Anyway, the affair puts money into my pocket, and does credit to my penetration as an uncommonly sharp man.

I have only one word more to add, and it is this: If any individual ventures to assert that Mr. Jay and his confederates are innocent of all share in the stealing of the cash-box, I, in return, defy that individual—though he may even be Chief Inspector Theakstone himself—to tell me who has committed the robbery at Rutherford Street, Soho.

I have the honour to be,
Your very obedient servant,
MATTHEW SHARPIN.

From Chief Inspector Theakstone to Sergeant Bulmer

BIRMINGHAM, 9th July.

SERGEANT BULMER,—That empty-headed puppy, Mr. Matthew Sharpin, has made a mess of the case at Rutherford

Street, exactly as I expected he would. Business keeps me in this town; so I write to you to set the matter straight. I enclose, with this, the pages of feeble scribble-scrabble which the creature, Sharpin, calls a report. Look them over; and when you have made your way through all the gabble, I think you will agree with me that the conceited booby has looked for the thief in every direction but the right one. You can lay your hand on the guilty person in five minutes, now. Settle the case at once; forward your report to me at this place; and tell Mr. Sharpin that he is suspended till further notice.

Yours,
FRANCIS THEAKSTONE.

From Sergeant Bulmer to Chief Inspector Theakstone

LONDON, 10th July.

INSPECTOR THEAKSTONE,—Your letter and enclosure came safe to hand. Wise men, they say, may always learn something, even from a fool. By the time I had got through Sharpin's maundering report of his own folly, I saw my way clear enough to the end of the Rutherford Street case, just as you thought I should. In half an hour's time I was at the house. The first person I saw there was Mr. Sharpin himself.

'Have you come to help me?' says he.

'Not exactly,' says I. 'I've come to tell you that you are suspended till further notice.'

'Very good,' says he, not taken down, by so much as a single peg, in his own estimation. 'I thought you would be jealous of me. It's very natural; and I don't blame you. Walk in, pray, and make yourself at home. I'm off to do a little detective business on my own account, in the neighbourhood of the Regent's Park. Ta-ta, sergeant, ta-ta!'

With those words he took himself out of the way—which was exactly what I wanted him to do.

As soon as the maid-servant had shut the door, I told her to inform her master that I wanted to say a word to him in private. She showed me into the parlour behind the shop; and there was Mr. Yatman, all alone, reading the newspaper.

'About this matter of the robbery, sir,' says I.

He cut me short, peevishly enough—being naturally a poor, weak, womanish sort of man. 'Yes, yes, I know,' says he. 'You have come to tell me that your wonderfully clever man, who has bored holes in my second-floor partition, has made a mistake, and is off the scent of the scoundrel who has stolen my money.'

'Yes, sir,' says I. 'That *is* one of the things I came to tell you. But I have got something else to say, besides that.'

'Can you tell me who the thief is?' says he, more pettish than ever.

'Yes, sir,' says I, 'I think I can.'

He put down the newspaper, and began to look rather anxious and frightened.

'Not my shopman?' says he. 'I hope, for the man's own sake, it's not my shopman.'

'Guess again, sir,' says I.

'That idle slut, the maid?' says he.

'She is idle, sir,' says I, 'and she is also a slut; my first inquiries about her proved as much as that. But she's not the thief.'

'Then in the name of Heaven, who is?' says he.

'Will you please to prepare yourself for a very disagreeable surprise, sir?' says I. 'And in case you lose your temper, will you excuse my remarking that I am the stronger man of the two, and that, if you allow yourself to lay hands on me, I may unintentionally hurt you, in pure self-defence?'

He turned as pale as ashes, and pushed his chair two or three feet away from me.

'You have asked me to tell you, sir, who has taken your money,' I went on. 'If you insist on my giving you an answer——'

'I do insist,' he said faintly. 'Who has taken it?'

'Your wife has taken it,' I said very quietly, and very positively at the same time.

He jumped out of the chair as if I had put a knife into him, and struck his fist on the table, so heavily that the wood cracked again.

'Steady, sir,' says I. 'Flying into a passion won't help you to the truth.'

'It's a lie!' says he, with another smack of his fist on the table—'a base, vile, infamous lie! How dare you——'

He stopped, and fell back into the chair again, looked about him in a bewildered way, and ended by bursting out crying.

'When your better sense comes back to you, sir,' says I, 'I am sure you will be gentleman enough to make an apology for the language you have just used. In the meantime, please to listen, if you can, to a word of explanation. Mr. Sharpin has sent in a report to our inspector, of the most irregular and ridiculous kind; setting down, not only all his own foolish doings and sayings, but the doings and sayings of Mrs. Yatman as well. In most cases, such a document would have been fit for the waste-paper basket; but, in this particular case, it so happens that Mr. Sharpin's budget of nonsense leads to a certain conclusion, which the simpleton of a writer has been quite innocent of suspecting from the beginning to the end. Of that conclusion I am so sure, that I will forfeit my place, if it does not turn out that Mrs. Yatman has been practising upon the folly and conceit of this young man, and that she has tried to shield herself from discovery by purposely encouraging him to suspect the wrong persons. I tell you that confidently; and I will even go further. I will undertake to give a decided opinion as to why Mrs. Yatman took the money, and what she has done with it, or with a part of it. Nobody can look at that lady, sir, without being struck by the great taste and beauty of her dress——'

As I said those last words, the poor man seemed to find his powers of speech again. He cut me short directly, as haughtily as if he had been a duke instead of a stationer.

'Try some other means of justifying your vile calumny against my wife,' says he. 'Her milliner's bill for the past year is on my file of receipted accounts at this moment.'

'Excuse me, sir,' says I, 'but that proves nothing. Milliners, I must tell you, have a certain rascally custom which comes within the daily experience of our office. A married lady who wishes it, can keep two accounts at her dressmaker's; one is the account which her husband sees and pays; the other is the private account, which contains all the extravagant items, and which the wife pays secretly,

by instalments, whenever she can.   According to our usual
experience, these instalments are mostly squeezed out of
the housekeeping money.   In your case, I suspect no
instalments have been paid; proceedings have been threa-
tened; Mrs. Yatman, knowing your altered circumstances,
has felt herself driven into a corner; and she has paid her
private account out of your cash-box.'

'I won't believe it,' says he.   'Every word you speak is
an abominable insult to me and to my wife.'

'Are you man enough, sir,' says I, taking him up short,
in order to save time and words, 'to get that receipted bill
you spoke of just now off the file, and come with me at
once to the milliner's shop where Mrs. Yatman deals?'

He turned red in the face at that, got the bill directly,
and put on his hat.   I took out of my pocket-book the
list containing the numbers of the lost notes, and we left
the house together immediately.

Arrived at the milliner's (one of the expensive West End
houses, as I expected), I asked for a private interview, on
important business, with the mistress of the concern.   It
was not the first time that she and I had met over the same
delicate investigation.   The moment she set eyes on me,
she sent for her husband.   I mentioned who Mr. Yatman
was, and what we wanted.

'This is strictly private?' inquires her husband.   I
nodded my head.

'And confidential?' says the wife.   I nodded again.

'Do you see any objection, dear, to obliging the sergeant
with a sight of the books?' says the husband.

'None in the world, love, if you approve of it,' says
the wife.

All this while poor Mr. Yatman sat looking the picture
of astonishment and distress, quite out of place at our
polite conference.   The books were brought — and one
minute's look at the pages in which Mrs. Yatman's name
figured was enough, and more than enough, to prove the
truth of every word I had spoken.

There, in one book, was the husband's account, which
Mr. Yatman had settled.   And there, in the other, was the
private account, crossed off also; the date of settlement
being the very day after the loss of the cash-box.   This

said private account amounted to the sum of a hundred and seventy-five pounds, odd shillings; and it extended over a period of three years. Not a single instalment had been paid on it. Under the last line was an entry to this effect: 'Written to for the third time, 23rd June.' I pointed to it, and asked the milliner if that meant 'last June.' Yes, it did mean last June; and she now deeply regretted to say that it had been accompanied by a threat of legal proceedings.

'I thought you gave good customers more than three years credit?' says I.

The milliner looks at Mr. Yatman, and whispers to me—'Not when a lady's husband gets into difficulties.'

She pointed to the account as she spoke. The entries after the time when Mr. Yatman's circumstances became involved were just as extravagant, for a person in his wife's situation, as the entries for the year before that period. If the lady had economized in other things, she had certainly not economized in the matter of dress.

There was nothing left now but to examine the cash-book, for form's sake. The money had been paid in notes, the amounts and numbers of which exactly tallied with the figures set down in my list.

After that, I thought it best to get Mr. Yatman out of the house immediately. He was in such a pitiable condition, that I called a cab and accompanied him home in it. At first he cried and raved like a child: but I soon quieted him —and I must add, to his credit, that he made me a most handsome apology for his language, as the cab drew up at his house door. In return, I tried to give him some advice about how to set matters right, for the future, with his wife. He paid very little attention to me, and went upstairs muttering to himself about a separation. Whether Mrs. Yatman will come cleverly out of the scrape or not seems doubtful. I should say, myself, that she will go into screeching hysterics, and so frighten the poor man into forgiving her. But this is no business of ours. So far as we are concerned, the case is now at an end; and the present report may come to a conclusion along with it.

I remain, accordingly, yours to command,

THOMAS BULMER.

PS. I have to add that, on leaving Rutherford Street, I met Mr. Matthew Sharpin coming to pack up his things.

'Only think!' says he, rubbing his hands in great spirits, 'I've been to the genteel villa-residence; and the moment I mentioned my business, they kicked me out directly. There were two witnesses of the assault; and it's worth a hundred pounds to me, if it's worth a farthing.'

'I wish you joy of your luck,' says I.

'Thank you,' says he. 'When may I pay you the same compliment on finding the thief?'

'Whenever you like,' says I, 'for the thief is found.'

'Just what I expected,' says he. 'I've done all the work; and now you cut in, and claim all the credit—Mr. Jay of course?'

'No,' says I.

'Who is it, then?' says he.

'Ask Mrs. Yatman,' says I. 'She's waiting to tell you.'

'All right! I'd much rather hear it from that charming woman than from you,' says he, and goes into the house in a mighty hurry.

What do you think of that, Inspector Theakstone? Would you like to stand in Mr. Sharpin's shoes? I shouldn't, I can promise you!

From Chief Inspector Theakstone to Mr. Matthew Sharpin

12th July.

SIR,—Sergeant Bulmer has already told you to consider yourself suspended until further notice. I have now authority to add, that your services as a member of the Detective Police are positively declined. You will please to take this letter as notifying officially your dismissal from the force.

I may inform you, privately, that your rejection is not intended to cast any reflection on your character. It merely implies that you are not quite sharp enough for our purpose. If we *are* to have a new recruit among us, we should infinitely prefer Mrs. Yatman.

Your obedient servant,

FRANCIS THEAKSTONE.

Note on the preceding correspondence, added by
Mr. Theakstone

The Inspector is not in a position to append any explanations of importance to the last of the letters. It has been discovered that Mr. Matthew Sharpin left the house in Rutherford Street five minutes after his interview outside of it with Seregant Bulmer—his manner expressing the liveliest emotions of terror and astonishment, and his left cheek displaying a bright patch of red, which might have been the result of a slap on the face from a female hand. He was also heard, by the shopman at Rutherford Street, to use a very shocking expression in reference to Mrs. Yatman; and was seen to clench his fist vindictively, as he ran round the corner of the street. Nothing more has been heard of him; and it is conjectured that he has left London with the intention of offering his valuable services to the provincial police.

On the interesting domestic subject of Mr. and Mrs. Yatman still less is known. It has, however, been positively ascertained that the medical attendant of the family was sent for in a great hurry, on the day when Mr. Yatman returned from the milliner's shop. The neighbouring chemist received, soon afterwards, a prescription of a soothing nature to make up for Mrs. Yatman. The day after, Mr. Yatman purchased some smelling-salts at the shop, and afterwards appeared at the circulating library to ask for a novel, descriptive of high life, that would amuse an invalid lady. It has been inferred from these circumstances, that he has not thought it desirable to carry out his threat of separating himself from his wife—at least in the present (presumed) condition of that lady's sensitive nervous system.

ROBERT LOUIS STEVENSON

WAS IT MURDER?

'My friend the count,' it was thus that he began his story, 'had for an enemy a certain German baron, a stranger in Rome. It matters not what was the ground of the count's enmity; but as he had a firm design to be revenged, and that with safety to himself, he kept it secret even from the baron. Indeed, that is the first principle of vengeance; and hatred betrayed is hatred impotent. The count was a man of a curious, searching mind; he had something of the artist; if anything fell for him to do, it must always be done with an exact perfection, not only as to the result, but in the very means and instruments, or he thought the thing miscarried. It chanced he was one day riding in the outer suburbs, when he came to a disused by-road branching off into the moor which lies about Rome. On the one hand was an ancient Roman tomb; on the other a deserted house in a garden of evergreen trees. This road brought him presently into a field of ruins, in the midst of which, in the side of a hill, he saw an open door, and, not far off, a single stunted pine no greater than a currant-bush. The place was desert and very secret; a voice spoke in the count's bosom that there was something here to his advantage. He tied his horse to the pine tree, took his flint and steel in his hand to make a light and entered into the hill. The doorway opened on a passage of old Roman masonry, which shortly after branched in two. The count took the turning to the right, and followed it, groping forward in the dark, till he was brought up by a kind of fence, about elbow high, which extended quite across the passage. Sounding forward with his foot, he found an edge of polished stone, and then vacancy. All his curiosity was now awakened, and, getting some rotten sticks that lay about the floor, he made a fire. In front of him was a profound well; doubtless some neighbouring peasant had once used it for his water, and it was he that had set up the fence.   A long while the count stood leaning on the rail and looking down into the pit.   It was of Roman foundation, and, like all that nation set their hands to, built as for eternity; the sides were still straight, and the joints smooth; to a man who should fall in no escape was possible.   "Now," the count was thinking, "a strong impulsion brought me to this place.   What for? what have I gained? why should I be sent to gaze into this well?" when the rail of the fence gave suddenly under his weight, and he came within an ace of falling headlong in.   Leaping back to save himself, he trod out the last flicker of his fire, which gave him thenceforth no more light, only an incommoding smoke.   "Was I sent here to my death?" says he, and shook from head to foot.   And then a thought flashed in his mind.   He crept forth on hands and knees to the brink of the pit, and felt above him in the air.   The rail had been fast to a pair of uprights; it had only broken from the one, and still depended from the other.   The count set it back again as he had found it, so that the place meant death to the first comer, and groped out of the catacomb like a sick man.   The next day, riding in the Corso with the baron, he purposely betrayed a strong preoccupation.   The other (as he had designed) inquired into the cause; and he, after some fencing, admitted that his spirits had been dashed by an unusual dream.   This was calculated to draw on the baron—a superstitious man, who affected the scorn of superstition.   Some rallying followed, and then the count, as if suddenly carried away, called on his friend to beware, for it was of him that he had dreamed.   You know enough of human nature, my excellent Mackellar, to be certain of one thing: I mean that the baron did not rest till he had heard the dream.   The count, sure that he would never desist, kept him in play till his curiosity was highly inflamed, and then suffered himself, with seeming reluctance, to be overborne.   "I warn you," says he, "evil will come of it; something tells me so.   But since there is to be no peace either for you or me except on this condition, the blame be on your own head!   This was the dream: I beheld you riding, I know not where, yet I think it must have been near Rome, for on your one hand was an ancient tomb, and on the other a garden of evergreen trees.   Methought I cried and cried upon you to came back in a very agony of terror; whether you heard me I know not, but you went doggedly on. The road brought you to a desert place among the ruins, where was a door in a hill-side, and hard by the door a misbegotten pine. Here you dismounted (I still crying on you to beware), tied your horse to the pine tree, and entered resolutely in by the door. Within, it was dark; but in my dream I could still see you and still besought you to hold back. You felt your way along the right-hand wall, took a branching passage to the right, and came to a little chamber, where was a well with a railing. At this—I know not why—my alarm for you increased a thousandfold, so that I seemed to scream myself hoarse with warnings, crying it was still time, and bidding you begone at once from that vestibule. Such was the word I used in my dream, and it seemed then to have a clear significancy; but to-day, and awake, I profess I know not what it means. To all my outcry you rendered not the least attention, leaning the while upon the rail and looking down intently in the water. And then there was made to you a communication; I do not think I even gathered what it was, but the fear of it plucked me clean out of my slumber, and I awoke shaking and sobbing. And now," continues the count, "I thank you from my heart for your insistency. This dream lay on me like a load; and now I have told it in plain words and in the broad daylight, it seems no great matter."—"I do not know," says the baron. "It is in some points strange. A communication, did you say? Oh, it is an odd dream. It will make a story to amuse our friends."—"I am not so sure," says the count. "I am sensible of some reluctancy. Let us rather forget it."—"By all means," says the baron. And (in fact) the dream was not again referred to. Some days after, the count proposed a ride in the fields, which the baron (since they were daily growing faster friends) very readily accepted. On the way back to Rome, the count led them insensibly by a particular route. Presently he reined in his horse, clapped his hand before his eyes, and cried out aloud. Then he showed his face again (which was now quite white, for he was a consummate actor), and stared upon the baron. "What ails you?" cries the baron. "What is wrong with you?"—

"Nothing," cries the count. "It is nothing. A seizure,
I know not what. Let us hurry back to Rome." But in
the meanwhile the baron had looked about him; and there,
on the left-hand side of the way as they went back to Rome,
he saw a dusty by-road with a tomb upon the one hand and a
garden of evergreen trees upon the other. "Yes," says he,
with a changed voice. "Let us by all means hurry back to
Rome. I fear you are not well in health." "Oh, for God's
sake!" cries the count, shuddering, "back to Rome and let
me get to bed." They made their return with scarce a
word; and the count, who should by rights have gone into
society, took to his bed and gave out he had a touch of
country fever. The next day the baron's horse was found
tied to the pine, but himself was never heard of from that
hour. And now, was that a murder?' says the Master,
breaking sharply off.

GILBERT KEITH CHESTERTON

THE MAN IN THE PASSAGE

Two men appeared simultaneously at the two ends of a sort of passage running along the side of the Apollo Theatre in the Adelphi. The evening daylight in the streets was large and luminous, opalescent and empty. The passage was comparatively long and dark, so each man could see the other as a mere black silhouette at the other end. Nevertheless, each man knew the other, even in that inky outline; for they were both men of striking appearance and they hated each other.

The covered passage opened at one end on one of the steep streets of the Adelphi, and at the other on a terrace overlooking the sunset-coloured river. One side of the passage was a blank wall, for the building it supported was an old unsuccessful theatre restaurant, now shut up. The other side of the passage contained two doors, one at each end. Neither was what was commonly called the stage door; they were a sort of special and private stage doors used by very special performers, and in this case by the star actor and actress in the Shakespearian performance of the day. Persons of that eminence often like to have such private exits and entrances, for meeting friends or avoiding them.

The two men in question were certainly two such friends, men who evidently knew the doors and counted on their opening, for each approached the door at the upper end with equal coolness and confidence. Not, however, with equal speed; but the man who walked fast was the man from the other end of the tunnel, so they both arrived before the secret stage door almost at the same instant. They saluted each other with civility, and waited a moment before one of them, the sharper walker, who seemed to have the shorter patience, knocked at the door.

In this and everything else each man was opposite and and neither could be called inferior. As private persons both were handsome, capable, and popular. As public persons, both were in the first public rank. But everything about them, from their glory to their good looks, was of a diverse and incomparable kind. Sir Wilson Seymour was the kind of man whose importance is known to everybody who knows. The more you mixed with the innermost ring in every polity or profession, the more often you met Sir Wilson Seymour. He was the one intelligent man on twenty unintelligent committees—on every sort of subject, from the reform of the Royal Academy to the project of bimetallism for Greater Britain. In the arts especially he was omnipotent. He was so unique, that nobody could quite decide whether he was a great aristocrat who had taken up art, or a great artist whom the aristocrats had taken up. But you could not meet him for five minutes without realizing that you had really been ruled by him all your life.

His appearance was 'distinguished' in exactly the same sense; it was at once conventional and unique. Fashion could have found no fault with his high silk hat; yet it was unlike any one else's hat—a little higher, perhaps, and adding something to his natural height. His tall, slender figure had a slight stoop, yet it looked the reverse of feeble. His hair was silver-grey, but he did not look old; it was worn longer than the common, yet he did not look effeminate; it was curly, but it did not look curled. His carefully pointed beard made him look more manly and militant rather than otherwise, as it does in those old admirals of Velazquez with whose dark portraits his house was hung. His grey gloves were a shade bluer, his silver-knobbed cane a shade longer than scores of such gloves and canes flapped and flourished about the theatres and the restaurants.

The other man was not so tall, yet would have struck nobody as short, but merely as strong and handsome. His hair also was curly, but fair and cropped close to a strong, massive head—the sort of head you break a door with, as Chaucer said of the Miller's. His military moustache and the carriage of his shoulders showed him a soldier, but he had a pair of those peculiar, frank and piercing blue eyes which are more common in sailors. His face was some-what square, his jaw was square, his shoulders were square, even his jacket was square.   Indeed, in the wild school of caricature then current, Mr. Max Beerbohm had represented him as a proposition in the fourth book of Euclid.

For he also was a public man, though with quite another sort of success.   You did not have to be in the best society to have heard of Captain Cutler, of the siege of Hong Kong, and the great march across China.   You could not get away from hearing of him wherever you were; his portrait was on every other post card, his maps and battles in every other illustrated paper; songs in his honour in every other music-hall turn or on every other barrel-organ.   His fame, though probably more temporary, was ten times more wide, popular, and spontaneous than the other man's.   In thousands of English homes he appeared enormous above England, like Nelson.   Yet he had infinitely less power in England than Sir Wilson Seymour.

The door was opened to them by an aged servant or 'dresser,' whose broken-down face and figure and black shabby coat and trousers contrasted queerly with the glittering interior of the great actress's dressing-room.   It was fitted and filled with looking-glasses at every angle of refraction, so that they looked like the hundred facets of one huge diamond—if one could get inside a diamond.   The other features of luxury, a few flowers, a few coloured cushions, a few scraps of stage costume, were multiplied by all the mirrors into the madness of the Arabian Nights, and danced and changed places perpetually as the shuffling attendant shifted a mirror outwards or shot one back against the wall.

They both spoke to the dingy dresser by name, calling him Parkinson, and asking for the lady as Miss Aurora Rome.   Parkinson said she was in the other room, but he would go and tell her.   A shade crossed the brow of both visitors; for the other room was the private room of the great actor with whom Miss Aurora was performing, and she was of the kind that does not inflame admiration without inflaming jealousy.   In about half a minute, however, the inner door opened, and she entered as she always did, even in private life, so that the very silence seemed to be a roar of applause, and one well-deserved.   She was clad in a somewhat strange garb of peacock green and peacock blue satins, that gleamed like blue and green metals, such as delight children and aesthetes, and her heavy, hot brown hair framed one of those magic faces which are dangerous to all men, but especially to boys and to men growing grey. In company with her male colleague, the great American actor, Isidore Bruno, she was producing a particularly poetical and fantastic interpretation of the *Midsummer Night's Dream*, in which the artistic prominence was given to Oberon and Titania, or in other words to Bruno and herself. Set in dreamy and exquisite scenery, and moving in mystical dances, the green costume, like burnished beetle-wings, expressed all the elusive individuality of an elfin queen. But when personally confronted in what was still broad daylight, a man looked only at the woman's face.

She greeted both men with the beaming and baffling smile which kept so many males at the same just dangerous distance from her. She accepted some flowers from Cutler, which were as tropical and expensive as his victories; and another sort of present from Sir Wilson Seymour, offered later on and more nonchalantly by that gentleman. For it was against his breeding to show eagerness, and against his conventional unconventionality to give anything so obvious as flowers. He had picked up a trifle, he said, which was rather a curiosity; it was an ancient Greek dagger of the Mycenean Epoch, and might well have been worn in the time of Theseus and Hippolyta. It was made of brass like all the Heroic weapons, but, oddly enough, sharp enough to prick any one still. He had really been attracted to it by the leaflike shape; it was as perfect as a Greek vase. If it was of any interest to Miss Rome or could come in anywhere in the play, he hoped she would——

The inner door burst open and a big figure appeared, who was more of a contrast to the explanatory Seymour than even Captain Cutler. Nearly six foot six, and of more than theatrical thews and muscles, Isidore Bruno, in the gorgeous leopard skin and golden-brown garments of Oberon, looked like a barbaric god. He leaned on a sort of hunting-spear, which across a theatre looked a slight, silvery wand, but which in the small and comparatively crowded room looked as plain as a pikestaff—and as menacing. His vivid black eyes rolled volcanically, his bronzed face, handsome as it

was, showed at that moment a combination of high cheek-
bones with set white teeth, which recalled certain American
conjectures about his origin in the Southern plantations.

'Aurora,' he began, in that deep voice like a drum of
passion that had moved so many audiences, 'will you——'

He stopped indecisively because a sixth figure had presented itself just inside the doorway—a figure so incongruous in the scene as to be almost comic. It was a very
short man in the black uniform of the Roman secular clergy,
and looking (especially in such a presence as Bruno's and
Aurora's) rather like the wooden Noah out of an ark. He
did not, however, seem conscious of any contrast, but said
with dull civility: 'I believe Miss Rome sent for me.'

A shrewd observer might have remarked that the
emotional temperature rather rose at so unemotional an
interruption. The detachment of a professional celibate
seemed to reveal to the others that they stood round the
woman as a ring of amorous rivals; just as a stranger
coming in with frost cn his coat will reveal that a room is
like a furnace. The presence of the one man who did not
care about her increased Miss Rome's sense that everybody
else was in love with her, and each in a somewhat dangerous
way: the actor with all the appetite of a savage and a spoilt
child; the soldier with all the simple selfishness of a man of
will rather than mind; Sir Wilson with that daily hardening
concentration with which old hedonists take to a hobby;
nay, even the abject Parkinson, who had known her before
her triumphs, and who followed her about the room with
eyes or feet, with the dumb fascination of a dog.

A shrewd person might also have noted a yet odder
thing. The man like a black wooden Noah (who was not
wholly without shrewdness) noted it with a considerable
but contained amusement. It was evident that the great
Aurora, though by no means indifferent to the admiration
of the other sex, wanted at this moment to get rid of all the
men who admired her and be left alone with the man who
did not—did not admire her in that sense at least; for the
little priest did admire and even enjoy the firm feminine
diplomacy with which she set about her task. There was,
perhaps, only one thing that Aurora Rome was clever about,
and that was one half of humanity—the other half. The

little priest watched, like a Napoleonic campaign, the
swift precision of her policy for expelling all while banishing
none. Bruno, the big actor, was so babyish that it was
easy to send him off in brute sulks, banging the door.
Cutler, the British officer, was pachydermatous to ideas,
but punctilious about behaviour. He would ignore all hints,
but he would die rather than ignore a definite commission
from a lady. As to old Seymour, he had to be treated
differently; he had to be left to the last. The only way to
move him was to appeal to him in confidence as an old
friend, to let him into the secret of the clearance. The
priest did really admire Miss Rome as she achieved all these
three objects in one selected action.

She went across to Captain Cutler and said in her sweetest
manner: 'I shall value all these flowers, because they must
be your favourite flowers. But they won't be complete,
you know, without *my* favourite flower. *Do* go over to that
shop round the corner and get me some lilies of the valley,
and then it will be *quite lovely*.'

The first object of her diplomacy, the exit of the enraged
Bruno, was at once achieved. He had already handed his
spear in a lordly style, like a sceptre, to the piteous Parkinson, and was about to assume one of the cushioned seats like
a throne. But at this open appeal to his rival there glowed
in his opal eyeballs all the sensitive insolence of the slave; he
knotted his enormous brown fists for an instant, and then,
dashing open the door, disappeared into his own apartments beyond. But meanwhile Miss Rome's experiment in
mobilizing the British Army had not succeeded so simply
as seemed probable. Cutler had indeed risen stiffly and
suddenly, and walked towards the door, hatless, as if at a
word of command. But perhaps there was something
ostentatiously elegant about the languid figure of Seymour
leaning against one of the looking-glasses, that brought him
up short at the entrance, turning his head this way and
that like a bewildered bulldog.

'I must show this stupid man where to go,' said Aurora
in a whisper to Seymour, and ran out to the threshold to
speed the parting guest.

Seymour seemed to be listening, elegant and unconscious
as was his posture, and he seemed relieved when he heard

the lady call out some last instructions to the captain, and
then turn sharply and run laughing down the passage towards the other end, the end on the terrace above the
Thames. Yet a second or two after, Seymour's brow
darkened again. A man in his position has so many rivals,
and he remembered that at the other end of the passage was
the corresponding entrance to Bruno's private room. He
did not lose his dignity; he said some civil words to Father
Brown about the revival of Byzantine architecture in the
Westmister Cathedral, and then, quite naturally, strolled
out himself into the upper end of the passage. Father
Brown and Parkinson were left alone, and they were neither
of them men with a taste for superfluous conversation.
The dresser went round the room, pulling out looking-glasses
and pushing them in again, his dingy dark coat and trousers
looking all the more dismal since he was still holding the
festive spear of King Oberon. Every time he pulled out
the frame of a new glass, a new black figure of Father
Brown appeared; the absurd glass chamber was full of
Father Browns, upside down in the air like angels, turning
somersaults like acrobats, turning their backs to everybody
like very rude persons.

Father Brown seemed quite unconscious of this cloud of
witnesses, but followed Parkinson with an idly attentive
eye till he took himself and his absurd spear into the farther
room of Bruno. Then he abandoned himself to such
abstract meditations as always amused him—calculating
the angles of the mirrors, the angles of each refraction, the
angle at which each must fit into the wall . . . when he
heard a strong but strangled cry.

He sprang to his feet and stood rigidly listening. At the
same instant Sir Wilson Seymour burst back into the room,
white as ivory. 'Who's that man in the passage?' he
cried. 'Where's that dagger of mine?'

Before Father Brown could turn in his heavy boots,
Seymour was plunging about the room looking for the
weapon. And before he could possibly find that weapon
or any other, a brisk running of feet broke upon the pavement outside, and the square face of Cutler was thrust into
the same doorway. He was still grotesquely grasping a
bunch of lilies of the valley. 'What's this?' he cried.

'What 's that creature down the passage? Is this some of your tricks?'

'My tricks!' hissed his pale rival, and made a stride towards him.

In the instant of time in which all this happened Father Brown stepped out into the top of the passage, looked down it, and at once walked briskly towards what he saw.

At this the other two men dropped their quarrel and darting after him, Cutler calling out: 'What are you doing? Who are you?'

'My name is Brown,' said the priest sadly, as he bent over something and straightened himself again. 'Miss Rome sent for me, and I came as quickly as I could. I have come too late.'

The three men looked down, and in one of them at least the life died in that late light of afternoon. It ran along the passage like a path of gold, and in the midst of it Aurora lay lustrous in her robes of green and gold, with her dead face turned upwards. Her dress was torn away as in a struggle, leaving the right shoulder bare, but the wound from which the blood was welling was on the other side. The brass dagger lay flat and gleaming a yard or so away.

There was a blank stillness for a measurable time; so that they could hear far off a flower-girl's laugh outside Charing Cross, and someone whistling furiously for a taxicab in one of the streets off the Strand. Then the captain, with a movement so sudden that it might have been passion or play-acting, took Sir Wilson Seymour by the throat.

Seymour looked at him steadily without either fight or fear. 'You need not kill me,' he said in a voice quite cold; 'I shall do that on my own account.'

The captain's hand hesitated and dropped; and the other added with the same icy candour: 'If I find I haven't the nerve to do it with that dagger, I can do it in a month with drink.'

'Drink isn't good enough for me,' replied Cutler, 'but I 'll have blood for this before I die. Not yours—but I think I know whose.'

And before the others could appreciate his intention he snatched up the dagger, sprang at the other door at the lower end of the passage, burst it open, bolt and all, and confronted Bruno in his dressing-room. As he did so, old Parkinson tottered in his wavering way out of the door and caught sight of the corpse lying in the passage. He moved shakily towards it; looked at it weakly with a working face; then moved shakily back into the dressing-room again, and sat down suddenly on one of the richly cushioned chairs. Father Brown instantly ran across to him, taking no notice of Cutler and the colossal actor, though the room already rang with their blows and they began to struggle for the dagger. Seymour, who retained some practical sense, was whistling for the police at the end of the passage.

When the police arrived it was to tear the two men from an almost apelike grapple; and, after a few formal inquiries, to arrest Isidore Bruno upon a charge of murder, brought against him by his furious opponent. The idea that the great national hero of the hour had arrested a wrongdoer with his own hand doubtless had its weight with the police, who are not without elements of the journalist. They treated Cutler with a certain solemn attention, and pointed out that he had got a slight slash on the hand. Even as Cutler bore him back across tilted chair and table, Bruno had twisted the dagger out of his grasp and disabled him just below the wrist. The injury was really slight, but till he was removed from the room the half-savage prisoner stared at the running blood with a steady smile.

'Looks a cannibal sort of chap, don't he?' said the constable confidentially to Cutler.

Cutler made no answer, but said sharply a moment after: 'We must attend to the . . . the death . . .' and his voice escaped from articulation.

'The two deaths,' came in the voice of the priest from the farther side of the room. 'This poor fellow was gone when I got across to him.' And he stood looking down at old Parkinson, who sat in a black huddle on the gorgeous chair. He also had paid his tribute, not without eloquence, to the woman who had died.

The silence was first broken by Cutler, who seemed not untouched by a rough tenderness. 'I wish I was him,' he said huskily. 'I remember he used to watch her wherever she walked more than—anybody. She was his air, and he's dried up. He's just dead.'

'We are all dead,' said Seymour in a strange voice, looking down the road.

They took leave of Father Brown at the corner of the road, with some random apologies for any rudeness they might have shown. Both their faces were tragic, but also cryptic.

The mind of the little priest was always a rabbit-warren of wild thoughts that jumped too quickly for him to catch them. Like the white tail of a rabbit he had the vanishing thought that he was certain of their grief, but not so certain of their innocence.

'We had better all be going,' said Seymour heavily; 'we have done all we can to help.'

'Will you understand my motives,' asked Father Brown quietly, 'if I say you have done all you can to hurt?'

They both started as if guiltily, and Cutler said sharply: 'To hurt whom?'

'To hurt yourselves,' answered the priest. 'I would not add to your troubles if it weren't common justice to warn you. You've done nearly everything you could do to hang yourselves, if this actor should be acquitted. They'll be sure to subpoena me; I shall be bound to say that after the cry was heard, each of you rushed into the room in a wild state and began quarrelling about a dagger. As far as my words on oath can go, you might either of you have done it. You hurt yourselves with that; and then Captain Cutler must hurt himself with the dagger.'

'Hurt myself!' exclaimed the captain, with contempt. 'A silly little scratch.'

'Which drew blood,' replied the priest, nodding. 'We know there's blood on the brass now. And so we shall never know whether there was blood on it before.'

There was a silence; and then Seymour said, with an emphasis quite alien to his daily accent: 'But I saw a man in the passage.'

''I know you did,' answered the cleric Brown with a face of wood, 'so did Captain Cutler. That's what seems so improbable.'

Before either could make sufficient sense of it even to answer, Father Brown had politely excused himself and gone stumping up the road with his stumpy old umbrella.

As modern newspapers are conducted, the most honest and most important news is the police news. If it be true that in the twentieth century more space was given to murder than to politics, it was for the excellent reason that murder is a more serious subject. But even this would hardly explain the enormous omnipresence and widely distributed detail of 'The Bruno Case,' or 'The Passage Mystery,' in the Press of London and the provinces. So vast was the excitement that for some weeks the Press really told the truth; and the reports of examination and cross-examination, if interminable, even if intolerable, are at least reliable. The true reason, of course, was the co-incidence of persons. The victim was a popular actress; the accused was a popular actor; and the accused had been caught red-handed, as it were, by the most popular soldier of the patriotic season. In those extraordinary circumstances the Press was paralysed into probity and accuracy; and the rest of this somewhat singular business can practically be recorded from the reports of Bruno's trial.

The trial was presided over by Mr. Justice Monkhouse, one of those who are jeered at as humorous judges, but who are generally much more serious than the serious judges, for their levity comes from a living impatience of professional solemnity; while the serious judge is really filled with frivolity, because he is filled with vanity. All the chief actors being of a worldly importance, the barristers were well balanced; the prosecutor for the Crown was Sir Walter Cowdray, a heavy but weighty advocate of the sort that knows how to seem English and trustworthy, and how to be rhetorical with reluctance. The prisoner was defended by Mr. Patrick Butler, K.C., who was mistaken for a mere *flâneur* by those who misunderstood the Irish character—and those who had not been examined by him. The medical evidence involved no contradictions, the doctor whom Seymour had summoned on the spot, agreeing with the eminent surgeon who had later examined the body. Aurora Rome had been stabbed with some sharp instrument such as a knife or dagger; some instrument at least, of which the blade was short. The wound was just over the heart, and she had died instantly. When the first doctor saw her she could hardly have been dead for twenty minutes. Therefore when Father Brown found her she could hardly have been dead for three.

Some official detective evidence followed, chiefly concerned with the presence or absence of any proof of a a struggle; the only suggestion of this was the tearing of the dress at the shoulder, and this did not seem to fit in particularly well with the direction and finality of the blow. When these details had been supplied, though not explained, the first of the important witnesses was called.

Sir Wilson Seymour gave evidence as he did everything else that he did at all—not only well, but perfectly. Though himself much more of a public man than the judge, he conveyed exactly the fine shade of self-effacement before the King's Justice; and though every one looked at him as they would at the Prime Minister or the Archbishop of Canterbury, they could have said nothing of his part in it but that it was that of a private gentleman, with an accent on the noun. He was also refreshingly lucid, as he was on the committees. He had been calling on Miss Rome at the theatre; he had met Captain Cutler there; they had been joined for a short time by the accused, who had then returned to his own dressing-room; they had been then joined by a Roman Catholic priest, who asked for the deceased lady and said his name was Brown. Miss Rome had then gone just outside the theatre to the entrance of the passage, in order to point out to Captain Cutler a flower-shop at which he was to buy her some more flowers; and the witness had remained in the room, exchanging a few words with the priest. He had then distinctly heard the deceased, having sent the captain on his errand, turn round laughing and run down the passage towards its other end, where was the prisoner's dressing-room. In idle curiosity as to the rapid movements of his friends, he had strolled out to the head of the passage himself and looked down it towards the prisoner's door. Did he see anything in the passage? Yes, he saw something in the passage.

Sir Walter Cowdray allowed an impressive interval, during which the witness looked down, and for all his usual composure seemed to have more than his usual pallor. Then the barrister said in a lower voice, which seemed at once sympathetic and creepy: 'Did you see it distinctly?'

Sir Wilson Seymour, however moved, had his excellent brains in full working order. 'Very distinctly as regards its outline, but quite indistinctly, indeed not at all, as regards the details inside the outline. The passage is of such length that any one in the middle of it appears quite black against the light at the other end.' The witness lowered his steady eyes once more and added: 'I had noticed the fact before, when Captain Cutler first entered it.' There was another silence, and the judge leaned forward and made a note.

'Well,' said Sir Walter patiently, 'what was the outline like? Was it, for instance, like the figure of the murdered woman?'

'Not in the least,' answered Seymour quietly.

'What did it look like?'

'It looked to me,' replied the witness, 'like a tall man.'

Every one in court kept his eyes riveted on his pen or his umbrella handle or his book or his boots or whatever he happened to be looking at. They seemed to be holding their eyes away from the prisoner by main force; but they felt this figure in the dock, and they felt it as gigantic. Tall as Bruno was to the eye, he seemed to swell taller and taller when all eyes had been torn away from him.

Cowdray was resuming his seat with his solemn face, smoothing his black silk robes and white silk whiskers. Sir Wilson was leaving the witness-box, after a few final particulars to which there were many other witnesses, when the counsel for the defence sprang up and stopped him.

'I shall only detain you a moment,' said Mr. Butler, who was a rustic-looking person with red eyebrows and an expression of partial slumber. 'Will you tell his lordship how you knew it was a man?'

A faint, refined smile seemed to pass over Seymour's features. 'I'm afraid it is the vulgar test of trousers,' he said. 'When I saw daylight between the long legs I was sure it was a man, after all.'

Butler's sleepy eyes opened as suddenly as some silent explosion. 'After all!' he repeated slowly. 'So you did think first it was a woman?'

Seymour looked troubled for the first time. 'It is

hardly a point of fact,' he said, 'but if his lordship would like me to answer for my impression, of course I shall do so. There was something about the thing that was not exactly a woman and yet was not quite a man; somehow the curves were different. And it had something that looked like long hair.'

'Thank you,' said Mr. Butler, K.C., and sat down suddenly, as if he had got what he wanted.

Captain Cutler was a far less plausible and composed witness than Sir Wilson, but his account of the opening incidents was solidly the same. He described the return of Bruno to his dressing-room, the dispatching of himself to buy a bunch of lilies of the valley, his return to the upper end of the passage, the thing he saw in the passage, his suspicion of Seymour, and his struggle with Bruno. But he could give little artistic assistance about the black figure that he and Seymour had seen. Asked about its outline, he said he was no art critic—with a somewhat too obvious sneer at Seymour. Asked it if was a man or a woman, he said it looked more like a beast—with a too obvious snarl at the prisoner. But the man was plainly shaken with sorrow and sincere anger, and Cowdray quickly excused him from confirming facts that were already fairly clear.

The defending counsel also was again brief in his cross-examination; although (as was his custom) even in being brief, he seemed to take a long time about it. 'You used a rather remarkable expression,' he said, looking at Cutler sleepily. 'What do you mean by saying that it looked more like a beast than a man or a woman?'

Cutler seemed seriously agitated. 'Perhaps I oughtn't to have said that,' he said, 'but when the brute has huge humped shoulders like a chimpanzee, and bristles sticking out of its head like a pig——'

Mr. Butler cut short his curious impatience in the middle. 'Never mind whether its hair was like a pig's,' he said; 'was it like a woman's?'

'A woman's!' cried the soldier. 'Great Scott, no!'

'The last witness said it was,' commented the counsel, with unscrupulous swiftness. 'And did the figure have any of those serpentine and semi-feminine curves to which eloquent allusion has been made? No? No feminine curves? The figure, if I understand you, was rather heavy and square than otherwise?'

'He may have been bending forward,' said Cutler, in a hoarse and rather faint voice.

'Or again, he may not,' said Mr. Butler, and sat down suddenly for the second time.

The third witness called by Sir Walter Cowdray was the little Catholic clergyman, so little, compared with the others, that his head seemed hardly to come above the box, so that it was like cross-examining a child. But unfortunately Sir Walter had somehow got it into his head (mostly by some ramifications of his family's religion) that Father Brown was on the side of the prisoner, because the prisoner was wicked and foreign and even partly black. Therefore he took Father Brown up sharply whenever that proud pontiff tried to explain anything; and told him to answer yes or no, and tell the plain facts without any jesuitry. When Father Brown began, in his simplicity, to say who he thought the man in the passage was, the barrister told him that he did not want his theories.

'A black shape was seen in the passage. And you say you saw the black shape. Well, what shape was it?'

Father Brown blinked as under rebuke; but he had long known the literal nature of obedience. 'The shape,' he said, 'was short and thick, but had two sharp, black projections curved upwards on each side of the head or top, rather like horns, and——'

'Oh! the devil with horns, no doubt,' ejaculated Cowdray, sitting down in triumphant jocularity. 'It was the devil come to eat Protestants.'

'No,' said the priest dispassionately; 'I know who it was.'

Those in court had been wrought up to an irrational, but real sense of some monstrosity. They had forgotten the figure in the dock and thought only of the figure in the passage. And the figure in the passage, described by three capable and respectable men who had all seen it, was a shifting nightmare: one called it a woman, and the other a beast, and the other a devil. . . .

The judge was looking at Father Brown with level and piercing eyes. 'You are a most extraordinary witness,' he said, 'but there is something about you that makes me think you are trying to tell the truth. Well, who was the man you saw in the passage?'

'He was myself,' said Father Brown.

Butler, K.C., sprang to his feet in an extraordinary stillness, and said quite calmly: 'Your lordship will allow me to cross-examine?' And then, without stopping, he shot at Brown the apparently disconnected question: 'You have heard about this dagger; you know the experts say the crime was committed with a short blade?'

'A short blade,' assented Brown, nodding solemnly like an owl, 'but a very long hilt.'

Before the audience could quite dismiss the idea that the priest had really seen himself doing murder with a short dagger with a long hilt (which seemed somehow to make it more horrible), he had himself hurried on to explain.

'I mean daggers aren't the only things with short blades. Spears have short blades. And spears catch at the end of the steel just like daggers, if they're that sort of fancy spear they have in theatres; like the spear poor old Parkinson killed his wife with, just when she 'd sent for me to settle their family troubles—and I came just too late, God forgive me! But he died penitent—he just died of being penitent. He couldn't bear what he 'd done.'

The general impression in court was that the little priest, who was gabbling away, had literally gone mad in the box. But the judge still looked at him with bright and steady eyes of interest; and the counsel for the defence went on with his questions unperturbed.

'If Parkinson did it with that pantomime spear,' said Butler, 'he must have thrust from four yards away. How do you account for signs of struggle, like the dress dragged off the shoulder?' He had slipped into treating this mere' witness as an expert; but no one noticed it now.

'The poor lady's dress was torn,' said the witness, 'because it was caught in a panel that slid to just behind her. She struggled to free herself, and as she did so Parkinson came out of the prisoner's room and lunged with the spear.'

'A panel?' repeated the barrister in a curious voice.

'It was a looking-glass on the other side,' explained Father Brown. 'When I was in the dressing-room I noticed that some of them could probably be slid out into the passage.'

There was another vast and unnatural silence, and this time it was the judge who spoke. 'So you really mean that when you looked down that passage, the man you saw was yourself—in a mirror?'

'Yes, my lord; that was what I was trying to say,' said Brown, 'but they asked me for the shape; and our hats have corners just like horns, and so I——'

The judge leaned forward, his old eyes yet more brilliant, and said in specially distinct tones: 'Do you really mean to say that when Sir Wilson Seymour saw that wild what-you-call-him with curves and a woman's hair and a man's trousers, what he saw was Sir Wilson Seymour?'

'Yes, my lord,' said Father Brown.

'And you mean to say that when Captain Cutler saw that chimpanzee with humped shoulders and hog's bristles, he simply saw himself?'

'Yes, my lord.'

The judge leaned back in his chair with a luxuriance in which it was hard to separate the cynicism and the admiration. 'And can you tell us why,' he asked, 'you should know your own figure in a looking-glass, when two such distinguished men don't?'

Father Brown blinked even more painfully than before; then he stammered: 'Really, my lord, I don't know . . . unless it 's because I don't look at it so often.'

EDMUND CLERIHEW BENTLEY

THE CLEVER COCKATOO

'WELL, that's my sister,' said Mrs. Lancey, in a low voice. 'What do you think of her, now you've spoken to her?'

Philip Trent, newly arrived from England, stood by his hostess within the loggia of an Italian villa looking out upon a prospect of such loveliness as has enchanted and enslaved the Northern mind from age to age. It was a country that looked good and gracious for men to live in. Not far below them lay the broad, still surface of a great lake, blue as the sky; beyond it, low mountains rose up from the distant shore, tilled and wooded to the summit, drinking the light and warmth, visibly storing up earthly energy, with little villages of white and red scattered about their slopes like children clustered round their mother's knees. Before the villa lay a long paved terrace, and by the balustrade of it a woman stood looking out over the lake and conversing with a tall, grey-haired man.

'Ten minutes is rather a short acquaintance,' Trent replied. 'Besides, I was attending rather more to her companion. Mynheer Scheffer is the first Dutchman I have met on social terms. One thing about Lady Bosworth is clear to me, though. She is the most beautiful thing in sight, which is saying a good deal. And as for that low, velvety voice of hers, if she asked me to murder my best friend, I should have to do it on the spot.'

Mrs. Lancey laughed.

'But I want you to take a personal interest in her, Philip; it means nothing, I know, when you talk like that. I care a great deal about Isabel; she is far more to me than any other woman. That's rather rare between sisters, I believe. And it makes me wretched to know that there's something wrong with her.'

'With her health, do you mean? One wouldn't think so.'

'Yes, but I fear it is that.'

'Is it possible?' said Trent. 'Why, Edith, the woman has the complexion of a child and the step of a race-horse and eyes like jewels. She looks like Atalanta in blue linen.'

'Did Atalanta marry an Egyptian mummy?' inquired Mrs. Lancey.

'It is true,' said Trent thoughtfully, 'that Sir Peregrine looks rather as if he had been dug up somewhere. But I think he owes much of his professional success to that. People like a great doctor to look more or less unhealthy.'

'Perhaps they do; but I don't think the doctor's wife enjoys it very much. Isabel is always happiest when away from him—if he were here now she would be quite different from what you see. You know, Philip, their marriage hasn't been a success—I always knew it wouldn't be.'

Trent shrugged his shoulders.

'Let us drop the subject, Edith. Tell me why you want me to know about Lady Bosworth having something the matter with her. I'm not a physician.'

'No; but there's something very puzzling about it, as you will see; and you are clever at getting at the truth about things other people don't understand. Now, I'll tell you no more. I only want you to observe Bella particularly at dinner this evening, and tell me afterwards what you think. You'll be sitting opposite to her, between me and Agatha Stone. Now go and talk to her and the Dutchman.'

'Scheffer's appearance interests me,' remarked Trent. 'He has a face curiously like Frederick the Great's, and yet there's a difference—he doesn't look quite as if his soul were lost for ever and ever.'

'Well, go and ask him about it,' suggested Mrs. Lancey.

When the party of seven sat down to dinner that evening, Lady Bosworth had just descended from her room. Trent perceived no change in her; she talked enthusiastically of the loveliness of the Italian evening, and joined in a conversation that was general and lively. It was only after some ten minutes that she fell silent, and that a new look came over her face.

Little by little all animation departed from it. Her eyes grew heavy and dull, her lips were parted in a foolish smile, and to the high, fresh tint of her cheek there succeeded a disagreeable pallor. There was nothing about this altered appearance in itself that could be called odious. Had she been so always, one would have set her down merely as a beautiful and stupid woman of lymphatic type. But there was something inexpressibly repugnant about such a change in such a being; it was as though the vivid soul had been withdrawn.

All charm, all personal force had departed. It needed an effort to recall her quaint, vivacious talk of an hour ago, now that she sat looking vaguely at the table before her, and uttering occasionally a blank monosyllable in reply to the discourse that Mr. Scheffer poured into her ear. It was not, Trent told himself, that anything abnormal was done. It was the staring fact that Lady Bosworth was not herself, but someone wholly of another kind, that opened a new and unknown spring of revulsion in the recesses of his heart.

An hour later Mrs. Lancey carried Trent off to a garden-seat facing the lake.

'Well?' she said quietly.

'It's very strange, and rather ghastly,' he answered, nursing his knee. 'But if you hadn't told me it puzzled you, I should have thought it was easy to find an explanation.'

'Drugs, you mean?'

He nodded.

'Of course everybody must think so. George does, I know. It's horrible!' declared Mrs. Lancey, with a thump on the arm of the seat. 'Agatha Stone began hinting at it after the first few days. Gossiping cat! She loathes Isabel, and she'll spread it round everywhere that my sister is a drug-fiend. Philip, I asked her point-blank if she was taking anything that could account for it. She was much offended at that; told me I had known her long enough to know she never had done, and never would do such a thing. And though Isabel has her faults, she's absolutely truthful.'

Trent looked on the ground. 'Yes; but you may have heard——'

'Oh, I know! They say that kind of habit makes people lie and deceive who never did before. But, you see, she is so completely herself, except just at this time. I simply couldn't make up my mind to disbelieve her. And, besides, if Bella is peculiar about anything, it 's clean, wholesome, hygienic living. She has every sort of carbolicky idea. She never uses scent or powder or any kind of before-and-after stuff, never puts anything on her hair; she is washing herself from morning till night, but she always uses ordinary yellow soap. She never touches anything alcoholic, or tea, or coffee. You wouldn't think she had that kind of fad to look at her and her clothes; but she has; and I can't think of anything in the world she would despise more than dosing herself with things.'

'Not any kind of cosmetic whatever? That is surprising. Well, it seems to suit her,' Trent remarked. 'When she isn't like this, she is one of the most radiant creatures I ever saw.'

'I know, and that 's what makes it so irritating for women like myself, who look absolute hags if they don't assist nature a little. She 's always been as strong as a horse and bursting with vitality, and her looks have never shown the slightest sign of going off. And now this thing has come to her, absolutely suddenly and without warning.'

'How long has it been going on?'

'This is the seventh evening. I entreated her to see a doctor; but she hates the idea of being doctored. She says it 's sure to pass off and that it doesn't make any difference to her general health. George, who has always been devoted to her, only talks to her now with an effort. Randolph Stone is just the same; and two days before you arrived the Illingworths and Captain Burrows both went earlier than they had intended—I 'm certain, because this change in Isabel was spoiling their visit for them.'

'She seems to get on remarkably well with Scheffer,' remarked Trent.

'I know—it 's extraordinary, but he seems more struck with her than ever.'

'Well, he is; but in a lizard-hearted way of his own. He and I were talking just now after you left the dining-room. He spoke of Lady Bosworth in a queer, semi-scientific sort of way, saying she was very interesting to a medical man like himself. You didn't tell me he was one.'

'I didn't know. George calls him an anthropologist, and disagrees with him about the races of Farther India.

It's the one thing George does know something about, having lived there twelve years governing the poor things. They took to each other at once when they met last year, and when I asked him to stay here he was quite delighted. He only begged to be allowed to bring his cockatoo, as it could not live without him.'

'Strange pet for a man,' Trent observed. 'He was showing off its paces to me this afternoon. Well, it seems he's greatly interested in these attacks of hers. He has seen nothing quite like them. But he is convinced the thing is due to what he calls a toxic agent of some sort. As to what, or how, or why, he is absolutely at a loss.'

'Then you must find out what, and how, and why, Philip. I'm glad Scheffer isn't so easily upset as the other men; it's so much better for Isabel. She finds him very interesting, of course; not only because he's the only man here who pays her a lot of attention, but because he's really a wonderful person. He's lived for years among the most appalling savages in Dutch New Guinea, doing scientific work for his government, and according to George they treat him like a sort of god; he's somehow got the reputation among them that he can kill a man by pointing his finger at him, and he can manage the natives as nobody else can. He's most attractive and quite kind really, I think, but there's something about him that makes me afraid of him.'

'What is it?'

'I think it is the frosty look in his eyes,' replied Mrs. Lancey, drawing her shoulders together in a shiver.

'Perhaps that is the feeling about him in Dutch New Guinea,' said Trent. 'Did you tell me, Edith, that your sister began to be like this the very first evening she came here?'

'Yes. And it had never happened before, she declares.'

'She came out from England with the Stones, didn't she?'

'Only the last part of the journey. They got on the train at Lucerne.'

Trent looked back into the drawing-room at the wistful face of Mrs. Stone, who was playing piquet with her host. She was slight and pretty, with large, appealing eyes that never lost their melancholy, though she was always smiling.

'You say she loathes Lady Bosworth,' he said. 'Why?'

'Well, I suppose it 's mainly Bella's own fault,' confessed Mrs. Lancey, with a grimace. 'You may as well know, Philip—you 'll soon find out, anyhow—the truth is she *will* flirt with any man that she doesn't actively dislike. She 's so brimful of life she can't hold herself in—or she won't, rather; she says there 's no harm in it, and she doesn't care if there is. Several times she has practised on Randolph, and, although he 's a perfectly safe old donkey if there ever was one, Agatha can't bear the sight of her.'

'She seems quite friendly with her,' Trent observed.

Mrs. Lancey produced through her delicate nostrils a sound that expressed a scorn for which there were no words.

'Well, what do you make of it, Philip?' his hostess asked, at length. 'Myself, I simply don't know what to think. These queer fits of hers frighten me horribly. There 's one dreadful idea, you see, that keeps occurring to me. Could it, perhaps, be'—Mrs. Lancey lowered her already low tone—'the beginning of insanity?'

He spoke reassuringly. 'Oh, I shouldn't cherish that fancy. There are other things much more likely and much less terrible. Look here, Edith, will you try to arrange certain things for to-morrow, without asking me why? And don't let anybody know I asked you to do it—not even George. Until later on, at least. Will you?'

'How exciting!' Mrs. Lancey breathed. 'Yes, of course, mystery-man. What do you want me to do?'

'Do you think you could manage things to-morrow so that you and I and Lady Bosworth could go out in the motor boat on the lake for an hour or two in the evening, getting back in time to change for dinner—just the three of us and the engineer?'

She pondered. 'It might be. George and Randolph are playing golf at Cadenabbia to-morrow. I might arrange an expedition in the afternoon for Agatha and Mr. Scheffer, and let Bella know I wanted her to stay with me. You could lose yourself after breakfast with your sketching things, I dare say, and return for tea. Then the three of us could run down in the boat to San Marmette—it 's a lovely little place—and be back before seven. In this weather it 's really the best time of day for the lake.'

'That would do admirably, if you could work it. And one thing more—if we do go as you suggest, I want you privately to tell your engineer to do just what I ask him to do—no matter what it is.'

Mrs. Lancey worked it without difficulty. At five o'clock the two ladies and Trent, with a powerful young man of superb manners at the steering-wheel, were gliding swiftly southward, mile after mile, down the long lake. They landed at the most picturesque, and perhaps the most dilapidated and dirtiest, of all the lakeside villages, where, in the tiny square above the landing-place, a score of dusky infants were treading the measures and chanting the words of one of the immemorial games of childhood. While Mrs. Lancey and her sister watched them in delight, Trent spoke rapidly to the young engineer, whose gleaming eyes and teeth flashed understanding.

Soon afterward they strolled through San Marmette, and up the mountain road to a little church, half a mile away, where a curious fresco could be seen.

It was close on half-past six when they returned, to be met by Giuseppe, voluble in excitement and apology. It appeared that while he had been fraternizing with the keeper of the inn by the landing-place certain *tristi individui* had, unseen by any one, been tampering maliciously with the engine of the boat, and had poured handfuls of dust into the delicate mechanism. Mrs. Lancey, who had received a private nod from Trent, reproved him bitterly for leaving the boat, and asked how long it would take to get the engine working again.

Giuseppe, overwhelmed with contrition, feared that it might be a matter of hours. Questioned, he said that the public steamer had arrived and departed twenty minutes since; the next one, the last of the day, was not due until after nine. Their excellencies could at least count on getting home by that, if the engine was not ready sooner. Questioned farther, he said that one could telephone from the post office, and that food creditably cooked was to be had at the *trattoria*.

Lady Bosworth was delighted. She declared that she would not have missed this occasion for anything. She had come to approve highly of Trent, who had made himself excellent company, and she saw her way to being quite admirable, for she was in dancing spirits. In ten minutes she was on the best of terms with the fat, vivacious woman at the inn. Trent, who had been dispatched to telephone their plight to George Lancey, and had added that they were enjoying it very much, returned to find Lady Bosworth in the little garden behind the inn, with her skirts pinned up, peeling potatoes and singing '*Il segreto per esser felice*,' while her sister beat up something in a bowl, and the landlady, busy with cooking, laughed and screamed cheerful observations from the kitchen. Seeing himself unemployable, Trent withdrew; sitting on a convenient wall, he took a leaf from his sketchbook and began to devise and decorate a *menu* of an absurdity suited to the spirit of the hour.

It was a more than cheerful dinner that they had under a canopy of vine leaves on a tiny terrace overlooking the lake. Twilight came on unnoticed, and soon afterwards appeared the passenger boat, by which, Giuseppe advising it, they decided to return. It was as they sought for places on the crowded upper deck that Mrs. Lancey put her hand on Trent's arm. 'There hasn't been a sign of it all the evening,' she whispered. 'What does that mean?'

'It means,' murmured Trent, 'that we got her away from the cause at the critical time, without anybody knowing we were going to do it.'

'Whom do you mean by "anybody"?'

'How on earth should I know? Here comes your sister.'

It was not until the following afternoon that Trent found an opportunity of being alone with his hostess in the garden.

'She is perfectly delighted at having escaped it last night,' said Mrs. Lancey. 'She says she knew it would pass off, but she hasn't the least notion how she was cured. Nor have I.'

'She isn't,' replied Trent. 'Last night was only a

beginning, and we can't get her unexpectedly stranded for
the evening every day.   The next move can be made now,
if you consent to it.   Lady Bosworth will be out until this
evening, I believe?'

'She 's gone shopping in the town.   What do you want
to do?'

'I want you to take me up to her room, and there I want
you to look very carefully through everything in the place—
in every corner of every box and drawer and bag and cupboard—and show me anything you find that might——'

'I should hate to do that!' Mrs. Lancey interrupted
him, her face flushing.

'You would hate much more to see your sister again this
evening as she was every evening before last night.   Look
here, Edith; the position is simple enough.   Every day,
about seven, Lady Bosworth goes into that room in her
normal state to dress for dinner.   Every day she comes out
of it apparently as she went in, but turns queer a little later.
Now is there any other place than that room where the
mischief could happen?'

Mrs. Lancey frowned dubiously.   'Her maid is with her
always.'

'I suppose so; but it doesn't make any difference to
the argument.   That room is the only place where Lady
Bosworth isn't with the rest of us, doing what we are doing,
eating the same food, breathing the same air, exposed to all
the same influences as we are.   Does anything take place
in that room to account for those strange seizures?'

Mrs. Lancey threw out her hands.   'I can't bear to
think that Isabel should be deceiving me.   And yet I
know—it 's a dreadful thing—and what else could happen
there?'

'That is what we may find out, if we do as I say.   You
must decide, but remember that you must think of Lady
Boswell as one whom you are trying to save from a subtle
evil.   You can't shrink from a step merely because you
wouldn't dream of taking it in the ordinary way.'

For a few moments she stood carefully boring a hole in
the gravel with one heel.   Then, 'Come along,' she said,
and led the way toward the house.

'Unless we take the floor up,' said Mrs. Lancey, seating

herself emphatically on the bed in her sister's room twenty minutes later, 'there's nowhere else to look. I've taken everything out and pried into every hole and corner. There isn't a single lockable thing that is locked. There isn't a bottle or phial or pill-box of any sort to be found. So much for your suspicions. What interests you about that nail-polishing pad? You must have seen one before, surely.'

'This ornamental design on hammered silver is very beautiful and original,' replied Trent, abstractedly. 'I have never seen anything quite like it.'

'The same design is on the whole of the toilet-set,' Mrs. Lancey observed tartly, 'and it shows to least advantage on the manicure things. You are talking rubbish; and yet,' she added slowly, 'you are looking rather pleased with yourself.'

Trent, his hands in his pockets, was balancing himself on his heels as he stared out of the window of the bedroom. His eyes were full of animation, and he was whistling almost inaudibly. He turned round slowly. 'I'm only thinking. Whose are the rooms on each side of this, Edith?'

'This side, the Stones's; that side, Mr. Scheffer's.'

'Then I will go for a walk all alone and think some more. Good-bye.'

'Yes,' declared Mrs. Lancey as he went out, 'it's plain enough you have picked up some scent or other.'

'It isn't scent exactly,' Trent replied, as he descended the stairs. 'Guess again.'

Trent was not in the house when, three hours later, a rousing tumult broke out on the upper floor. Those below in the loggia heard first a piercing scream, then a clatter of feet on parquet flooring, then more sounds of feet, excited voices, other screams of harsh, inhuman quality, and a lively scuffling and banging. Mr. Scheffer, with a volley of guttural words of which it was easy to gather the general sense, headed the rush of the company upstairs.

'Gisko! Gisko!' he shouted, at the head of the stairway. There was another ear-splitting screech, and the cockatoo came scuttling and fluttering out of Lady Bosworth's room, pursued by three vociferating women servants. The bird's yellow crest was erect and quivering with agitation; it screeched furious defiance again as it leapt upon its master's outstretched wrist.

'Silence, devil!' exclaimed Mr. Scheffer, seizing it by the head and shaking it violently. 'I know not how to apologize, Lancey,' he declared. 'The accursed bird has somehow slipped from his chain away. I left him in my room secure just before we had tea.'

'Never mind, never mind!' replied his host, who seemed rather pleased than otherwise with this small diversion. 'I don't suppose he's done any harm beyond frightening the women. Anything wrong, Edith?' he asked, as they approached the open door of the bedroom, to which the ladies had already hurried. Lady Bosworth's maid was telling a voluble story.

'When she came in just now to get the room ready for Isabel to dress,' Mrs. Lancey summarized, 'she suddenly heard a voice say something, and saw the bird perched on top of the mirror, staring at her. It gave her such a shock that she dropped the water-can and fled; then the two other girls came and helped her, trying to drive it out. They hadn't the sense to send for Mr. Scheffer.'

'Apologize, carrion!' commanded Gisko's master. The cockatoo uttered a string of Dutch words in a subdued croak. 'He says he asks one thousand pardons, and he will sin no more,' Mr. Scheffer translated. 'Miserable brigand! Traitor!'

Lady Bosworth hurried out of her room.

'I won't hear the poor thing scolded like that,' she protested. 'How was he to know my maid would be frightened? He looks so wretched! Take him away, Mr. Scheffer, and cheer him up.'

It was half an hour later that Mrs. Lancey came to her husband in his dressing-room.

'I must say Bella was very decent about Scheffer's horrid bird,' she began. 'Do you know what the little fiend had done?'

'No my dear. I thought he had confined himself to frightening the maid out of her skin.'

'Not at all. He had been having the time of his life. Bella saw at once that he had been up to mischief, but she pretended there was nothing. Now it turns out he has

bitten the buttons off two pairs of gloves, chewed up a lot
of hair-pins, and spoiled her pretty little manicure set.
He 's torn the lining out of the case, the silver handles are
covered with beak-marks, two or three of the things he
seems to have hidden somewhere, and the polishing-pad is
a ruin.'

'It 's too bad!' declared Mr. Lancey, bending over a
shoe.

'I believe you're laughing, George,' said his wife coldly.

He began to do so audibly. 'You must admit it 's funny
to think of the bird going solemnly through a programme
of mischief like that. I wish I could have seen the little
beggar at it. Well, we shall have to get Bella a new
nail-outfit. I 'm glad she held her tongue about it just
now.'

'Why?'

'Because, my dear, we don't ask people to the house to
make them feel uncomfortable—especially foreigners.'

'Bella wasn't thinking of your ideal of hospitality. She
held her tongue because she 's taken a fancy to Scheffer.
But, George, how do you suppose the little pest got in?
The window was shut, and Hignett declares the door was
too, when she went to the room.'

'Then I expect Hignett deceives herself. Anyway, what
does it matter? What I am anxious about is your sister's
little peculiarity. As I 've told you, I don't at all like the
look of her having been quite normal yesterday evening,
the one evening when she was away from the house by
accident. I really am feeling miserably depressed, Edith.
What I 'm dreading now is a repetition of the usual ghastly
performance to-night.'

But neither that night, nor any night after, was that
performance repeated. Lady Bosworth, free now of all
apprehension, renewed and redoubled the life of the little
company. And the lips of Trent were obstinately sealed.

Three weeks later Trent was shown into the consulting-
room of Sir Peregrine Bosworth. The famous physician
was a tall, stooping man of exaggarated gauntness, narrow-
jawed, and high-nosed. He was courteous of manner and
smiled readily; but his face was set in unhappy lines.

'Will you sit down, Mr. Trent?' said Sir Peregrine. 'You wrote that you wished to see me upon a private matter concerning myself. I am at a loss to imagine what it can be, but, knowing your name, I had no hesitation in making an appointment.'

Trent inclined his head. 'I am obliged to you, Sir Peregrine. The matter is really important, and also quite private—so private that no person whatever knows the material facts besides myself. I won't waste words. I have lately been staying with the Lanceys, whom you know, in Italy. Lady Bosworth was also a guest there. For some days before my arrival she had suffered each evening from a curious attack of lassitude and vacancy of mind. I don't know what it was. Perhaps you do.'

Sir Peregrine, immovably listening, smiled grimly. 'The description of symptoms is a little vague. I have heard nothing of this, I must say, from my wife.'

'It always came on at a certain time of the day, and only then. That time was a few minutes after eight, at the beginning of dinner. The attack passed off gradually after two hours or so.'

The physician laid his clenched hand on the table between them. 'You are not a medical man, Mr. Trent, I believe. What concern have you with all this?' His voice was coldly hostile now.

'Lots,' answered Trent briefly. Then he added, as Sir Peregrine got to his feet with a burning eye, 'I know nothing of medicine, but I cured Lady Bosworth.'

The other sat down again suddenly. His open hands fell upon the table and his dark face became very pale. 'You ——' he began with difficulty.

'I and no other, Sir Peregrine. And in a curiously simple way. I found out what was causing the trouble, and without her knowledge I removed it. It was—oh, the devil!' Trent exclaimed in a lower tone. For Sir Peregrine Bosworth, with a brow gone suddenly white and clammy, had first attempted to rise and then sunk forward with his head on the table.

Trent, who had seen such things before, hurried to him, pulled his chair from the table, and pressed his head down to his knees. Within a minute the stricken man was leaning

back in his chair. He inspired deeply from a small bottle
he had taken from his pocket.

'You have been overworking, perhaps,' Trent said.
'Something is wrong. I think I had better not——'

Sir Peregrine had pulled himself together. 'I know very
well what is wrong with me, sir,' he interrupted brusquely. 'It
is my business to know. That will not happen again. I wish
to hear what you have to say, before you leave this house.'

'Very well.' Trent took a tone of colourless precision.
'I was asked by Lady Bosworth's sister, Mrs. Lancey, to
help in trying to trace the source of the disorder which
attacked her every evening. I need not describe the signs
of it, and I will not trouble you with an account of how
I reasoned on the matter. But I found out that Lady
Bosworth was, on these occasions, under the influence of a
drug, which had the effect of lowering her vitality and
clogging her brain, without producing stupefaction or sleep;
and I was led to the conclusion that she was administering
this drug to herself without knowing it.'

He paused, and felt in his waistcoat pocket. 'When Mrs.
Lancey and I were making a search for something of the
kind in her room, my attention was caught by the fine work-
manship of a manicure set on the dressing-table. I took
up the little round box meant to contain nail-polishing
paste, admiring its shape and decoration, and on looking
inside it found it half-full of paste. But I have often
watched the process of beautifying finger-nails, and it
seemed to me that the stuff was of a deeper red than the
usual pink confection; and I saw next that the polish-pad
of the set, though well-worn, had never been used with
paste, which leaves a sort of dark incrustation on the pad.
Yet it was evident that the paste in the little box had been
used. It is useful sometimes, you see, to have a mind that
notices trifles. So I jumped to the conclusion that the paste
that was not employed as nail-polish was employed for some
other purpose; and when I reached that point I simply put
the box in my pocket and went away with it. I may say
that Mrs. Lancey knew nothing of this, or of what I did
afterwards.'

'And what was that?' Sir Peregrine appeared now to
be following the story with an ironic interest.

'Naturally, knowing nothing of such matters, I took it to the place that called itself "English Pharmacy" in the town, and asked the proprietor what the stuff was. He looked at it, took a little on his finger, smelt it, and said it was undoubtedly lip-salve.

'It was then I remembered how, when I saw Lady Bosworth during one of her attacks, her lips were brilliantly red, though all the colour had departed from her face. That had struck me as very odd, because I am a painter, and naturally I could not miss an abnormality like that. Then I remembered another thing. One evening, when Lady Bosworth, her sister, and myself were prevented from returning to the house for dinner, and dined at a country inn, there had been no sign of her trouble; but I had noticed that she moistened her lips again and again with her tongue.'

'You are observant,' remarked Sir Peregrine dispassionately, and again had recourse to his smelling-bottle.

'You are good enough to say so,' Trent replied, with a wooden face. 'On thinking these things over, it seemed to me probable that Lady Bosworth was in the habit of putting on a little lip-salve when she dressed for dinner in the evening; perhaps finding that her lips at that time of day tended to become dry, or perhaps not caring to use it in daylight, when its presence would be much more easily detected. For I had learned that she made some considerable parade of not using any kind of cosmetics or artificial aids to beauty; and that, of course, accounted for her carrying it in a box meant for manicure-paste, which might be represented as merely a matter of cleanliness, and at any rate was not to be classed with paint and powder. It was not pleasant to me to have surprised this innocent little deception; but it was as well that I did so, for I soon ascertained beyond doubt that the stuff had been tampered with.

'When I left the chemist's I went and sat in a quiet corner of the Museum grounds. There I put the least touch of the salve on my tongue, and awaited result. In five minutes I had lost all power of connected thought or will; I no longer felt any interest in my own experiment. I was conscious. I felt no discomfort, and no loss of the power of movement. Only my intelligence seemed to be paralysed.

For an hour I was looking out upon the world with the soul of an ox, placid and blank.'

Trent now opened his fingers and showed a little round box of hammered silver, with a delicate ornamentation running round the lid. It was of about the bigness of a pill-box.

'It seemed best to me that this box should simply disappear, and in some quite natural, unsuspicious way. Merely to remove the salve would have drawn Lady Bosworth's attention to it and set her guessing. She did not suspect the stuff as yet, I was fully convinced; and I thought it well that the affair of her seizures should remain a mystery. Your eyes ask why. Just because I did not want a painful scandal in Mrs. Lancey's family—we are old friends, you see. And now here I am with the box, and neither Lady Bosworth nor any other person has the smallest inkling of its crazy secret but you and I.'

He stopped again and looked in Sir Peregrine's eyes. They remained fixed upon him with the gaze of a statue.

'It was plain, of course,' Trent continued, 'that someone had got at the stuff immediately before she went out to Italy, or immediately on her arrival. The attacks began on the first evening there, two hours after reaching the house. Therefore any tampering with the salve after her arrival was practically impossible. When I asked myself who should have tampered with it before Lady Bosworth left this house to go out to Italy, I was led to form a very unpleasant conjecture.'

Sir Peregrine stirred in his chair. 'You had been told the truth—or a part of the truth—about our married life, I suppose?'

Trent inclined his head. 'Three days ago I arrived in London, and showed a little of this paste to a friend of mine who is an expert analyst. He has sent me a report, which I have here.' He handed an envelope across the table. 'He was deeply interested in what he found, but I have not satisfied his curiosity. He found the salve to be evenly impregnated with a very slight quantity of a rare alkaloid body called "purvisine." Infinitesimal doses of it produce effects on the human organism which he describes, as I can testify, with considerable accuracy. It was discovered, he notes, by Henry Purvis twenty-five years ago; and you will

remember, Sir Peregrine, what I only found out by inquiry
—that you were assistant to Purvis about that time in
Edinburgh, where he had the chair of medical jurisprudence
and toxicology.'

He ceased to speak, and there was a short silence. Sir
Peregrine gazed at the table before him. Once or twice he
drew breath deeply, and at length began to speak calmly.

'I shall not waste words,' he said, 'in trying to explain
fully my state of mind or my action in this matter. But I
will tell you enough for your imagination to do the rest. My
feeling for my wife was an infatuation from the beginning,
and is still. I was too old for her. I don't think now that
she ever cared for me greatly; but she was too strong-
minded ever to marry a wealthy fool. By the time we had
been married a year I could no longer hide from myself that
she had an incurable weakness for philandering. She has
surrendered herself to it with less and less restraint, and
without any attempt to deceive me on the subject. If I
tried to tell you what torture it has been to me, you wouldn't
understand. The worst was when she was away from me,
staying with her friends. At length I took the step you
know. It was undeniably an act of baseness, and we will
leave it at that, if you please. If you should ever suffer as
I do, you will modify your judgment upon me. I knew of
my wife's habit, discovered by you, of using lip-salve at her
evening toilette. On the night before her departure I took
what was in that box and combined it with a preparation of
the drug purvisine. The infinitesimal amount which would
pass into the mouth after the application of the salve was
calculated to produce for an hour or two the effects you
have described, without otherwise doing any harm. But I
knew the impression that would be produced upon normal
men and women by the sight of any one in such a state. I
wanted to turn her attractiveness into repulsiveness, and I
seem to have succeeded. I was mad when I did it. I have
been aghast at my own action ever since. I am glad it has
been frustrated. And now I should like to know what you
intend to do.'

Trent took up the box. 'If you agree, Sir Peregrine, I
shall drop this from Westminster Bridge to-night. And so
long as nothing of the sort is practised again, the whole affair

shall be buried. Yours is a wretched story, and I don't suppose any of us would find our moral fibre improved by such a situation. I have no more to say.'

He rose and moved to the door. Sir Peregrine rose also and stood with lowered eyes, apparently deep in thought.

'I am obliged to you, Mr. Trent,' he said, formally. 'I may say, too, that your account of your proceedings interested me deeply. I should like to ask a question. How did you contrive that her box should disappear without its owner seeing anything remarkable in its absence?'

'Oh, easily,' Trent replied, his hand on the door-knob. 'After experimenting on myself, I went back to the house before tea-time, when no one happened to be in. I went upstairs to a room where a cockatoo was kept—a mischievous brute—took him off his chain, and carried him into Lady Bosworth's room. There I put him on the dressing-table, and teased him a little with the manicure things to interest him in them. Then I took away one of the pairs of scissors, so that the box shouldn't be the one thing missing, and left him shut in there to do his worst, while I went out of the house again. When I went he was ripping out the silk lining of the case, and had chewed up the silver handles of the things pretty well. After I had gone he went on to destroy various other things. In the riot that took place when he was found, the disappearance of the little box and scissors became a mere detail. Certainly Lady Bosworth suspected nothing.

'I suppose,' he added, thoughtfully, 'that occasion would be the only time a cockatoo was of any particular use.'

And Trent went out.

ERNEST BRAMAH

THE GHOST AT MASSINGHAM MANSIONS

'Do you believe in ghosts, Max?' inquired Mr. Carlyle.

'Only as ghosts,' replied Carrados with decision.

'Quite so,' assented the private detective with the air of acquiescence with which he was wont to cloak his moments of obfuscation. Then he added cautiously: 'And how don't you believe in them, pray?'

'As public nuisances—or private ones for that matter,' replied his friend. 'So long as they are content to behave as ghosts I am with them. When they begin to meddle with a state of existence that is outside their province—to interfere in business matters and depreciate property—to rattle chains, bang doors, ring bells, predict winners, and to edit magazines—and to attract attention instead of shunning it, I cease to believe. My sympathies are entirely with the sensible old fellow who was awakened in the middle of the night to find a shadowy form standing by the side of his bed and silently regarding him. For a few minutes the disturbed man waited patiently, expecting some awful communication, but the same profound silence was maintained. "Well," he remarked at length, "if you have nothing to do, I have," and turning over went to sleep again.'

'I have been asked to take up a ghost,' Carlyle began to explain.

'Then I don't believe in it,' declared Carrados.

'Why not?'

'Because it is a pushful, notoriety-loving ghost, or it would not have gone so far. Probably it wants to get into the *Daily Mail*. The other people, whoever they are, don't believe in it, either, Louis, or they wouldn't have called you in. They would have gone to Sir Oliver Lodge for an explanation, or to the nearest priest for a stoup of holy water.'

'I admit that I shall direct my researches towards the forces of this world before I begin to investigate any other,' conceded Louis Carlyle. 'And I don't doubt,' he added, with his usual bland complacence, 'that I shall hale up some mischievous or aggrieved individual before the ghost is many days older. Now that you have brought me so far, do you care to go on round to the place with me, Max, to hear what they have to say about it?'

Carrados agreed with his usual good nature. He rarely met his friend without hearing the details of some new case, for Carlyle's practice had increased vastly since the night when chance had led him into the blind man's study. They discussed the cases according to their interest, and there the matter generally ended so far as Max Carrados was concerned, until he casually heard the result subsequently from Carlyle's lips or learned the sequel from the newspaper. But these pages are primarily a record of the methods of the one man whose name they bear and therefore for the occasional case that Carrados completed for his friend there must be assumed the unchronicled scores which the inquiry agent dealt capably with himself. This reminder is perhaps necessary to dissipate the impression that Louis Carlyle was a pretentious humbug. He was, as a matter of fact, in spite of his amiable foibles and the self-assurance that was, after all, merely an asset of his trade, a shrewd and capable business man of his world, and behind his office manner nothing concerned him more than to pocket fees for which he felt that he had failed to render value.

Massingham Mansions proved to be a single block of residential flats overlooking a recreation ground. It was, as they afterwards found, an adjunct to a larger estate of similar property situated down another road. A porter, residing in the basement, looked after the interests of Massingham Mansions; the business office was placed among the other flats. On that morning it presented the appearance of a well-kept, prosperous enough place, a little dull, a little unfinished, a little depressing perhaps; in fact faintly reminiscent of the superfluous mansions that stand among broad, weedy roads on the outskirts of overgrown seaside resorts; but it was persistently raining at the time when Mr. Carlyle had his first view of it.

'It is early to judge,' he remarked, after stopping the car in order to verify the name on the brass plate, 'but, upon my word, Max, I really think that our ghost might have discovered more appropriate quarters.'

At the office, to which the porter had directed them, they found a managing clerk and two coltish youths in charge. Mr. Carlyle's name produced an appreciable flutter.

'The governor isn't here just now, but I have this matter in hand,' said the clerk with an easy air of responsibility—an effect unfortunately marred by a sudden irrepressible giggle from the least overawed of the colts. 'Will you kindly step into our private room?' He turned at the door of the inner office and dropped a freezing eye on the offender. 'Get those letters copied before you go out to lunch, Binns,' he remarked in a sufficiently loud voice. Then he closed the door quickly, before Binns could find a suitable retort.

So far it had been plain sailing, but now, brought face to face with the necessity of explaining, the clerk began to develop some hesitancy in beginning.

'It's a funny sort of business,' he remarked, skirting the difficulty.

'Perhaps,' admitted Mr. Carlyle; 'but that will not embarrass us. Many of the cases that pass through my hands are what you would call "funny sorts of business."'

'I suppose so,' responded the young man, 'but not through ours. Well, this is at 11 Massingham. A few nights ago—I suppose it must be more than a week now—Willett, the estate porter, was taking up some luggage to 75 Northanger for the people there when he noticed a light in one of the rooms at 11 Massingham. The backs face, though about twenty or thirty yards away. It struck him as curious, because 11 Massingham is empty and locked up. Naturally he thought at first that the porter at Massingham or one of us from the office had gone up for something. Still it was so unusual—being late at night—that it was his business to look into it. On his way round—you know where Massingham Mansions are?—he had to pass here. It was dark, for we'd all been gone hours, but Willett has duplicate keys and he let himself in. Then he began to think that something must be wrong, for here, hanging up

against their number on the board, were the only two keys
of 11 Massingham that there are supposed to be. He put
the keys in his pocket and went on to Massingham. Green,
the resident porter there, told him that he hadn't been into
No. 11 for a week. What was more, no one had passed the
outer door, in or out, for a good half-hour. He knew that,
because the door "springs" with a noise when it is opened,
no matter how carefully. So the two of them went up.
The door of No. 11 was locked and inside everything was
as it should be. There was no light then, and after looking
well round with the lanterns that they carried they were
satisfied that no one was concealed there.'

'You say lanterns,' interrupted Mr. Carlyle. 'I suppose
they lit the gas, or whatever it is there, as well?'

'It is gas, but they could not light it because it was cut
off at the meter. We always cut it off when a flat becomes
vacant.'

'What sort of a light was it, then, that Willett saw?'

'It was gas, Mr. Carlyle. It is possible to see the bracket
in that room from 75 Northanger. He saw it burning.'

'Then the meter had been put on again?'

'It is in a locked cupboard in the basement. Only the
office and the porters have keys. They tried the gas in the
room and it was dead out; they looked at the meter in the
basement afterwards and it was dead off.'

'Very good,' observed Mr. Carlyle, noting the facts in his
pocket-book. 'What next?'

'The next,' continued the clerk, 'was something that had
really happened before. When they got down again—
Green and Willett—Green was rather chipping Willett
about seeing the light, you know, when he stopped suddenly. He'd remembered something. The day before
the servant at 12 Massingham had asked him who it was
that was using the bathroom at No. 11—she of course
knowing that it was empty. He told her that no one used
the bathroom. "Well," she said, "we hear the water
running and splashing almost every night and it's funny
with no one there." He had thought nothing of it at the
time, concluding—as he told her—that it must be the water
in the bathroom of one of the underneath flats that they
heard. Of course he told Willett then and they went up

again and examined the bathroom more closely. Water
had certainly been run there, for the sides of the bath were
still wet. They tried the taps and not a drop came. When
a flat is empty we cut off the water like the gas.'

'At the same place—the cupboard in the basement?'
inquired Carlyle.

'No; at the cistern in the roof. The trap is at the top of
the stairs and you need a longish ladder to get there. The
next morning Willett reported what he'd seen and the
governor told me to look into it. We didn't think much of
it so far. That night I happened to be seeing some friends
to the station here—I live not so far off—and I thought I
might as well take a turn round here on my way home. I
knew that if a light was burning I should be able to see the
window lit up from the yard at the back, although the gas
itself would be out of sight. And, sure enough, there was
the light blazing out of one of the windows of No. 11. I
won't say that I didn't feel a bit home-sick then, but I'd
made up my mind to go up.'

'Good man,' murmured Mr. Carlyle approvingly.

'Wait a bit,' recommended the clerk, with a shamefaced
laugh. 'So far I had only had to make my mind up. It
was then close on midnight and not a soul about. I came
here for the keys, and I also had the luck to remember an
old revolver that had been lying about in a drawer of the
office for years. It wasn't loaded, but it didn't seem quite
so lonely with it. I put it in my pocket and went on to
Massingham, taking another turn into the yard to see that
the light was still on. Then I went up the stairs as quietly
as I could and let myself into No. 11.'

'You didn't take Willett or Green with you?'

The clerk gave Mr. Carlyle a knowing look, as of one smart
man who will be appreciated by another.

'Willett's a very trustworthy chap,' he replied, 'and we
have every confidence in him. Green also, although he has
not been with us so long. But I thought it just as well to
do it on my own, you understand, Mr. Carlyle. You didn't
look in at Massingham on your way? Well, if you had you
would have seen that there is a pane of glass above every
door, frosted glass to the hall doors and plain over each of
those inside. It's to light the halls and passages, you

know. Each flat has a small square hall and a longish
passage leading off it. As soon as I opened the door I
could tell that one of the rooms down the passage was lit
up, though I could not see the door of it from there. Then
I crept very quietly through the hall into the passage. A
regular stream of light was shining from above the end door
on the left. The room, I knew, was the smallest in the flat
—it's generally used for a servant's bedroom or sometimes
for a box-room. It was a bit thick, you'll admit—right
at the end of a long passage and midnight, and after what
the others had said.'

'Yes, yes,' assented the inquiry agent. 'But you went
on?'

'I went on, tiptoeing without a sound. I got to the door,
took out my pistol, put my hand almost on the handle and
then——'

'Well, well,' prompted Mr. Carlyle, as the narrator
paused provokingly, with the dramatic instinct of an expert
raconteur, 'what then?'

'Then the light went out; while my hand was within an
inch of the handle the light went out, as clean as if I had
been watched all along and the thing timed. It went out
all at once, without any warning and without the slightest
sound from the beastly room beyond. And then it was as
black as hell in the passage and something seemed to be
going to happen.'

'What did you do?'

'I did a slope,' acknowledged the clerk frankly. 'I
broke all the records down that passage, I bet you. You'll
laugh, I dare say, and think you would have stood, but you
don't know what it was like. I'd been screwing myself
up, wondering what I should see in that lighted room when
I opened the door, and then the light went out like a knife,
and for all I knew the next second the door would open on
me in the dark and Christ only knows what come out.'

'Probably I should have run also,' conceded Mr. Carlyle
tactfully. 'And you, Max?'

'You see, I always feel at home in the dark,' apologized
the blind man. 'At all events, you got safely away,
Mr.——?'

'My name's Elliott,' responded the clerk. 'Yes, you

may bet I did. Whether the door opened and anybody or anything came out or not I can't say. I didn't look. I certainly did get an idea that I heard the bath water running and swishing as I snatched at the hall door, but I didn't stop to consider that either, and if it was, the noise was lost in the slam of the door and my clatter as I took about twelve flights of stairs six steps at a time. Then when I was safely out I did venture to go round to look up again, and there was that damned light full on again.'

'Really?' commented Mr. Carlyle. 'That was very audacious of him.'

'Him? Oh, well, yes, I suppose so. That's what the governor insists, but he hasn't been up there himself in the dark.'

'Is that as far as you have got?'

'It's as far as we can get. The bally thing goes on just as it likes. The very next day we tied up the taps of the gas-meter and the water cistern and sealed the string. Bless you, it didn't make a ha'porth of difference. Scarcely a night passes without the light showing, and there's no doubt that the water runs. We've put copying ink on the door handles and the taps and got into it ourselves until there isn't a man about the place that you couldn't implicate.'

'Has any one watched up there?'

'Willett and Green together did one night. They shut themselves up in the room opposite from ten till twelve and nothing happened. I was watching the window with a pair of opera-glasses from an empty flat here—85 Northanger. Then they chucked it, and before they could have been down the steps the light was there—I could see the gas as plain as I can see this inkstand. I ran down and met them coming to tell me that nothing had happened. The three of us sprinted up again and the light was out and the flat as deserted as a churchyard. What do you make of that?'

'It certainly requires looking into,' replied Mr. Carlyle diplomatically.

'Looking into! Well, you're welcome to look all day and all night too, Mr. Carlyle. It isn't as though it was an old baronial mansion, you see, with sliding panels and secret passages. The place has the date over the front door, 1882

—1882 and haunted, by gosh! It was built for what it is, and there isn't an inch unaccounted for between the slates and the foundation.'

'These two things—the light and the water running— are the only indications there have been?' asked Mr. Carlyle.

'So far as we ourselves have seen or heard. I ought perhaps to tell you of something else, however. When this business first started I made a few casual inquiries here and there among the tenants. Among others I saw Mr. Belting, who occupies 9 Massingham—the flat directly beneath No. 11. It didn't seem any good making up a cock-and-bull story, so I put it to him plainly—had he been annoyed by anything unusual going on at the empty flat above?'

'"If you mean your confounded ghost up there, I have not been particularly annoyed," he said at once, "but Mrs. Belting has, and I should advise you to keep out of her way, at least until she gets another servant." Then he told me that their girl, who slept in the bedroom underneath the little one at No. 11, had been going on about noises in the room above—footsteps and tramping and a bump on the floor—for some time before we heard anything of it. Then one day she suddenly said that she'd had enough of it and bolted. That was just before Willett first saw the light.'

'It is being talked about, then—among the tenants?'

'You bet!' assented Mr. Elliott pungently. 'That's what gets the governor. He wouldn't give a continental if no one knew, but you can't tell where it will end. The people at Northanger don't half like it either. All the children are scared out of their little wits and none of the slaveys will run errands after dark. It 'll give the estate a bad name for the next three years if it isn't stopped.'

'It shall be stopped,' declared Mr. Carlyle impressively. 'Of course we have our methods for dealing with this sort of thing, but in order to make a clean sweep it is desirable to put our hands on the offender *in flagrante delicto*. Tell your—er—principal not to have any further concern in the matter. One of my people will call here for any further details that he may require during the day. Just leave

everything as it is in the meanwhile.   Good morning, Mr.
Elliott, good morning. . . . A fairly obvious game, I
imagine, Max,' he commented as they got into the car,
'although the details are original and the motive not dis-
closed as yet.   I wonder how many of them are in it?'

'Let me know when you find out,' said Carrados, and
Mr. Carlyle promised.

Nearly a week passed and the expected revelation failed
to make its appearance.   Then, instead, quite a different
note arrived:

'MY DEAR MAX,

'I wonder if you formed any conclusion of that Massingham Mansions affair from Mr. Elliott's refined
narrative of the circumstances?

'I begin to suspect that Trigget, whom I put on, is
somewhat of an ass, though a very remarkable circumstance has come to light which might—if it wasn't a
matter of business—offer an explanation of the whole
business by stamping it as inexplicable.

'You know how I value your suggestions.   If you
happen to be in the neighbourhood—not otherwise, Max,
I protest—I should be glad if you would drop in for a
chat.

'Yours sincerely,

'LOUIS CARLYLE.'

Carrados smiled at the ingenuous transparency of the
note.   He had thought several times of the case since the
interview with Elliott, chiefly because he was struck by
certain details of the manifestation that divided it from the
ordinary methods of the bogy-raiser, an aspect that had
apparently made no particular impression on his friend.
He was sufficiently interested not to let the day pass without
'happening' to be in the neighbourhood of Bampton Street.

'Max,' exclaimed Mr. Carlyle, raising an accusing forefinger, 'you have come on purpose.'

'If I have,' replied the visitor, 'you can reward me with
a cup of that excellent beverage that you were able to
conjure up from somewhere down in the basement on a
former occasion.   As a matter of fact, I have.'

Mr. Carlyle transmitted the order and then demanded his friend's serious attention.

'That ghost at Massingham Mansions——'

'I still don't believe in that particular ghost, Louis,' commented Carrados in mild speculation.

'I never did, of course,' replied Carlyle, 'but, upon my word, Max, I shall have to very soon as a precautionary measure. Triggett has been able to do nothing and now he has as good as gone on strike.'

'Downed—now what on earth can an inquiry man down to go on strike, Louis? Note-books? So Trigget has got a chill, like our candid friend Elliott, eh?'

'He started all right—said that he didn't mind spending a night or a week in a haunted flat, and, to do him justice, I don't believe he did at first. Then he came across a very curious piece of forgotten local history, a very remarkable —er—coincidence in the circumstances, Max.'

'I was wondering,' said Carrados, 'when we should come up against that story, Louis.'

'Then you know of it?' exclaimed the inquiry agent in surprise.

'Not at all. Only I guessed it must exist. Here you have the manifestation associated with two things which in themselves are neither usual nor awe-inspiring—the gas and the water. It requires some association to connect them up, to give them point and force. That is the story.'

'Yes,' assented his friend, 'that is the story, and, upon my soul, in the circumstances—well, you shall hear it. It comes partly from the newspapers of many years ago, but only partly, for the circumstances were successfully hushed up in a large measure and it required the stimulated memories of ancient scandalmongers to fill in the details. Oh, yes, it was a scandal, Max, and would have been a great sensation too, I do not doubt, only they had no proper pictorial Press in those days, poor beggars. It was very soon after Massingham Mansions had been erected—they were called Enderby House in those days, by the way, for the name was changed on account of this very business. The household at No. 11 consisted of a comfortable, middle-aged married couple and one servant, a quiet and attractive young creature, one is led to understand. As a matter of fact, I think they were the first tenants of that flat.'

'The first occupants give the soul to a new house,' remarked the blind man gravely. 'That is why empty houses have their different characters.'

'I don't doubt it for a moment,' assented Mr. Carlyle in his incisive way, 'but none of our authorities on this case made any reference to the fact. They did say, however, that the man held a good and responsible position—a position for which high personal character and strict morality were essential. He was also well known and regarded in quiet but substantial local circles where serious views prevailed. He was, in short, a man of notorious "respectability."

'The first chapter of the tragedy opened with the painful death of the prepossessing handmaiden—suicide, poor creature. She didn't appear one morning and the flat was full of the reek of gas. With great promptitude the master threw all the windows open and called up the porter. They burst open the door of the little bedroom at the end of the passage, and there was the thing as clear as daylight for any coroner's jury to see. The door was locked on the inside, and the extinguished gas was turned full on. It was only a tiny room, with no fireplace, and the ventilation of a closed well-fitting door and window was negligible in the circumstances. At all events the girl was proved to have been dead for several hours when they reached her, and the doctor who conducted the autopsy crowned the convincing fabric of circumstances when he mentioned as delicately as possible that the girl had a very pressing reason for dreading an inevitable misfortune that would shortly overtake her. The jury returned the obvious verdict.

'There have been many undiscovered crimes in the history of mankind, Max, but it is by no means every ingenious plot that carries. After the inquest, at which our gentleman doubtless cut a very proper and impressive figure, the barbed whisper began to insinuate and to grow in freedom. It is sheerly impossible to judge how these things start, but we know that when once they have been begun they gather material like an avalanche. It was remembered by someone at the flat underneath that late on the fatal night a window in the principal bedroom above had been heard to open, top and bottom, very quietly. Certain other sounds of movement in the night did not tally with the tale of sleep-wrapped innocence. Sceptical busy-bodies were anxious to demonstrate practically to those who differed from them on this question that it was quite easy to extinguish a gas-jet in one room by blowing down the gas-pipe in another; and in this connection there was evidence that the lady of the flat had spoken to her friends more than once of her sentimental young servant's extravagant habit of reading herself to sleep occasionally with the light full on. Why was nothing heard at the inquest, they demanded, of the curious fact that an open novelette lay on the counterpane when the room was broken into? A hundred trifling circumstances were adduced — arrange-ments that the girl had been making for the future down to the last evening of her life—interpretable hints that she had dropped to her acquaintances—her views on suicide and the best means to that end: a favourite topic, it would seem, among her class—her possession of certain com-paratively expensive trinkets on a salary of a very few shillings a week, and so on. Finally, some rather more definite and important piece of evidence must have been conveyed to the authorities, for we know now that one fine day a warrant was issued. Somehow rumour preceded its execution. The eminently respectable gentleman with whom it was concerned did not wait to argue out the merits of the case. He locked himself in the bathroom, and when the police arrived they found that instead of an arrest they had to arrange the details for another inquest.'

'A very convincing episode,' conceded Carrados in re-sponse to his friend's expectant air. 'And now her spirit passes the long winter evenings turning the gas on and off, and the one amusement of his consists in doing the same with the bath-water — or the other way about, Louis. Truly, one half the world knows not how the other half lives!'

'All your cheap humour won't induce Trigget to spend another night in that flat, Max,' retorted Mr. Carlyle. 'Nor, I am afraid, will it help me through this business in any other way.'

'Then I 'll give you a hint that may,' said Carrados. 'Try your respectable gentleman's way of settling difficulties.'

'What is that?' demanded his friend.

'Blow down the pipes, Louis.'

'Blow down the pipes?' repeated Carlyle.

'At all events try it. I infer that Mr. Trigget has not experimented in that direction.'

'But what will it do, Max?'

'Possibly it will demonstrate where the other end goes to.'

'But the other end goes to the meter.'

'I suggest not—not without some interference with its progress. I have already met your Mr. Trigget, you know, Louis. An excellent and reliable man within his limits, but he is at his best posted outside the door of a hotel waiting to see the co-respondent go in. He hasn't enough imagination for this case—not enough to carry him away from what would be his own obvious method of doing it to what is someone else's equally obvious but quite different method. Unless I am doing him an injustice, he will have spent most of his time trying to catch someone getting into the flat to turn the gas and water on and off, whereas I conjecture that no one does go into the flat because it is perfectly simple—ingenious but simple—to produce these phenomena without. Then when Mr. Trigget has satisfied himself that it is physically impossible for any one to be going in and out, and when, on the top of it, he comes across this roman- tic tragedy—a tale that might psychologically explain the ghost, simply because the ghost is moulded on the tragedy —then, of course, Mr. Trigget's mental process is swept away from its moorings and his feet begin to get cold.'

'This is very curious and suggestive,' said Mr. Carlyle. 'I certainly assumed—— But shall we have Trigget up and question him on the point? I think he ought to be here now—if he isn't detained at the "Bull."'

Carrados assented, and in a few minutes Mr. Trigget presented himself at the door of the private office. He was a melancholy-looking middle-aged little man, with an ineradicable air of being exactly what he was, and the searcher for deeper or subtler indications of character would only be rewarded by a latent pessimism grounded on the depressing probability that he would never be anything else.

'Come in, Trigget,' called out Mr. Carlyle when his employee diffidently appeared. 'Come in. Mr. Carrados would like to hear some of the details of the Massingham Mansions case.'

'Not the first time I have availed myself of the benefit of your inquiries, Mr. Trigget,' nodded the blind man. 'Good afternoon.'

'Good afternoon, sir,' replied Trigget with gloomy deference. 'It's very handsome of you to put it in that way, Mr. Carrados, sir. But this isn't another Tarporley-Templeton case, if I may say so, sir. That was as plain as a pikestaff after all, sir.'

'When we saw the pikestaff, Mr. Trigget; yes, it was,' admitted Carrados, with a smile. 'But this is insoluble? Ah, well. When I was a boy I used to be extraordinarily fond of ghost stories, I remember, but even while reading them I always had an uneasy suspicion that when it came to the necessary detail of explaining the mystery I should be defrauded with some subterfuge as "by an ingenious arrangement of hidden wires the artful Muggles had contrived," etc., or "an optical illusion effected by means of concealed mirrors revealed the *modus operandi* of the apparition." I thought that I had been swindled. I think so still. I hope there are no ingenious wires or concealed mirrors here, Mr. Trigget?'

Mr. Trigget looked mildly sagacious but hopelessly puzzled. It was his misfortune that in him the necessities of his business and the proclivities of his nature were at variance, so that he ordinarily presented the curious anomaly of looking equally alert and tired.

'Wires, sir?' he began, with faint amusement.

'Not only wires, but anything that might account for what is going on,' interposed Mr. Carlyle. 'Mr. Carrados means this, Trigget: you have reported that it is impossible for any one to be concealed in the flat or to have secret access to it——'

'I have tested every inch of space in all the rooms, Mr. Carrados, sir,' protested the hurt Trigget. 'I have examined every board and, you may say, every nail in the floor, the skirting-boards, the window frames, and, in fact, wherever a board or a nail exists. There are no secret ways in or out.

Then I have taken the most elaborate precautions against the doors and windows being used for surreptitious ingress and egress. They have not been used, sir. For the past week I am the only person who has been in and out of the flat, Mr. Carrados, and yet night after night the gas that is cut off at the meter is lit and turned out again, and the water that is cut off at the cistern splashes about in the bath up to the second I let myself in. Then it 's as quiet as the grave and everything is exactly as I left it. It isn't human, Mr. Carrados, sir, and flesh and blood can't stand it—not in the middle of the night, that is to say.'

'You see nothing further, Mr. Trigget?'

'I don't indeed, Mr. Carrados. I would suggest doing away with the gas in that room altogether. As a box-room it wouldn't need one.'

'And the bathroom?'

'That might be turned into a small bedroom and all the water fittings removed. Then to provide a bathroom——'

'Yes, yes,' interrupted Mr. Carlyle impatiently, 'but we are retained to discover who is causing this annoyance and to detect the means, not to suggest structural alterations in the flat, Trigget. The fact is that after having put in a week on this job you have failed to bring us an inch nearer its solution. Now Mr. Carrados has suggested'—Mr. Carlyle was not usually detained among the finer shades of humour, but some appreciation of the grotesqueness of the advice required him to control his voice as he put the matter in its baldest form—'Mr. Carrados has suggested that instead of spending the time measuring the chimneys and listening to the wall-paper, if you had simply blown down the gas-pipe——'

Carrados was inclined to laugh, although he thought it rather too bad of Louis.

'Not quite in those terms, Mr. Trigget,' he interposed.

'Blow down the gas-pipe, sir?' repeated the amazed man. 'What for?'

'To ascertain where the other end comes out,' replied Carlyle.

'But don't you see, sir, that that is a detail until you ascertain how it is being done? The pipe may be tapped between the bath and the cistern. Naturally, I considered that. As a matter of fact, the water-pipe isn't tapped. It goes straight up from the bath to the cistern in the attic above, a distance of only a few feet, and I have examined it. The gas-pipe, it is true, passes through a number of flats, and without pulling up all the floors it isn't practicable to trace it. But how does that help us, Mr. Carrados? The gas-tap has to be turned on and off; you can't do that with these hidden wires. It has to be lit. I've never heard of lighting gas by optical illusions, sir. Somebody must get in and out of the flat or else it isn't human. I've spent a week, a very trying week, sir, in endeavouring to ascertain how it could be done. I haven't shirked cold and wet and solitude, sir, in the discharge of my duty. I've freely placed my poor gifts of observation and intelligence, such as they are, sir, at the service——'

'Not "freely," Trigget,' interposed his employer with decision.

'I am speaking under a deep sense of injury, Mr. Carlyle,' retorted Mr. Trigget, who, having had time to think it over, had now come to the conclusion that he was not appreciated. 'I am alluding to a moral attitude such as we all possess. I am very grieved by what has been suggested. I didn't expect it of you, Mr. Carlyle, sir; indeed I did not. For a week I have done everything that it has been possible to do, everything that a long experience could suggest, and now, as I understand it, sir, you complain that I didn't blow down the gas-pipe, sir. It's hard, sir; it's very hard.'

'Oh, well, for heaven's sake don't cry about it, Trigget,' exclaimed Mr. Carlyle. 'You're always sobbing about the place over something or other. We know you did your best—God help you!' he added aside.

'I did, Mr. Carlyle; indeed I did, sir. And I thank you for that appreciative tribute to my services. I value it highly, very highly indeed, sir.' A tremulous note in the rather impassioned delivery made it increasingly plain that Mr. Trigget's regimen had not been confined entirely to solid food that day. His wrongs were forgotten and he approached Mr. Carrados with an engaging air of secrecy.

'What is this tip about blowing down the gas-pipe, sir?'

he whispered confidentially. 'The old dog 's always willing to learn something new.'

'Max,' said Mr. Carlyle curtly, 'is there anything more that we need detain Trigget for?'

'Just this,' replied Carrados after a moment's thought. 'The gas-bracket—it has a mantle attachment on?'

'Oh, no, Mr. Carrados,' confided the old dog with the affectation of imparting rather valuable information, 'not a mantle on. Oh, certainly no mantle. Indeed—indeed, not a mantle at all.'

Mr. Carlyle looked at his friend curiously. It was half evident that something might have miscarried. Furthermore, it was obvious that the warmth of the room and the stress of emotion were beginning to have a disastrous effect on the level of Mr. Trigget's ideas and speech.

'A globe?' suggested Carrados.

'A globe? No, sir, not even a globe, in the strict sense of the word. No globe, that is to say, Mr. Carrados. In fact nothing like a globe.'

'What is there, then?' demanded the blind man without any break in his unruffled patience. 'There may be another way—but surely—surely there must be some attachment?'

'No,' said Mr. Trigget with precision, 'no attachment at all; nothing at all; nothing whatsoever. Just the ordinary or common or penny plain gas-jet, and above it the whayou-maycallit thingamabob.'

'The shade — gas consumer — of course!' exclaimed Carrados. 'That is it.'

'The tin thingamabob,' insisted Mr. Trigget with slow dignity. 'Call it what you will. Its purpose is self-evident. It acts as a dispirator—a distributor, that is to say——'

'Louis,' struck in Carrados joyously, 'are you good for settling it to-night?'

'Certainly, my dear fellow, if you can really give the time.'

'Good; it 's years since I last tackled a ghost. What about——?' His look indicated the other member of the council.

'Would he be of any assistance?'

'Perhaps—then.'

'What time?'

'Say eleven-thirty.'

'Trigget,' rapped out his employer sharply, 'meet us at the corner of Middlewood and Enderby Roads at half-past eleven sharp to-night. If you can't manage it I shall not require your services again.'

'Certainly, sir; I shall not fail to be punctual,' replied Trigget without a tremor. The appearance of an almost incredible sobriety had possessed him in the face of warning, and both in speech and manner he was again exactly the man as he had entered the room. 'I regard it as a great honour, Mr. Carrados, to be associated with you in this business, sir.'

'In the meanwhile,' remarked Carrados, 'if you find the time hang heavy on your hands you might look up the subject of "platinum black." It may be the new tip you want.'

'Certainly, sir. But do you mind giving me a hint as to what "platinum black" is?'

'It is a chemical that has the remarkable property of igniting hydrogen or coal gas by mere contact,' replied Carrados. 'Think how useful that may be if you haven't got a match!'

To mark the happy occasion Mr. Carlyle had insisted on taking his friend off to witness a popular musical comedy. Carrados had a few preparations to make, a few accessories to procure for the night's work, but the whole business had come within the compass of an hour and the theatre spanned the interval between dinner at the Palm Tree and the time when they left the car at the appointed meeting-place. Mr. Trigget was already there, in an irreproachable state of normal dejection. Parkinson accompanied the party, bringing with him the baggage of the expedition.

'Anything going on, Trigget?' inquired Mr. Carlyle.

'I've made a turn round the place, sir, and the light was on,' was the reply. 'I didn't go up for fear of disturbing the conditions before you saw them. That was about ten minutes ago. Are you going into the yard to look again? I have all the keys, of course.'

'Do we, Max?' queried Mr. Carlyle.

'Mr. Trigget might. We need not all go. He can catch us up again.'

He caught them up again before they had reached the outer door.

'It's still on, sir,' he reported.

'Do we use any special caution, Max?' asked Carlyle.

'Oh, no. Just as though we were friends of the ghost, calling in the ordinary way.'

Trigget, who retained the keys, preceded the party up the stairs till the top was reached. He stood a moment at the door of No. 11 examining, by the light of the electric lamp he carried, his private marks there and pointing out to the others in a whisper that they had not been tampered with. All at once a most dismal wail, lingering, piercing, and ending in something like a sob that died away because the life that gave it utterance had died with it, drawled forebodingly through the echoing emptiness of the deserted flat. Trigget had just snapped off his light and in the darkness a startled exclamation sprang from Mr. Carlyle's lips.

'It's all right, sir,' said the little man, with a private satisfaction that he had the diplomacy to conceal. 'Bit creepy, isn't it? Especially when you hear it by yourself up here for the first time. It's only the end of the bathwater running out.'

He had opened the door and was conducting them to the room at the end of the passage. A faint aurora had been visible from that direction when they first entered the hall, but it was cut off before they could identify its source.

'That's what happens,' muttered Trigget.

He threw open the bedroom door without waiting to examine his marks there and they crowded into the tiny chamber. Under the beams of the lamps they carried it was brilliantly though erratically illuminated. All turned towards the central object of their quest, a tarnished gas-bracket of the plainest description. A few inches above it hung the metal disk that Trigget had alluded to, for the ceiling was low and at that point it was brought even nearer to the gas by corresponding with the slant of the roof outside.

With the prescience so habitual with him that it had

ceased to cause remark among his associates Carrados walked straight to the gas-bracket and touched the burner.

'Still warm,' he remarked. 'And so are we getting now. A thoroughly material ghost, you perceive, Louis.'

'But still turned off, don't you see, Mr. Carrados, sir,' put in Trigget eagerly. 'And yet no one's passed out.'

'Still turned off—and still turned on,' commented the blind man.

'What do you mean, Max?'

'The small screwdriver, Parkinson,' requested Carrados.

'Well, upon my word!' dropped Mr. Carlyle expressively. For in no longer time than it takes to record the fact Max Carrados had removed a screw and then knocked out the tap. He held it up towards them and they all at once saw that so much of the metal had been filed away that the gas passed through no matter how the tap stood. 'How on earth did you know of that?'

'Because it wasn't practicable to do the thing in any other way. Now unhook the shade, Parkinson—carefully.'

The warning was not altogether unnecessary, for the man had to stand on tiptoes before he could comply. Carrados received the dingy metal cone and lightly touched its inner surface.

'Ah, here, at the apex, to be sure,' he remarked. 'The gas is bound to get there. And there, Louis, you have an ever-lit and yet a truly "safety" match—so far as gas is concerned. You can buy the thing for a shilling, I believe.'

Mr. Carlyle was examining the tiny apparatus with interest. So small that it might have passed for the mummy of a midget hanging from a cobweb, it appeared to consist of an insignificant black pellet and an inch of the finest wire.

'Um, I've never heard of it. And this will really light the gas?'

'As often as you like. That is the whole bag of tricks.'

Mr. Carlyle turned a censorious eye upon his lieutenant, but Trigget was equal to the occasion and met it without embarrassment.

'I hadn't heard of it either, sir,' he remarked conversationally. 'Gracious, what won't they be getting out next, Mr. Carlyle!'

'Now for the mystery of the water.' Carrados was finding his way to the bathroom and they followed him down the passage and across the hall. 'In its way I think that this is really more ingenious than the gas, for, as Mr. Trigget has proved for us, the water does not come from the cistern. The taps, you perceive, are absolutely dry.'

'It is forced up?' suggested Mr. Carlyle, nodding towards the outlet.

'That is the obvious alternative. We will test it presently.' The blind man was down on his hands and knees following the lines of the different pipes. 'Two degrees more cold are not conclusive, because in any case the water has gone out that way. Mr. Trigget, you know the ropes, will you be so obliging as to go up to the cistern and turn the water on.'

'I shall need a ladder, sir.'

'Parkinson.'

'We have a folding ladder out here,' said Parkinson, touching Mr. Trigget's arm.

'One moment,' interposed Carrados, rising from his investigation among the pipes; 'this requires some care. I want you to do it without making a sound or showing a light, if that is possible. Parkinson will help you. Wait until you hear us raising a diversion at the other end of the flat. Come, Louis.'

The diversion took the form of tapping the wall and skirting-board in the other haunted room. When Trigget presented himself to report that the water was now on Carrados put him to continue the singular exercise with Mr. Carlyle while he himself slipped back to the bathroom.

'The pump, Parkinson,' he commanded in a brisk whisper to his man, who was waiting in the hall.

The appliance was not unlike a powerful tyre pump with some modifications. One tube from it was quickly fitted to the outlet pipe of the bath, another trailed a loose end into the bath itself, ready to take up the water. There were a few other details, the work of moments. Then Carrados turned on the tap, silencing the inflow by the attachment of a short length of rubber tube. When the water had risen a few inches he slipped off to the other room, told his rather mystified confederates there that he wanted a little more noise and bustle put into their performance, and was back again in the bathroom.

'Now, Parkinson,' he directed, and turned off the tap. There was about a foot of water in the bath.

Parkinson stood on the broad base of the pump and tried to drive down the handle. It scarcely moved.

'Harder,' urged Carrados, interpreting every detail of sound with perfect accuracy.

Parkinson set his teeth and lunged again. Again he seemed to come up against a solid wall of resistance.

'Keep trying; something must give,' said his master encouragingly. 'Here, let me——' He threw his weight into the balance and for a moment they hung like a group poised before action. Then, somewhere, something did give and the sheathing plunger 'drew.'

'Now like blazes till the bath is empty. Then you can tell the others to stop hammering.' Parkinson, looking round to acquiesce, found himself alone, for with silent step and quickened senses Carrados was already passing down the dark flights of the broad stone stairway.

It was perhaps three minutes later when an excited gentleman in the state of disrobement that is tacitly regarded as falling upon the *punctum caecum* in time of fire, flood, and nocturnal emergency shot out of the door of No. 7 and bounding up the intervening flights of steps pounded with the knocker on the door of No. 9. As someone did not appear with the instantaneity of a jack-in-the-box, he proceeded to repeat the summons, interspersing it with an occasional 'I say!' shouted through the letter-box.

The light above the door made it unconvincing to affect that no one was at home. The gentleman at the door trumpeted the fact through his channel of communication and demanded instant attention. So immersed was he with his own grievance, in fact, that he failed to notice the approach of someone on the other side, and the sudden opening of the door, when it did take place, surprised him on his knees at his neighbour's doorstep, a large and conse-quential-looking personage as revealed in the light from the hall, wearing the silk hat that he had instinctively snatched up, but with his braces hanging down.

'Mr. Tupworthy of No. 7, isn't it?' quickly interposed the

new man before his visitor could speak. 'But why this—homage? Permit me to raise you, sir.'

'Confound it all,' snorted Mr. Tupworthy indignantly, 'you 're flooding my flat. The water 's coming through my bathroom ceiling in bucketfuls. The plaster 'll fall next. Can't you stop it? Has a pipe burst or something?'

'Something, I imagine,' replied No. 9 with serene detachment. 'At all events it appears to be over now.'

'So I should hope,' was the irate retort. 'It 's bad enough as it is. I shall go round to the office and complain. I 'll tell you what it is, Mr. Belting: these mansions are becoming a pandemonium, sir, a veritable pandemonium.'

'Capital idea; we 'll go together and complain: two will be more effective,' suggested Mr. Belting. 'But not to-night, Mr. Tupworthy. We should not find any one there. The office will be closed. Say to-morrow——'

'I had no intention of anything so preposterous as going there to-night. I am in no condition to go. If I don't get my feet into hot water at once I shall be laid up with a severe cold. Doubless you haven't noticed it, but I am wet through to the skin, saturated, sir.'

Mr. Belting shook his head sagely.

'Always a mistake to try to stop water coming through the ceiling,' he remarked. 'It will come, you know. Finds its own level and all that.'

'I did not try to stop it—at least not voluntarily. A temporary emergency necessitated a slight rearrangement of our accommodation. I—I tell you this in confidence—I was sleeping in the bathroom.'

At the revelation of so notable a catastrophe Mr. Belting actually seemed to stagger. Possibly his eyes filled with tears; certainly he had to turn and wipe away his emotion before he could proceed.

'Not—not right under it?' he whispered.

'I imagine so,' replied Mr. Tupworthy. 'I do not conceive that I could have been placed more centrally. I received the full cataract in the region of the ear. Well, if I may rely on you that it has stopped, I will terminate our interview for the present.'

'Good night,' responded the still tremulous Belting. 'Good night—or good morning, to be exact.' He waited

with the door open to light the first flight of stairs for Mr.
Tupworthy's descent. Before the door was closed another
figure stepped down quietly from the obscurity of the steps
leading upwards.

'Mr. Belting, I believe?' said the stranger. 'My name is
Carrados. I have been looking over the flat above. Can
you spare me a few minutes?'

'What, Mr. Max Carrados?'

'The same,' smiled the owner of the name.

'Come in, Mr. Carrados,' exclaimed Belting, not only
without embarrassment, but with positive affection in his
voice. 'Come in by all means. I've heard of you more
than once. Delighted to meet you. This way. I know—
I know.' He put a hand on his guest's arm and insisted
on steering his course until he deposited him in an easy-
chair before a fire. 'This looks like being a great night.
What will you have?'

Carrados put the suggestion aside and raised a corner of
the situation.

'I'm afraid that I don't come altogether as a friend,' he
hinted.

'It's no good,' replied his host. 'I can't regard you in
any other light after this. You heard Tupworthy? But
you haven't seen the man, Mr. Carrados. I know—I've
heard—but no wealth of the imagination can ever really
quite reconstruct Tupworthy, the shoddy magnifico, in
his immense porcine complacency, his monumental self-
importance. And sleeping right underneath! Gods, but
we have lived to-night! Why—why ever did you stop?'

'You associate me with this business?'

'Associate you! My dear Mr. Carrados, I give you the
full glorious credit for the one entirely successful piece of low
comedy humour in real life that I have ever encountered.
Indeed, in a legal and pecuniary sense, I hold you absolutely
responsible.'

'Oh!' exclaimed Carrados, beginning to laugh quietly.
Then he continued: 'I think that I shall come through that
all right. I shall refer you to Mr. Carlyle, the private
inquiry agent, and he will doubtless pass you on to your
landlord, for whom he is acting, and I imagine that he in
turn will throw all the responsibility on the ingenious

gentleman who has put them to so much trouble. Can you guess the result of my investigation in the flat above?'

'Guess, Mr. Carrados? I don't need to guess: I *know*. You don't suppose I thought for a moment that such transparent devices as two intercepted pipes and an automatic gas-lighter would impose on a man of intelligence? They were only contrived to mystify the credulous imagination of clerks and porters.'

'You admit it, then?'

'Admit! Good gracious, of course I admit it, Mr. Carrados. What's the use of denying it?'

'Precisely. I am glad you see that. And yet you seem far from being a mere practical joker. Does your confidence extend to the length of letting me into your object?'

'Between ourselves,' replied Mr. Belting, 'I haven't the least objection. But I wish that you would have—say a cup of coffee. Mrs. Belting is still up, I believe. She would be charmed to have the opportunity ——No? Well, just as you like. Now, my object? You must understand, Mr. Carrados, that I am a man of sufficient leisure and adequate means for the small position we maintain. But I am not unoccupied—not idle. On the contrary, I am always busy. I don't approve of any man passing his time aimlessly. I have a number of interests in life—hobbies, if you like. You should appreciate that, as you are a private criminologist. I am—among other things which don't concern us now—a private retributionist. On every side people are becoming far too careless and negligent. An era of irresponsibility has set in. Nobody troubles to keep his word, to carry out literally his undertakings. In my small way I try to set that right by showing them the logical development of their ways. I am, in fact, the sworn enemy of anything approaching sloppiness. You smile at that?'

'It is a point of view,' replied Carrados. 'I was wondering how the phrase at this moment would convey itself, say, to Mr. Tupworthy's ear.'

Mr. Belting doubled up.

'But don't remind me of Tupworthy or I can't get on,' he said. 'In my method I follow the system of Herbert Spencer towards children. Of course you are familiar with his treatise on *Education*? If a rough boy persists, after warnings, in tearing or soiling all his clothes, don't scold him for what, after all, is only a natural and healthy instinct overdone. But equally, of course, don't punish yourself by buying him other clothes. When the time comes for the children to be taken to an entertainment little Tommy cannot go with them. It would not be seemly, and he is too ashamed, to go in rags. He begins to see the force of practical logic. Very well. If a tradesman promises—promises explicitly—delivery of his goods by a certain time and he fails, he finds that he is then unable to leave them. I pay on delivery, by the way. If a man undertakes to make me an article like another—I am painstaking, Mr. Carrados: I point out at the time how exactly like I want it—and if it is (as it generally is) on completion something quite different, I decline to be easy-going and to be put off with it. I take the simplest and most obvious instances; I could multiply indefinitely. It is, of course, frequently inconvenient to me, but it establishes a standard.'

'I see that you are a dangerous man, Mr. Belting,' remarked Carrados. 'If most men were like you our national character would be undermined. People would have to behave properly.'

'If most men were like me we should constitute an intolerable nuisance,' replied Belting seriously. 'A necessary reaction towards sloppiness would set in and find me at its head. I am always with minorities.'

'And the case in point?'

'The present trouble centres round the kitchen sink. It is cracked and leaks. A trivial cause for so elaborate an outcome, you may say, but you doubtless remember that two men quarrelling once at a spring as to who should use it first involved half Europe in a war, and the whole tragedy of *Lear* sprang from a silly business round a word. I hadn't noticed the sink when we took this flat, but the landlord had solemnly sworn to do everything that was necessary. Is a new sink necessary to replace a cracked one? Obviously. Well, you know what landlords are: possibly you are one yourself. They promise you heaven until you have signed the agreement and then they tell you to go to hell.

Suggested that we 'd probably broken the sink ourselves and would certainly be looked to to replace it. An excellent servant caught a cold standing in the drip and left. Was I to be driven into paying for a new sink myself? Very well, I thought, if the reasonable complaint of one tenant is nothing to you, see how you like the unreasonable complaints of fifty. The method served a useful purpose too. When Mrs. Belting heard that old tale about the tragedy at No. 11 she was terribly upset; vowed that she couldn't stay alone in here at night on any consideration.

'"My dear," I said, "don't worry yourself about ghosts. I 'll make as good a one as ever lived, and then when you see how it takes other people in, just remember next time you hear of another that someone's pulling the string." And I really don't think that she 'll ever be afraid of ghosts again.'

'Thank you,' said Carrados, rising. 'Altogether I have spent a very entertaining evening, Mr. Belting. I hope your retaliatory method won't get you into serious trouble this time.'

'Why should it?' demanded Belting quickly.

'Oh, well, tenants are complaining, the property is being depreciated. The landlord may think that he has legal redress against you.'

'But surely I am at liberty to light the gas or use the bath in my own flat when and how I like?'

A curious look had come into Mr. Belting's smiling face; a curious note must have sounded in his voice. Carrados was warned and, being warned, guessed.

'You are a wonderful man,' he said with upraised hand. 'I capitulate. Tell me how it is, won't you?'

'I knew the man at No. 11. His tenancy isn't really up till March, but he got an appointment in the north and had to go. His two unexpired months weren't worth troubling about, so I got him to sublet the flat to me—all quite regularly—for a nominal consideration, and not to mention it.'

'But he gave up the keys?'

'No. He left them in the door and the porter took them away. Very unwarrantable of him; surely I can keep my keys where I like? However, as I had another . . . Really,

Mr. Carrados, you hardly imagine that unless I had an absolute right to be there I should penetrate into a flat, tamper with the gas and water, knock the place about, tramp up and down——'

'I go,' said Carrados, 'to get our people out in haste. Good night.'

'Good night, Mr. Carrados. It's been a great privilege to meet you. Sorry I can't persuade you . . .'

EDGAR JEPSON AND ROBERT EUSTACE

THE TEA-LEAF

ARTHUR KELSTERN and Hugh Willoughton met in the Turkish bath in Duke Street, St. James's, and rather more than a year later in that Turkish bath they parted. Both of them were bad-tempered men, Kelstern cantankerous and Willoughton violent. It was, indeed, difficult to decide which was the worse-tempered; and when I found that they had suddenly become friends, I gave that friendship three months. It lasted nearly a year.

When they did quarrel they quarrelled about Kelstern's daughter Ruth. Willoughton fell in love with her and she with him, and they became engaged to be married. Six months later, in spite of the fact that'they were plainly very much in love with one another, the engagement was broken off. Neither of them gave any reason for breaking it off. My belief was that Willoughton had given Ruth a taste of his infernal temper and got as good as he gave.

Not that Ruth was at all a Kelstern to look at. Like the members of most of the old Lincolnshire families, descendants of the Vikings and the followers of Canute, one Kelstern is very like another Kelstern, fair-haired, clear-skinned, with light blue eyes and a good bridge to the nose. But Ruth had taken after her mother; she was dark, with a straight nose, dark-brown eyes of the kind often described as liquid, dark-brown hair, and as kissable lips as ever I saw. She was a proud, self-sufficing, high-spirited girl, with a temper of her own. She needed it to live with that cantankerous old brute Kelstern. Oddly enough, in spite of the fact that he always would try to bully her, she was fond of him; and I will say for him that he was very fond of her. Probably she was the only creature in the world of whom he was really fond. He was an expert in the application of scientific discoveries to industry; and she worked with him in his laboratory. He paid her five hundred a year, so that she must have been uncommonly good.

He took the breaking off of the engagement very hard indeed. He would have it that Willoughton had jilted her. Ruth took it hard, too; her warm colouring lost some of its warmth; her lips grew less kissable and set in a thinner line. Willoughton's temper grew worse than ever; he was like a bear with a perpetually sore head. I tried to feel my way with both him and Ruth with a view to help to bring about a reconciliation. To put it mildly, I was rebuffed. Willoughton swore at me; Ruth flared up and told me not to meddle in matters that didn't concern me. Nevertheless, my strong impression was that they were missing one another badly and would have been glad enough to come together again if their stupid vanity could have let them.

Kelstern did his best to keep Ruth furious with Willoughton. One night I told him—it was no business of mine; but I never did give a tinker's curse for his temper—that he was a fool to meddle and had much better leave them alone. It made him furious, of course; he would have it that Willoughton was a dirty hound and a low blackguard—at least those were about the mildest things he said of him. Given his temper and the provocation, nothing less could be expected. Moreover, he was looking a very sick man and depressed.

He took immense trouble to injure Willoughton. At his clubs, the Athenaeum, the Devonshire, and the Savile, he would display considerable ingenuity in bringing the conversation round to him; then he would declare that he was a scoundrel of the meanest type. Of course, it did Willoughton harm, though not nearly as much as Kelstern desired, for Willoughton knew his job as few engineers knew it; and it is very hard indeed to do much harm to a man who really knows his job. People have to have him. But of course it did him some harm; and Willoughton knew that Kelstern was doing it. I came across two men who told me that they had given him a friendly hint. That did not improve *his* temper.

An expert in the construction of those ferro-concrete buildings which are rising up all over London, he was as distinguished in his sphere as Kelstern in his. They were alike not only in the matters of brains and bad temper; but I think that their minds worked in very much the same way. At any rate, both of them seemed determined not to change their ordinary course of life because of the breaking off of that engagement.

It had been the habit of both of them to have a Turkish bath, at the baths in Duke Street, at four in the afternoon on the second and last Tuesday in every month. To that habit they stuck. The fact that they must meet on those Tuesdays did not cause either of them to change his hour of taking his Turkish bath by the twenty minutes which would have given them no more than a passing glimpse of one another. They continued to take it, as they always had, simultaneously. Thick-skinned? They were thick-skinned. Neither of them pretended that he did not see the other; he scowled at him; and he scowled at him most of the time. I know this, for sometimes I had a Turkish bath myself at that hour.

It was about three months after the breaking off of the engagement that they met for the last time at that Turkish bath, and there parted for good.

Kelstern had been looking ill for about six weeks; there was a greyness and a drawn look to his face; and he was losing weight. On the second Tuesday in October he arrived at the bath punctually at four, bringing with him, as was his habit, a thermos flask full of a very delicate China tea. If he thought that he was not perspiring freely enough he would drink it in the hottest room; if he did perspire freely enough, he would drink it after his bath. Willoughton arrived about two minutes later. Kelstern finished undressing and went into the bath a couple of minutes before Willoughton. They stayed in the hot room about the same time; Kelstern went into the hottest room about a minute after Willoughton. Before he went into it he sent for his thermos flask, which he had left in the dressing-room, and took it into the hottest room with him.

As it happened, they were the only two people in the hottest room; and they had not been in it two minutes before the four men in the hot room heard them quarrelling.

They heard Kelstern call Willoughton a dirty hound and a low blackguard, among other things, and declare he would do him in yet. Willoughton told him to go to the devil twice. Kelstern went on abusing him, and presently Willoughton fairly shouted: 'Oh, shut up, you old fool! Or I'll make you!'

Kelstern did not shut up. About two minutes later Willoughton came out of the hottest room, scowling, walked through the hot room into the shampooing room, and put himself into the hands of one of the shampooers. Two or three minutes after that a man of the name of Helston went into the hottest room and fairly yelled. Kelstern was lying back on a couch, with the blood still flowing from a wound over his heart.

There was a devil of a hullabaloo. The police were called in; Willoughton was arrested. Of course he lost his temper and, protesting furiously that he had had nothing whatever to do with the crime, abused the police. That did not incline them to believe him.

After examining the room and the dead body the detective-inspector in charge of the case came to the conclusion that Kelstern had been stabbed as he was drinking his tea. The thermos flask lay on the floor and some of the tea had evidently been spilt, for some tea-leaves—the tea in the flask must have been carelessly strained off the leaves by the maid who filled it—lay on the floor about the mouth of the empty flask. It looked as if the murderer had taken advantage of Kelstern's drinking his tea to stab him while the flask rather blocked his vision and prevented him from seeing what he would be at.

The case would have been quite plain sailing but for the fact that they could not find the weapon. It had been easy enough for Willoughton to take it into the bath in the towel in which he was draped. But how had he got rid of it? Where had he hidden it? A Turkish bath is no place to hide anything in. It is as bare as an empty barn—if anything barer; and Willoughton had been in the barest part of it. The police searched every part of it—not that there was much point in doing that, for Willoughton had come out of the hottest room and gone through the hot room into the shampooers' room. When Helston started shouting

'Murder!' he had rushed back with the shampooers to
the hottest room and there he had stayed. Since it was
obvious that he had committed the murder, the shampooers
and the bathers had kept their eyes on him. They were
all of them certain that he had not left them to go to
the dressing-room; they would not have allowed him to
do so.

It was obvious that he must have carried the weapon
into the bath, hidden in the folds of the towel in which he
was draped, and brought it away in the folds of that towel.
He had laid the towel down beside the couch on which he
was being shampooed; and there it still lay when they came
to look for it, untouched, with no weapon in it, with no
traces of blood on it. There was not much in the fact
that it was not stained with blood, since Willoughton could
have wiped the knife, or dagger, or whatever weapon he
used, on the couch on which Kelstern lay. There were no
marks of any such wiping on the couch; but the blood,
flowing from the wound, might have covered them up.
But why was the weapon not in the towel?

There was no finding that weapon.

Then the doctors who made the autopsy came to the
conclusion that the wound had been inflicted by a circular,
pointed weapon nearly three-quarters of an inch in diameter. It had penetrated rather more than three inches,
and, supposing that its handle was only four inches long,
it must have been a sizable weapon, quite impossible to
overlook. The doctors also discovered a further proof of
the theory that Kelstern had been drinking tea when he
was stabbed. Half-way down the wound they found two
halves of a tea-leaf which had evidently fallen on to
Kelstern's body, been driven into the wound, and cut in
half by the weapon. Also they discovered that Kelstern
was suffering from cancer. This fact was not published
in the papers; I heard it at the Devonshire.

Willoughton was brought before the magistrates, and
to most people's surprise did not reserve his defence. He
went into the witness-box and swore that he had never
touched Kelstern, that he had never had anything to touch
him with, that he had never taken any weapon into the
Turkish bath and so had had no weapon to hide, that he

had never even seen any such weapon as the doctors described. He was committed for trial.

The papers were full of the crime; every one was discussing it; and the question which occupied every one's mind was: where had Willoughton hidden the weapon? People wrote to the papers to suggest that he had ingeniously put it in some place under everybody's eyes and that it had been overlooked because it was so obvious. Others suggested that, circular and pointed, it must be very like a thick lead-pencil, that it was a thick lead-pencil; and that was why the police had overlooked it in their search. The police had not overlooked any thick lead-pencil; there had been no thick lead-pencil to overlook. They hunted England through—Willoughton did a lot of motoring—to discover the man who had sold him this curious and uncommon weapon. They did not find the man who had sold it to him; they did not find a man who sold such weapons at all. They came to the conclusion that Kelstern had been murdered with a piece of steel, or iron, rod filed to a point like a pencil.

In spite of the fact that only Willoughton *could* have murdered Kelstern, I could not believe that he had done it. The fact that Kelstern was doing his best to injure him professionally and socially was by no means a strong enough motive. Willoughton was far too intelligent a man not to be very well aware that people do not take much notice of statements to the discredit of a man whom they need to do a job for them; and for the social injury he would care very little. Besides, he might very well injure, or even kill, a man in one of his tantrums; but his was not the kind of bad temper that plans a cold-blooded murder; and if ever a murder had been deliberately planned, Kelstern's had.

I was as close a friend as Willoughton had, and I went to visit him in prison. He seemed rather touched by my doing so, and grateful. I learnt that I was the only person who had done so. He was subdued and seemed much gentler. It might last. He discussed the murder readily enough, and naturally with a harassed air. He said quite frankly that he did not expect me, in the circumstances, to believe that he had not committed it; but he had not, and he could not for the life of him conceive who had. I did believe that he had not committed it; there was something in his way of discussing it that wholly convinced me. I told him that I was quite sure that he had not killed Kelstern; and he looked at me as if he did not believe the assurance. But again he looked grateful.

Ruth was grieving for her father; but Willoughton's very dangerous plight to some degree distracted her mind from her loss. A woman can quarrel with a man bitterly without desiring to see him hanged; and Willoughton's chance of escaping hanging was not at all a good one. But she would not believe for a moment that he had murdered her father.

'No; there's nothing in it—nothing whatever,' she said firmly. 'If dad had murdered Hugh I could have understood it. He had reasons—or at any rate he had persuaded himself that he had. But whatever reason had Hugh for murdering dad? It's all nonsense to suppose that he'd mind dad's trying all he knew to injure him as much as that. All kinds of people are going about trying to injure other people in that way, but they don't really injure them very much; and Hugh knows that quite well.'

'Of course they don't; and Hugh wouldn't really believe that your father was injuring him much,' I said. 'But you're forgetting his infernal temper.'

'No, I'm not,' she protested. 'He might kill a man in one of his rages on the spur of the moment. But this wasn't the spur of the moment. Whoever did it had worked the whole thing out and came along with the weapon ready.'

I had to admit that that was reasonable enough. But who had done it? I pointed out to her that the police had made careful inquiries about every one in the bath at the time, the shampooers and the people taking their baths, but they found no evidence whatever that any one of them had at any time had any relations, except that of shampooer, with her father.

'Either it was one of them, or somebody else who just did it and got right away, or there's a catch somewhere,' she said, frowning thoughtfully.

'I can't see how there can possibly have been any one

in the bath, except the people who are known to have been there,' said I. 'In fact, there can't have been.'

Then the Crown subpoenaed her as a witness for the prosecution. It seemed rather unnecessary and even a bit queer, for it could have found plenty of evidence of bad blood between the two men without dragging her into it. Plainly it was bent on doing all it knew to prove motive enough. Ruth worked her brain so hard trying to get to the bottom of the business that there came a deep vertical wrinkle just above her right eyebrow that stayed there.

On the morning of the trial I called for her after breakfast to drive her down to the New Bailey. She was pale and looked as if she had had a poor night's rest, and, naturally enough, she seemed to be suffering from an excitement she found hard to control. It was not like her to show any excitement she might be feeling.

She said in an excited voice: 'I think I've got it!' and would say no more.

We had, of course, been in close touch with Willoughton's solicitor, Hamley; and he had kept seats for us just behind him. He wished to have Ruth to hand to consult should some point turn up on which she could throw light, since she knew more than any one about the relations between Willoughton and her father. I had timed our arrival very well; the jury had just been sworn in. Of course, the court was full of women, the wives of peers and bookmakers and politicians, most of them overdressed and over-scented.

Then the judge came in; and with his coming the atmosphere of the court became charged with that sense of anxious strain peculiar to trials for murder. It was rather like the atmosphere of a sick-room in a case of fatal illness, but worse.

Willoughton came into the dock looking under the weather and very much subdued. But he was certainly looking dignified, and he said that he was not guilty in a steady enough voice.

Greatorex, the leading counsel for the Crown, opened the case for the prosecution. There was no suggestion in his speech that the police had discovered any new fact. He begged the jury not to lay too much stress on the fact that the weapon had not been found. He had to, of course.

Then Hèlston gave evidence of finding that Kelstern had been stabbed, and he and the other three men who had been with him in the hot room gave evidence of the quarrel they had overheard between Willoughton and the dead man, and that Willoughton came out of the hottest room scowling and obviously furious. One of them, a fussy old gentleman of the name of Underwood, declared that it was the bitterest quarrel he had ever heard. None of the four of them could throw any light on the matter of whether Willoughton was carrying the missing weapon in the folds of the towel in which he was draped; all of them were sure that he had nothing in his hands.

The medical evidence came next. In cross-examining the doctors who had made the autopsy, Hazeldean, Willoughton's counsel, established the fact quite definitely that the missing weapon was of a fair size; that its rounded blade must have been over half an inch in diameter and between three and four inches long. They were of the opinion that to drive a blade of that thickness into the heart a handle of at least four inches in length would be necessary to give a firm enough grip. They agreed that it might very well have been a piece of a steel, or iron, rod sharpened like a pencil. At any rate, it was certainly a sizable weapon, not one to be hidden quickly or to disappear wholly in a Turkish bath. Hazeldean could not shake their evidence about the tea-leaf; they were confident that it had been driven into the wound and cut in half by the blade of the missing weapon, and that went to show that the wound had been inflicted while Kelstern was drinking his tea.

Detective-Inspector Brackett, who was in charge of the case, was cross-examined at great length about his search for the missing weapon. He made it quite clear that it was nowhere in that Turkish bath, neither in the hot rooms, nor the shampooing room, nor the dressing-rooms, nor the vestibule, nor the office. He had had the plunge bath emptied; he had searched the roofs, though it was practically certain that the skylight above the hot room, not the hottest, had been shut at the time of the crime.

In re-examination he scouted the idea of Willoughton's having had an accomplice who had carried away the weapon for him. He had gone into that matter most carefully.

The shampooer stated that Willoughton came to him scowling so savagely that he wondered what had put him into such a bad temper. In cross-examining him, Arbuthnot, Hazeldean's junior, made it clearer than ever that, unless Willoughton had already hidden the weapon in the bare hottest room, it was hidden in the towel. Then he drew from the shampooer the definite statement that Willoughton had set down the towel beside the couch on which he was shampooed; that he had hurried back to the hot rooms in front of the shampooer; that the shampooer had come back from the hot rooms, leaving Willoughton still in them discussing the crime, to find the towel lying just as Willoughton had set it down, with no weapon in it and no trace of blood on it.

Since the inspector had disposed of the possibility that an accomplice had slipped in, taken the weapon from the towel, and slipped out of the bath with it, this evidence really made it clear that the weapon had never left the hottest room.

Then the prosecution called evidence of the bad terms on which Kelstern and Willoughton had been. Three well-known and influential men told the jury about Kelstern's efforts to prejudice Willoughton in their eyes and the damaging statements he had made about him. One of them had felt it to be his duty to tell Willoughton about this; and Willoughton had been very angry. Arbuthnot, in cross-examining, elicited the fact that any damaging statement that Kelstern made about any one was considerably discounted by the fact that every one knew him to be in the highest degree cantankerous.

I noticed that during the end of the cross-examination of the shampooer and during this evidence Ruth had been fidgeting and turning to look impatiently at the entrance to the court, as if she were expecting someone. Then, just as she was summoned to the witness-box, there came in a tall, stooping, grey-headed, grey-bearded man of about sixty, carrying a brown-paper parcel. His face was familiar to me, but I could not place him. He caught her eye and nodded to her. She breathed a sharp sigh of relief, and bent over and handed a letter she had in her hand to Willoughton's solicitor and pointed out the grey-bearded man to him. Then she went quietly to the witness-box.

Hamley read the letter and at once bent over and handed it to Hazeldean and spoke to him. I caught a note of excitement in his hushed voice. Hazeldean read the letter and appeared to grow excited too. Hamley slipped out of his seat and went to the grey-bearded man, who was still standing just inside the door of the porch, and began to talk to him earnestly.

Greatorex began to examine Ruth; and naturally I turned my attention to her. His examination was directed also to show on what bad terms Kelstern and Willoughton had been. Ruth was called on to tell the jury some of Kelstern's actual threats. Then he questioned Ruth about her own relations with Willoughton and the breaking off of the engagement and its infuriating effect on her father. She admitted that he had been very bitter about it, and had told her that he was resolved to do his best to do Willoughton in. I thought that she went out of her way to emphasize this resolve of Kelstern's. It seemed to me likely to prejudice the jury still more against Willoughton, making them sympathize with a father's righteous indignation, and making yet more obvious that he was a dangerous enemy. Yet she would not admit that her father was right in believing that Willoughton had jilted her.

Hazeldean rose to cross-examine Ruth with a wholly confident air. He drew from her the fact that her father had been on excellent terms with Willoughton until the breaking off of the engagement.

Then Hazeldean asked: 'Is it a fact that since the breaking off of your engagement the prisoner has more than once begged you to forgive him and renew it?'

'Four times,' said Ruth.

'And you refused?'

Yes,' said Ruth. She looked at Willoughton queerly and added: 'He wanted a lesson.'

The judge asked: 'Did you intend, then, to forgive him ultimately?'

Ruth hesitated; then she rather evaded a direct answer; she scowled frankly at Willoughton, and said: 'Oh, well, there was no hurry. He would always marry me if I changed my mind and wanted to.'

'And did your father know this?' asked the judge.

'No. I didn't tell him. I was angry with Mr. Willoughton,' Ruth replied.

There was a pause. Then Hazeldean started on a fresh line.

In sympathetic accents he asked: 'Is it a fact that your father was suffering from cancer in a painful form?'

'It was beginning to grow very painful,' said Ruth sadly.

'Did he make a will and put all his affairs in order a few days before he died?'

'Three days,' said Ruth.

'Did he ever express an intention of committing suicide?'

'He said that he would stick it out for a little while and then end it all,' said Ruth. She paused and added: '*And that is what he did do.*'

One might almost say that the court started. I think that every one in it moved a little, so that there was a kind of rustling murmur.

'Will you tell the court your reasons for that statement?' said Hazeldean.

Ruth seemed to pull herself together—she was looking very tired—then she began in a quiet, even voice: 'I never believed for a moment that Mr. Willoughton murdered my father. If my father had murdered Mr. Willoughton it would have been a different matter. Of course, like everybody else, I puzzled over the weapon; what it was and where it had got to. I did not believe that it was a pointed piece of a half-inch steel rod. If anybody had come to the Turkish bath meaning to murder my father and hide the weapon, they wouldn't have used one so big and so difficult to hide, when a hat-pin would have done just as well and could be hidden much more easily. But what puzzled me most was the tea-leaf in the wound. All the other tea-leaves that came out of the flask were lying on the floor. Inspector Brackett told me they were. And I couldn't believe that one tea-leaf had fallen on to my father at the very place above his heart at which the point of the weapon had penetrated the skin and got driven in by it. It was too much of a coincidence for me to swallow. But I got no nearer understanding it than any one else.'

She paused to ask if she might have a glass of water, for she had been up all night and was very tired. It was brought to her.

Then she went on in the same quiet voice: 'Of course, I remembered that dad had talked of putting an end to it; but no one with a wound like that could get up and hide the weapon. So it was impossible that he had committed suicide. Then, the night before last, I dreamt that I went into the laboratory and saw a piece of steel rod, pointed, lying on the table at which my father used to work.'

'Dreams!' murmured Greatorex, a trifle pettishly, as if he was not pleased with the way things were going.

'I didn't think much of the dream, of course,' Ruth went on. 'I had been puzzling about it all so hard for so long that it was only natural to dream about it. But after breakfast I had a sudden feeling that the secret was in the laboratory if I could only find it. I did not attach any importance to the feeling; but it went on growing stronger; and after lunch I went to the laboratory and began to hunt.

'I looked through all the drawers and could find nothing. Then I went round the room looking at everything and into everything, instruments and retorts and tubes and so on. Then I went into the middle of the floor and looked slowly round the room pretty hard. Against the wall, near the door, lying ready to be taken away, was a gas cylinder. I rolled it over to see what gas had been in it and found no label on it.'

She paused to look round the court as if claiming its best attention; then she went on: 'Now that was very queer, because every gas cylinder must have a label on it—so many gases are dangerous. I turned on the tap of the cylinder and nothing came out of it. It was quite empty. Then I went to the book in which all the things which come in are entered, and found that ten days before dad died he had had a cylinder of CO_2 and seven pounds of ice. Also he had had seven pounds of ice every day till the day of his death. It was the ice and the CO_2 together that gave me the idea. CO_2, carbon dioxide, has a very low freezing-

point—eighty degrees centigrade—and as it comes out of
the cylinder and mixes with the air it turns into very fine
snow; and that snow, if you compress it, makes the hardest
and toughest ice possible. It flashed on me that dad could
have collected this snow and forced it into a mould and
made a weapon that would not only inflict that wound but
would evaporate very quickly! Indeed, in that heat you'd
have to see the wound inflicted to know what had done it.'

She paused again to look round the court at about as rapt
a lot of faces as any narrator could desire. Then she went
on: 'I knew that that was what he had done. I knew it for
certain. Carbon dioxide ice would make a hard, tough
dagger, and it would evaporate quickly in the hottest room
of a Turkish bath and leave no smell because it is scentless.
So there wouldn't be any weapon. And it explained the
tea-leaf, too. Dad had made a carbon dioxide dagger perhaps a week before he used it, perhaps only a day. And he
had put it into the thermos flask as soon as he had made it.
The thermos flask keeps out the heat as well as the cold, you
know. But to make sure that it couldn't melt at all, he
kept the flask in ice till he was ready to use the dagger.
It's the only way you can explain that tea-leaf. It came
out of the flask sticking to the point of the dagger and was
driven into the wound!'

She paused again, and one might almost say that the
court heaved a deep sigh of relief.

'But why didn't you go straight to the police with this
theory?' asked the judge.

'But that wouldn't have been any good,' she protested
quickly. 'It was no use my knowing it myself; I had to
make other people believe it; I had to find evidence. I
began to hunt for it. I felt in my bones that there was
some. What I wanted was the mould in which dad compressed the carbon dioxide snow and made the dagger.
I found it!'

She uttered the words in a tone of triumph and smiled at
Willoughton; then she went on: 'At least, I found bits of it.
In the box into which we used to throw odds and ends,
scraps of material, damaged instruments, and broken test-
tubes, I found some pieces of vulcanite; and I saw at once
that they were bits of a vulcanite container. I took some

wax and rolled it into a rod about the right size, and then
I pieced the container together on the outside of it—at least
most of it—there are some small pieces missing. It took
me nearly all night. But I found the most important bit
—*the pointed end*!'

She dipped her hand into her handbag and drew out a
black object about nine inches long and three-quarters of
an inch thick, and held it up for every one to see.

Someone, without thinking, began to clap; and there
came a storm of applause that drowned the voice of the
clerk calling for order.

When the applause died down, Hazeldean, who never
misses the right moment, said: 'I have no more questions
to ask the witness, my lord,' and sat down.

That action seemed to clinch it in my eyes, and I have
no doubt it clinched it in the eyes of the jury.

The judge leant forward and said to Ruth in a rather
shocked voice: 'Do you expect the jury to believe that
a well-known man like your father died in the act of deliberately setting a trap to hang the prisoner?'

Ruth looked at him, shrugged her shoulders, and said,
with a calm acceptance of the facts of human nature one
would expect to find only in a much older woman: 'Oh,
well, daddy was like that. And he certainly believed he
had very good reasons for killing Mr. Willoughton.'

There was that in her tone and manner which made it
absolutely certain that Kelstern was not only like that,
but that he had acted according to his nature.

Greatorex did not re-examine Ruth; he conferred with
Hazeldean. Then Hazeldean rose to open the case for the
defence. He said that he would not waste the time of the
court, and that, in view of the fact that Miss Kelstern had
solved the problem of her father's death, he would only call
one witness, Professor Mozley.

The grey-headed, grey-bearded, stooping man, who had
come to the court so late, went into the witness-box. Of
course his face had been familiar to me; I had seen his
portrait in the newspapers a dozen times. He still carried
the brown-paper parcel.

In answer to Hazeldean's questions he stated that it was
possible, not even difficult, to make a weapon of carbon

dioxide hard enough and tough enough and sharp enough
to inflict such a wound as that which had caused Kelstern's
death. The method of making it was to fold a piece of
chamois leather into a bag, hold that bag with the left
hand, protected by a glove, over the nozzle of a cylinder
containing liquid carbon dioxide, and open the valve with
the right hand. Carbon dioxide evaporates so quickly that
its freezing-point, eighty degrees centigrade, is soon reached;
and it solidifies in the chamois-leather bag as a deposit of
carbon dioxide snow. Then turn off the gas, spoon that
snow into a vulcanite container of the required thickness,
and ram it down with a vulcanite plunger into a rod of the
required hardness. He added that it was advisable to pack
the container in ice while filling it and ramming down the
snow. Then put the rod into a thermos flask; and keep it
till it is needed.

'And you have made such a rod?' said Hazeldean.

'Yes,' said the professor, cutting the string of the brown-
paper parcel. 'When Miss Kelstern hauled me out of bed
at half-past seven this morning to tell me her discoveries,
I perceived at once that she had found the solution of the
problem of her father's death, which had puzzled me considerably. I had breakfast quickly and got to work to
make such a weapon myself for the satisfaction of the court.
Here it is.'

He drew a thermos flask from the brown paper, unscrewed
the top of it, and inverted it. There dropped into his gloved
hand a white rod, with a faint sparkle to it, about eight
inches long. He held it out for the jury to see, and said:

'This carbon dioxide ice is the hardest and toughest ice
we know of; and I have no doubt that Mr. Kelstern killed
himself with a similar rod. The difference between the rod
he used and this is that his rod was pointed. I had no
pointed vulcanite container; but the container that Miss
Kelstern pieced together is pointed. Doubtless Mr. Kelstern had it specially made, probably by Messrs. Hawkins
and Spender.'

He dropped the rod back into the thermos flask and
screwed on the top.

Hazeldean sat down, Greatorex rose.

'With regard to the point of the rod, Professor Mozley,

would it remain sharp long enough to pierce the skin in that heat?' he asked.

'In my opinion it would,' said the professor. 'I have been considering that point, and bearing in mind the facts that Mr. Kelstern would from his avocation be very deft with his hands, and being a scientific man would know exactly what to do, he would have the rod out of the flask and the point in position in very little more than a second —perhaps less. He would, I think, hold it in his left hand and drive it home by striking the butt of it hard with his right. The whole thing would not take him two seconds. Besides, if the point of the weapon had melted the tea-leaf would have fallen off it.'

'Thank you,' said Greatorex, and turned and conferred with the Crown solicitors.

Then he said: 'We do not propose to proceed with the case, my lord.'

The foreman of the jury rose quickly and said: 'And the jury doesn't want to hear anything more, my lord. We're quite satisfied that the prisoner isn't guilty.'

'Very good,' said the judge, and he put the question formally to the jury, who returned a verdict of 'Not guilty.' He discharged Willoughton.

I came out of the court with Ruth and we waited for Willoughton.

Presently he came out of the door and stopped and shook himself. Then he saw Ruth and came to her. They did not greet one another. She just slipped her hand through his arm; and they walked out of the New Bailey together.

We made a good deal of noise, cheering them.

RICHARD AUSTIN FREEMAN

THE CONTENTS OF A MARE'S NEST

'IT is very unsatisfactory,' said Mr. Stalker, of the "Griffin" Life Assurance Company, at the close of a consultation on a doubtful claim. 'I suppose we shall have to pay up.'

'I am sure you will,' said Thorndyke. 'The death was properly certified, the deceased is buried, and you have not a single fact with which to support an application for further inquiry.'

'No,' Stalker agreed. 'But I am not satisfied. I don't believe that doctor really knew what she died from. I wish cremation were more usual.'

'So, I have no doubt, has many a poisoner,' Thorndyke remarked dryly.

Stalker laughed, but stuck to his point. 'I know you don't agree,' said he, 'but from our point of view it is much more satisfactory to know that the extra precautions have been taken. In a cremation case, you have not to depend on the mere death certificate; you have the cause of death verified by an independent authority, and it is difficult to see how any miscarriage can occur.'

Thorndyke shook his head. 'It is a delusion, Stalker. You can't provide in advance for unknown contingencies. In practice, your special precautions degenerate into mere formalities. If the circumstances of a death appear normal, the independent authority will certify; if they appear abnormal, you won't get a certificate at all. And if suspicion arises only after the cremation has taken place, it can neither be confirmed nor rebutted.'

'My point is,' said Stalker, 'that the searching examination would lead to discovery of a crime before cremation.'

'That is the intention,' Thorndyke admitted. 'But no examination, short of an exhaustive post-mortem, would make it safe to destroy a body so that no reconsideration of the cause of death would be possible.'

Stalker smiled as he picked up his hat. 'Well,' he said, 'to a cobbler there is nothing like leather, and I suppose that to a toxicologist, there is nothing like an exhumation,' and with this parting shot he took his leave.

We had not seen the last of him, however. In the course of the same week he looked in to consult us on a fresh matter.

'A rather queer case has turned up,' said he. 'I don't know that we are deeply concerned in it, but we should like to have your opinion as to how we stand. The position is this: Eighteen months ago, a man named Ingle insured with us for fifteen hundred pounds, and he was then accepted as a first-class life. He has recently died—apparently from heart failure, the heart being described as fatty and dilated—and his wife, Sibyl, who is the sole legatee and executrix, has claimed payment. But just as we were making arrangements to pay, a caveat has been entered by a certain Margaret Ingle, who declares that she is the wife of the deceased and claims the estate as next-of-kin. She states that the alleged wife, Sibyl, is a widow named Huggard who contracted a bigamous marriage with the deceased, knowing that he had a wife living.'

'An interesting situation,' commented Thorndyke, 'but, as you say, it doesn't particularly concern you. It is a matter for the Probate Court.'

'Yes,' agreed Stalker. 'But that is not all. Margaret Ingle not only charges the other woman with bigamy; she accuses her of having made away with the deceased.'

'On what grounds?'

'Well, the reasons she gives are rather shadowy. She states that Sibyl's husband, James Huggard, died under suspicious circumstances—there seems to have been some suspicion that he had been poisoned—and she asserts that Ingle was a healthy, sound man and could not have died from the causes alleged.'

'There is some reason in that,' said Thorndyke, 'if he was really a first-class life only eighteen months ago. As to the first husband, Huggard, we should want some particulars: as to whether there was an inquest, what was the alleged cause of death, and what grounds there were for suspecting that he had been poisoned. If there really were any suspicious circumstances, it would be advisable to apply to the Home Office for an order to exhume the body of Ingle and verify the cause of death.'

Stalker smiled somewhat sheepishly. 'Unfortunately,' said he, 'that is not possible. Ingle was cremated.'

'Ah!' said Thorndyke, 'that is, as you say, unfortunate. It clearly increases the suspicion of poisoning, but destroys the means of verifying that suspicion.'

'I should tell you,' said Stalker, 'that the cremation was in accordance with the provisions of the will.'

'That is not very material,' replied Thorndyke. 'In fact, it rather accentuates the suspicious aspect of the case; for the knowledge that the death of the deceased would be followed by cremation might act as a further inducement to get rid of him by poison. There were two death certificates, of course?'

'Yes. The confirmatory certificate was given by Dr. Halbury, of Wimpole Street. The medical attendant was a Dr. Barber, of Howland Street. The deceased lived in Stock Orchard Crescent, Holloway.'

'A good distance from Howland Street,' Thorndyke remarked. 'Do you know if Halbury made a post-mortem? I don't suppose he did.'

'No, he didn't,' replied Stalker.

'Then,' said Thorndyke, 'his certificate is worthless. You can't tell whether a man has died from heart failure by looking at his dead body. He must have just accepted the opinion of the medical attendant. Do I understand that you want me to look into this case?'

'If you will. It is not really our concern whether or not the man was poisoned, though I suppose we should have a claim on the estate of the murderer. But we should like you to investigate the case; though how the deuce you are going to do it I don't quite see.'

'Neither do I,' said Thorndyke. 'However, we must get into touch with the doctors who signed the certificates, and possibly they may be able to clear the whole matter up.'

'Of course,' said I, 'there is the other body—that of Huggard — which might be exhumed — unless he was cremated, too.'

'Yes,' agreed Thorndyke; 'and for the purposes of the criminal law, evidence of poisoning in that case would be sufficient. But it would hardly help the Griffin Company, which is concerned exclusively with Ingle deceased. Can you let us have a précis of the facts relating to this case, Stalker?'

'I have brought one with me,' was the reply; 'a short statement, giving names, addresses, dates, and other particulars. Here it is'; and he handed Thorndyke a sheet of paper bearing a tabulated statement.

When Stalker had gone Thorndyke glanced rapidly through the précis and then looked at his watch. 'If we make our way to Wimpole Street at once,' said he, 'we ought to catch Halbury. That is obviously the first thing to do. He signed the "C" certificate, and we shall be able to judge from what he tells us whether there is any possibility of foul play. Shall we start now?'

As I assented, he slipped the précis in his pocket and we set forth. At the top of Middle Temple Lane we chartered a taxi by which we were shortly deposited at Dr. Halbury's door, and a few minutes later were ushered into his consulting room, and found him shovelling a pile of letters into the waste-paper basket.

'How d' ye do?' he said briskly, holding out his hand. 'I 'm up to my eyes in arrears, you see. Just back from my holiday. What can I do for you?'

'We have called,' said Thorndyke, 'about a man named Ingle.'

'Ingle—Ingle,' repeated Halbury. 'Now, let me see——'

'Stock Orchard Crescent, Holloway,' Thorndyke explained.

'Oh, yes. I remember him. Well, how is he?'

'He 's dead,' replied Thorndyke.

'Is he really?' exclaimed Halbury. 'Now that shows how careful one should be in one's judgments. I half suspected that fellow of malingering. He was supposed to have a dilated heart, but I couldn't make out any appreciable dilation. There was excited, irregular action. That was all. I had a suspicion that he had been dosing himself with trinitrine. Reminded me of the cases of cordite chewing that I used to meet with in South Africa. So he 's

dead, after all.   Well, it's queer.   Do you know what the
exact cause of death was?'

'Failure of a dilated heart is the cause stated on the
certificates—the body was cremated; and the "C" Certificate was signed by you.'

'By me!' exclaimed the physician.   'Nonsense! It's a
mistake.   I signed a certificate for a Friendly Society—
Mrs. Ingle brought it here for me to sign—but I didn't even
know he was dead.   Besides, I went away for my holiday
a few days after I saw the man, and only came back yesterday.   What makes you think I signed the death certificate?'

Thorndyke produced Stalker's précis and handed it to
Halbury, who read out his own name and address with a
puzzled frown.   'This is an extraordinary affair,' said he.
'It will have to be looked into.'

'It will, indeed,' assented Thorndyke; 'especially as a
suspicion of poisoning has been raised.'

'Ha!' exclaimed Halbury.   'Then it was trinitrine, you
may depend.   But I suspected him unjustly.   It was
somebody else who was dosing him; perhaps that sly-
looking baggage of a wife of his.   Is any one in particular
suspected?'

'Yes.   The accusation, such as it is, is against the wife.'

'H'm.   Probably a true bill.   But she's done us.   Artful
devil.   You can't get much evidence out of an urnful of
ashes.   Still, somebody has forged my signature.   I suppose that is what the hussy wanted that certificate for—to
get a specimen of my handwriting.   I see the "B" certificate was signed by a man named Meeking.   Who's he?   It
was Barber who called me in for an opinion.'

'I must find out who he is,' replied Thorndyke.   'Possibly
Dr. Barber will know.   I shall go and call on him now.'

'Yes,' said Dr. Halbury, shaking hands as we rose to
depart, 'you ought to see Barber.   He knows the history
of the case, at any rate.'

From Wimpole Street we steered a course for Howland
Street, and here we had the good fortune to arrive just as
Dr. Barber's car drew up at the door.   Thorndyke intro-
duced himself and me, and then introduced the subject of
his visit, but said nothing, at first, about our call on Dr.
Halbury.

'Ingle,' repeated Dr. Barber. 'Oh, yes, I remember him. And you say he is dead. Well, I 'm rather surprised. I didn't regard his condition as serious.'

'Was his heart dilated?' Thorndyke asked.

'Not appreciably. I found nothing organic; no valvular disease. It was more like a tobacco heart. But it 's odd that Meeking didn't mention the matter to me—he was my locum, you know. I handed the case over to him when I went on my holiday. And you say he signed the death certificate?'

'Yes; and the "B" certificate for cremation, too.'

'Very odd,' said Dr. Barber. 'Just come in and let us have a look at the day book.'

We followed him into the consulting room, and there, while he was turning over the leaves of the day book, I ran my eye along the shelf over the writing-table from which he had taken it; on which I observed the usual collection of case books and books of certificates and notification forms, including the book of death certificates.

'Yes,' said Dr. Barber, 'here we are: "Ingle, Mr., Stock Orchard Crescent." The last visit was on the 4th of September, and Meeking seems to have given some sort of certificate. Wonder if he used a printed form.' He took down two of the books and turned over the counterfoils.

'Here we are,' he said presently; "'Ingle, Jonathan, 4th September. Now recovered and able to resume duties." That doesn't look like dying, does it? Still, we may as well make sure.'

He reached down the book of death certificates and began to glance through the most recent entries.

'No,' he said, turning over the leaves, there doesn't seem to be—— Hallo! What 's this? Two blank counterfoils; and about the date, too; between the 2nd and 13th of September. Extraordinary! Meeking is such a careful, reliable man.'

He turned back to the day book and read through the fortnight's entries. Then he looked up with an anxious frown.

'I can't make this out,' he said. 'There is no record of any patient having died in that period.'

'Where is Dr. Meeking at present?' I asked.

'Somewhere in the South Atlantic,' replied Barber. 'He left here three weeks ago to take up a post on a Royal Mail boat. So he couldn't have signed the certificate in any case.'

That was all that Dr. Barber had to tell us, and a few minutes later we took our departure.

'This case looks pretty fishy,' I remarked, as we turned down Tottenham Court Road.

'Yes,' Thorndyke agreed. 'There is evidently something radically wrong. And what strikes me especially is the cleverness of the fraud; the knowledge and judgment and foresight that are displayed.'

'She took pretty considerable risks,' I observed.

'Yes, but only the risks that were unavoidable. Everything that could be foreseen has been provided for. All the formalities have been complied with—in appearance. And you must notice, Jervis, that the scheme did actually succeed. The cremation has taken place. Nothing but the incalculable accident of the appearance of the real Mrs. Ingle and her vague and apparently groundless suspicions, prevented the success from being final. If she had not come on the scene, no questions would ever have been asked.'

'No,' I agreed. 'The discovery of the plot is a matter of sheer bad luck. But what do you suppose has really happened?'

Thorndyke shook his head.

'It is very difficult to say. The mechanism of the affair is obvious enough, but the motives and purpose are rather incomprehensible. The illness was apparently a sham, the symptoms being produced by nitro-glycerine or some similar heart poison. The doctors were called in, partly for the sake of appearances and partly to get specimens of their handwriting. The fact that both the doctors happened to be away from home and one of them at sea at the time when verbal questions might have been asked—by the undertaker, for instance—suggests that this had been ascertained in advance. The death certificate forms were pretty certainly stolen by the woman when she was left alone in Barber's consulting room, and, of course, the cremation certificates could be obtained on application to the crematorium authorities. That is all plain sailing. The mystery is, what is it all about? Barber or Meeking would almost certainly have given a death certificate, although the death was unexpected, and I don't suppose Halbury would have refused to confirm it. They would have assumed that their diagnosis had been at fault.'

'Do you think it could have been suicide, or an inadvertent overdose of trinitrine?'

'Hardly. If it was suicide, it was deliberate, for the purpose of getting the insurance money for the woman, unless there was some further motive behind. And the cremation, with all its fuss and formalities, is against suicide; while the careful preparation seems to exclude inadvertent poisoning. Then, what was the motive for the sham illness except as a preparation for an abnormal death?'

'That is true,' said I. 'But if you reject suicide, isn't it rather remarkable that the victim should have provided for his own cremation?'

'We don't know that he did,' replied Thorndyke. 'There is a suggestion of a capable forger in this business. It is quite possible that the will itself is a forgery.'

'So it is!' I exclaimed. 'I hadn't thought of that.'

'You see,' continued Thorndyke, 'the appearances suggest that cremation was a necessary part of the programme; otherwise these extraordinary risks would not have been taken. The woman was sole executrix and could have ignored the cremation clause. But if the cremation was necessary, why was it necessary? The suggestion is that there was something suspicious in the appearance of the body; something that the doctors would certainly have observed or that would have been discovered if an exhumation had taken place.'

'You mean some injury or visible signs of poisoning?'

'I mean something discoverable by examination even after burial.'

'But what about the undertaker? Wouldn't he have noticed anything palpably abnormal?'

'An excellent suggestion, Jervis. We must see the undertaker. We have his address: Kentish Town Road—a long way from deceased's house, by the way. We had better get on a bus and go there now.'

A yellow omnibus was approaching as he spoke. We hailed it and sprang on, continuing our discussion as we were borne northward.

Mr. Burrell, the undertaker, was a pensive-looking, profoundly civil man who was evidently in a small way, for he combined with his funeral functions general carpentry and cabinet making. He was perfectly willing to give any required information, but he seemed to have very little to give.

'I never really saw the deceased gentleman,' he said in reply to Thorndyke's cautious inquiries. 'When I took the measurements, the corpse was covered with a sheet; and as Mrs. Ingle was in the room, I made the business as short as possible.'

'You didn't put the body in the coffin, then?'

'No. I left the coffin at the house, but Mrs. Ingle said that she and the deceased gentleman's brother would lay the body in it.'

'But didn't you see the corpse when you screwed the coffin-lid down?'

'I didn't screw it down. When I got there it was screwed down already. Mrs. Ingle said they had to close up the coffin, and I dare say it was necessary. The weather was rather warm; and I noticed a strong smell of formalin.'

'Well,' I said, as we walked back down the Kentish Town Road, 'we haven't got much more forward.'

'I wouldn't say that,' replied Thorndyke. 'We have a further instance of the extraordinary adroitness with which this scheme was carried out; and we have confirmation of our suspicion that there was something unusual in the appearance of the body. It is evident that this woman did not dare to let even the undertaker see it. But one can hardly help admiring the combination of daring and caution, the boldness with which these risks were taken, and the care and judgment with which they were provided against. And again I point out that the risks were justified by the result. The secret of that man's death appears to have been made secure for all time.'

It certainly looked as if the mystery with which we were concerned were beyond the reach of investigation. Of course, the woman could be prosecuted for having forged the death certificates, to say nothing of the charge of bigamy. But that was no concern of ours or Stalker's. Jonathan Ingle was dead, and no one could say how he died.

On our arrival at our chambers we found a telegram that had just arrived, announcing that Stalker would call on us in the evening; and as this seemed to suggest that he had some fresh information we looked forward to his visit with considerable interest. Punctually at six o'clock he made his appearance and at once opened the subject.

'There are some new developments in this Ingle case,' said he. 'In the first place, the woman, Huggard, has bolted. I went to the house to make a few inquiries and found the police in possession. They had come to arrest her on the bigamy charge, but she had got wind of their intentions and cleared out. They made a search of the premises, but I don't think they found anything of interest except a number of rifle cartridges; and I don't know that they are of much interest either, for she could hardly have shot him with a rifle.'

'What kind of cartridges were they?' Thorndyke asked.

Stalker put his hand in his pocket.

'The inspector let me have one to show you,' said he; and he laid on the table a military cartridge of the pattern of some twenty years ago. Thorndyke picked it up, and taking from a drawer a pair of pliers drew the bullet out of the case and inserted into the latter a pair of dissecting forceps. When he withdrew the forceps, their points grasped one or two short strings of what looked like cat-gut.

'Cordite!' said I. 'So Halbury was probably right, and this is how she got her supply.' Then, as Stalker looked at me inquiringly, I gave him a short account of the results of our investigations.

'Ha!' he exclaimed, 'the plot thickens. This juggling with the death certificates seems to connect itself with another kind of juggling that I came to tell you about. You know that Ingle was secretary and treasurer to a company that bought and sold land for building estates. Well, I called at their office after I left you and had a little talk with the chairman. From him I learned that Ingle had practically complete control of the financial affairs of the company, that he received and paid all moneys and kept the books.   Of late, however, some of the directors have had a suspicion that all was not well with the finances, and at last it was decided to have the affairs of the company thoroughly overhauled by a firm of chartered accountants. This decision was communicated to Ingle, and a couple of days later a letter arrived from his wife saying that he had had a severe heart attack and asking that the audit of the books might be postponed until he recovered and was able to attend at the office.'

'And was it postponed?' I asked.

'No,' replied Stalker.   'The accountants were asked to get to work at once, which they did; with the result that they discovered a number of discrepancies in the books and a sum of about three thousand pounds unaccounted for. It isn't quite obvious how the frauds were carried out, but it is suspected that some of the returned cheques are fakes with forged endorsements.'

'Did the company communicate with Ingle on the subject?' asked Thorndyke.

'No.   They had a further letter from Mrs. Ingle—that is, Huggard—saying that Ingle's condition was very serious; so they decided to wait until he had recovered.   Then, of course, came the announcement of his death, on which the matter was postponed pending the probate of the will.   I suppose a claim will be made on the estate, but as the executrix has absconded, the affair has become rather complicated.'

'You were saying,' said Thorndyke, 'that the fraudulent death certificates seem to be connected with these frauds on the company.   What kind of connection do you assume?'

'I assume—or, at least, suggest,' replied Stalker, 'that this was a case of suicide.   The man, Ingle, saw that his frauds were discovered, or were going to be, and that he was in for a long term of penal servitude, so he just made away with himself.   And I think that if the murder charge could be dropped, Mrs. Huggard might be induced to come forward and give evidence as to the suicide.'

Thorndyke shook his head.

'The murder charge couldn't be dropped,' said he. 'If it was suicide, Huggard was certainly an accessory; and in law, an accessory to suicide is an accessory to murder.

But, in fact, no official charge of murder has been made, and at present there are no means of sustaining such a charge. The identity of the ashes might be assumed to be that stated in the cremation order, but the difficulty is the cause of death. Ingle was admittedly ill. He was attended for heart disease by three doctors. There is no evidence that he did not die from that illness.'

'But the illness was due to cordite poisoning,' said I.

'That is what we believe. But no one could swear to it. And we certainly could not swear that he died from cordite poisoning.'

'Then,' said Stalker, 'apparently there is no means of finding out whether his death was due to natural causes, suicide, or murder?'

'There is only one chance,' replied Thorndyke. 'It is just barely possible that the cause of death might be ascertainable by an examination of the ashes.'

'That doesn't seem very hopeful,' said I. 'Cordite poisoning would certainly leave no trace.'

'We mustn't assume that he died from cordite poisoning,' said Thorndyke. 'Probably he did not. That may have masked the action of a less obvious poison, or death might have been produced by some new agent.'

'But,' I objected, 'how many poisons are there that could be detected in the ashes? No organic poison would leave any traces, nor would metallic poisons such as mercury, antimony, or arsenic.'

'No,' Thorndyke agreed. 'But there are other metallic poisons which could be easily recovered from the ashes; lead, tin, gold, and silver, for instance. But it is useless to discuss speculative probabilities. The only chance that we have of obtaining any new facts is by an examination of the ashes. It seems infinitely improbable that we shall learn anything from it, but there is the bare possibility and we ought not to leave it untried.'

Neither Stalker nor I made any further remark, but I could see that the same thought was in both our minds. It was not often that Thorndyke was 'gravelled'; but apparently the resourceful Mrs. Huggard had set him a problem that was beyond even his powers. When an investigator of crime is reduced to the necessity of examining a potful of ashes in the wild hope of ascertaining from them how the deceased met his death, one may assume that he is at the very end of his tether. It is a forlorn hope indeed.

Nevertheless, Thorndyke seemed to view the matter quite cheerfully, his only anxiety being lest the Home Secretary should refuse to make the order authorizing the examination. And this anxiety was dispelled a day or two later by the arrival of a letter giving the necessary authority, and informing him that a Dr. Hemming—known to us both as an expert pathologist—had been deputed to be present at the examination and to confer with him as to the necessity for a chemical analysis.

On the appointed day Dr. Hemming called at our chambers and we set forth together for Liverpool Street; and as we drove thither it became evident to me that his view of our mission was very similar to my own. For, though he talked freely enough, and on professional topics, he maintained a most discreet silence on the subject of the forthcoming inspection; indeed, the first reference to the subject was made by Thorndyke himself just as the train was approaching Corfield, where the crematorium was situated.

'I presume,' said he, 'you have made all necessary arrangements, Hemming?'

'Yes,' was the reply. 'The superintendent will meet us and will conduct us to the catacombs, and there, in our presence, will take the casket from its niche in the columbarium, and have it conveyed to the office, where the examination will be made. I thought it best to use these formalities, though, as the casket is sealed and bears the name of the deceased, there is not much point in them.'

'No,' said Thorndyke, 'but I think you were right. It would be easy to challenge the identity of a mass of ashes if all precautions were not taken, seeing that the ashes themselves are unidentifiable.'

'That was what I felt,' said Hemming; and then, as the train slowed down, he added: 'This is our station, and that gentleman on the platform, I suspect, is the superintendent.'

The surmise turned out to be correct; but the cemetery official was not the only one present bearing that title; for

as we were mutually introducing ourselves, a familiar tall
figure approached up the platform from the rear of the train
—our old friend Superintendent Miller of the Criminal
Investigation Department.

'I don't wish to intrude,' said he, as he joined the group
and was presented by Thorndyke to the strangers, 'but
we were notified by the Home Office that an investigation
was to be made, so I thought I would be on the spot to pick
up any crumbs of information that you may drop. Of
course, I am not asking to be present at the examination.'

'You may as well be present as an additional witness to
the removal of the urn,' said Thorndyke; and Miller
accordingly joined the party, which now made its way from
the station to the cemetery.

The catacombs were in a long, low arcaded building at
the end of the pleasantly-wooded grounds, and on our way
thither we passed the crematorium, a smallish, church-like
edifice with a perforated chimney-shaft partly concealed
by the low spire. Entering the catacombs, we were conducted to the 'columbarium,' the walls of which were
occupied by a multitude of niches or pigeon-holes, each
niche accommodating a terra-cotta urn or casket. The
superintendent proceeded to near the end of the gallery,
where he halted, and opening the register, which he had
brought with him, read out a number and the name
'Jonathan Ingle,' and then led us to a niche bearing that
number and name in which reposed a square casket, on
which was inscribed the name and date of death. When
we had verified these particulars, the casket was tenderly
lifted from its place by two attendants, who carried it to a
well-lighted room at the end of the building, where a large
table by a window had been covered with white paper.
Having placed the casket on the table, the attendants
retired, and the superintendent then broke the seals and
removed the cover.

For a while we all stood looking in at the contents of the
casket without speaking; and I found myself contrasting
them with what would have been revealed by the lifting of
a coffin-lid. Truly corruption had put on incorruption.
The mass of snow-white, coral-like fragments, delicate,
fragile, and lace-like in texture, so far from being repulsive

in aspect, were almost attractive. I ran my eye, with
an anatomist's curiosity, over these dazzling remnants of
what had lately been a man, half-unconsciously seeking to
identify and give a name to particular fragments, and a
little surprised at the difficulty of determining that this or
that irregularly-shaped white object was a part of any
one of the bones with which I had thought myself so
familiar.

Presently Hemming looked up at Thorndyke and asked:
'Do you observe anything abnormal in the appearance of
these ashes? I don't.'

'Perhaps,' replied Thorndyke, 'we had better turn
them out on to the table, so that we can see the whole of
them.'

This was done very gently, and then Thorndyke proceeded to spread out the heap, touching the fragments with
the utmost delicacy—for they were extremely fragile and
brittle—until the whole collection was visible.

'Well,' said Hemming, when we had once more looked
them over critically, 'what do you say? I can see no trace
of any foreign substance. Can you?'

'No,' replied Thorndyke. 'And there are some other
things that I can't see. For instance, the medical referee
reported that the proposer had a good set of sound teeth.
Where are they? I have not seen a single fragment of a
tooth. Yet teeth are far more resistant to fire than bones,
especially the enamel caps.'

Hemming ran a searching glance over the mass of fragments and looked up with a perplexed frown.

'I certainly can't see any sign of teeth,' he admitted;
'and it is rather curious, as you say. Does the fact suggest
any particular significance to you?'

By way of reply, Thorndyke delicately picked up a flat
fragment and silently held it out towards us. I looked at
it and said nothing; for a very strange suspicion was
beginning to creep into my mind.

'A piece of a rib,' said Hemming. 'Very odd that it
should have broken across so cleanly. It might have been
cut with a saw.'

Thorndyke laid it down and picked up another, larger
fragment, which I had already noticed.

'Here is another example,' said he, handing it to our colleague.

'Yes,' agreed Hemming. 'It is really rather extraordinary. It looks exactly as if it had been sawn across.'

'It does,' agreed Thorndyke. 'What bone should you say it is?'

'That is what I was just asking myself,' replied Hemming, looking at the fragment with a sort of half-vexed smile. 'It seems ridiculous that a competent anatomist should be in any doubt with as large a portion as this, but really I can't confidently give it a name. The shape seems to me to suggest a tibia, but of course it is much too small. Is it the upper end of the ulna?'

'I should say no,' answered Thorndyke. Then he picked out another of the larger fragments, and handing it to Hemming, asked him to name it.

Our friend began to look somewhat worried.

'It is an extraordinary thing, you know,' said he, 'but I can't tell you what bone it is part of. It is clearly the shaft of a long bone, but I'm hanged if I can say which. It is too big for a metatarsal and too small for any of the main limb bones. It reminds one of a diminutive thigh bone.'

'It does,' agreed Thorndyke; 'very strongly.' While Hemming had been speaking he had picked out four more large fragments, and these he now laid in a row with the one that had seemed to resemble a tibia in shape. Placed thus together, and the fragments bore an obvious resemblance.

'Now,' said he, 'look at these. There are five of them. They are parts of limb bones, and the bones of which they are parts were evidently exactly alike, excepting that three were apparently from the left side and two from the right. Now, you know, Hemming, a man has only four limbs, and of those only two contain similar bones. Then two of them show distinct traces of what looks like a saw-cut.'

Hemming gazed at the row of fragments with a frown of deep cogitation.

'It is very mysterious,' he said. 'And looking at them in a row they strike me as curiously like tibiae—in shape; not in size.'

'The size,' said Thorndyke, 'is about that of a sheep's tibia.'

'A sheep's!' exclaimed Hemming, staring in amazement, first at the calcined bones and then at my colleague.

'Yes; the upper half, sawn across in the middle of the shank.'

Hemming was thunderstruck.

'It is an astounding affair!' he exclaimed. 'You mean to suggest——'

'I suggest, said Thorndyke, 'that there is not a sign of a human bone in the whole collection. But there are very evident traces of at least five legs of mutton.'

For a few moments there was a profound silence, broken only by a murmur of astonishment from the cemetery official and a low chuckle from Superintendent Miller, who had been listening with absorbed interest. At length Hemming spoke.

'Then, apparently, there was no corpse in the coffin at all?'

'No,' answered Thorndyke. 'The weight was made up, and the ashes furnished, by joints of butcher's meat. I dare say, if we go over the ashes carefully, we shall be able to judge what they were. But it is hardly necessary. The presence of five legs of mutton and the absence of a single recognizable fragment of a human skeleton, together with the forged certificates, gives us a pretty conclusive case. The rest, I think, we can leave to Superintendent Miller.'

'I take it, Thorndyke,' said I, as the train moved out of the station, 'that you came here expecting to find what you did find?'

'Yes,' he replied. 'It seemed to me the only possibility, having regard to all the known facts.'

'When did it first occur to you?'

'It occurred to me as a possibility as soon as we discovered that the cremation certificates had been forged; but it was the undertaker's statement that seemed to clench the matter.'

'But he distinctly stated that he measured the body.'

'True. But there was nothing to show that it was a dead body. What was perfectly clear was that there was something that must on no account be seen; and when

Stalker told us of the embezzlement we had a body of evidence that could point to only one conclusion. Just consider that evidence.

'Here we had a death, preceded by an obviously sham illness and followed by cremation with forged certificates. Now, what was it that had happened? There were four possible hypotheses. Normal death, suicide, murder, and fictitious death. Which of these hypotheses fitted the facts?

'Normal death was apparently excluded by the forged certificates.

'The theory of suicide did not account for the facts. It did not agree with the careful, elaborate preparation. And why the forged certificates? If Ingle had really died, Meeking would have certified the death. And why the cremation? There was no purpose in taking those enormous risks.

'The theory of murder was unthinkable. These certificates were almost certainly forged by Ingle himself, who we know was a practised forger. But the idea of the victim arranging for his own cremation is an absurdity.

'There remained only the theory of fictitious death; and that theory fitted all the facts perfectly. First, as to the motive. Ingle had committed a felony. He had to disappear. But what kind of disappearance could be so effectual as death and cremation? Both the prosecutors and the police would forthwith write him off and forget him. Then there was the bigamy—a criminal offence in itself. But death would not only wipe that off; after "death" he could marry Huggard regularly under another name, and he would have shaken off his deserted wife for ever. And he stood to gain fifteen hundred pounds from the insurance company. Then see how this theory explained the other facts. A fictitious death made necessary a fictitious illness. It necessitated the forged certificates, since there was no corpse. It made cremation highly desirable; for suspicion might easily have arisen, and then the exhumation of a coffin containing a dummy would have exploded the fraud. But successful cremation would cover up the fraud for ever. It explained the concealment of the corpse from the undertaker, and it even explained the smell of formalin which he noticed.'

'How did it?' I asked.

'Consider, Jervis,' he replied. 'The dummy in this coffin had to be a dummy of flesh and bone which would yield the correct kind of ash. Joints of butcher's meat would fulfil the conditions. But the quantity required would be from a hundred and fifty to two hundred pounds. Now Ingle could not go to the butcher and order a whole sheep to be sent the day before the funeral. The joints would have to be bought gradually and stored. But the storage of meat in warm weather calls for some kind of preservative; and formalin is highly effective, as it leaves no trace after burning.

'So you see that the theory of fictitious death agreed with all the known circumstances, whereas the alternative theories presented inexplicable discrepancies and contradictions. Logically, it was the only possible theory, and as you have seen, experiment proved it to be the true one.'

As Thorndyke concluded, Dr. Hemming took his pipe from his mouth and laughed softly.

'When I came down to-day,' said he, 'I had all the facts which you had communicated to the Home Office, and I was absolutely convinced that we were coming to examine a mare's nest. And yet, now I have heard your exposition, the whole thing looks perfectly obvious.'

'That is usually the case with Thorndyke's conclusions,' said I. 'They are perfectly obvious — when you have heard the explanation.'

Within a week of our expedition, Ingle was in the hands of the police. The apparent success of the cremation adventure had misled him to a sense of such complete security that he had neglected to cover his tracks, and he had accordingly fallen an easy prey to our friend Superintendent Miller. The police were highly gratified, and so were the directors of the Griffin Life Assurance Company.

THOMAS BURKE

THE HANDS OF MR. OTTERMOLE

At six o'clock of a January evening Mr. Whybrow was walking home through the cobweb alleys of London's East End. He had left the golden clamour of the great High Street to which the tram had brought him from the river and his daily work, and was now in the chess-board of byways that is called Mallon End. None of the rush and gleam of the High Street trickled into these byways. A few paces south—a flood-tide of life, foaming and beating. Here—only slow shuffling figures and muffled pulses. He was in the sink of London, the last refuge of European vagrants.

As though in tune with the street's spirit, he too walked slowly, with head down. It seemed that he was pondering some pressing trouble, but he was not. He had no trouble. He was walking slowly because he had been on his feet all day, and he was bent in abstraction because he was wondering whether the Missis would have herrings for his tea, or haddock; and he was trying to decide which would be the more tasty on a night like this. A wretched night it was, of damp and mist, and the mist wandered into his throat and his eyes, and the damp had settled on pavement and roadway, and where the sparse lamplight fell it sent up a greasy sparkle that chilled one to look at. By contrast it made his speculation more agreeable, and made him ready for that tea—whether herring or haddock. His eye turned from the glum bricks that made his horizon, and went forward half a mile. He saw a gas-lit kitchen, a flamy fire and a spread tea-table. There was toast in the hearth and a singing kettle on the side and a piquant effusion of herrings, or maybe of haddock, or perhaps sausages. The vision gave his aching feet a throb of energy. He shook imperceptible damp from his shoulders, and hastened towards its reality.

But Mr. Whybrow wasn't going to get any tea that evening—or any other evening. Mr. Whybrow was going to die. Somewhere within a hundred yards of him another man was walking: a man much like Mr. Whybrow and much like any other man, but without the only quality that enables mankind to live peaceably together and not as madmen in a jungle. A man with a dead heart eating into itself and bringing forth the foul organisms that arise from death and corruption. And that thing in man's shape, on a whim or a settled idea—one cannot know—had said within himself that Mr. Whybrow should never taste another herring. Not that Mr. Whybrow had injured him. Not that he had any dislike of Mr. Whybrow. Indeed, he knew nothing of him save as a familiar figure about the streets. But, moved by a force that had taken possession of his empty cells, he had picked on Mr. Whybrow with that blind choice that makes us pick one restaurant table that has nothing to mark it from four or five other tables, or one apple from a dish of half a dozen equal apples; or that drives Nature to send a cyclone upon one corner of this planet, and destroy five hundred lives in that corner, and leave another five hundred in the same corner unharmed. So this man had picked on Mr. Whybrow, as he might have picked on you or me, had we been within his daily observation; and even now he was creeping through the blue-toned streets, nursing his large white hands, moving ever closer to Mr. Whybrow's tea-table, and so closer to Mr. Whybrow himself.

He wasn't, this man, a bad man. Indeed, he had many of the social and amiable qualities, and passed as a respectable man, as most successful criminals do. But the thought had come into his mouldering mind that he would like to murder somebody, and, as he held no fear of God or man, he was going to do it, and would then go home to *his* tea. I don't say that flippantly, but as a statement of fact. Strange as it may seem to the humane, murderers must and do sit down to meals after a murder. There is no reason why they shouldn't, and many reasons why they should. For one thing, they need to keep their physical and mental vitality at full beat for the business of covering their crime. For another, the strain of their effort makes them hungry, and satisfaction at the accomplishment of a desired thing brings a feeling of relaxation towards human pleasures. It is accepted among non - murderers that the murderer is always overcome by fear for his safety and horror at his act; but this type is rare. His own safety is, of course, his immediate concern, but vanity is a marked quality of most murderers, and that, together with the thrill of conquest, makes him confident that he can secure it, and when he has restored his strength with food he goes about securing it as a young hostess goes about the arranging of her first big dinner—a little anxious, but no more. Criminologists and detectives tell us that *every* murderer, however intelligent or cunning, always makes one slip in his tactics—one little slip that brings the affair home to him. But that is only half true. It is true only of the murderers who are caught. Scores of murderers are not caught: therefore scores of murderers do not make any mistake at all. This man didn't.

As for horror or remorse, prison chaplains, doctors, and lawyers have told us that of murderers they have interviewed under condemnation and the shadow of death, only one here and there has expressed any contrition for his act, or shown any sign of mental misery. Most of them display only exasperation at having been caught when so many have gone undiscovered, or indignation at being condemned for a perfectly reasonable act. However normal and humane they may have been before the murder, they are utterly without conscience after it. For what is conscience? Simply a polite nickname for superstition, which is a polite nickname for fear. Those who associate remorse with murder are, no doubt, basing their ideas on the world-legend of the remorse of Cain, or are projecting their own frail minds into the mind of the murderer, and getting false reactions. Peaceable folk cannot hope to make contact with this mind, for they are not merely different in mental type from the murderer: they are different in their personal chemistry and construction. Some men can and do kill, not one man, but two or three, and go calmly about their daily affairs. Other men could not, under the most agonizing provocation, bring themselves even to wound. It is men of this sort who imagine the murderer in torments of remorse and fear of the law, whereas he is actually sitting down to his tea.

The man with the large white hands was as ready for his tea as Mr. Whybrow was, but he had something to do before he went to it. When he had done that something, and made no mistake about it, he would be even more ready for it, and would go to it as comfortably as he went to it the day before, when his hands were stainless.

Walk on, then Mr. Whybrow, walk on; and as you walk, look your last upon the familiar features of your nightly journey. Follow your jack-o'-lantern tea-table. Look well upon its warmth and colour and kindness; feed your eyes with it, and tease your nose with its gentle domestic odours; for you will never sit down to it. Within ten minutes' pacing of you a pursuing phantom has spoken in his heart, and you are doomed. There you go—you and phantom—two nebulous dabs of mortality, moving through green air along pavements of powder-blue, the one to kill, the other to be killed. Walk on. Don't annoy your burning feet by hurrying, for the more slowly you walk, the longer you will breathe the green air of this January dusk, and see the dreamy lamplight and the little shops, and hear the agreeable commerce of the London crowd and the haunting pathos of the street-organ. These things are dear to you, Mr. Whybrow. You don't know it now, but in fifteen minutes you will have two seconds in which to realize how inexpressibly dear they are.

Walk on, then, across this crazy chess-board. You are in Lagos Street now, among the tents of the wanderers of Eastern Europe. A minute or so, and you are in Loyal Lane, among the lodging-houses that shelter the useless and the beaten of London's camp-followers. The lane holds the smell of them, and its soft darkness seems heavy with the wail of the futile. But you are not sensitive to impalpable things, and you plod through it, unseeing, as you do every evening, and come to Blean Street, and plod through that. From basement to sky rise the tenements of an alien colony. Their windows slit the ebony of their walls with lemon. Behind those windows strange life is moving, dressed with forms that are not of London or of England, yet, in essence, the same agreeable life that you have been living, and to-night will live no more. From high above you comes a voice crooning *The Song of Katta*. Through a window you see a family keeping a religious rite. Through another you see a woman pouring out tea for her husband. You see a man mending a pair of boots; a mother bathing her baby. You have seen all these things before, and never noticed them. You do not notice them now, but if you knew that you were never going to see them again, you would notice them. You never *will* see them again, not because your life has run its natural course, but because a man whom you have often passed in the street has at his own solitary pleasure decided to usurp the awful authority of nature, and destroy you. So perhaps it 's as well that you don't notice them, for your part in them is ended. No more for you these pretty moments of our earthly travail: only one moment of terror, and then a plunging darkness.

Closer to you this shadow of massacre moves, and now he is twenty yards behind you. You can hear his footfalls, but you do not turn your head. You are familiar with foot-falls. You are in London, in the easy security of your daily territory, and footfalls behind you, your instinct tells you, are no more than a message of human company.

But can't you hear something in those footfalls—something that goes with a widdershins beat? Something that says: *Look out, look out. Beware, beware.* Can't you hear the very syllables of *murd-er-er, murd-er-er*? No; there is nothing in footfalls. They are neutral. The foot of villainy falls with the same quiet note as the foot of honesty. But those footfalls, Mr. Whybrow, are bearing on to you a pair of hands, and there *is* something in hands. Behind you that pair of hands is even now stretching its muscles in prepara-tion for your end. Every minute of your days you have been seeing human hands. Have you ever realized the sheer horror of hands—those appendages that are a symbol for our moments of trust and affection and salutation? Have you thought of the sickening potentialities that lie within the scope of that five-tentacled member? No, you never have; for all the human hands that you have seen have been stretched to you in kindness or fellowship. Yet, though the eyes can hate, and the lips can sting, it is only that dangling member that can gather the accumulated essence of evil, and electrify it into currents of destruction.

Satan may enter into man by many doors, but in the hands alone can he find the servants of his will.

Another minute, Mr. Whybrow, and you will know all about the horror of human hands.

You are nearly home now. You have turned into your street—Caspar Street—and you are in the centre of the chess-board. You can see the front window of your little four-roomed house. The street is dark, and its three lamps give only a smut of light that is more confusing than darkness. It is dark—empty, too. Nobody about; no lights in the front parlours of the houses, for the families are at tea in their kitchens; and only a random glow in a few upper rooms occupied by lodgers. Nobody about but you and your following companion, and you don't notice him. You see him so often that he is never seen. Even if you turned your head and saw him, you would only say 'Good evening' to him, and walk on. A suggestion that he was a possible murderer would not even make you laugh. It would be too silly.

And now you are at your gate. And now you have found your door key. And now you are in, and hanging up your hat and coat. The Missis has just called a greeting from the kitchen, whose smell is an echo of that greeting (herring!) and you have answered it, when the door shakes under a sharp knock.

Go away, Mr. Whybrow. Go away from that door. Don't touch it. Get right away from it. Get out of the house. Run with the Misses to the back garden, and over the fence. Or call the neighbours. But don't touch that door. Don't, Mr. Whybrow, don't open . . .

Mr. Whybrow opened the door.

That was the beginning of what became known as London's Strangling Horrors. Horrors they were called because they were something more than murders: they were motiveless, and there was an air of black magic about them. Each murder was committed at a time when the street where the bodies were found was empty of any perceptible or possible murderer. There would be an empty alley. There would be a policeman at its end. He would turn his back on the empty alley for less than a minute. Then he would look

round and run into the night with news of another strangling. And in any direction he looked nobody to be seen
and no report to be had of anybody being seen. Or he
would be on duty in a long quiet street, and suddenly be
called to a house of dead people whom a few seconds earlier
he had seen alive. And, again, whichever way he looked
nobody to be seen; and although police whistles put an
immediate cordon around the area, and all houses were
searched, no possible murderer to be found.

The first news of the murder of Mr. and Mrs. Whybrow
was brought by the station sergeant. He had been walking
through Caspar Street on his way to the station for duty,
when he noticed the open door of No. 98. Glancing in, he
saw by the gaslight of the passage a motionless body on the
floor. After a second look he blew his whistle, and when
the constables answered him he took one to join him in a
search of the house, and sent others to watch all neighbouring streets, and make inquiries at adjoining houses. But
neither in the house nor in the streets was anything found
to indicate the murderer. Neighbours on either side, and
opposite, were questioned, but they had seen nobody about,
and had heard nothing. One had heard Mr. Whybrow
come home—the scrape of his latchkey in the door was so
regular an evening sound, he said, that you could set your
watch by it for half-past six—but he had heard nothing
more than the sound of the opening door until the sergeant's
whistle. Nobody had been seen to enter the house or leave
it, by front or back, and the necks of the dead people carried
no finger-prints or other traces. A nephew was called in to
go over the house, but he could find nothing missing; and
anyway his uncle possessed nothing worth stealing. The
little money in the house was untouched, and there were no
signs of any disturbance of the property, or even of struggle.
No signs of anything but brutal and wanton murder.

Mr. Whybrow was known to neighbours and work-mates
as a quiet, likeable, home-loving man; such a man as could
not have any enemies. But, then, murdered men seldom
have. A relentless enemy who hates a man to the point of
wanting to hurt him seldom wants to murder him, since to
do that puts him beyond suffering. So the police were left
with an impossible situation: no clue to the murderer and

no motive for the murders; only the fact that they had
been done.

The first news of the affair sent a tremor through London
generally, and an electric thrill through all Mallon End.
Here was murder of two inoffensive people, not for gain
and not for revenge; and the murderer, to whom, apparently, killing was a casual impulse, was at large. He had
left no traces, and, provided he had no companions, there
seemed no reason why he should not remain at large. Any
clear-headed man who stands alone, and has no fear of
God or man, can, if he chooses, hold a city, even a nation,
in subjection; but your everyday criminal is seldom clear-
headed, and dislikes being lonely. He needs, if not the
support of confederates, at least somebody to talk to; his
vanity needs the satisfaction of perceiving at first hand the
effect of his work. For this he will frequent bars and
coffee-shops and other public places. Then, sooner or
later, in a glow of comradeship, he will utter the one word
too much; and the nark, who is everywhere, has an easy job.

But though the doss-houses and saloons and other places
were 'combed' and set with watches, and it was made
known by whispers that good money and protection were
assured to those with information, nothing attaching to the
Whybrow case could be found. The murderer clearly had
no friends and kept no company. Known men of this type
were called up and questioned, but each was able to give a
good acount of himself; and in a few days the police were
at a dead end. Against the constant public gibe that the
thing had been done almost under their noses, they became
restive, and for four days each man of the force was working his daily beat under a strain. On the fifth day they
became still more restive.

It was the season of annual teas and entertainments for
the children of the Sunday Schools, and on an evening of
fog, when London was a world of groping phantoms, a
small girl, in the bravery of best Sunday frock and shoes,
shining face and new-washed hair, set out from Logan
Passage for St. Michael's Parish Hall. She never got there.
She was not actually dead until half-past six, but she was
as good as dead from the moment she left her mother's
door. Somebody like a man, pacing the street from which

the Passage led, saw her come out; and from that moment she was dead. Through the fog somebody's large white hands reached after her, and in fifteen minutes they were about her.

At half-past six a whistle screamed trouble, and those answering it found the body of little Nellie Vrinoff in a warehouse entry in Minnow Street. The sergeant was first among them, and he posted his men to useful points, ordering them here and there in the tart tones of repressed rage, and berating the officer whose beat the street was. 'I saw you, Magson, at the end of the lane. What were you up to there? You were there ten minutes before you turned.' Magson began an explanation about keeping an eye on a suspicious-looking character at that end, but the sergeant cut him short: 'Suspicious characters be damned. You don't want to look for suspicious characters. You want to look for *murderers*. Messing about . . . and then this happens right where you ought to be. Now think what they 'll say.'

With the speed of ill news came the crowd, pale and perturbed; and on the story that the unknown monster had appeared again, and this time to a child, their faces streaked the fog with spots of hate and horror. But then came the ambulance and more police, and swiftly they broke up the crowd; and as it broke the sergeant's thought was thickened into words, and from all sides came low murmurs of 'Right under their noses.' Later inquiries showed that four people of the district, above suspicion, had passed that entry at intervals of seconds before the murder, and seen nothing and heard nothing. None of them had passed the child alive or seen her dead. None of them had seen anybody in the street except themselves. Again the police were left with no motive and with no clue.

And now the district, as you will remember, was given over, not to panic, for the London public never yields to that, but to apprehension and dismay. If these things were happening in their familiar streets, then anything might happen. Wherever people met—in the streets, the markets and the shops—they debated the one topic. Women took to bolting their windows and doors at the first fall of dusk. They kept their children closely under their eye. They did their shopping before dark, and watched anxiously, while pretending they weren't watching, for the return of their husbands from work. Under the Cockney's semi-humorous resignation to disaster, they hid an hourly foreboding. By the whim of one man with a pair of hands the structure and tenor of their daily life were shaken, as they always can be shaken by any man contemptuous of humanity and fearless of its laws. They began to realize that the pillars that supported the peaceable society in which they lived were mere straws that anybody could snap; that laws were powerful only so long as they were obeyed; that the police were potent only so long as they were feared. By the power of his hands this one man had made a whole community do something new: he had made it think, and left it gasping at the obvious.

And then, while it was yet gasping under his first two strokes, he made his third. Conscious of the horror that his hands had created, and hungry as an actor who has once tasted the thrill of the multitude, he made fresh advertisement of his presence; and on Wednesday morning, three days after the murder of the child, the papers carried to the breakfast-tables of England the story of a still more shocking outrage.

At 9.32 on Tuesday night a constable was on duty in Jarnigan Road, and at that time spoke to a fellow-officer named Peterson at the top of Clemming Street. He had seen this officer walk down that street. He could swear that the street was empty at that time, except for a lame boot-black whom he knew by sight, and who passed him and entered a tenement on the side opposite that on which his fellow-officer was walking. He had the habit, as all constables had just then, of looking constantly behind him and around him, whichever way he was walking, and he was certain that the street was empty. He passed his sergeant at 9.33, saluted him, and answered his inquiry for anything seen. He reported that he had seen nothing, and passed on. His beat ended at a short distance from Clemming Street, and, having paced it, he turned and came again at 9.34 to the top of the street. He had scarcely reached it before he heard the hoarse voice of the sergeant: 'Gregory! You there? Quick. Here's another. My God, it's Peterson! Garrotted. Quick, call 'em up!'

That was the third of the Strangling Horrors, of which there were to be a fourth and a fifth; and the five horrors were to pass into the unknown and unknowable. That is, unknown as far as authority and the public were concerned. The identity of the murderer *was* known, but to two men only. One was the murderer himself; the other was a young journalist.

This young man, who was covering the affairs for his paper, the *Daily Torch*, was no smarter than the other zealous newspaper men who were hanging about these by-ways in the hope of a sudden story. But he was patient, and he hung a little closer to the case than the other fellows, and by continually staring at it he at last raised the figure of the murderer like a genie from the stones on which he had stood to do his murders.

After the first few days the men had given up any attempt at exclusive stories, for there was none to be had. They met regularly at the police station, and what little information there was they shared. The officials were agreeable to them, but no more. The sergeant discussed with them the details of each murder; suggested possible explanations of the man's methods; recalled from the past those cases that had some similarity; and on the matter of motive reminded them of the motiveless Neil Cream and the wanton John Williams, and hinted that work was being done which would soon bring the business to an end; but about that work he would not say a word. The inspector, too, was gracefully garrulous on the theme of murder, but whenever one of the party edged the talk towards what was being done in this immediate matter, he glided past it. Whatever the officials knew, they were not giving it to newspaper men. The business had fallen heavily upon them, and only by a capture made by their own efforts could they rehabilitate themselves in official and public esteem. Scotland Yard, of course, was at work, and had all the station's material; but the station's hope was that they themselves would have the honour of settling the affair; and however useful the co-operation of the Press might be in other cases they did not want to risk a defeat by a premature disclosure of their theories and plans.

So the sergeant talked at large, and propounded one

interesting theory after another, all of which the newspaper men had thought of themselves.

The young man soon gave up these morning lectures on the Philosophy of Crime, and took to wandering about the streets and making bright stories out of the effect of the murders on the normal life of the people.   A melancholy job made more melancholy by the district.   The littered roadways, the crestfallen houses, the bleared windows— all held the acid misery that evokes no sympathy: the misery of the frustrated poet.   The misery was the creation of the aliens, who were living in this makeshift fashion because they had no settled homes, and would neither take the trouble to make a home where they *could* settle, nor get on with their wandering.

There was little to be picked up.   All he saw and heard were indignant faces and wild conjectures of the murderer's identity and of the secret of his trick of appearing and disappearing unseen.   Since a policeman himself had fallen a victim, denunciations of the force had ceased, and the unknown was now invested with a cloak of legend.   Men eyed other men, as though thinking: It might be *him*.   It might be *him*.   They were no longer looking for a man who had the air of a Madame Tussaud murderer; they were looking for a man, or perhaps some harridan woman, who had done these particular murders.   Their thoughts ran mainly on the foreign set.   Such ruffianism could scarcely belong to England, nor could the bewildering cleverness of the thing.   So they turned to Rumanian gipsies and Turkish carpet-sellers.   There, clearly, would be found the 'warm' spot.   These Eastern fellows—they knew all sorts of tricks, and they had no real religion—nothing to hold them within bounds.   Sailors returning from those parts had told tales of conjurors who made themselves invisible; and there were tales of Egyptian and Arab potions that were used for abysmally queer purposes.   Perhaps it *was* possible to them; you never knew.   They were so slick and cunning, and they had such gliding movements; no Englishman could melt away as they could.   Almost certainly the murderer would be found to be one of that sort—with some dark trick of his own—and just because they were sure that he *was* a magician, they felt that it was useless to look for him.   He was a power, able to hold them in subjection and to hold himself untouchable. Superstition, which so easily cracks the frail shell of reason, had got into them. He could do anything he chose; he would never be discovered. These two points they settled, and they went about the streets in a mood of resentful fatalism.

They talked of their ideas to the journalist in half-tones, looking right and left, as though *HE* might overhear them and visit them. And though all the district was thinking of him and ready to pounce upon him, yet, so strongly had he worked upon them, that if any man in the street—say, a small man of commonplace features and form—had cried '*I* am the monster!' would their stifled fury have broken into flood and have borne him down and engulfed him? Or would they not suddenly have seen something unearthly in that everyday face and figure, something unearthly in his everyday boots, something unearthly about his hat, something that marked him as one whom none of their weapons could alarm or pierce? And would they not momentarily have fallen back from this devil, as the devil fell back from the cross made by the sword of Faust, and so have given him time to escape? I do not know; but so fixed was their belief in his invincibility that it is at least likely that they would have made this hesitation, had such an occasion arisen. But it never did. To-day this common-place fellow, his murder-lust glutted, is still seen and ob-served among them as he was seen and observed all the time; but because nobody then dreamt, or now dreams, that he was what he was, they observed him then, and observe him now, as people observe a lamp-post.

Almost was their belief in his invincibility justified; for five days after the murder of the policeman Petersen, when the experience and inspiration of the whole detective force of London were turned towards his identification and capture, he made his fourth and fifth strokes.

At nine o'clock that evening, the young newspaper man who hung about every night until his paper was away, was strolling along Richards Lane. Richards Lane is a narrow street, partly a stall-market, and partly residential. The young man was in the residential section, which carries on one side small working-class cottages, and on the other the wall of a railway goods yard. The great wall hung a blanket of shadow over the lane, and the shadow and the cadaverous outline of the now deserted market stalls gave it the appearance of a living lane that had been turned to frost in the moment between breath and death. The very lamps, that elsewhere were nimbuses of gold, had here the rigidity of gems. The journalist, feeling this message of frozen eternity, was telling himself that he was tired of the whole thing, when in one stroke the frost was broken. In the moment between one pace and another silence and darkness were racked by a high scream and through the scream a voice: 'Help! help! *He's here!*'

Before he could think what movement to make, the lane came to life. As though its invisible populace had been waiting on that cry, the door of every cottage was flung open, and from them and from the alleys poured shadowy figures bent in question-mark form. For a second or so they stood as rigid as the lamps; then a police whistle gave them direction, and the flock of shadows sloped up the street. The journalist followed them, and others followed him. From the main street and from surrounding streets they came, some risen from unfinished suppers, some disturbed in their ease of slippers and shirt-sleeves, some stumbling on infirm limbs, and some upright, and armed with pokers or the tools of their trade. Here and there above the wavering cloud of heads moved the bold helmets of policemen. In one dim mass they surged upon a cottage whose doorway was marked by the sergeant and two constables; and voices of those behind urged them on with 'Get in! Find him! Run round the back! Over the wall!' and those in front cried: 'Keep back! Keep back!'

And now the fury of a mob held in thrall by unknown peril broke loose. He was here—on the spot. Surely this time he *could not* escape. All minds were bent upon the cottage; all energies thrust towards its doors and windows and roof; all thought was turned upon one unknown man and his extermination. So that no one man saw any other man. No man saw the narrow, packed lane and the mass of struggling shadows, and all forgot to look among themselves for the monster who never lingered upon his victims. All forgot, indeed, that they, by their mass crusade of vengeance, were affording him the perfect hiding-place. They saw only the house, and they heard only the rending of woodwork and the smash of glass at back and front, and the police giving orders or crying with the chase; and they pressed on.

But they found no murderer. All they found was news of murder and a glimpse of the ambulance, and for their fury there was no other object than the police themselves, who fought against this hampering of their work.

The journalist managed to struggle through to the cottage door, and to get the story from the constable stationed there. The cottage was the home of a pensioned sailor and his wife and daughter. They had been at supper, and at first it appeared that some noxious gas had smitten all three in mid-action. The daughter lay dead on the hearth-rug, with a piece of bread and butter in her hand. The father had fallen sideways from his chair, leaving on his plate a filled spoon of rice-pudding. The mother lay half under the table, her lap filled with the pieces of a broken cup and splashes of cocoa. But in three seconds the idea of gas was dismissed. One glance at their necks showed that this was the Strangler again; and the police stood and looked at the room and momentarily shared the fatalism of the public. They were helpless.

This was his fourth visit, making seven murders in all. He was to do, as you know, one more—and to do it that night; and then he was to pass into history as the unknown London horror, and return to the decent life that he had always led, remembering little of what he had done, and worried not at all by the memory. Why did he stop? Impossible to say. Why did he begin? Impossible again.' It just happened like that; and if he thinks at all of those days and nights, I surmise that he thinks of them as we think of foolish or dirty little sins that we committed in childhood. We say that they were not really sins, because we were not then consciously ourselves: we had not come to realization; and we look back at that foolish little creature that we once were, and forgive him because he didn't know. So, I think, with this man.

There are plenty like him. Eugene Aram, after the murder of Daniel Clark, lived a quiet, contented life for fourteen

years, unhaunted by his crime and unshaken in his self-
esteem.   Dr. Crippen murdered his wife, and then lived
pleasantly with his mistress in the house under whose floor
he had buried his wife.   Constance Kent, found Not Guilty
of the murder of her young brother, led a peaceful life for
five years before she confessed.   George Joseph Smith and
William Palmer lived amiably among their fellows un-
troubled by fear or by remorse for their poisonings and
drownings.   Charles Peace, at the time he made his one
unfortunate essay, had settled down into a respectable
citizen with an interest in antiques.   It happened that,
after a lapse of time, these men were discovered, but more
murderers than we guess are living decent lives to-day, and
will die in decency, undiscovered and unsuspected.   As this
man will.

But he had a narrow escape, and it was perhaps this
narrow escape that brought him to a stop.   The escape was
due to an error of judgment on the part of the journalist.

As soon as he had the full story of the affair, which took
some time, he spent fifteen minutes on the telephone, sending the story through, and at the end of the fifteen minutes,
when the stimulus of the business had left him, he felt
physically tired and mentally dishevelled.   He was not
yet free to go home; the paper would not go away for
another hour; so he turned into a bar for a drink and
some sandwiches.

It was then, when he had dismissed the whole business
from his mind, and was looking about the bar and admiring
the landlord's taste in watch-chains and his air of domina-
tion, and was thinking that the landlord of a well-conducted
tavern had a more comfortable life than a newspaper man,
that his mind received from nowhere a spark of light.   He
was not thinking about the Strangling Horrors; his mind
was on his sandwich.   As a public-house sandwich, it was a
curiosity.   The bread had been thinly cut, it was buttered,
and the ham was not two months stale; it was ham as it
should be.   His mind turned to the inventor of this refreshment, the Earl of Sandwich, and then to George the Fourth,
and then to the Georges, and to the legend of that George
who was worried to know how the apple got into the apple-
dumpling.   He wondered whether George would have

been equally puzzled to know how the ham got into the ham sandwich, and how long it would have been before it occurred to him that the ham could not have got there unless somebody had put it there. He got up to order another sandwich, and in that moment a little active corner of his mind settled the affair. If there was ham in his sandwich, somebody must have put it there. If seven people had been murdered, somebody must have been there to murder them. There was no aeroplane or automobile that would go into a man's pocket; therefore that somebody must have escaped either by running away or standing still; and again therefore——

He was visualizing the front page story that his paper would carry if his theory were correct, and if—a matter of conjecture—his editor had the necessary nerve to make a bold stroke, when a cry of 'Time, gentlemen, please! All out!' reminded him of the hour. He got up and went out into a world of mist, broken by the ragged disks of roadside puddles and the streaming lightning of motor buses. He was certain that he had *the* story, but, even if it were proved, he was doubtful whether the policy of his paper would permit him to print it. It had one great fault. It was truth, but it was impossible truth. It rocked the foundations of everything that newspaper readers believed and that newspaper editors helped them to believe. They might believe that Turkish carpet-sellers had the gift of making themselves invisible. They would not believe this.

As it happened, they were not asked to, for the story was never written. As his paper had by now gone away, and as he was nourished by his refreshment and stimulated by his theory, he thought he might put in an extra half-hour by testing that theory. So he began to look about for the man he had in mind—a man with white hair, and large white hands; otherwise an everyday figure whom nobody would look twice at. He wanted to spring his idea on this man without warning, and he was going to place himself within reach of a man armoured in legends of dreadfulness and grue. This might appear to be an act of supreme courage —that one man, with no hope of immediate outside support, should place himself at the mercy of one who was holding a whole parish in terror. But it wasn't. He didn't think about the risk. He didn't think about his duty to his employers or loyalty to his paper. He was moved simply by an instinct to follow a story to its end.

He walked slowly from the tavern and crossed into Fingal Street, making for Deever Market, where he had hope of finding his man. But his journey was shortened. At the corner of Lotus Street he saw him—or a man who looked like him. This street was poorly lit, and he could see little of the man: but he *could* see white hands. For some twenty paces he stalked him; then drew level with him; and at a point where the arch of a railway crossed the street, he was sure that this was his man. He approached him with the current conversational phrase of the district: 'Well, seen anything of the murderer?' The man stopped to look sharply at him; then, satisfied that the journalist was not the murderer, said:

'Eh? No, nor 's anybody else, curse it. Doubt if they ever will.'

'I don't know. I've been thinking about them, and I've got an idea.'

'So?'

'Yes. Came to me all of a sudden. Quarter of an hour ago. And I'd felt that we'd all been blind. It's been staring us in the face.'

The man turned again to look at him, and the look and the movement held suspicion of this man who seemed to know so much. 'Oh? Has it? Well, if you're so sure, why not give us the benefit of it?'

'I'm going to.' They walked level, and were nearly at the end of the little street where it meets Deever Market, when the journalist turned casually to the man. He put a finger on his arm. 'Yes, it seems to me quite simple now. But there's still one point I don't understand. One little thing I'd like to clear up. I mean the motive. Now, as man to man, tell me, Sergeant Ottermole, just *why* did you kill those inoffensive people?'

The sergeant stopped, and the journalist stopped. There was just enough light from the sky, which held the reflected light of the continent of London, to give him a sight of the sergeant's face, and the sergeant's face was turned to him with a wide smile of such urbanity and charm that the journalist's eyes were frozen as they met it. The smile stayed for some seconds. Then said the sergeant: 'Well, to tell you the truth, Mister Newspaper Man, I don't know. I really don't know. In fact, I 've been worried about it myself. But I 've got an idea—just like you. Everybody knows that we can't control the workings of our minds. Don't they? Ideas come into our minds without asking. But everybody 's supposed to be able to control his body. Why? Eh? We get our minds from lord-knows-where—from people who were dead hundreds of years before we were born. Mayn't we get our bodies in the same way? Our faces—our legs—our heads—they aren't completely ours. We don't make 'em. They come to us. And couldn't ideas come into our bodies like ideas come into our minds? Eh? Can't ideas live in nerve and muscle as well as in brain? Couldn't it be that parts of our bodies aren't really us, and couldn't ideas come into those parts all of a sudden, like ideas come into—into'—he shot his arms out, showing the great white-gloved hands and hairy wrists; shot them out so swiftly to the journalist's throat that his eyes never saw them—'into *my hands.*'

FATHER RONALD KNOX

SOLVED BY INSPECTION

MILES BREDON, the eminently indefatigable inquiry agent, was accustomed to describe himself as a perfect fool at his job. Here he was in agreement with his wife Angela; where he differed from her was in really regarding himself as a fool at his job. There she knew better; and so, fortunately for both of them, did the Indescribable—that vast insurance company which employed him to investigate the more questionable transactions of its clients, and saved itself about five thousand a year by doing so. On one occasion, however, Bredon did claim to have really solved a problem by inspection, without any previous knowledge to put him on the right track. Indeed, since he seldom read the cheaper kind of newspaper, it is probable that he had never heard of the eccentric millionaire, Herbert Jervison, until Herbert Jervison was found dead in his bed. He was only supplied with the facts of the situation as he travelled down in the train to Wiltshire with Dr. Simmonds, the expensive medical man whom the Indescribable valued almost as much as Bredon himself. It was a bright summer's morning, and the dewy fields, horizoned by lazy stretches of canal, would have been food enough for meditation if Simmonds had not been so confoundedly anxious to impart information.

'You must have heard of him,' he was saying. 'He was a newspaper boom long before he was a casualty. The Million and a Half Mystic—that was the sort of thing they called him. Why is it that the grossly rich never have the least idea of how to spend money? This Jervison had pottered about in the East, and had got caught with all that esoteric bilge—talked about Mahatmas and Yogis and things till even the most sanguine of his poor relations wouldn't ask him to stay. So he settled down at Yewbury here with some Indian frauds he had picked up, and said he was the Brotherhood of Light. Had it printed on his note-paper, which was dark green. Ate nuts and did automatic writing and made all sorts of psychic experiments, till the papers were all over him; that sort of stuff gets them where they live. And then, you see, he went and died.'

'That 's a kind of publicity we all achieve sooner or later. If they all did it later, our job with the Indescribable would be a soft one. Anyhow, why did they send for me? He probably choked on a Brazil nut or something. No question of muder or suicide or anything, is there?'

'That 's just the odd part about it. He died suddenly, of starvation.'

'I suppose you want me to say that 's impossible. No medical man myself, I am astute enough to see that my leg is being pulled. Let 's hear more about it. Did you ever see the fellow?'

'Not till he came in to be vetted for his insurance. I 've been kicking myself over that; because, you see, I thought he was about the soundest life I 'd ever struck. He was only fifty-three, and of course these people who go in for Oriental food-fads do sometimes pull off a longevity record. In fact, he had the cheek to ask for a specially low premium, because he said he was in a fair way to discovering the secret of immortality—which, as he pointed out, would make his premium a permanent asset to the company. And then he goes and kills himself by refusing his mash. Mark you, I 'm not sure I wouldn't sooner starve than eat the sort of muck he ate; but then, he seemed to flourish on it.'

'And there was really nothing wrong with him? What about his top story?'

'Well, he admitted to nerves, and I must say he showed up badly over some of the nerve tests. You know we take the nervy people up to the top of the Indescribable building nowadays, to see whether it gives them the jim-jams. Well, this fellow was at the end of his tether; you couldn't get him to look over the edge for love or money. But if his relations had wanted him certified — and they 'd every reason to—I couldn't have done it. Colney Hatch wasn't on the map; I 'd swear to that, even at a directors' meeting.'

'So he went off and died suddenly of starvation. Could you amplify that statement a bit?'

'Well, what really happened was that he shut himself up
for ten days or so in the room he calls his laboratory. I
haven't seen it, but it's an old gymnasium or racket-
court, they tell me. There was nothing queer in that,
because he was always shutting himself up to do his fool
experiments; locked himself in and wasn't to be disturbed
on any account. Probably thought his astral body was
wandering about in Thibet. But—this is the odd thing—
he was fully victualled, so I hear, for a fortnight. And at
the end of ten days he was found dead in his bed. The
local doctor, who has been out in the East and served a
famine area, says it's the clearest case of starvation he's
ever met.'

'And the food?'

'The food was untouched. I say, this is Westbury, where
the car's going to meet us. I didn't tell Dr. Mayhew I was
bringing a friend; how exactly am I going to explain you?'

'Tell him I'm the representative of the company. That
always fetches them. Hallo, there's a black man on the
platform.'

'That'll be the chauffeur. . . . No, thanks, no luggage. . . .
Good morning, are you from Yewbury? Dr. Simmonds,
my name is; I think Dr. Mayhew expects me. Outside, is
he? Good. Come along, Bredon.'

Dr. Mayhew was a little round-faced man who seemed
incapable of suspicion and radiated hospitality. You saw
at once that he was the kind of country doctor who suffers
from having too little company, and can scarcely be got to
examine your symptoms because he is so anxious to exchange all the news first. He outdid Simmonds himself in
his offhand way of referring to the tragedy.

'Awfully good of you fellows to come,' he said. 'Not
that I'm anxious for a second opinion here. Nine cases out
of ten, *you* know that well enough, one signs the death
certificate on an off-chance; but there ain't any doubt
about this poor devil. I've been in a famine area, you
know, and seen the symptoms often enough to make you
dream of it; not pleasant, are they? I expect Mr.—oh, yes,
Bredon, to be sure; Mr. Bredon won't want to see the corpus.
They've got it parked up at the Brotherhood House,
ready to be disposed of when it's finished with; the—er—

symptoms come on rather suddenly, you know, Mr. Bredon,
in these cases. What about coming round to my house and
having a spot of something on the way? Sure you won't?
Oh, very well. Yes, they 've got to bury him in some
special way of their own, tuck him up with his feet towards
Jericho, I expect, or something of that sort. Hope these
niggers 'll clear out after this,' he added, lowering his voice
for fear the driver should overhear him. 'The neighbours
don't like 'em, and that 's a fact. They 're not pukka
Indians, you know; he picked them up in San Francisco or
somewhere; lascars, I should call 'em.'

'I don't know that you're likely to be rid of them, doctor,'
explained Bredon. 'I suppose you realize that they benefit
heavily under Jervison's will? At least, his insurance
policy is made out in favour of the Brotherhood, and I suppose there 'll be a tidy piece of his own money coming to
them as well.'

'And your company pays up, does it, Mr. Bredon?' said
the little doctor. 'Gad, I wonder if they 'd let me into the
Brotherhood? There are only four of them in it, and I
could do with a few extra thousands.'

'Well,' explained Bredon, 'that 's what we're here about.
If it 's suicide, you see, they can't touch the money. Our
policies don't cover suicide; it would be too much of a
temptation.'

'That so? Well, then, you 're on velvet. The thing can
only be suicide, and unsound mind at that. There 's Yewbury, up on the hill. Queer place; very rich man had it,
name of Rosenbach, and fitted it all up like a palace, with
a real racket-court; that 's the roof of it you see there.
Then he crashed, and the place was sold for next to nothing;
taken on as a preparatory school, it was, by a young fellow
called Enstone; I liked him, but he never could make the
place pay properly, one way and another, so he sold out
and went to the South Coast, and then Jervison took it on.
Well, here we are. Would you like to wander about the
grounds, Mr. Bredon, while we go in and look at the remains,
or what?'

'I think I 'd like to go into the room where he was found.
Perhaps one of these natives would take me in; I 'd like to
have a chance of talking to one of them.'

The arrangement was made without difficulty, though Bredon found his guide a source of embarrassment, almost of nervousness. The driver of the car had worn an ordinary dark suit, but this other representative of the community was dressed in flowing white robes, with a turban to match, and seemed covered all over with cabalistic emblems. He was tall and strongly built; his manner was at once impassive and continually alert; nothing seemed to disturb him, yet you felt that nothing escaped him. And when he spoke, he belied his whole appearance by talking English with a violently American intonation.

The racket-court stood at a considerable distance from the main block of buildings; perhaps five hundred yards away. The gallery which had once existed close to the door had been cleared away to make space when it had been turned into a gymnasium, and you entered directly into a huge oblong room, with something of a cathedral vastness in its effects of distance and of silence. The floor had been fitted with shiny red oil-cloth, so that your footsteps were deadened, and the echoes of the place awoke only at the sound of your voice. The light came chiefly, and the ventilation entirely, from a well in the centre of the roof; the top of this was of fixed glass, and only the iron slats at the side were capable of letting in air. There were still memories of the gymnasium period; at four points in the ceiling were iron rings, which looked as if ropes had hung down from them by hooks, and there were lockers at one side which still seemed to demand the presence of juvenile boots. Little had been done since in the way of furnishing; the eccentric had evidently used the place when he wanted to be separated from his kind, with the thick walls shutting out the sounds of the countryside, the heavy locked doors preventing intrusion. Bredon could not help wondering if the owner had felt safer sleeping in here than under the same roof with his questionable protégés.

But two pieces of furniture there were, which attracted attention almost equally as symptoms of the recent tragedy. One was a bed, standing out in the very middle of the floor; a temporary arrangement, apparently, since it was a wheeled bed with iron railings, of the type common in hospitals, and the wheels had dragged lines across the linoleum, which still shone from their passage. The bed itself was absolutely bare; even the under-blanket had been torn out from its position, and lay, with the other blankets and the sheets, on and around the bed in grotesque confusion. It had the air, Bredon felt, of a bed from which the occupant has been pulled out, rather than of one which the occupant has left, in whatever hurry or excitement, of his own free will. Beyond the bed, against the wall furthest from the entrance, stood a sideboard, plentifully laden with vegetarian food. There was a loaf of bread, made of some very coarse grain, a honeycomb in a glass dish, a box of dates, some biscuits which looked brittle as glue, even, in witness of Simmonds's accuracy, some nuts. It was not a room in which the ordinary man would have sat down cheerfully to a meal; but, what was more important, it was a room in which you could not possibly starve.

Bredon went to the sideboard first of all, and gave the exhibits a careful scrutiny. He felt the outside of the bread, and satisfied himself, from the hardness of the 'fly-walk,' that it had remained for several days untasted. He tried some milk from a jug which stood there, and found it, as he had expected, thoroughly sour. 'Did Mr. Jervison always have sour milk?' he asked of his guide, who was watching all his movements with grave interest. 'No, sir,' was the answer. 'I took that milk in myself, the evening when we last saw the prophet alive. It was sweet milk, fresh from the dairy. It has not been drunk, not one drop of it, till you tasted it, sir, just now.' The box of dates, though it was opened, contained its full complement of fruit. The honey was thick, and furred over with dust. The place on which the biscuits lay was not covered with crumbs, as it should have been if any of them had been broken. Altogether, it seemed a safe conclusion that the dead man had starved in sight of plenty.

'I want to ask some questions, if I may,' said Bredon, turning to the native. 'My company wishes to satisfy itself whether Mr. Jervison died by misadventure, or took his own life. You will not mind helping me?'

'I will tell you whatever you wish to know. I am sure you are a very just man.'

'Look here, then—did Jervison often sleep here? And

why did he want to sleep there that night—the night when
you last saw him?'

'Never before; but that night he was trying a very special
experiment; you do not understand these things here in the
West. He was meaning to take a narcotic drug, one which
he had prepared himself, which would set his soul free from
his body. But because it is very dangerous to be disturbed
from outside, while the soul is away from the body, he
wanted to sleep here, where nobody could disturb him,
and we wheeled that bed in from the house. All this you
will find written in his diary; he was very careful to do that,
because, he said, if any harm came to him from the experiment, he wished it to be known that it was no fault of ours.
I will show you the diary myself.'

'Oh, he was drugged, was he, that first night? You
don't think he may have taken an overdose of the drug,
and died from that?'

The Indian smiled ever so slightly, and shrugged his
shoulders. 'But the doctor has told us that he starved to
death. Your friend is a doctor also; he will tell you the
same. No, I will tell you what I think. The prophet fasted
very often, especially when he wished his soul to be free.
And I think that when he woke up from his sleep he had
had some revelation which made him want to go deeper
into these mysteries; and therefore he fasted; only this
time he fasted too long. He fasted perhaps till he fainted,
and was too weak to reach his food, or to come out and find
help. And we waited in the house, doing our own studies,
while the prophet was dying in here. It was fated that it
should be so.'

Bredon was less interested in the theological bearings of
the question than in its legal aspect. Is a man who starves
himself without meaning to kill himself a suicide? Anyhow,
that was for the lawyers. 'Thank you,' he said, 'I will wait
for my friend here; don't let me keep you.' The Indian
bowed, and left him — with some reluctance, Bredon
thought. But he was determined to search this room
thoroughly; he did not like the look of things. The lock
on the door—no, that did not seem to have been tampered
with, unless there were a second key. The walls? You do
not make secret doors in a racket-court. The windows?

None, except those slats underneath the skylight, at the sides of the well; only just room for a man to put his hand in there, and that would be about forty feet up. Hang it all, the man had been alone for ten days; he had left the food untasted, and he had made no effort to get out. There was even a writing-tablet with a pencil tied to it, not far from the bed; he had meant, Bredon supposed, to write down his revelations on it as he woke from sleep; yet the dust stood on the top sheet, and the dead man had left no message. Could it really be madness? Or was the Indian right in his guess? Or was it even possible . . . one heard of strange tricks these Eastern jugglers played; was it possible that these four adepts had managed to tamper with the inside of the room without entering it?

And then Bredon noticed something on the floor which interested him; and when Simmonds came back with the little doctor they found him on all fours beside the bed, and the face he turned towards them as they came in was a very grave one, yet with a light in the eyes that suggested the anticipation of a victory.

'What a time you 've been!' he said reproachfully.

'There 's been a good deal in the way of alarms and excursions,' exclaimed Simmonds. 'Your friends the police have been round, and they 've just taken off the whole Brotherhood in a suitably coloured Maria. Apparently they are known in Chicago. But I 'm dashed if I see how they are going to fix anything on them over this business. The man starved to death. Don't talk to me about drugs, Bredon; there simply isn't any question of that.'

'It 's murder, though,' said Bredon cheerfully. 'Look here!' And he pointed to the shiny tracks drawn across the oil-cloth by the movement of the bed's wheels. 'You see those tracks? They don't lead right up to the place where the bed stands; they stop about two inches short of it. And that means murder, and a dashed ingenious kind of murder too. By rights, the police oughtn't to be able to fix it on them, as you say. But that 's the bother about a murder which takes four men to do it; one of them is certain to break down under examination, and give the others away. I was wondering, Dr. Mayhew—when your friend Enstone

left, did he take the fixtures away with him?   The fixtures
of this gymnasium, for example?'

'Sold the whole place, lock, stock, and barrel.   He needed
all the money he could get, and the Brotherhood weren't
particular.   There's a sort of shed at the back, you know,
where Enstone used to keep odds and ends, and I shouldn't
be a bit surprised if you find the parallel bars and what
not tidied away in there.   Were you thinking of giving us a
gymnastic display?   Because I should suggest some lunch
first.'

'I just thought I'd like to look at them, that's all.   And
then, as you say, lunch.'   Dr. Mayhew's prophecy proved
accurate.   The shed at the back was plentifully littered
with the appropriate debris.   A vaulting-horse stood there,
mutely reproachful at having been so long turned out to
grass; the parallel bars were still shiny from youthful hands;
the horizontal ladder, folded in three, was propped at an
uneasy angle, and the floor was a network of ropes and rings.
Bredon took up a rope at random and brought it out into
the daylight.   'You see,' he said, passing his hands down it;
'it's frayed all along.   Boys don't fray ropes when they
climb up them; they wear gym-shoes.   Besides, the fraying
is quite fresh; looks only a day or two old.   Yes, that's
what they did; and I suppose we had better tell the police
about it.   The company stands to lose, of course; but I
don't see what is to be done with the policy now, unless
they erect a mausoleum over the Brotherhood with it.
There won't be any more Brotherhood now, Dr. Mayhew.'

'You must excuse him,' apologized Simmonds; 'he is like
this sometimes.   I hate to say it, Bredon, but I haven't
completely followed your train of thought.   How did these
fellows get at Jervison, when he was locked up in his gymnasium?   You can't kill a man by starvation, unless you
shut him up without any food, or hold him down so that
he can't get at it.'

'You're wrong there,' objected Bredon.   'There are all
sorts of ways.   You can poison the food, and tell him it
is poisoned.   Not that that happened here, because I've
tasted some of the milk myself, and here I am.   Besides,
I think a starving man would always risk it when it came
to the point.   You can hypnotize the man, in theory, and

persuade him that the food isn't there, or that it isn't food at all. But that's only in theory; you never hear of a crime like that being pulled off in real life. No, the Indians had their alibi all right, when poor Jervison died.'

'You mean they starved him somewhere else, and brought his body in here afterwards?'

'Hardly that. You see, it would be very much simpler to starve your man in here, and bring the food in afterwards to look as if he'd starved himself deliberately. But to do either of those things you must have access to the building. Do you happen to know, Dr. Mayhew, who it was that first found the body? And what sort of difficulty they had in making their way into the gymnasium?'

'The door was locked, and the key fixed on the inside. We had to take the lock off. I was one of the party myself. The police, of course, had charge of things; but the Indians had called me in as well, the moment they got the idea that something was wrong.'

'Really? Now, that's very instructive. It shows how criminals always overdo these things. You or I, if a friend locked himself up and didn't appear for ten days, would shout through the keyhole and then send for a locksmith. Whereas these gentlemen sent off at once for a doctor and the police, as if they knew that both would be wanted. That's the worst of thinking that you've covered your tracks.'

'My dear Bredon, we're still taking your word for it that it *is* murder. If it is, I should say the murderers covered their tracks quite remarkably well. It looks to me the clearest possible case of lunacy and suicide.'

'You're wrong there. Did you notice that there was a writing-tablet and a pencil by the side of the bed? Now, what madman ever resisted the temptation to scrawl something on any odd piece of paper he came across? Especially if he thought he was being starved, or poisoned. That applies, too, if he were really making some fasting experiment; he would have left us a last message. And what did you make of the way the bed-clothes were piled on and round the bed? Nobody, mad or sane, wants to get out of bed that way.'

'Well, tell us all about it if you must. You may be mad

or I may be mad, but I see no reason why either of us should starve, and we are keeping Dr. Mayhew from his lunch.'

'Well, the outlines of the thing are simple.   Jervison had picked up these rogues somewhere in America, and they were no more mystics than you or I are; they could talk the patter, that's all.   They knew he was rich, and they stuck to him because they saw there was money to be made out of him.   When they found he had made the Brotherhood his heirs, there remained nothing except to eliminate him; they went over the plan of the ground, and determined to make the fullest use of the weapons that lay ready to hand. Always a mistake to bring in weapons from outside; study your man's habits, and kill him along his own lines, so to speak.   All they had to do was to encourage him in making these fool experiments, and to supply him with some ordinary kind of sleeping-draught which pretended to have a magical effect; probably it was they who suggested his retiring to the gymnasium, where he could be quiet, and they who insisted on wheeling his bed out into the middle of the room, telling him that he ought to catch the noonday sun, or some nonsense of that kind.   Who ever heard of a man wanting to have his bed out in the middle of the room? It's human nature to want it next to the wall, though why, I've no idea.'

'And then?'

'They waited, that night, till the sleeping-draught had taken its full effect; waited till it was early dawn, and they could see what was happening without being noticed by inquisitive neighbours.   They tied ladders together, or more probably used that horizontal ladder, stretched out into a straight line, and climbed up on to the roof.   All they took with them was ropes—the four ropes that used to hang from those hooks in the ceiling.   They still had iron hooks on them; I dare say they tied handkerchiefs round the hooks to prevent any noise.   Through the skylight, they could look down on the sleeping man; between the iron slats they could let down the four ropes.   The hooks acted as grapnels, and it did not take much fishing before they hooked the iron rails at the head and foot of the bed. Very quietly, very evenly, they pulled up the ropes; it was

like a profane and ghastly parody of a scene you may remember in the Gospels. And still poor Jervison slept on,
under the influence of his drug; dreaming, perhaps, that
he was being levitated, and had at last got rid of the burden
of the flesh. He nearly had.

'He slept on, and when he woke, he was hung up forty
feet in the air, still in his bed. The bed-clothes had been
removed; it would not do to let him have a chance of
climbing down. He hung there for over a week; and if his
cries reached the outside world at all, they only reached
the ears of four pitiless men, his murderers. Perhaps a
braver man would have jumped for it, and preferred to
end his life that way. But Jervison, you told me yourself,
Simmonds, was a coward about heights; he couldn't jump.'

'And if he had?'

'He would have been found dead, either from his fall or
from its effects. And the Indians would have told us,
gravely enough, that the prophet must have been making
an experiment in levitation, or something of that kind. As
it was, all they had to do was to come back when all was
safely over, to let down the ropes again, to throw his bed-
clothes in through the slats, falling where they would, and
to take their ropes and ladder down again the way they
had come. Only, as was natural, they did not bother to
pay out the ropes quite evenly this time, and the bed came
down in the wrong place, about two inches from where it
had stood originally. So that it didn't fit in with the tracks
across the oil-cloth, and it was that, somehow, which gave
me a notion of what had happened. The bed, evidently,
had been lifted; and you do not lift a wheeled bed unless
you have a special purpose to be served, as these devils
had. Jervison was a fool, but I hate to think of the way he
died, and I am going to do my best to see these four fellows
hanged. If I had my way with them, I would spare them
the drop.'

AGATHA CHRISTIE

PHILOMEL COTTAGE

'Good-bye, darling.'

'Good-bye, sweetheart.'

Alix Martin stood leaning over the small rustic gate, watching the retreating figure of her husband as he walked down the road in the direction of the village.

Presently he turned a bend and was lost to sight, but Alix still stayed in the same position, absent-mindedly smoothing a lock of the rich brown hair which had blown across her face, her eyes far away and dreamy.

Alix Martin was not beautiful, nor even, strictly speaking, pretty. But her face, the face of a woman no longer in her first youth, was irradiated and softened until her former colleagues of the old office days would hardly have recognized her. Miss Alix King had been a trim business-like young woman, efficient, slightly brusque in manner, obviously capable and matter-of-fact.

Alix had graduated in a hard school. For fifteen years, from the age of eighteen until she was thirty-three, she had kept herself (and for seven years of the time an invalid mother) by her work as a shorthand-typist. It was the struggle for existence which had hardened the soft lines of her girlish face.

True, there had been romance—of a kind—Dick Windyford, a fellow clerk. Very much of a woman at heart, Alix had always known without seeming to know that he cared. Outwardly they had been friends, nothing more. Out of his slender salary Dick had been hard put to it to provide for the schooling of a younger brother. For the moment he could not think of marriage.

And then suddenly deliverance from daily toil had come to the girl in the most unexpected manner. A distant cousin had died, leaving her money to Alix—a few thousand pounds, enough to bring in a couple of hundred a year. To

Alix it was freedom, life, independence. Now she and Dick need wait no longer.

But Dick reacted unexpectedly. He had never directly spoken of his love to Alix; now he seemed less inclined to do so than ever. He avoided her, became morose and gloomy. Alix was quick to realize the truth. She had become a woman of means. Delicacy and pride stood in the way of Dick's asking her to be his wife.

She liked him none the worse for it, and was indeed deliberating as to whether she herself might not take the first step, when for the second time the unexpected descended upon her.

She met Gerald Martin at a friend's house. He fell violently in love with her, and within a week they were engaged. Alix, who had always considered herself 'not the falling-in-love kind,' was swept clean off her feet.

Unwittingly she had found the way to arouse her former lover. Dick Windyford had come to her stammering with rage and anger.

'The man's a perfect stranger to you! You know nothing about him!'

'I know that I love him.'

'How can you know—in a week?'

'It doesn't take every one eleven years to find out that they're in love with a girl,' cried Alix angrily.

His face went white.

'I've cared for you ever since I met you. I thought that you cared also.'

Alix was truthful.

'I thought so too,' she admitted. 'But that was because I didn't know what love was.'

Then Dick had burst out again. Prayers, entreaties, even threats—threats against the man who had supplanted him. It was amazing to Alix to see the volcano that existed beneath the reserved exterior of the man she had thought she knew so well.

Her thoughts went back to that interview now, on this sunny morning, as she leant on the gate of the cottage. She had been married a month, and she was idyllically happy. Yet, in the momentary absence of her husband who was everything to her, a tinge of anxiety invaded her perfect happiness. And the cause of that anxiety was Dick Windyford.

Three times since her marriage she had dreamed the same dream. The environment differed, but the main facts were always the same. *She saw her husband lying dead and Dick Windyford standing over him, and she knew clearly and distinctly that his was the hand which had dealt the fatal blow.*

But horrible though that was, there was something more horrible still—horrible, that was, on awakening, for in the dream it seemed perfectly natural and inevitable. *She, Alix Martin, was glad that her husband was dead*; she stretched out grateful hands to the murderer, sometimes she thanked him. The dream always ended the same way, with herself clasped in Dick Windyford's arms.

She had said nothing of this dream to her husband, but secretly it had perturbed her more than she liked to admit. Was it a warning—a warning against Dick Windyford?

Alix was roused from her thoughts by the sharp ringing of the telephone bell from within the house. She entered the cottage and picked up the receiver. Suddenly she swayed, and put out a hand against the wall.

'Who did you say was speaking?'

'Why, Alix, what's the matter with your voice? I wouldn't have known it. It's Dick.'

'Oh!' said Alix. 'Oh! Where—where are you?'

'At the "Traveller's Arms"—that's the right name, isn't it? Or don't you even know of the existence of your village pub? I'm on my holiday—doing a bit of fishing here. Any objections to my looking you two good people up this evening after dinner?'

'No,' said Alix sharply. 'You mustn't come.'

There was a pause, and then Dick's voice, with a subtle alteration in it, spoke again.

'I beg your pardon,' he said formally. 'Of course I won't bother you——'

Alix broke in hastily. He must think her behaviour too extraordinary. It *was* extraordinary. Her nerves must be all to pieces.

'I only meant that we were — engaged to - night,' she

explained, trying to make her voice sound as natural as possible. 'Won't you — won't you come to dinner to-morrow night?'

But Dick evidently noticed the lack of cordiality in her tone.

'Thanks very much,' he said, in the same formal voice, 'but I may be moving on any time. Depends if a pal of mine turns up or not. Good-bye, Alix.' He paused, and then added hastily, in a different tone: 'Best of luck to you, my dear.'

Alix hung up the receiver with a feeling of relief.

'He mustn't come here,' she repeated to herself. 'He mustn't come here. Oh, what a fool I am! To imagine myself into a state like this. All the same, I'm glad he's not coming.'

She caught up a rustic rush hat from a table, and passed out into the garden again, pausing to look up at the name carved over the porch: Philomel Cottage.

'Isn't it a very fanciful name?' she had said to Gerald once before they were married. He had laughed.

'You little Cockney,' he had said affectionately. 'I don't believe you have ever heard a nightingale. I'm glad you haven't. Nightingales should sing only for lovers. We'll hear them together on a summer's evening outside our own home.'

And at the remembrance of how they had indeed heard them, Alix, standing in the doorway of her home, blushed happily.

It was Gerald who had found Philomel Cottage. He had come to Alix bursting with excitement. He had found the very spot for them—unique—a gem—the chance of a life-time. And when Alix had seen it she too was captivated. It was true that the situation was rather lonely—they were two miles from the nearest village—but the cottage itself was so exquisite, with its old-world appearance and its solid comfort of bathrooms, hot-water system, electric light, and telephone, that she fell a victim to its charm immediately. And then a hitch occurred. The owner, a rich man who had made it his whim, declined to let it. He would only sell.

Gerald Martin, though possessed of a good income, was unable to touch his capital. He could raise at most a thousand pounds. The owner was asking three. But Alix, who had set her heart on the place, came to the rescue. Her own capital was easily realized, being in bearer bonds. She would contribute half of it to the purchase of the home. So Philomel Cottage became their very own, and never for a minute had Alix regretted the choice. It was true that servants did not appreciate the rural solitude—indeed, at the moment they had none at all—but Alix, who had been starved of domestic life, thoroughly enjoyed cooking dainty little meals and looking after the house.

The garden, which was magnificently stocked with flowers, was attended to by an old man from the village who came twice a week.

As she rounded the corner of the house, Alix was surprised to see the old gardener in question busy over the flower beds. She was surprised because his days for work were Mondays and Fridays, and to-day was Wednesday.

'Why, George, what are you doing here?' she asked, as she came towards him.

The old man straightened up with a chuckle, touching the brim of an aged cap.

'I thought as how you 'd be surprised, ma'am. But 'tis this way. There be a fête over to Squire's on Friday, and I sez to myself, I sez, neither Mr. Martin nor yet his good lady won't take it amiss if I comes for once on a Wednesday instead of a Friday.'

'That 's quite all right,' said Alix. 'I hope you 'll enjoy yourself at the fête.'

'I reckon to,' said George simply. 'It 's a fine thing to be able to eat your fill and know all the time as it 's not you as is paying for it. Squire allus has a proper sit-down tea for 'is tenants. Then I thought too, ma'am, as I might as well see you before you goes away so as to learn your wishes for the borders. You 'll have no idea when you 'll be back, ma'am, I suppose?'

'But I 'm not going away.'

George stared at her.

'Bain't you going to Lunnon to-morrow?'

'No. What put such an idea into your head?'

George jerked his head over his shoulder.

'Met maister down to village yesterday. He told me you

was both going away to Lunnon to-morrow, and it was uncertain when you 'd be back again.'

'Nonsense,' said Alix, laughing. 'You must have mis-understood him.'

All the same, she wondered exactly what it could have been that Gerald had said to lead the old man into such a curious mistake. Going to London? She never wanted to go to London again.

'I hate London,' she said suddenly and harshly.

'Ah!' said George placidly. 'I must have been mistook somehow, and yet he said it plain enough, it seemed to me. I 'm glad you 're stopping on here. I don't hold with all this gallivanting about, and I don't think nothing of Lunnon. *I* 've never needed to go there. Too many moty cars—that 's the trouble nowadays. Once people have got a moty car, blessed if they can stay still any-wheres. Mr. Ames, wot used to have this house—nice, peaceable sort of gentleman he was until he bought one of them things. Hadn't had it a month before he put up this cottage for sale. A tidy lot he 'd spent on it, too, with taps in all the bedrooms, and the electric light and all. "You 'll never see your money back," I sez to him. "But," he sez to me, "I 'll get every penny of two thousand pounds for this house." And sure enough, he did.'

'He got three thousand,' said Alix, smiling.

'Two thousand,' repeated George. 'The sum he was asking was talked of at the time.'

'It really was three thousand,' said Alix.

'Ladies never understand figures,' said George, uncon-vinced. 'You 'll not tell me that Mr. Ames had the face to stand up to you, and say three thousand brazen-like in a loud voice?'

'He didn't say it to me,' said Alix; 'he said it to my husband.'

George stooped again to his flower bed.

'The price was two thousand,' he said obstinately.

Alix did not trouble to argue with him. Moving to one of the further beds, she began to pick an armful of flowers.

As she moved with her fragrant posy towards the house, Alix noticed a small, dark-green object peeping from between some leaves in one of the beds. She stopped and picked it up, recognizing it for her husband's pocket diary.

She opened it, scanning the entries with some amusement. Almost from the beginning of their married life she had realized that the impulsive and emotional Gerald had the uncharacteristic virtues of neatness and method. He was extremely fussy about meals being punctual, and always planned his day ahead with the accuracy of a time-table.

Looking through the diary, she was amused to notice the entry on the date of 14th May: 'Marry Alix St. Peter's 2.30.'

'The big silly,' murmured Alix to herself, turning the pages. Suddenly she stopped.

'"Wednesday, 18th June"—why, that's to-day.'

In the space for that day was written in Gerald's neat, precise hand: '9 p.m.' Nothing else. What had Gerald planned to do at 9 p.m.? Alix wondered. She smiled to herself as she realized that had this been a story, like those she had so often read, the diary would doubtless have furnished her with some sensational revelation. It would have had in it for certain the name of another woman. She fluttered the back pages idly. There were dates, appointments, cryptic references to business deals, but only one woman's name—her own.

Yet as she slipped the book into her pocket and went on with her flowers to the house, she was aware of a vague uneasiness. Those words of Dick Windyford's recurred to her almost as though he had been at her elbow repeating them: 'The man's a perfect stranger to you. You know nothing about him.'

It was true. What did she know about him? After all, Gerald was forty. In forty years there must have been women in his life. . . . .

Alix shook herself impatiently. She must not give way to these thoughts. She had a far more instant preoccupation to deal with. Should she, or should she not, tell her husband that Dick Windyford had rung her up?

There was the possibility to be considered that Gerald might have already run across him in the village. But in that case he would be sure to mention it to her immediately upon his return, and matters would be taken out of her hands. Otherwise—what? Alix was aware of a distinct desire to say nothing about it.

If she told him, he was sure to suggest asking Dick Windyford to Philomel Cottage. Then she would have to explain that Dick had proposed himself, and that she had made an excuse to prevent his coming. And when he asked her why she had done so, what could she say? Tell him her dreams? But he would only laugh—or, worse, see that she attached an importance to it which he did not.

In the end, rather shamefacedly, Alix decided to say nothing. It was the first secret she had ever kept from her husband, and the consciousness of it made her feel ill at ease.

When she heard Gerald returning from the village shortly before lunch, she hurried into the kitchen and pretended to be busy with the cooking so as to hide her confusion.

It was evident at once that Gerald had seen nothing of Dick Windyford. Alix felt at once relieved and embarrassed. She was definitely committed now to a policy of concealment.

It was not until after their simple evening meal, when they were sitting in the oak-beamed living-room with the windows thrown open to let in the sweet night air scented with the perfume of the mauve and white stocks outside, that Alix remembered the pocket diary.

'Here's something you've been watering the flowers with,' she said, and threw it into his lap.

'Dropped it in the border, did I?'

'Yes; I know all your secrets now.'

'Not guilty,' said Gerald, shaking his head.

'What about your assignation at nine o'clock to-night?'

'Oh! that——' He seemed taken aback for a moment, then he smiled as though something afforded him particular amusement. 'It's an assignation with a particularly nice girl, Alix. She's got brown hair and blue eyes and she's very like you.'

'I don't understand,' said Alix, with mock severity. 'You're evading the point.'

'No, I'm not. As a matter of fact, that's a reminder that I'm going to develop some negatives to-night, and I want you to help me.'

Gerald Martin was an enthusiastic photographer. He had a somewhat old-fashioned camera, but with an excellent lens, and he developed his own plates in a small cellar which he had had fitted up as a dark room.

'And it must be done at nine o'clock precisely,' said Alix teasingly.

Gerald looked a little vexed.

'My dear girl,' he said, with a shade of testiness in his manner, 'one should always plan a thing for a definite time. Then one gets through one's work properly.'

Alix sat for a minute or two in silence, watching her husband as he lay in his chair smoking, his dark head flung back and the clear-cut lines of his clean-shaven face showing up against the sombre background. And suddenly, from some unknown source, a wave of panic surged over her, so that she cried out before she could stop herself: 'Oh, Gerald, I wish I knew more about you!'

Her husband turned an astonished face upon her.

'But, my dear Alix, you do know all about me. I've told you of my boyhood in Northumberland, of my life in South Africa, and these last ten years in Canada which have brought me success.'

'Oh! business!' said Alix scornfully.

Gerald laughed suddenly.

'I know what you mean—love affairs. You women are all the same. Nothing interests you but the personal element.'

Alix felt her throat go dry, as she muttered indistinctly: 'Well, but there must have been—love affairs. I mean—if I only knew——'

There was silence again for a minute or two. Gerald Martin was frowning, a look of indecision on his face. When he spoke it was gravely, without a trace of his former bantering manner.

'Do you think it wise, Alix, this—Bluebeard's chamber business? There have been women in my life; yes, I don't deny it. You wouldn't believe me if I did deny it. But I can swear to you truthfully that not one of them meant anything to me.'

There was a ring of sincerity in his voice which comforted the listening wife.

'Satisfied, Alix?' he asked with a smile. Then he looked at her with a shade of curiosity.

'What has turned your mind on to these unpleasant subjects to-night of all nights?'

Alix got up and began to walk about restlessly.

'Oh, I don't know,' she said. 'I've been nervy all day.'

'That's odd,' said Gerald, in a low voice, as though speaking to himself. 'That's very odd.'

'Why is it odd?'

'Oh, my dear girl, don't flash out at me so. I only said it was odd because as a rule you're so sweet and serene.'

Alix forced a smile.

'Everything's conspired to annoy me to-day,' she confessed. 'Even old George had got some ridiculous idea into his head that we were going away to London. He said you had told him so.'

'Where did you see him?' asked Gerald sharply.

'He came to work to-day instead of Friday.'

'Damned old fool,' said George angrily.

Alix stared in surprise. Her husband's face was convulsed with rage. She had never seen him so angry. Seeing her astonishment Gerald made an effort to regain control of himself.

'Well, he is a damned old fool,' he protested.

'What can you have said to make him think that?'

'I? I never said anything. At least—oh, yes, I remember; I made some weak joke about being "off to London in the morning," and I suppose he took it seriously. Or else he didn't hear properly. You undeceived him, of course?'

He waited anxiously for her reply.

'Of course, but he's the sort of old man who if once he gets an idea in his head—well, it isn't easy to get it out again.'

Then she told him of George's insistence on the sum asked for the cottage.

Gerald was silent for a minute or two, then he said slowly:

'Ames was willing to take two thousand in cash and the remaining thousand on mortgage. That's the origin of that mistake, I fancy.'

'Very likely,' agreed Alix.

Then she looked up at the clock, and pointed to it with a mischievous finger.

'We ought to be getting down to it, Gerald. Five minutes behind schedule.'

A very peculiar smile came over Gerald Martin's face.

'I've changed my mind,' he said quietly; 'I shan't do any photography to-night.'

A woman's mind is a curious thing. When she went to bed that Wednesday night Alix's mind was contented and at rest. Her momentarily assailed happiness reasserted itself, triumphant as of yore.

But by the evening of the following day she realized that some subtle forces were at work undermining it. Dick Windyford had not rung up again, nevertheless she felt what she supposed to be his influence at work. Again and again those words of his recurred to her: '*The man's a perfect stranger. You know nothing about him.*' And with them came the memory of her husband's face, photographed clearly on her brain, as he said: 'Do you think it wise, Alix, this—Bluebeard's chamber business?' Why had he said that?

There had been warning in them—a hint of menace. It was as though he had said in effect: 'You had better not pry into my life, Alix. You may get a nasty shock if you do.'

By Friday morning Alix had convinced herself that there *had* been a woman in Gerald's life—a Bluebeard's chamber that he had sedulously sought to conceal from her. Her jealousy, slow to awaken, was now rampant.

Was it a woman he had been going to meet that night at 9 p.m.? Was his story of photographs to develop a lie invented upon the spur of the moment?

Three days ago she would have sworn that she knew her husband through and through. Now it seemed to her that he was a stranger of whom she knew nothing. She remembered his unreasonable anger against old George, so at variance with his usual good-tempered manner. A small thing, perhaps, but it showed her that she did not really know the man who was her husband.

There were several little things required on Friday from the village. In the afternoon Alix suggested that she should go for them whilst Gerald remained in the garden; but somewhat to her surprise he opposed this plan vehemently, and insisted on going himself whilst she remained at home. Alix was forced to give way to him, but his insistence surprised and alarmed her. Why was he so anxious to prevent her going to the village?

Suddenly an explanation suggested itself to her which made the whole thing clear. Was it not possible that, whilst saying nothing to her, Gerald had indeed come across Dick Windyford? Her own jealousy, entirely dormant at the time of their marriage, had only developed afterwards. Might it not be the same with Gerald? Might he not be anxious to prevent her seeing Dick Windyford again? This explanation was so consistent with the facts, and so comforting to Alix's perturbed mind, that she embraced it eagerly.

Yet when tea-time had come and passed she was restless and ill at ease. She was struggling with a temptation that had assailed her ever since Gerald's departure. Finally, pacifying her conscience with the assurance that the room did need a thorough tidying, she went upstairs to her husband's dressing-room. She took a duster with her to keep up the pretence of housewifery.

'If I were only sure,' she repeated to herself. 'If I could only be *sure*.'

In vain she told herself that anything compromising would have been destroyed ages ago. Against that she argued that men do sometimes keep the most damning piece of evidence through an exaggerated sentimentality.

In the end Alix succumbed. Her cheeks burning with the shame of her action, she hunted breathlessly through packets of letters and documents, turned out the drawers, even went through the pockets of her husband's clothes. Only two drawers eluded her: the lower drawer of the chest of drawers and the small right-hand drawer of the writing-desk were both locked. But Alix was by now lost to all shame. In one of those drawers she was convinced that she would find evidence of this imaginary woman of the past who obsessed her.

She remembered that Gerald had left his keys lying carelessly on the sideboard downstairs. She fetched them and tried them one by one. The third key fitted the writing-table drawer. Alix pulled it open eagerly. There was a cheque-book and a wallet well stuffed with notes, and at the back of the drawer a packet of letters tied up with a piece of tape.

Her breath coming unevenly, Alix untied the tape. Then a deep, burning blush overspread her face, and she dropped the letters back into the drawer, closing and relocking it. For the letters were her own, written to Gerald Martin before she married him.

She turned now to the chest of drawers, more with a wish to feel that she had left nothing undone than from any expectation of finding what she sought.

To her annoyance none of the keys on Gerald's bunch fitted the drawer in question. Not to be defeated, Alix went into the other rooms and brought back a selection of keys with her. To her satisfaction the key of the spare room wardrobe also fitted the chest of drawers. She unlocked the drawer and pulled it open. But there was nothing in it but a roll of newspaper clippings already dirty and discoloured with age.

Alix breathed a sigh of relief. Nevertheless, she glanced at the clippings, curious to know what subject had interested Gerald so much that he had taken the trouble to keep the dusty roll. They were nearly all American papers, dated some seven years ago, and dealing with the trial of the notorious swindler and bigamist, Charles Lemaitre. Lemaitre had been suspected of doing away with his women victims. A skeleton had been found beneath the floor of one of the houses he had rented, and most of the women he had 'married' had never been heard of again.

He had defended himself from the charge with consummate skill, aided by some of the best legal talent in the United States. The Scottish verdict of 'Not Proven' might perhaps have stated the case best. In its absence, he was found Not Guilty on the capital charge, though sentenced to a long term of imprisonment on the other charges preferred against him.

Alix remembered the excitement caused by the case at the time, and also the sensation aroused by the escape of Lemaitre some three years later. He had never been recaptured. The personality of the man and his extraordinary power over women had been discussed at great length in the English papers at the time, together with an account of his excitability in court, his passionate protestations, and his occasional sudden physical collapses, due to the fact that he had a weak heart, though the ignorant accredited it to his dramatic powers.

There was a picture of him in one of the clippings Alix held, and she studied it with some interest—a long-bearded, scholarly looking gentleman.

Who was it the face reminded her of? Suddenly, with a shock, she realized that it was Gerald himself. The eyes and brow bore a strong resemblance to his. Perhaps he had kept the cutting for that reason. Her eyes went on to the paragraph beside the picture. Certain dates, it seemed, had been entered in the accused's pocket-book, and it was contended that these were dates when he had done away with his victims. Then a woman gave evidence and identified the prisoner positively by the fact that he had a mole on his left wrist, just below the palm of the hand.

Alix dropped the papers and swayed as she stood. *On his left wrist, just below the palm, her husband had a small scar.*

The room whirled round her. Afterwards it struck her as strange that she should have leaped at once to such absolute certainty. Gerald Martin was Charles Lemaitre! She knew it, and accepted it in a flash. Disjointed fragments whirled through her brain, like pieces of a jig-saw puzzle fitting into place.

The money paid for the house—her money—her money only; the bearer bonds she had entrusted to his keeping. Even her dream appeared in its true significance. Deep down in her, her subconscious self had always feared Gerald Martin and wished to escape from him. And it was to Dick Windyford this self of hers had looked for help. That, too, was why she was able to accept the truth so easily, without doubt or hesitation. She was to have been another of Lemaitre's victims. Very soon, perhaps . . .

A half-cry escaped her as she remembered something. *Wednesday 9 p.m.* The cellar, with the flagstones that were so easily raised! Once before he had buried one of his

victims in a cellar.   It had been all planned for Wednesday
night.   But to write it down beforehand in that methodical
manner—insanity! No, it was logical. Gerald always made
a memorandum of his engagements: murder was to him a
business proposition like any other.

But what had saved her?   What could possibly have
saved her?   Had he relented at the last minute?   No.   In
a flash the answer came to her—*old George.*

She understood now her husband's uncontrollable anger.
Doubtless he had paved the way by telling every one he
met that they were going to London the next day.   Then
George had come to work unexpectedly, had mentioned
London to her, and she had contradicted the story.   Too
risky to do away with her that night, with old George
repeating that conversation.   But what an escape! If she
had not happened to mention that trivial matter—Alix
shuddered.

But there was no time to be lost.   She must get away at
once—before he came back.   She hurriedly replaced the
roll of clippings in the drawer, shut it, and locked it.

And then she stayed motionless as though frozen to stone.
She heard the creak of the gate into the road.   *Her husband
had returned.*

For a moment Alix stayed as though petrified, then she
crept on tiptoe to the window, looking out from behind
the shelter of the curtain.

Yes, it was her husband.   He was smiling to himself and
humming a little tune.   In his hand he held an object which
almost made the terrified girl's heart stop beating.   It was
a brand-new spade.

Alix leaped to a knowledge born of instinct.   *It was to be
to-night.*

But there was still a chance.   Gerald, humming his little
tune, went round to the back of the house.

Without hesitating a moment, she ran down the stairs
and out of the cottage.   But just as she emerged from the
door, her husband came round the other side of the house.

'Hallo,' he said, 'where are you running off to in such a
hurry?'

Alix strove desperately to appear calm and as usual.   Her
chance was gone for the moment, but if she was careful not

to arouse his suspicions, it would come again later. Even now, perhaps . . .

'I was going to walk to the end of the lane and back,' she said in a voice that sounded weak and uncertain to her own ears.

'Right,' said Gerald. 'I'll come with you.'

'No — please, Gerald. I'm — nervy, headachy — I'd rather go alone.'

He looked at her attentively. She fancied a momentary suspicion gleamed in his eye.

'What's the matter with you, Alix? You're pale — trembling.'

'Nothing.' She forced herself to be brusque—smiling. 'I've got a headache, that's all. A walk will do me good.'

'Well, it's no good your saying you don't want me,' declared Gerald, with his easy laugh. 'I'm coming, whether you want me or not.'

She dared not protest further. If he suspected that she *knew* . . .

With an effort she managed to regain something of her normal manner. Yet she had an uneasy feeling that he looked at her sideways every now and then, as though not quite satisfied. She felt that his suspicions were not completely allayed.

When they returned to the house he insisted on her lying down, and brought some eau-de-Cologne to bathe her temples. He was, as ever, the devoted husband. Alix felt herself as helpless as though bound hand and foot in a trap.

Not for a minute would he leave her alone. He went with her into the kitchen and helped her to bring in the simple cold dishes she had already prepared. Supper was a meal that choked her, yet she forced herself to eat, and even to appear gay and natural. She knew now that she was fighting for her life. She was alone with this man, miles from help, absolutely at his mercy. Her only chance was so to lull his suspicions that he would leave her alone for a few moments—long enough for her to get to the telephone in the hall and summon assistance. That was her only hope now.

A momentary hope flashed over her as she remembered

how he had abandoned his plan before. Suppose she told him that Dick Windyford was coming up to see them that evening?

The words trembled on her lips—then she rejected them hastily. This man would not be baulked a second time. There was a determination, an elation, underneath his calm bearing that sickened her. She would only precipitate the crime. He would murder her there and then, and calmly ring up Dick Windyford with a tale of having been suddenly called away. Oh! if only Dick Windyford were coming to the house this evening! If Dick . . .

A sudden idea flashed into her mind. She looked sharply sideways at her husband as though she feared that he might read her mind. With the forming of a plan, her courage was reinforced. She became so completely natural in manner that she marvelled at herself.

She made the coffee and took it out to the porch where they often sat on fine evenings.

'By the way,' said Gerald suddenly, 'we'll do those photographs later.'

Alix felt a shiver run through her, but she replied, nonchalantly: 'Can't you manage alone? I'm rather tired to-night.'

'It won't take long.' He smiled to himself. 'And I can promise you you won't be tired afterwards.'

The words seemed to amuse him. Alix shuddered. Now or never was the time to carry out her plan.

She rose to her feet.

'I'm just going to telephone to the butcher,' she announced nonchalantly. 'Don't you bother to move.'

'To the butcher? At this time of night?'

'His shop's shut, of course, silly. But he's in his house all right. And to-morrow's Saturday, and I want him to bring me some veal cutlets early, before someone else grabs them off him. The old dear will do anything for me.'

She passed quickly into the house, closing the door behind her. She heard Gerald say: 'Don't shut the door,' and was quick with her light reply: 'It keeps the moths out. I hate moths. Are you afraid I'm going to make love to the butcher, silly?'

Once inside, she snatched down the telephone receiver

and gave the number of the 'Traveller's Arms.' She was put through at once.

'Mr. Windyford? Is he still there? Can I speak to him?'

Then her heart gave a sickening thump. The door was pushed open and her husband came into the hall.

'Do go away, Gerald,' she said pettishly. 'I hate any one listening when I'm telephoning.'

He merely laughed and threw himself into a chair.

'Sure it really is the butcher you're telephoning to?' he quizzed.

Alix was in despair. Her plan had failed. In a minute Dick Windyford would come to the phone. Should she risk all and cry out an appeal for help?

And then, as she nervously depressed and released the little key in the receiver she was holding, which permits the voice to be heard or not heard at the other end, another plan flashed into her head.

'It will be difficult,' she thought to herself. 'It means keeping my head, and thinking of the right words, and not faltering for a moment, but I believe I could do it. I *must* do it.'

And at that minute she heard Dick Windyford's voice at the other end of the 'phone.

Alix drew a deep breath. Then she depressed the key firmly and spoke.

'*Mrs. Martin speaking—from Philomel Cottage. Please come* (she released the key) to-morrow morning with six nice veal cutlets (she depressed the key again). *It's very important* (she released the key). Thank you so much, Mr. Hexworthy; you don't mind my ringing you up so late, I hope, but those veal cutlets are really a matter of (she depressed the key again) *life or death* (she released it). Very well—to-morrow morning (she depressed it) *as soon as possible*.

She replaced the receiver on the hook and turned to face her husband, breathing hard.

'So that's how you talk to your butcher, is it?' said Gerald.

'It's the feminine touch,' said Alix lightly.

She was simmering with excitement. He had suspected nothing. Dick, even if he didn't understand, would come.

She passed into the sitting-room and switched on the electric light. Gerald followed her.

'You seem very full of spirits now?' he said, watching her curiously.

'Yes,' said Alix. 'My headache's gone.'

She sat down in her usual seat and smiled at her husband as he sank into his own chair opposite her. She was saved. It was only five-and-twenty past eight. Long before nine o'clock Dick would have arrived.

'I didn't think much of that coffee you gave me,' complained Gerald. 'It tasted very bitter.'

'It's a new kind I was trying. We won't have it again if you don't like it, dear.'

Alix took up a piece of needlework and began to stitch. Gerald read a few pages of his book. Then he glanced up at the clock and tossed the book away.

'Half-past eight. Time to go down to the cellar and start work.'

The sewing slipped from Alix's fingers.

'Oh, not yet. Let us wait until nine o'clock.'

'No, my girl—half-past eight. That's the time I fixed. You'll be able to get to bed all the earlier.'

'But I'd rather wait until nine.'

'You know when I fix a time, I always stick to it. Come along, Alix. I'm not going to wait a minute longer.'

Alix looked up at him, and in spite of herself she felt a wave of terror slide over her. The mask had been lifted. Gerald's hands were twitching, his eyes were shining with excitement, he was continually passing his tongue over his dry lips. He no longer cared to conceal his excitement.

Alix thought: 'It's true—*he can't wait*—he's like a madman.'

He strode over to her, and jerked her on to her feet with a hand on her shoulder.

'Come on, my girl—or I'll carry you there.'

His tone was gay, but there was an undisguised ferocity behind it that appalled her. With a supreme effort she jerked herself free and clung cowering against the wall. She was powerless. She couldn't get away—she couldn't do anything—and he was coming towards her.

'Now, Alix——'

'No—no.'

She screamed, her hands held out impotently to ward him off.

'Gerald—stop—I've got something to tell you, something to confess——'

He did stop.

'To confess?' he said curiously.

'Yes, to confess.' She had used the words at random, but she went on desperately, seeking to hold his arrested attention.

A look of contempt swept over his face.

'A former lover, I suppose,' he sneered.

'No,' said Alix. 'Something else. You'd call it, I expect—yes, you'd call it a crime.'

And at once she saw that she had struck the right note. Again his attention was arrested, held. Seeing that, her nerve came back to her. She felt mistress of the situation once more.

'You had better sit down again,' she said quietly.

She herself crossed the room to her old chair and sat down. She even stooped and picked up her needlework. But behind her calmness she was thinking and inventing feverishly; for the story she invented must hold his interest until help arrived.

'I told you,' she said slowly, 'that I had been a shorthand-typist for fifteen years. That was not entirely true. There were two intervals. The first occurred when I was twenty-two. I came across a man, an elderly man with a little property. He fell in love with me and asked me to marry him. I accepted. We were married.' She paused. 'I induced him to insure his life in my favour.'

She saw a sudden keen interest spring up in her husband's face, and went on with renewed assurance:

'During the war I worked for a time in a hospital dispensary. There I had the handling of all kinds of rare drugs and poisons.'

She paused reflectively. He was keenly interested now, not a doubt of it. The murderer is bound to have an interest in murder. She had gambled on that, and succeeded. She stole a glance at the clock. It was five-and-twenty to nine.

'There is one poison—it is a little white powder. A pinch of it means death. You know something about poisons, perhaps?'

She put the question is some trepidation. If he did, she would have to be careful.

'No,' said Gerald; 'I know very little about them.'

She drew a breath of relief.

'You have heard of hyoscine, of course? This is a drug that acts much the same way, but is absolutely untraceable. Any doctor would give a certificate of heart failure. I stole a small quantity of this drug and kept it by me.'

She paused, marshalling her forces.

'Go on,' said Gerald.

'No. I'm afraid. I can't tell you. Another time.'

'Now,' he said impatiently. 'I want to hear.'

'We had been married a month. I was very good to my elderly husband, very kind and devoted. He spoke in praise of me to all the neighbours. Every one knew what a devoted wife I was. I always made his coffee myself every evening. One evening, when we were alone together, I put a pinch of the deadly alkaloid in his cup——'

Alix paused, and carefully re-threaded her needle. She, who had never acted in her life, rivalled the greatest actress in the world at this moment. She was actually living the part of the cold-blooded poisoner.

'It was very peaceful. I sat watching him. Once he gasped a little and asked for air. I opened the window. Then he said he could not move from his chair. *Presently he died.*'

She stopped, smiling. It was a quarter to nine. Surely they would come soon.

'How much,' said Gerald, 'was the insurance money?'

'About two thousand pounds. I speculated with it, and lost it. I went back to my office work. But I never meant to remain there long. Then I met another man. I had stuck to my maiden name at the office. He didn't know I had been married before. He was a younger man, rather good-looking, and quite well off. We were married quietly in Sussex. He didn't want to insure his life, but of course he made a will in my favour. He liked me to make his coffee myself just as my first husband had done.'

Alix smiled reflectively, and added simply: 'I make very good coffee.'

Then she went on:

'I had several friends in the village where we were living. They were very sorry for me, with my husband dying suddenly of heart failure one evening after dinner. I didn't quite like the doctor. I don't think he suspected me, but he was certainly very surprised at my husband's sudden death. I don't quite know why I drifted back to the office again. Habit, I suppose. My second husband left about four thousand pounds. I didn't speculate with it this time; I invested it. Then, you see——'

But she was interrupted. Gerald Martin, his face suffused with blood, half choking, was pointing a shaking forefinger at her.

'The coffee—my God! the coffee!'

She stared at him.

'I understand now why it was bitter. You devil! You 've been up to your tricks again.'

His hands gripped the arms of his chair. He was ready to spring upon her.

'You 've poisoned me.'

Alix had retreated from him to the fire-place. Now, terrified, she opened her lips to deny—and then paused. In another minute he would spring upon her. She summoned all her strength. Her eyes held his steadily, compellingly.

'Yes,' she said. 'I poisoned you. Already the poison is working. At this minute you can't move from your chair—you can't move——'

If she could keep him there—even a few minutes . . .

Ah! what was that? Footsteps on the road. The creak of the gate. Then footsteps on the path outside. The outer door opening.

'*You can't move,*' she said again.

Then she slipped past him and fled headlong from the room to fall fainting into Dick Windyford's arms.

'My God! Alix,' he cried.

Then he turned to the man with him, a tall, stalwart figure in policeman's uniform.

'Go and see what 's been happening in that room.'

He laid Alix carefully down on a couch and bent over her.

'My little girl,' he murmured. 'My poor little girl. What have they been doing to you?'

Her eyelids fluttered and her lips just murmured his name.

Dick was aroused by the policeman's touching him on the arm.

'There's nothing in that room, sir, but a man sitting in a chair. Looks as though he'd had some kind of bad fright, and——'

'Yes?'

'Well, sir, he's—dead.'

They were startled by hearing Alix's voice. She spoke as though in some kind of dream, her eyes still closed.

'*And presently*,' she said, almost as though she were quoting from something, '*he died*——'

ANTHONY BERKELEY

THE AVENGING CHANCE

ROGER SHERINGHAM was inclined to think afterwards that the Poisoned Chocolates Case, as the papers called it, was perhaps the most perfectly planned murder he had ever encountered. The motive was so obvious, when you knew where to look for it—but you didn't know; the method was so significant, when you had grasped its real essentials—but you didn't grasp them; the traces were so thinly covered, when you had realized what was covering them—but you didn't realize. But for a piece of the merest bad luck, which the murderer could not possibly have foreseen, the crime must have been added to the classical list of great mysteries.

This is the gist of the case, as Chief Inspector Moresby told it one evening to Roger in the latter's rooms in the Albany a week or so after it happened:

On Friday morning, the fifteenth of November, at half-past ten in the morning, in accordance with his invariable custom, Sir William Anstruther walked into his club in Piccadilly, the very exclusive Rainbow Club, and asked for his letters. The porter handed him three and a small parcel. Sir William walked over to the fire-place in the big lounge hall to open them.

A few minutes later another member entered the club, a Mr. Graham Beresford. There were a letter and a couple of circulars for him, and he also strolled over to the fire-place, nodding to Sir William, but not speaking to him. The two men only knew each other very slightly, and had probably never exchanged more than a dozen words in all.

Having glanced through his letters, Sir William opened the parcel and, after a moment, snorted with disgust. Beresford looked at him, and with a grunt Sir William thrust out a letter which had been enclosed in the parcel. Concealing a smile (Sir William's ways were a matter of some amusement to his fellow-members), Beresford read the letter. It was from a big firm of chocolate manufacturers, Mason & Sons, and set forth that they were putting on the market a new brand of liqueur-chocolates designed especially to appeal to men; would Sir William do them the honour of accepting the enclosed two-pound box and letting the firm have his candid opinion on them?

'Do they think I'm a blank chorus-girl?' fumed Sir William. 'Write 'em testimonials about their blank chocolates, indeed! Blank 'em! I'll complain to the blank committee. That sort of blank thing can't blank well be allowed here.'

'Well, it's an ill wind so far as I'm concerned,' Beresford soothed him. 'It's reminded me of something. My wife and I had a box at the Imperial last night. I bet her a box of chocolates to a hundred cigarettes that she wouldn't spot the villain by the end of the second act. She won. I must remember to get them. Have you seen it—*The Creaking Skull*? Not a bad show.'

Sir William had not seen it, and said so with force.

'Want a box of chocolates, did you say?' he added, more mildly. 'Well, take this blank one. I don't want it.'

For a moment Beresford demurred politely and then, most unfortunately for himself, accepted. The money so saved meant nothing to him for he was a wealthy man; but trouble was always worth saving.

By an extraordinarily lucky chance neither the outer wrapper of the box nor its covering letter were thrown into the fire, and this was the more fortunate in that both men had tossed the envelopes of their letters into the flames. Sir William did, indeed, make a bundle of the wrapper, letter, and string, but he handed it over to Beresford, and the latter simply dropped it inside the fender. This bundle the porter subsequently extracted and, being a man of orderly habits, put it tidily away in the waste-paper basket, whence it was retrieved later by the police.

Of the three unconscious protagonists in the impending tragedy, Sir William was without doubt the most remarkable. Still a year or two under fifty, he looked, with his flaming red face and thick-set figure, a typical country squire of the old school, and both his manners and his language were in accordance with tradition. His habits, especially as regards women, were also in accordance with tradition—the tradition of the bold, bad baronet which he undoubtedly was.

In comparison with him, Beresford was rather an ordinary man, a tall, dark, not unhandsome fellow of two-and-thirty, quiet and reserved. His father had left him a rich man, but idleness did not appeal to him, and he had a finger in a good many business pies.

Money attracts money, Graham Beresford had inherited it, he made it, and, inevitably, he had married it, too. The daughter of a late shipowner in Liverpool, with not far off half a million in her own right. But the money was incidental, for he needed her and would have married her just as inevitably (said his friends) if she had not had a farthing. A tall, rather serious-minded, highly cultured girl, not so young that her character had not had time to form (she was twenty-five when Beresford married her, three years ago), she was the ideal wife for him. A bit of a Puritan perhaps in some ways, but Beresford, whose wild oats, though duly sown, had been a sparse crop, was ready enough to be a Puritan himself by that time if she was. To make no bones about it, the Beresfords succeeded in achieving that eighth wonder of the modern world, a happy marriage.

And into the middle of it there dropped with irretrievable tragedy, the box of chocolates.

Beresford gave them to her after lunch as they sat over their coffee, with some jesting remark about paying his honourable debts, and she opened the box at once. The top layer, she noticed, seemed to consist only of kirsch and maraschino. Beresford, who did not believe in spoiling good coffee, refused when she offered him the box, and his wife ate the first one alone. As she did so she exclaimed in surprise that the filling seemed exceedingly strong and positively burnt her mouth.

Beresford explained that they were samples of a new brand and then, made curious by what his wife had said, took one too. A burning taste, not intolerable but much too strong to be pleasant, followed the release of the liquid, and the almond flavouring seemed quite excessive.

'By Jove,' he said, 'they are strong. They must be filled with neat alcohol.'

'Oh, they wouldn't do that, surely,' said his wife, taking another. 'But they are very strong. I think I rather like them, though.'

Beresford ate another, and disliked it still more. 'I don't,' he said with decision. 'They make my tongue feel quite numb. I shouldn't eat any more of them if I were you, I think there's something wrong with them.'

'Well, they're only an experiment, I suppose,' she said. 'But they do burn. I'm not sure whether I like them or not.'

A few minutes later Beresford went out to keep a business appointment in the City. He left her still trying to make up her mind whether she liked them, and still eating them to decide. Beresford remembered that scrap of conversation afterwards very vividly, because it was the last time he saw his wife alive.

That was roughly half-past two. At a quarter to four Beresford arrived at his club from the City in a taxi, in a state of collapse. He was helped into the building by the driver and the porter, and both described him subsequently as pale to the point of ghastliness, with staring eyes and livid lips, and his skin damp and clammy. His mind seemed unaffected, however, and when they had got him up the steps he was able to walk, with the porter's help, into the lounge.

The porter, thoroughly alarmed, wanted to send for a doctor at once, but Beresford, who was the last man in the world to make a fuss, refused to let him, saying that it must be indigestion and he would be all right in a few minutes. To Sir William Anstruther, however, who was in the lounge at the time, he added after the porter had gone:

'Yes, and I believe it was those infernal chocolates you gave me, now I come to think of it. I thought there was something funny about them at the time. I'd better go and find out if my wife——' He broke off abruptly. His body, which had been leaning back limply in his chair, suddenly heaved rigidly upright; his jaws locked together, the livid lips drawn back in a horrible grin, and his hands clenched on the arms of his chair. At the same time Sir

William became aware of an unmistakable smell of bitter almonds.

Thoroughly alarmed, believing indeed that the man was dying under his eyes, Sir William raised a shout for the porter and a doctor. The other occupants of the lounge hurried up, and between them they got the convulsed body of the unconscious man into a more comfortable position. Before the doctor could arrive a telephone message was received at the club from an agitated butler asking if Mr. Beresford was there, and if so would he come home at once as Mrs. Beresford had been taken seriously ill. As a matter of fact she was already dead.

Beresford did not die. He had taken less of the poison than his wife, who after his departure must have eaten at least three more of the chocolates, so that its action was less rapid and the doctor had time to save him. As a matter of fact it turned out afterwards that he had not had a fatal dose. By about eight o'clock that night he was conscious; the next day he was practically convalescent.

As for the unfortunate Mrs. Beresford, the doctor had arrived too late to save her, and she passed away very rapidly in a deep coma.

The police had taken the matter in hand as soon as Mrs. Beresford's death was reported to them and the fact of poison established, and it was only a very short time before things had become narrowed down to the chocolates as the active agent.

Sir William was interrogated, the letter and wrapper were recovered from the waste-paper basket, and, even before the sick man was out of danger, a detective inspector was asking for an interview with the managing director of Mason & Sons. Scotland Yard moves quickly.

It was the police theory at this stage, based on what Sir William and the two doctors had been able to tell them, that by an act of criminal carelessness on the part of one of Mason's employees, an excessive amount of oil of bitter almonds had been included in the filling mixture of the chocolates, for that was what the doctors had decided must be the poisoning ingredient. However, the managing director quashed this idea at once: oil of bitter almonds, he asserted, was never used by Mason's.

He had more interesting news still. Having read with undisguised astonishment the covering letter, he at once declared that it was a forgery. No such letter, no such samples had been sent out by the firm at all; a new variety of liqueur-chocolates had never even been mooted. The fatal chocolates were their ordinary brand.

Unwrapping and examining one more closely, he called the inspector's attention to a mark on the underside, which he suggested was the remains of a small hole drilled in the case, through which the liquid could have been extracted and the fatal filling inserted, the hole afterwards being stopped up with softened chocolate, a perfectly simple operation.

He examined it under a magnifying-glass and the inspector agreed. It was now clear to him that somebody had been trying deliberately to murder Sir William Anstruther.

Scotland Yard doubled its activities. The chocolates were sent for analysis, Sir William was interviewed again, and so was the now conscious Beresford. From the latter the doctor insisted that the news of his wife's death must be kept till the next day, as in his weakened condition the shock might be fatal, so that nothing very helpful was obtained from him.

Nor could Sir William throw any light on the mystery or produce a single person who might have any grounds for trying to kill him. He was living apart from his wife, who was the principal beneficiary in his will, but she was in the South of France, as the French police subsequently confirmed. His estate in Worcestershire, heavily mortgaged, was entailed and went to a nephew; but as the rent he got for it barely covered the interest on the mortgage, and the nephew was considerably better off than Sir William himself, there was no motive there. The police were at a dead end.

The analysis brought one or two interesting facts to light. Not oil of bitter almonds but nitrobenzine, a kindred substance, chiefly used in the manufacture of aniline dyes, was the somewhat surprising poison employed. Each chocolate in the upper layer contained exactly six minims of it, in a mixture of kirsch and maraschino. The chocolates in the other layers were harmless.

As to the other clues, they seemed equally useless. The sheet of Mason's notepaper was identified by Merton's, the printers, as of their work, but there was nothing to show how it had got into the murderer's possession. All that could be said was that, the edges being distinctly yellowed, it must be an old piece. The machine on which the letter had been typed, of course, could not be traced. From the wrapper, a piece of ordinary brown paper with Sir William's address hand-printed on it in large capitals, there was nothing to be learnt at all beyond that the parcel had been posted at the office in Southampton Street between the hours of 8.30 and 9.30 on the previous evening.

Only one thing was quite clear. Whoever had coveted Sir William's life had no intention of paying for it with his or her own.

'And now you know as much as we do, Mr. Sheringham,' concluded Chief Inspector Moresby, 'and if you can say who sent those chocolates to Sir William, you'll know a good deal more.'

Roger nodded thoughtfully.

'It's a brute of a case. I met a man only yesterday who was at school with Beresford. He didn't know him well because Beresford was on the modern side and my friend was a classical bird, but they were in the same house. He says Beresford's absolutely knocked over by his wife's death. I wish you could find out who sent those chocolates, Moresby.'

'So do I, Mr. Sheringham,' said Moresby gloomily.

'It might have been any one in the whole world,' Roger mused. 'What about feminine jealousy, for instance? Sir William's private life doesn't seem to be immaculate. I dare say there's a good deal of off with the old light-o'-love and on with the new.'

'Why, that's just what I've been looking into, Mr. Sheringham, sir,' retorted Chief Inspector Moresby reproachfully. 'That was the first thing that came to me. Because if anything does stand out about this business it is that it's a woman's crime. Nobody but a woman would send poisoned chocolates to a man. Another man would send a poisoned sample of whisky, or something like that.'

'That's a very sound point, Moresby,' Roger meditated. 'Very sound indeed. And Sir William couldn't help you?'

'Couldn't,' said Moresby, not without a trace of resentment, 'or wouldn't. I was inclined to believe at first that he might have his suspicions and was shielding some woman. But I don't think so now.'

'Humph!' Roger did not seem quite so sure. 'It's reminiscent, this case, isn't it? Didn't some lunatic once send poisoned chocolates to the Commissioner of Police himself? A good crime always gets imitated, as you know.'

Moresby brightened.

'It's funny you should say that, Mr. Sheringham, because that's the very conclusion I've come to. I've tested every other theory, and so far as I know there's not a soul with an interest in Sir William's death, whether from motives of gain, revenge, or what you like, whom I haven't had to rule quite out of it. In fact, I've pretty well made up my mind that the person who sent those chocolates was some irresponsible lunatic of a woman, a social or religious fanatic who's probably never even seen him. And if that's the case,' Moresby sighed, 'a fat chance I have of ever laying hands on her.'

'Unless Chance steps in, as it so often does,' said Roger brightly, 'and helps you. A tremendous lot of cases get solved by a stroke of sheer luck, don't they? *Chance the Avenger*. It would make an excellent film-title. But there's a lot of truth in it. If I were superstitious, which I'm not, I should say it wasn't chance at all, but Providence avenging the victim.'

'Well, Mr. Sheringham,' said Moresby, who was not superstitious either, 'to tell the truth, I don't mind what it is, so long as it lets me get my hands on the right person.'

If Moresby had paid his visit to Roger Sheringham with any hope of tapping that gentleman's brains, he went away disappointed.

To tell the truth, Roger was inclined to agree with the chief inspector's conclusion, that the attempt on the life of Sir William Anstruther and the actual murder of the unfortunate Mrs. Beresford must be the work of some unknown criminal lunatic. For this reason, although he thought about it a good deal during the next few days, he made no attempt to take the case in hand. It was the sort of affair, necessitating endless inquiries that a private person would have neither the time nor the authority to carry out, which can be handled only by the official police. Roger's interest in it was purely academic.

It was hazard, a chance encounter nearly a week later, which translated this interest from the academic into the personal.

Roger was in Bond Street, about to go through the distressing ordeal of buying a new hat. Along the pavement he suddenly saw bearing down on him Mrs. Verreker-le-Flemming. Mrs. Verreker-le-Flemming was small, exquisite, rich, and a widow, and she sat at Roger's feet whenever he gave her the opportunity. But she talked. She talked, in fact, and talked, and talked. And Roger, who rather liked talking himself, could not bear it. He tried to dart across the road, but there was no opening in the traffic stream. He was cornered.

Mrs. Verreker-le-Flemming fastened on him gladly.

'Oh, Mr. Sheringham! *Just* the person I wanted to see. Mr. Sheringham, *do* tell me. In confidence. *Are* you taking up this dreadful business of poor Joan Beresford's death?'

Roger, the frozen and imbecile grin of civilized intercourse on his face, tried to get a word in; without result.

'I was horrified when I heard of it—simply horrified. You see, Joan and I were such *very* close friends. Quite intimate. And the awful thing, the truly *terrible* thing is that Joan brought the whole business on herself. Isn't that *appalling*?'

Roger no longer wanted to escape.

'What did you say?' he managed to insert incredulously.

'I suppose it's what they call tragic irony,' Mrs. Verreker-le-Flemming chattered on. 'Certainly it was tragic enough, and I've never heard anything so terribly ironical. You know about that bet she made with her husband, of course, so that he had to get her a box of chocolates, and if he hadn't Sir William would never have given him the poisoned ones and he'd have eaten them and died himself and good riddance? Well, Mr. Sheringham——' Mrs. Verreker-le-Flemming lowered her voice to a conspirator's whisper and glanced about her in the approved manner. 'I've never told anybody else this, but I 'm telling you because I know you 'll appreciate it. *Joan wasn't playing fair.*'

'How do you mean?' Roger asked, bewildered.

Mrs. Verreker-le-Flemming was artlessly pleased with her sensation.

'Why, she 'd seen the play before. We went together, the very first week it was on. She *knew* who the villain was all the time.'

'By Jove!' Roger was as impressed as Mrs. Verreker-le-Flemming could have wished. 'Chance the Avenger! We 're none of us immune from it.'

'Poetic justice, you mean?' twittered Mrs. Verreker-le-Flemming, to whom these remarks had been somewhat obscure. 'Yes, but Joan Beresford of all people! That 's the extraordinary thing. I should never have thought Joan *would* do a thing like that. She was such a *nice* girl. A little close with money, of course, considering how well off they are, but that isn't anything. Of course it was only fun, and pulling her husband's leg, but I always used to think Joan was such a *serious* girl, Mr. Sheringham. I mean, ordinary people don't talk about honour and truth, and playing the game, and all those things one takes for granted. But Joan did. She was always saying that this wasn't honourable, or that wouldn't be playing the game. Well, she paid herself for not playing the game, poor girl, didn't she? Still, it all goes to show the truth of the old saying, doesn't it?'

'What old saying?' said Roger, hypotized by this flow.

'Why, that still waters run deep. Joan must have been deep, I 'm afraid.' Mrs. Verreker-le-Flemming sighed. It was evidently a social error to be deep. 'I mean, she certainly took me in. She can't have been quite so honourable and truthful as she was always pretending, can she? And I can't help wondering whether a girl who 'd deceived her husband in a little thing like that might not—oh, well, I don't want to say anything against poor Joan now she 's dead, poor darling, but she can't have been *quite* such a plaster saint after all, can she? I mean,' said Mrs. Verreker-le-Flemming, in hasty extenuation of these suggestions, 'I do think psychology is so very interesting, don't you, Mr. Sheringham?'

'Sometimes, very,' Roger agreed gravely. 'But you mentioned Sir William Anstruther just now. Do you know him, too?'

'I used to,' Mrs. Verreker-le-Flemming replied, without particular interest. 'Horrible man! Always running after some woman or other. And when he's tired of her, just drops her—biff!—like that. At least,' added Mrs. Verreker-le-Flemming somewhat hastily, 'so I've heard.'

'And what happens if she refuses to be dropped?'

'Oh dear, I'm sure I don't know. I suppose you've heard the latest?'

Mrs. Verreker-le-Flemming hurried on, perhaps a trifle more pink than the delicate aids to nature on her cheeks would have warranted.

'He's taken up with that Bryce woman now. You know, the wife of the oil man, or petrol, or whatever he made his money in. It began about three weeks ago. You'd have thought that dreadful business of being responsible, in a way, for poor Joan Beresford's death would have sobered him up a little, wouldn't you? But not a bit of it; he——'

Roger was following another line of thought.

'What a pity you weren't at the Imperial with the Beresfords that evening. She'd never have made that bet if you had been.' Roger looked extremely innocent. 'You weren't, I suppose?'

'I?' queried Mrs. Verreker-le-Flemming in surprise, 'Good gracious, no. I was at the new revue at the Pavilion. Lady Gavelstroke had a box and asked me to join her party.'

'Oh, yes. Good show, isn't it? I thought that sketch *The Sempiternal Triangle* very clever. Didn't you?'

'*The Sempiternal Triangle?*' wavered Mrs. Verreker-le-Flemming.

'Yes, in the first half.'

'Oh! Then I didn't see it. I got there disgracefully late, I'm afraid. But then,' said Mrs. Verreker-le-Flemming with pathos, 'I always do seem to be late for simply everything.'

Roger kept the rest of the conversation resolutely upon theatres. But before he left her he had ascertained that she had photographs of both Mrs. Beresford and Sir William Anstruther and had obtained permission to borrow them some time. As soon as she was out of view he hailed a taxi and gave Mrs. Verreker-le-Flemming's address. He thought it better to take advantage of her permission at a time when he would not have to pay for it a second time over.

The parlour-maid seemed to think there was nothing odd in his mission, and took him up to the drawing-room at once. A corner of the room was devoted to the silver-framed photographs of Mrs. Verreker-le-Flemming's friends, and there were many of them. Roger examined them with interest, and finally took away with him not two photographs but six, those of Sir William, Mrs. Beresford, Beresford, two strange males who appeared to belong to the Sir William period, and, lastly a likeness of Mrs. Verreker-le-Flemming herself. Roger liked confusing his trail.

For the rest of the day he was very busy.

His activities would have no doubt seemed to Mrs. Verreker-le-Flemming not merely baffling but pointless. He paid a visit to a public library, for instance, and consulted a work of reference, after which he took a taxi and drove to the offices of the Anglo-Eastern Perfumery Company, where he inquired for a certain Mr. Joseph Lea Hardwick and seemed much put out on hearing that no such gentleman was known to the firm and was certainly not employed in any of their branches. Many questions had to be put about the firm and its branches before he consented to abandon the quest.

After that he drove to Messrs. Weall & Wilson, the well-known institution which protects the trade interests of individuals and advises its subscribers regarding investments. Here he entered his name as a subscriber, and explaining that he had a large sum of money to invest, filled in one of the special inquiry-forms which are headed Strictly Confidential.

Then he went to the Rainbow Club, in Piccadilly.

Introducing himself to the porter without a blush as connected with Scotland Yard, he asked the man a number of questions, more or less trivial, concerning the tragedy.

'Sir William, I understand,' he said finally, as if by the way, 'did not dine here the evening before?'

There it appeared that Roger was wrong. Sir William had dined in the club, as he did about three times a week.

'But I quite understood he wasn't here that evening?' Roger said plaintively.

The porter was emphatic. He remembered quite well. So did a waiter, whom the porter summoned to corroborate him. Sir William had dined, rather late, and had not left the dining-room till about nine o'clock. He spent the evening there, too, the waiter knew, or at least some of it, for he himself had taken him a whisky-and-soda in the lounge not less than half an hour later.

Roger retired.

He retired to Merton's in a taxi.

It seemed that he wanted some new notepaper printed, of a very special kind, and to the young woman behind the counter he specified at great length and in wearisome detail exactly what he did want. The young woman handed him the books of specimen pieces and asked him to see if there was any style there which would suit him. Roger glanced through them, remarking garrulously to the young woman that he had been recommended to Merton's by a very dear friend, whose photograph he happened to have on him at that moment. Wasn't that a curious coincidence? The young woman agreed that it was.

'About a fortnight ago, I think, my friend was in here last,' said Roger, producing the photograph. 'Recognize this?'

The young woman took the photograph, without apparent interest.

'Oh, yes. I remember. About some notepaper, too, wasn't it? So that's your friend. Well, it's a small world. Now this is a line we're selling a good deal of just now.'

Roger went back to his rooms to dine. Afterwards, feeling restless, he wandered out of the Albany and turned up Piccadilly. He wandered round the Circus, thinking hard, and paused for a moment out of habit to inspect the photographs of the new revue hung outside the Pavilion. The next thing he realized was that he had got as far as Jermyn Street and was standing outside the Imperial Theatre. Glancing at the advertisements of *The Creaking*

Skull, he saw that it began at half-past eight. Glancing at his watch, he saw that the time was twenty-nine minutes past that hour. He had an evening to get through somehow. He went inside.

The next morning, very early for Roger, he called on Moresby at Scotland Yard.

'Moresby,' he said without preamble, 'I want you to do something for me. Can you find me a taximan who took a fare from Piccadilly Circus or its neighbourhood at about ten past nine on the evening before the Beresford crime, to the Strand somewhere near the bottom of Southampton Street, and another who took a fare back between those points. I'm not sure about the first. Or one taxi might have been used for the double journey, but I doubt that. Anyhow, try to find out for me, will you?'

'What are you up to now, Mr. Sheringham?' Moresby asked suspiciously.

'Breaking down an interesting alibi,' replied Roger serenely. 'By the way, I know who sent those chocolates to Sir William. I'm just building up a nice structure of evidence for you. Ring up my rooms when you've got those taximen.'

He strolled out, leaving Moresby positively gaping after him.

The rest of the day he spent apparently trying to buy a second-hand typewriter. He was very particular that it should be a Hamilton No. 4. When the shop-people tried to induce him to consider other makes he refused to look at them, saying that he had had the Hamilton No. 4 so strongly recommended to him by a friend, who had bought one about three weeks ago. Perhaps it was at this very shop? No? They hadn't sold a Hamilton No. 4 for the last three months? How odd!

But at one shop they had sold a Hamilton No. 4 within the last month, and that was odder still.

At half-past four Roger got back to his rooms to await the telephone message from Moresby. At half-past five it came.

'There are fourteen taxi-drivers here, littering up my office,' said Moresby offensively. 'What do you want me to do with 'em?'

'Keep them till I come, Chief Inspector,' returned Roger with dignity.

The interview with the fourteen was brief enough, however. To each man in turn Roger showed a photograph, holding it so that Moresby could not see it, and asked if he could recognize his fare. The ninth man did so, without hesitation.

At a nod from Roger, Moresby dismissed them, then sat at his table and tried to look official. Roger seated himself on the table, looking most unofficial, and swung his legs. As he did so, a photograph fell unnoticed out of his pocket and fluttered, face downwards, under the table. Moresby eyed it but did not pick it up.

'And now, Mr. Sheringham, sir,' he said, 'perhaps you 'll tell me what you 've been doing?'

'Certainly, Moresby,' said Roger blandly. 'Your work for you. I really have solved the thing, you know. Here 's your evidence.' He took from his note-case an old letter and handed it to the Chief Inspector. 'Was that typed on the same machine as the forged letter from Mason's, or was it not?'

Moresby studied it for a moment, then drew the forged letter from a drawer of his table and compared the two minutely.

'Mr. Sheringham,' he said soberly, 'where did you get hold of this?'

'In a second-hand typewriter shop in St. Martin's Lane. The machine was sold to an unknown customer about a month ago. They identified the customer from that same photograph. As it happened, this machine had been used for a time in the office after it was repaired, to see that it was O.K., and I easily got hold of that specimen of its work.'

'And where is the machine now?'

'Oh, at the bottom of the Thames, I expect,' Roger smiled. 'I tell you, this criminal takes no unnecessary chances. But that doesn't matter. There 's your evidence.'

'Humph! It 's all right so far as it goes,' conceded Moresby. 'But what about Mason's paper?'

'That,' said Roger calmly, 'was extracted from Merton's book of sample notepapers, as I 'd guessed from the very yellowed edges might be the case. I can prove contact of the criminal with the book, and there is a page which will certainly turn out to have been filled by that piece of paper.'

'That's fine,' Moresby said more heartily.

'As for that taximan, the criminal had an alibi. You've heard it broken down. Between ten past nine and twenty-five past, in fact during the time when the parcel must have been posted, the murderer took a hurried journey to that neighbourhood, going probably by bus or underground, but returning as I expected, by taxi, because time would be getting short.'

'And the murderer, Mr. Sheringham?'

'The person whose photograph is in my pocket,' Roger said unkindly. 'By the way, do you remember what I was saying the other day about Chance the Avenger, my excellent film-title? Well, it's worked again. By a chance meeting in Bond Street with a silly woman I was put, by the merest accident, in possession of a piece of information which showed me then and there who had sent those chocolates addressed to Sir William. There were other possibilities, of course, and I tested them, but then and there on the pavement I saw the whole thing, from first to last.'

'Who was the murderer, then, Mr. Sheringham?' repeated Moresby.

'It was so beautifully planned,' Roger went on dreamily. 'We never grasped for one moment that we were making the fundamental mistake that the murderer all along intended us to make.'

'And what was that?' asked Moresby.

'Why, that the plan had miscarried. That the wrong person had been killed. That was just the beauty of it. The plan had *not* miscarried. It had been brilliantly successful. The wrong person was *not* killed. Very much the right person was.'

Moresby gaped.

'Why, how on earth do you make that out, sir?'

'Mrs. Beresford was the objective all the time. That's why the plot was so ingenious. Everything was anticipated. It was perfectly natural that Sir William should hand the chocolates over to Beresford. It was foreseen that we should look for the criminal among Sir William's associates and not the dead woman's. It was probably even foreseen that the crime would be considered the work of a woman!'

Moresby, unable to wait any longer, snatched up the photograph.

'Good heavens! But Mr. Sheringham, you don't mean to tell me that . . . Sir William himself!'

'He wanted to get rid of Mrs. Beresford,' Roger continued. 'He had liked her well enough at the beginning, no doubt, though it was her money he was after all the time.

'But the real trouble was that she was too close with her money. He wanted it, or some of it, pretty badly; and she wouldn't part. There 's no doubt about the motive. I made a list of the firms he 's interested in and got a report on them. They 're all rocky, every one. He 'd got through all his own money, and he had to get more.

'As for the nitrobenzine which puzzled us so much, that was simple enough. I looked it up and found that beside the uses you told me, it 's used largely in perfumery. And he 's got a perfumery business. The Anglo-Eastern Perfumery Company. That 's how he 'd know about it being poisonous, of course. But I shouldn't think he got his supply from there. He 'd be cleverer than that. He probably made the stuff himself. And schoolboys know how to treat benzol with nitric acid to get nitrobenzine.'

'But,' stammered Moresby, 'but Sir William . . . He was at Eton.'

'Sir William?' said Roger sharply. 'Who 's talking about Sir William? I told you the photograph of the murderer was in my pocket.' He whipped out the photograph in question and confronted the astounded chief inspector with it. 'Beresford, man! Beresford 's the murderer of his own wife.

'Beresford, who still had hankerings after a gay life,' he went on more mildly, 'didn't want his wife but did want her money. He contrived this plot, providing as he thought against every contingency that could possibly arise. He established a mild alibi, if suspicion ever should arise, by taking his wife to the Imperial, and slipped out of the theatre at the first interval. (I sat through the first act of the dreadful thing myself last night to see when the interval came.)

Then he hurried down to the Strand, posted his parcel, and took a taxi back. He had ten minutes, but nobody would notice if he got back to the box a minute late.

'And the rest simply followed. He knew Sir William came to the club every morning at ten-thirty, as regularly as clockwork; he knew that for a psychological certainty he could get the chocolates handed over to him if he hinted for them; he knew that the police would go chasing after all sorts of false trails starting from Sir William. And as for the wrapper and the forged letter he carefully didn't destroy them because they were calculated not only to divert suspicion but actually to point away from him to some anonymous lunatic.'

'Well, it's very smart of you, Mr. Sheringham,' Moresby said, with a little sigh, but quite ungrudgingly. 'Very smart indeed. What was it the lady told you that showed you the whole thing in a flash?'

'Why, it wasn't so much what she actually told me as what I heard between her words, so to speak. What she told me was that Mrs. Beresford knew the answer to that bet; what I deduced was that, being the sort of person she was, it was quite incredible that she should have made a bet to which she knew the answer. *Ergo*, she didn't. *Ergo*, there never was such a bet. *Ergo*, Beresford was lying. *Ergo*, Beresford wanted to get hold of those chocolates for some reason other than he stated. After all, we only had Beresford's word for the bet, hadn't we?

'Of course he wouldn't have left her that afternoon till he'd seen her take, or somehow made her take, at least six of the chocolates, more than a lethal dose. That's why the stuff was in those meticulous six-minim doses. And so that he could take a couple himself, of course. A clever stroke, that.'

Moresby rose to his feet.

'Well, Mr. Sheringham, I'm much obliged to you sir. And now I shall have to get busy myself.' He scratched his head. 'Chance the Avenger, eh? Well, I can tell one pretty big thing Beresford left to Chance the Avenger, Mr. Sheringham. Suppose Sir William hadn't handed over the chocolates after all? Supposing he'd kept 'em, to give to one of his own ladies?'

Roger positively snorted. He felt a personal pride in Beresford by this time.

'Really, Moresby! It wouldn't have had any serious results if Sir William had. Do give my man credit for being what he is. You don't imagine he sent the poisoned ones to Sir William, do you? Of course not! He'd send harmless ones, and exchange them for the others on his way home. Dash it all, he wouldn't go right out of his way to present opportunities to Chance.

'If,' added Roger, 'Chance really is the right word.'

FREEMAN WILLS CROFTS

THE MYSTERY OF THE SLEEPING-CAR EXPRESS [1]

No one who was in England in the autumn of 1909 can
fail to remember the terrible tragedy which took place in
a North-Western express between Preston and Carlisle.
The affair attracted enormous attention at the time, not
only because of the arresting nature of the events themselves, but even more for the absolute mystery in which
they were shrouded.

Quite lately a singular chance has revealed to me the
true explanation of the terrible drama, and it is at the
express desire of its chief actor that I now take upon
myself to make the facts known. As it is a long time since
1909, I may, perhaps, be pardoned if I first recall the
events which came to light at the time.

One Thursday, then, early in November of the year in
question, the 10.30 p.m. sleeping-car train left Euston as
usual for Edinburgh, Glasgow, and the North. It was
generally a heavy train, being popular with business men
who liked to complete their day's work in London, sleep
while travelling, and arrive at their northern destination
with time for a leisurely bath and breakfast before office
hours. The night in question was no exception to the rule,
and two engines hauled behind them eight large sleeping-
cars, two firsts, two thirds, and two vans, half of which
went to Glasgow, and the remainder to Edinburgh.

It is essential to the understanding of what follows that
the composition of the rear portion of the train should be
remembered. At the extreme end came the Glasgow van,
a long, eight-wheeled, bogie vehicle, with Guard Jones in
charge. Next to the van was one of the third-class
coaches, and immediately in front of it came a first-
class, both labelled for the same city. These coaches were
fairly well filled, particularly the third-class. In front of

[1] See diagram on page 230.

the first-class came the last of the four Glasgow sleepers. The train was corridor throughout, and the officials could, and did, pass through it several times during the journey.

It is with the first-class coach that we are principally concerned, and it will be understood from the above that it was placed in between the sleeping-car in front and the third-class behind, the van following immediately behind the third. It had a lavatory at each end and six compartments, the last two, next the third-class, being smokers, the next three non-smoking, and the first, immediately beside the sleeping-car, a 'Ladies Only.' The corridors in both it and the third-class coach were on the left-hand side in the direction of travel—that is, the compartments were on the side of the double line.

The night was dark as the train drew out of Euston, for there was no moon and the sky was overcast. As was remembered and commented on afterwards, there had been an unusually long spell of dry weather, and, though it looked like rain earlier in the evening, none fell till the next day, when, about six in the morning, there was a torrential downpour.

As the detectives pointed out later, no weather could have been more unfortunate from their point of view, as, had footmarks been made during the night, the ground would have been too hard to take good impressions, while even such traces as remained would more than likely have been blurred by the rain.

The train ran to time, stopping at Rugby, Crewe, and Preston. After leaving the latter station Guard Jones found he had occasion to go forward to speak to a ticket-collector in the Edinburgh portion. He accordingly left his van in the rear and passed along the corridor of the third-class carriage adjoining.

At the end of this corridor, beside the vestibule joining it to the first-class, were a lady and gentleman, evidently husband and wife, the lady endeavouring to soothe the cries of a baby she was carrying. Guard Jones addressed some civil remark to the man, who explained that their child had been taken ill, and they had brought it out of their compartment as it was disturbing the other passengers.

With an expression of sympathy, Jones unlocked the two

doors across the corridor at the vestibule between the
carriages, and, passing on into the first-class coach, re-
closed them behind him. They were fitted with spring
locks, which became fast on the door shutting.

The corridor of the first-class coach was empty, and as
Jones walked down it he observed that the blinds of all
the compartments were lowered, with one exception—that
of the 'Ladies Only.' In this compartment, which contained three ladies, the light was fully on, and the guard
noticed that two out of the three were reading.

Continuing his journey, Jones found that the two doors
at the vestibule between the first-class coach and the sleeper
were also locked, and he opened them and passed through,
shutting them behind him. At the sleeping-car attendant's
box, just inside the last of these doors, two car attendants
were talking together. One was actually inside the box,
the other standing in the corridor. The latter moved
aside to let the guard pass, taking up his former position
as, after exchanging a few words, Jones moved on.

His business with the ticket-collector finished, Guard
Jones returned to his van. On this journey he found the
same conditions obtaining as on the previous—the two
attendants were at the rear end of the sleeping-car, the
lady and gentleman with the baby in the front end of
the third-class coach, the first-class corridor deserted, and
both doors at each end of the latter coach locked. These
details, casually remarked at the time, became afterwards
of the utmost importance, adding as they did to the
mystery in which the tragedy was enveloped.

About an hour before the train was due at Carlisle, while
it was passing through the wild moorland country of the
Westmorland highlands, the brakes were applied—at first
gently, and then with considerable power. Guard Jones,
who was examining parcel waybills in the rear end of his
van, supposed it to be a signal check, but as such was
unusual at this place, he left his work and, walking down
the van, lowered the window at the left-hand side and
looked out along the train.

The line happened to be in a cutting, and the railway
bank for some distance ahead was dimly illuminated by the
light from the corridors of the first- and third-class coaches

immediately in front of his van. As I have said, the night was dark, and, except for this bit of bank, Jones could see nothing ahead. The railway curved away to the right, so, thinking he might see better from the other side, he crossed the van and looked out of the opposite window, next the up line.

There were no signal lights in view, nor anything to suggest the cause of the slack, but as he ran his eye along the train he saw that something was amiss in the first-class coach. From the window at its rear end figures were leaning, gesticulating wildly, as if to attract attention to some grave and pressing danger. The guard at once ran through the third-class to this coach, and there he found a strange and puzzling state of affairs.

The corridor was still empty, but the centre blind of the rear compartment—that is, the first reached by the guard —had been raised. Through the glass Jones could see that the compartment contained four men. Two were leaning out of the window on the opposite side, and two were fumbling at the latch of the corridor door, as if trying to open it. Jones caught hold of the outside handle to assist, but they pointed in the direction of the adjoining compartment, and the guard, obeying their signs, moved on to the second door.

The centre blind of this compartment had also been pulled up, though here, again, the door had not been opened. As the guard peered in through the glass he saw that he was in the presence of a tragedy.

Tugging desperately at the handle of the corridor door stood a lady, her face blanched, her eyes starting from her head, and her features frozen into an expression of deadly fear and horror. As she pulled she kept glancing over her shoulder, as if some dreadful apparition lurked in the shadows behind. As Jones sprang forward to open the door his eyes followed the direction of her gaze, and he drew in his breath sharply.

At the far side of the compartment, facing the engine and huddled down in the corner, was the body of a woman. She lay limp and inert, with head tilted back at an un-natural angle into the cushions and a hand hanging help-lessly down over the edge of the seat. She might have been thirty years of age, and was dressed in a reddish-brown fur coat with toque to match. But these details the guard hardly glanced at, his attention being riveted to her forehead. There, above the left eyebrow, was a sinister little hole, from which the blood had oozed down the coat and formed a tiny pool on the seat. That she was dead was obvious.

But this was not all. On the seat opposite her lay a man, and, as far as Guard Jones could see, he also was dead.

He apparently had been sitting in the corner seat, and had fallen forward so that his chest lay across the knees of the woman and his head hung down towards the floor. He was all bunched and twisted up—just a shapeless mass in a grey frieze overcoat, with dark hair at the back of what could be seen of his head. But under that head the guard caught the glint of falling drops, while a dark, ominous stain grew on the floor beneath.

Jones flung himself on the door, but it would not move. It stood fixed, an inch open, jammed in some mysterious way, imprisoning the lady with her terrible companions.

As she and the guard strove to force it open, the train came to a standstill. At once it occurred to Jones that he could now enter the compartment from the opposite side.

Shouting to reassure the now almost frantic lady, he turned back to the end compartment, intending to pass through it on to the line and so back to that containing the bodies. But here he was again baffled, for the two men had not succeeded in sliding back their door. He seized the handle to help them, and then he noticed their companions had opened the opposite door and were climbing out on to the permanent way.

It flashed through his mind that an up-train passed about this time, and, fearing an accident, he ran down the corridor to the sleeping-car, where he felt sure he would find a door that would open. That at the near end was free, and he leaped out on to the track. As he passed he shouted to one of the attendants to follow him, and to the other to remain where he was and let no one pass. Then he joined the men who had already alighted, warned them about the up-train, and the four opened the outside door of the compartment in which the tragedy had taken place.

Their first concern was to get the uninjured lady out, and
here a difficult and ghastly task awaited them. The door
was blocked by the bodies, and its narrowness prevented
more than one man from working. Sending the car
attendant to search the train for a doctor, Jones clambered
up, and, after warning the lady not to look at what he
was doing, he raised the man's body and propped it back
in the corner seat.

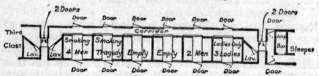

The face was a strong one with clean-shaven but rather
coarse features, a large nose, and a heavy jaw. In the
neck, just below the right ear, was a bullet hole which,
owing to the position of the head, had bled freely. As
far as the guard could see, the man was dead. Not without
a certain shrinking, Jones raised the feet, first of the man,
and then of the woman, and placed them on the seats, thus
leaving the floor clear except for its dark, creeping pool.
Then, placing his handkerchief over the dead woman's face,
he rolled back the end of the carpet to hide its sinister stain.

'Now, ma'am, if you please,' he said; and keeping the
lady with her back to the more gruesome object on the
opposite seat, he helped her to the open door, from where
willing hands assisted her to the ground.

By this time the attendant had found a doctor in the
third-class coach, and a brief examination enabled him to
pronounce both victims dead. The blinds in the compartment having been drawn down and the outside door

locked, the guard called to those passengers who had alighted to resume their seats, with a view to continuing their journey.

The fireman had meantime come back along the train to ascertain what was wrong, and to say the driver was unable completely to release the brake. An examination was therefore made, and the tell-tale disk at the end of the first-class coach was found to be turned, showing that someone in that carriage had pulled the communication chain. This, as is perhaps not generally known, allows air to pass between the train pipe and the atmosphere, thereby gently applying the brake and preventing its complete release. Further investigation showed that the slack of the chain was hanging in the end smoking-compartment, indicating that the alarm must have been operated by one of the four men who travelled there. The disk was then turned back to normal, the passengers reseated, and the train started, after a delay of about fifteen minutes.

Before reaching Carlisle, Guard Jones took the name and address of every one travelling in the first- and third-class coaches, together with the numbers of their tickets. These coaches, as well as the van, were thoroughly searched, and it was established beyond any doubt that no one was concealed under the seats, in the lavatories, behind luggage, or, in fact, anywhere about them.

One of the sleeping-car attendants having been in the corridor in the rear of the last sleeper from the Preston stop till the completion of this search, and being positive no one except the guard had passed during that time, it was not considered necessary to take the names of the passengers in the sleeping-cars, but the numbers of their tickets were noted.

On arrival at Carlisle the matter was put into the hands of the police. The first-class carriage was shunted off, the doors being locked and sealed, and the passengers who had travelled in it were detained to make their statements. Then began a most careful and searching investigation, as a result of which several additional facts became known.

The first step taken by the authorities was to make an examination of the country surrounding the point at which the train had stopped, in the hope of finding traces of some stranger on the line. The tentative theory was that a murder had been committed and that the murderer had escaped from the train when it stopped, struck across the country, and, gaining some road, had made good his escape.

Accordingly, as soon as it was light, a special train brought a force of detectives to the place, and the railway, as well as a tract of ground on each side of it, were subjected to a prolonged and exhaustive search. But no traces were found. Nothing that a stranger might have dropped was picked up, no footsteps were seen, no marks discovered. As has already been stated, the weather was against the searchers. The drought of the previous days had left the ground hard and unyielding, so that clear impressions were scarcely to be expected, while even such as might have been made were not likely to remain after the downpour of the early morning.

Baffled at this point, the detectives turned their attention to the stations in the vicinity. There were only two within walking distance of the point of the tragedy, and at neither had any stranger been seen. Further, no trains had stopped at either of these stations; indeed, not a single train, either passenger or goods, had stopped anywhere in the neighbourhood since the sleeping-car express went through. If the murderer had left the express, it was, therefore, out of the question that he could have escaped by rail.

The investigators then turned their attention to the country roads and adjoining towns, trying to find the trail —if there was a trail—while it was hot. But here, again, no luck attended their efforts. If there were a murderer, and if he had left the train when it stopped, he had vanished into thin air. No traces of him could anywhere be discovered.

Nor were their researches in other directions much more fruitful.

The dead couple were identified as a Mr. and Mrs. Horatio Llewelyn, of Gordon Villa, Broad Road, Halifax. Mr. Llewelyn was the junior partner of a large firm of Yorkshire ironfounders. A man of five-and-thirty, he moved in good society and had some claim to wealth. He was of kindly though somewhat passionate disposition, and, so far as could be learnt, had not an enemy in the world. His

firm was able to show that he had had business appointments in London on the Thursday and in Carlisle on the
Friday, so that his travelling by the train in question was
quite in accordance with his known plans.

His wife was the daughter of a neighbouring merchant,
a pretty girl of some seven - and - twenty. They had been
married only a little over a month, and had, in fact, only
a week earlier returned from their honeymoon. Whether
Mrs. Llewelyn had any definite reason for accompanying
her husband on the fatal journey could not be ascertained.
She also, so far as was known, had no enemy, nor could
any motive for the tragedy be suggested.

The extraction of the bullets proved that the same weapon
had been used in each case—a revolver of small bore and
modern design. But as many thousands of similar revolvers
existed, this discovery led to nothing.

Miss Blair-Booth, the lady who had travelled with the
Llewelyns, stated she had joined the train at Euston, and
occupied one of the seats next the corridor. A couple of
minutes before starting the deceased had arrived, and they
sat in the two opposite corners. No other passengers had
entered the compartment during the journey, nor had any
of the three left it; in fact, except for the single visit of
the ticket-collector shortly after leaving Euston, the door
into the corridor had not been even opened.

Mr. Llewelyn was very attentive to his young wife, and
they had conversed for some time after starting, then, after
consulting Miss Blair-Booth, he had pulled down the blinds
and shaded the light, and they had settled down for the
night. Miss Blair-Booth had slept at intervals, but each
time she wakened she had looked round the compartment,
and everything was as before. Then she was suddenly
aroused from a doze by a loud explosion close by.

She sprang up, and as she did so a flash came from
somewhere near her knee, and a second explosion sounded.
Startled and trembling, she pulled the shade off the lamp,
and then she noticed a little cloud of smoke just inside the
corridor door, which had been opened about an inch, and
smelled the characteristic odour of burnt powder. Swinging
round, she was in time to see Mr. Llewelyn dropping
heavily forward across his wife's knees, and then she

observed the mark on the latter's forehead and realized they had both been shot.

Terrified, she raised the blind of the corridor door which covered the handle and tried to get out to call assistance. But she could not move the door, and her horror was not diminished when she found herself locked in with what she rightly believed were two dead bodies. In despair she pulled the communication chain, but the train did not appear to stop, and she continued struggling with the door till, after what seemed to her hours, the guard appeared, and she was eventually released.

In answer to a question, she further stated that when her blind went up the corridor was empty, and she saw no one till the guard came.

The four men in the end compartment were members of one party travelling from London to Glasgow. For some time after leaving they had played cards, but, about midnight, they, too, had pulled down their blinds, shaded their lamp, and composed themselves to sleep. In this case also, no person other than the ticket-collector had entered the compartment during the journey. But after leaving Preston the door had been opened. Aroused by the stop, one of the men had eaten some fruit, and having thereby soiled his fingers, had washed them in the lavatory. The door then opened as usual. This man saw no one in the corridor, nor did he notice anything out of the common.

Some time after this all four were startled by the sound of two shots. At first they thought of fog signals, then, realizing they were too far from the engine to hear such, they, like Miss Blair-Booth, unshaded their lamp, raised the blind over their corridor door, and endeavoured to leave the compartment. Like her, they found themselves unable to open their door, and, like her also, they saw that there was no one in the corridor. Believing something serious had happened, they pulled the communication chain, at the same time lowering the outside window and waving from it in the hope of attracting attention. The chain came down easily as if slack, and this explained the apparent contradiction between Miss Blair-Booth's statement that she had pulled it, and the fact that the slack was found hanging in the end compartment. Evidently the lady had pulled it first, applying the brake, and the second pull had simply transferred the slack from one compartment to the next.

The two compartments in front of that of the tragedy were found to be empty when the train stopped, but in the last of the non-smoking compartments were two gentlemen, and in the 'Ladies Only,' three ladies. All these had heard the shots, but so faintly above the noise of the train that the attention of none of them was specially arrested, nor had they attempted any investigation. The gentlemen had not left their compartment or pulled up their blinds between the time the train left Preston and the emergency stop, and could throw no light whatever on the matter.

The three ladies in the end compartment were a mother and two daughters, and had got in at Preston. As they were alighting at Carlisle they had not wished to sleep, so they had left their blinds up and their light unshaded. Two of them were reading, but the third was seated at the corridor side, and this lady stated positively that no one except the guard had passed while they were in the train.

She described his movements—first, towards the engine, secondly, back towards the van, and a third time, running, towards the engine after the train had stopped—so accurately in accord with the other evidence that considerable reliance was placed on her testimony. The stoppage and the guard's haste had aroused her interest, and all three ladies had immediately come out into the corridor, and had remained there till the train proceeded, and all three were satisfied that no one else had passed during that time.

An examination of the doors which had jammed so mysteriously revealed the fact that a small wooden wedge, evidently designed for the purpose, had been driven in between the floor and the bottom of the framing of the door, holding the latter rigid. It was evident therefore that the crime was premeditated, and the details had been carefully worked out beforehand. The most careful search of the carriage failed to reveal any other suspicious object or mark.

On comparing the tickets issued with those held by the passengers, a discrepancy was discovered. All were accounted for except one. A first single for Glasgow had been issued at Euston for the train in question, which had not been collected. The purchaser had therefore either not travelled at all, or had got out at some intermediate station. In either case no demand for a refund had been made.

The collector who had checked the tickets after the train left London believed, though he could not speak positively, that two men had then occupied the non-smoking compartment next to that in which the tragedy had occurred, one of whom held a Glasgow ticket, and the other a ticket for an intermediate station. He could not recollect which station nor could he describe either of the men, if indeed they were there at all.

But the ticket-collector's recollection was not at fault, for the police succeeded in tracing one of these passengers, a Dr. Hill, who had got out at Crewe. He was able, partially at all events, to account for the missing Glasgow ticket. It appeared that when he joined the train at Euston, a man of about five-and-thirty was already in the compartment. This man had fair hair, blue eyes, and a full moustache, and was dressed in dark, well-cut clothes. He had no luggage, but only a waterproof and a paper-covered novel. The two travellers had got into conversation, and on the stranger learning that the doctor lived at Crewe, said he was alighting there also, and asked to be recommended to an hotel. He then explained that he had intended to go on to Glasgow and had taken a ticket to that city, but had since decided to break his journey to visit a friend in Chester next day. He asked the doctor if he thought his ticket would be available to complete the journey the following night, and if not, whether he could get a refund.

When they reached Crewe, both these travellers had alighted, and the doctor offered to show his acquaintance the entrance to the 'Crewe Arms,' but the stranger, thanking him, declined, saying he wished to see to his luggage. Dr. Hill saw him walking towards the van as he left the platform.

Upon interrogating the staff on duty at Crewe at the time, no one could recall seeing such a man at the van, nor had any inquiries about luggage been made. But as these facts did not come to light until several days after the tragedy, confirmation was hardly to be expected.

A visit to all the hotels in Crewe and Chester revealed the fact that no one in any way resembling the stranger had stayed there, nor could any trace whatever be found of him.

Such were the principal facts made known at the adjourned inquest on the bodies of Mr. and Mrs. Llewelyn. It was confidently believed that a solution to the mystery would speedily be found, but as day after day passed away without bringing to light any fresh information, public interest began to wane, and became directed into other channels.

But for a time controversy over the affair waxed keen. At first it was argued that it was a case of suicide, some holding that Mr. Llewelyn had shot first his wife and then himself; others that both had died by the wife's hand. But this theory had only to be stated to be disproved.

Several persons hastened to point out that not only had the revolver disappeared, but on neither body was there powder blackening, and it was admitted that such a wound could not be self-inflicted without leaving marks from this source. That murder had been committed was therefore clear.

Rebutted on this point, the theorists then argued that Miss Blair-Booth was the assassin. But here again the suggestion was quickly negatived. The absence of motive, her known character, and the truth of such of her statements as could be checked were against the idea. The disappearance of the revolver was also in her favour. As it was not in the compartment nor concealed about her person, she could only have rid herself of it out of the window. But the position of the bodies prevented access to the window, and, as her clothes were free from any stain of blood, it was impossible to believe she had moved these grim relics, even had she been physically able.

But the point that finally demonstrated her innocence was the wedging of the corridor door. It was obvious she could not have wedged the door on the outside and then passed through it. The belief was universal that whoever wedged the door fired the shots, and the fact that the former was wedged an inch open strengthened that view, as the motive was clearly to leave a slot through which to shoot.

Lastly, the medical evidence showed that if the Llewelyns were sitting where Miss Blair-Booth stated, and the shots were fired from where she said, the bullets would have entered the bodies from the direction they were actually found to have done.

But Miss Blair-Booth's detractors were loath to recede from the position they had taken up. They stated that of the objections to their theory only one—the wedging of the doors—was overwhelming. And they advanced an ingenious theory to meet it. They suggested that before leaving Preston Miss Blair-Booth had left the compartment, closing the door after her, that she had then wedged it, and that, on stopping at the station, she had passed out through some other compartment, re-entering her own through the outside door.

In answer to this it was pointed out that the gentleman who had eaten the fruit had opened his door *after* the Preston stop, and if Miss Blair-Booth was then shut into her compartment she could not have wedged the other door. That two people should be concerned in the wedging was unthinkable. It was therefore clear that Miss Blair-Booth was innocent, and that some other person had wedged both doors, in order to prevent his operations in the corridor being interfered with by those who would hear the shots.

It was recognized that similar arguments applied to the four men in the end compartment—the wedging of the doors cleared them also.

Defeated on these points the theorists retired from the field. No further suggestions were put forward by the public or the daily Press. Even to those behind the scenes the case seemed to become more and more difficult the longer it was pondered.

Each person known to have been present came in turn under the microscopic eye of New Scotland Yard, but each in turn had to be eliminated from suspicion, till it almost seemed proved that no murder could have been committed at all. The prevailing mystification was well summed up by the chief at the Yard in conversation with the inspector in charge of the case.

'A troublesome business, certainly,' said the great man, 'and I admit that your conclusions seem sound. But let us go over it again. There *must* be a flaw somewhere.'

'There must, sir. But I 've gone over it and over it till I 'm stupid, and every time I get the same result.'

'We 'll try once more. We begin, then, with a murder in a railway carriage. We 're sure it was a murder, of course?'

'Certain, sir. The absence of the revolver and of powder blackening and the wedging of the doors prove it.'

'Quite. The murder must therefore have been committed by some person who was either in the carriage when it was searched, or had left before that. Let us take these two possibilities in turn. And first, with regard to the searching. Was that efficiently done?'

'Absolutely, sir. I have gone into it with the guard and attendants. No one could have been overlooked.'

'Very good. Taking first, then, those who were in the carriage. There were six compartments. In the first were the four men, and in the second Miss Blair-Booth. Are you satisfied these were innocent?'

'Perfectly, sir. The wedging of the doors eliminated them.'

'So I think. The third and fourth compartments were empty, but in the fifth there were two gentlemen. What about them?'

'Well, sir, you know who they were. Sir Gordon M'Clean, the great engineer, and Mr. Silas Hemphill, the professor of Aberdeen University. Both utterly beyond suspicion.'

'But, as you know, inspector, *no one* is beyond suspicion in a case of this kind.'

'I admit it, sir, and therefore I made careful inquiries about them. But I only confirmed my opinion.'

'From inquiries I also have made I feel sure you are right. That brings us to the last compartment, the "Ladies Only." What about those three ladies?'

'The same remarks apply. Their characters are also beyond suspicion, and, as well as that, the mother is elderly and timid, and couldn't brazen out a lie. I question if the daughters could either. I made inquiries all the same, and found not the slightest ground for suspicion.'

'The corridors and lavatories were empty?'

'Yes, sir.'

'Then every one found in the coach when the train stopped may be definitely eliminated?'

'Yes. It is quite impossible it could have been any that we have mentioned.'

'Then the murderer must have left the coach?'

'He must; and that's where the difficulty comes in.'

'I know, but let us proceed. Our problem then really becomes—*how* did he leave the coach?'

'That's so, sir, and I have never been against anything stiffer.'

The chief paused in thought, as he absently selected and lit another cigar. At last he continued:

'Well, at any rate, it is clear he did not go through the roof or the floor, or any part of the fixed framing or sides. Therefore he must have gone in the usual way—through a door. Of these, there is one at each end and six at each side. He therefore went through one of these fourteen doors. Are you agreed, inspector?'

'Certainly, sir.'

'Very good. Take the ends first. The vestibule doors were locked?'

'Yes, sir, at both ends of the coach. But I don't count that much. An ordinary carriage key opened them and the murderer would have had one.'

'Quite. Now, just go over again our reasons for thinking he did not escape to the sleeper.'

'Before the train stopped, sir, Miss Bintley, one of the three in the 'Ladies Only,' was looking out into the corridor, and the two sleeper attendants were at the near end of their coach. After the train stopped, all three ladies were in the corridor, and one attendant was at the sleeper vestibule. All these persons swear most positively that no one but the guard passed between Preston and the searching of the carriage.'

'What about these attendants? Are they reliable?'

'Wilcox has seventeen years' service, and Jeffries six, and both bear excellent characters. Both, naturally, came under suspicion of the murder, and I made the usual investigation. But there is not a scrap of evidence against them, and I am satisfied they are all right.'

'It certainly looks as if the murderer did not escape towards the sleeper.'

'I am positive of it. You see, sir, we have the testimony of two separate lots of witnesses, the ladies and the attendants. It is out of the question that these parties would agree to deceive the police. Conceivably one or other might, but not both.'

'Yes, that seems sound. What, then, about the other end—the third-class end?'

'At that end,' replied the inspector, 'were Mr. and Mrs. Smith with their sick child. They were in the corridor close by the vestibule door, and no one could have passed without their knowledge. I had the child examined, and its illness was genuine. The parents are quiet persons, of exemplary character, and again quite beyond suspicion. When they said no one but the guard had passed I believed them. However, I was not satisfied with that, and I examined every person that travelled in the third-class coach, and established two things: first, that no one was in it at the time it was searched who had not travelled in it from Preston; and secondly, that no one except the Smiths had left any of the compartments during the run between Preston and the emergency stop. That proves beyond question that no one left the first-class coach for the third after the tragedy.'

'What about the guard himself?'

'The guard is also a man of good character, but he is out of it, because he was seen by several passengers as well as the Smiths running through the third-class after the brakes were applied.'

'It is clear, then, the murderer must have got out through one of the twelve side doors. Take those on the compartment side first. The first, second, fifth, and sixth compartments were occupied, therefore he could not have passed through them. That leaves the third and fourth doors. Could he have left by either of these?'

The inspector shook his head.

'No, sir,' he answered, 'that is equally out of the question.

You will recollect that two of the four men in the end compartment were looking out along the train from a few seconds after the murder until the stop. It would not have been possible to open a door and climb out on to the footboard without being seen by them. Guard Jones also looked out at that side of the van and saw no one. After the stop these same two men, as well as others, were on the ground, and all agree that none of these doors were opened at any time.'

'H'm,' mused the chief, 'that also seems conclusive, and it brings us definitely to the doors on the corridor side. As the guard arrived on the scene comparatively early, the murderer must have got out while the train was running at a fair speed. He must therefore have been clinging on to the outside of the coach while the guard was in the corridor working at the sliding doors. When the train stopped all attention was concentrated on the opposite, or compartment, side, and he could easily have dropped down and made off. What do you think of that theory, inspector?'

'We went into that pretty thoroughly, sir. It was first objected that the blinds of the first and second compartments were raised too soon to give him time to get out without being seen. But I found this was not valid. At least fifteen seconds must have elapsed before Miss Blair-Booth and the men in the end compartment raised their blinds, and that would easily have allowed him to lower the window, open the door, pass out, raise the window, shut the door, and crouch down on the footboard out of sight. I estimate also that nearly thirty seconds passed before Guard Jones looked out of the van at that side. As far as time goes he could have done what you suggest. But another thing shows he didn't. It appears that when Jones ran through the third-class coach, while the train was stopping, Mr. Smith, the man with the sick child, wondering what was wrong, attempted to follow him into the first-class. But the door slammed after the guard before the other could reach it, and, of course, the spring lock held it fast. Mr. Smith therefore lowered the end corridor window and looked out ahead, and he states positively no one was on the footboard of the first-class.

To see how far Mr. Smith could be sure of this, on a dark
night we ran the same carriage, lighted in the same way,
over the same part of the line, and we found a figure
crouching on the footboard was clearly visible from the
window. It showed a dark mass against the lighted side
of the cutting. When we remember that Mr. Smith was
specially looking out for something abnormal, I think we
may accept his evidence.'

'You are right. It is convincing. And, of course, it is
supported by the guard's own testimony. He also saw
no one when he looked out of his van.'

'That is so, sir. And we found a crouching figure was
visible from the van also, owing to the same cause —
lighted bank.'

'And the murderer could not have got out while the
guard was passing through the third-class?'

'No, because the corridor blinds were raised before the
guard looked out.'

The chief frowned.

'It is certainly puzzling,' he mused. There was silence
for some moments, and then he spoke again.

'Could the murderer, immediately after firing the shots,
have concealed himself in a lavatory and then, during
the excitement of the stop, have slipped out unperceived
through one of these corridor doors and, dropping on the
line, moved quietly away?'

'No, sir, we went into that also. If he had hidden in a
lavatory he could not have got out again. If he had gone
towards the third-class the Smiths would have seen him,
and the first-class corridor was under observation during
the entire time from the arrival of the guard till the search.
We have proved the ladies entered the corridor *immediately*
the guard passed their compartment, and two of the four
men in the end smoker were watching through their door
till considerably after the ladies had come out.'

Again silence reigned while the chief smoked thoughtfully.

'The coroner had some theory, you say?' he said at last.

'Yes, sir. He suggested the murderer might have,
immediately after firing, got out by one of the doors on
the corridor side—probably the end one—and from there
climbed on the outside of the coach to some place from

which he could not be seen from a window, dropping to the ground when the train stopped. He suggested the roof, the buffers, or the lower step. This seemed likely at first sight, and I tried therefore the experiment. But it was no good. The roof was out of the question. It was one of those high curved roofs—not a flat clerestory—and there was no hand-hold at the edge above the doors. The buffers were equally inaccessible. From the handle and guard of the end door to that above the buffer on the corner of the coach was seven feet two inches. That is to say, a man could not reach from one to the other, and there was nothing he could hold on to while passing along the step. The lower step was not possible either. In the first place it was divided—there was only a short step beneath each door—not a continuous board like the upper one—so that no one could pass along the lower while holding on to the upper, and secondly, I couldn't imagine any one climbing down there, and knowing that the first platform they came to would sweep him off.'

'That is to say, inspector, you have proved the murderer was in the coach at the time of the crime, that he was not in it when it was searched, and that he did not leave it in the interval. I don't know that that is a very creditable conclusion.'

'I know, sir. I regret it extremely, but that's the difficulty I have been up against from the start.'

The chief laid his hand on his subordinate's shoulder.

'It won't do,' he said kindly. 'It really won't do. You try again. Smoke over it, and I'll do the same, and come in and see me again to-morrow.'

But the conversation had really summed up the case justly. My Lady Nicotine brought no inspiration, and, as time passed without bringing to light any further facts, interest gradually waned till at last the affair took its place among the long list of unexplained crimes in the annals of New Scotland Yard.

And now I come to the singular coincidence referred to earlier whereby I, an obscure medical practitioner, came to learn the solution of this extraordinary mystery. With the case itself I had no connection, the details just given being taken from the official reports made at the time, to which I was allowed access in return for the information I brought. The affair happened in this way.

One evening just four weeks ago, as I lit my pipe after a long and tiring day, I received an urgent summons to the principal inn of the little village near which I practised. A motor cyclist had collided with a car at a cross-roads and had been picked up terribly injured. I saw almost at a glance that nothing could be done for him, in fact, his life was a matter of a few hours. He asked coolly how it was with him, and, in accordance with my custom in such cases, I told him, inquiring was there any one he would like sent for. He looked me straight in the eyes and replied:

'Doctor, I want to make a statement. If I tell it you will you keep it to yourself while I live and then inform the proper authorities and the public?'

'Why, yes,' I answered; 'but shall I not send for some of your friends or a clergyman?'

'No,' he said, 'I have no friends, and I have no use for parsons. You look a white man; I would rather tell you.'

I bowed and fixed him up as comfortably as possible, and he began, speaking slowly in a voice hardly above a whisper.

'I shall be brief for I feel my time is short. You remember some few years ago a Mr. Horatio Llewelyn and his wife were murdered in a train on the North-Western some fifty miles south of Carlisle?'

I dimly remembered the case.

'"The sleeping-car express mystery," the papers called it?' I asked.

'That's it,' he replied. 'They never solved the mystery and they never got the murderer. But he's going to pay now. I am he.'

I was horrified at the cool, deliberate way he spoke. Then I remembered that he was fighting death to make his confession and that, whatever my feelings, it was my business to hear and record it while yet there was time. I therefore sat down and said as gently as I could:

'Whatever you tell me I shall note carefully, and at the proper time shall inform the police.'

His eyes, which had watched me anxiously, showed relief.

'Thank you. I shall hurry. My name is Hubert Black,

and I live at 24 Westbury Gardens, Hove. Until ten years and two months ago I lived at Bradford, and there I made the acquaintance of what I thought was the best and most wonderful girl on God's earth—Miss Gladys Wentworth. I was poor, but she was well off. I was diffident about approaching her, but she encouraged me till at last I took my courage in both hands and proposed. She agreed to marry me, but made it a condition our engagement was to be kept secret for a few days. I was so mad about her I would have agreed to anything she wanted, so I said nothing, though I could hardly behave like a sane man from joy.

'Some time before this I had come across Llewelyn, and he had been very friendly, and had seemed to like my company. One day we met Gladys, and I introduced him. I did not know till later that he had followed up the acquaintanceship.

'A week after my acceptance there was a big dance at Halifax. I was to have met Gladys there, but at the last moment I had a wire that my mother was seriously ill, and I had to go. On my return I got a cool little note from Gladys saying she was sorry, but our engagement had been a mistake, and I must consider it at an end. I made a few inquiries, and then I learnt what had been done. Give me some stuff, doctor; I'm going down.'

I poured out some brandy and held it to his lips.

'That's better,' he said, continuing with gasps and many pauses: 'Llewelyn, I found out, had been struck by Gladys for some time. He knew I was friends with her, and so he made up to me. He wanted the introduction I was fool enough to give him, as well as the chances of meeting her he would get with me. Then he met her when he knew I was at my work, and made hay while the sun shone. Gladys spotted what he was after, but she didn't know if he was serious. Then I proposed, and she thought she would hold me for fear the bigger fish would get off. Llewelyn was wealthy, you understand. She waited till the ball, then she hooked him, and I went overboard. Nice, wasn't it?'

I did not reply, and the man went on:

'Well, after that I just went mad. I lost my head and

went to Llewelyn, but he laughed in my face. I felt I wanted to knock his head off, but the butler happened by, so I couldn't go on and finish him then. I needn't try to describe the hell I went through—I couldn't anyway. But I was blind mad, and lived only for revenge. And then I got it. I followed them till I got a chance, and then I killed them. I shot them in that train. I shot her first and then, as he woke and sprang up, I got him too.'

The man paused.

'Tell me the details,' I asked; and after a time he went on in a weaker voice:

'I had worked out a plan to get them in a train, and had followed them all through their honeymoon, but I never got a chance till then. This time the circumstances fell out to suit. I was behind him at Euston and heard him book to Carlisle, so I booked to Glasgow. I got into the next compartment. There was a talkative man there, and I tried to make a sort of alibi for myself by letting him think I would get out at Crewe. I did get out, but I got in again, and travelled on in the same compartment with the blinds down. No one knew I was there. I waited till we got to the top of Shap, for I thought I could get away easier in a thinly populated country. Then, when the time came, I fixed the compartment doors with wedges, and shot them both. I left the train and got clear of the railway, crossing the country till I came on a road. I hid during the day and walked at night till after dark on the second evening I came to Carlisle. From there I went by rail quite openly. I was never suspected.'

He paused, exhausted, while the Dread Visitor hovered closer.

'Tell me,' I said, 'just a word. How did you get out of the train?'

He smiled faintly.

'Some more of your stuff,' he whispered; and when I had given him a second dose of brandy he went on feebly and with long pauses which I am not attempting to reproduce:

'I had worked the thing out beforehand. I thought if I could get out on the buffers while the train was running and before the alarm was raised, I should be safe. No one looking out of the windows could see me, and when the train stopped, as I knew it soon would, I could drop down and make off. The difficulty was to get from the corridor to the buffers. I did it like this:

'I had brought about sixteen feet of fine, brown silk cord, and the same length of thin silk rope. When I got out at Crewe I moved to the corner of the coach and stood close to it by way of getting shelter to light a cigarette. Without any one seeing what I was up to I slipped the end of the cord through the bracket handle above the buffers. Then I strolled to the nearest door, paying out the cord, but holding on to its two ends. I pretended to fumble at the door as if it was stiff to open, but all the time I was passing the cord through the handle-guard, and knotting the ends together. If you 've followed me you 'll understand this gave me a loop of fine silk connecting the handles at the corner and the door. It was the colour of the carriage, and was nearly invisible. Then I took my seat again.

'When the time came to do the job, I first wedged the corridor doors. Then I opened the outside window and drew in the end of the cord loop and tied the end of the rope to it. I pulled one side of the cord loop and so got the rope pulled through the corner bracket handle and back again to the window. Its being silk made it run easily, and without marking the bracket. Then I put an end of the rope through the handle-guard, and after pulling it tight, knotted the ends together. This gave me a loop of rope tightly stretched from the door to the corner.

'I opened the door and then pulled up the window. I let the door close up against a bit of wood I had brought. The wind kept it to, and the wood prevented it from shutting.

'Then I fired. As soon as I saw that both were hit I got outside. I kicked away the wood and shut the door. Then with the rope for handrail I stepped along the footboard to the buffers. I cut both the cord and the rope and drew them after me, and shoved them in my pocket. This removed all traces.

'When the train stopped I slipped down on the ground. The people were getting out at the other side so I had only to creep along close to the coaches till I got out of their light, then I climbed up the bank and escaped.'

The man had evidently made a desperate effort to finish, for as he ceased speaking his eyes closed, and in a few minutes he fell into a state of coma which shortly preceded his death.

After communicating with the police I set myself to carry out his second injunction, and this statement is the result.

JOHN RHODE

THE ELUSIVE BULLET

'By the way, professor, there's something in the evening papers that might interest you,' said Inspector Hanslet, handing over as he spoke the copy he had been holding in his hand. 'There you are, "Prominent City Merchant found dead." Read it, it sounds quite interesting.'

Dr. Priestley adjusted his spectacles and began to read the paragraph. The professor and myself, Harold Merefield, who had been his secretary for a couple of years, had been sitting in the study of Dr. Priestley's house in Westbourne Terrace, one fine June evening after dinner, when Inspector Hanslet had been announced. The inspector was an old friend of ours, who availed himself of the professor's hobby, which was the mathematical detection of crime, to discuss with him any investigations upon which he happened to be engaged. He had just finished giving the professor an outline of a recent burglary case, over which the police had confessed themselves puzzled, and had risen to go, when the item in the newspaper occurred to him.

'This does not appear to me to be particularly interesting,' said the professor. 'It merely states that on the arrival of the 3.20 train this afternoon at Tilbury station a porter, in examining the carriages, found the dead body of a man, since identified as a Mr. Farquharson, lying in a corner of a first-class carriage. This Mr. Farquharson appears to have met his death through a blow on the side of the head, although no weapon capable of inflicting such a blow has so far been found. I can only suggest that if the facts are as reported, there are at least a dozen theories which could be made to fit in with them.'

'Such as?' inquired Hanslet tentatively.

The professor frowned. 'You know perfectly well, inspector, that I most strongly deprecate all conjecture,' he replied severely. 'Conjecture, unsupported by a thorough examination of facts, has been responsible for more than half the errors made by mankind throughout the ages. But, to demonstrate my meaning, I will outline a couple of theories which fit in with all the reported facts. Mr. Farquharson may have been struck by an assailant who left the train before its arrival at Tilbury, and who disposed of the weapon in some way. On the other hand, he may have leant out of the window, and been struck by some object at the side of the line, or even by a passing train, if he was at the right-hand side of the carriage, looking in the direction in which the train was going. Of course, as I wish to emphasize, a knowledge of *all* the facts, not only those contained in this brief paragraph, would probably render both these theories untenable.'

Hanslet smiled. He knew well enough from experience the professor's passion for facts and his horror of conjecture.

'Well, I don't suppose the case will come my way,' he said as he turned towards the door. 'But if it does I'll let you know what transpires. I shouldn't wonder if we know the whole story in a day or two. It looks simple enough. Well good night, sir.'

The professor waited till the front door had closed behind him. 'I have always remarked that Hanslet's difficulties are comparatively easy of solution, but that what he calls simple problems completely baffle his powers of reasoning. I should not be surprised if we heard from him again very shortly.'

As usual, the professor was right. Hanslet's first visit had been on Saturday evening. On the following Tuesday, at about the same time, he called again, with a peculiarly triumphant expression on his face.

'You remember that Farquharson business, don't you, professor?' he began without preliminary. 'Well, it did come my way, after all. The Essex police called Scotland Yard in, and I was put on to it. I've solved the whole thing in under forty-eight hours. Not a bad piece of work, eh? Mr. Farquharson was murdered by——'

Dr. Priestley held up his hand protestingly. 'My dear inspector, I am not the least concerned with the murderer of this Mr. Farquharson. As I have repeatedly told you, my interest in these matters is purely theoretical, and confined to the processes of deduction. You are beginning your story at the wrong end. If you wish me to listen to it, you must first tell me the full facts, then explain the course of your investigations, step by step.'

'Very well, sir,' replied Hanslet, somewhat crestfallen. 'The first fact I learnt was how Farquharson was killed. It appeared at first sight that he had been struck a terrific blow by some weapon like a pole-axe. There was a wound about two inches across on the right side of his head. But, at the post-mortem, this was found to have been caused by a bullet from an ordinary service rifle, which was found embedded in his brain.'

'Ah!' remarked the professor. 'A somewhat unusual instrument of murder, surely? What position did the body occupy in the carriage when it was found?'

'Oh, in the right-hand corner, facing the engine, I believe,' replied Hanslet impatiently. 'But that's of no importance, as you'll see. The next step, obviously, was to find out something about Farquharson, and why any one should want to murder him. The discovery of a motive is a very great help in an investigation like this. Farquharson lived with his daughter in a biggish house near a place called Stanford-le-Hope, on the line between Tilbury and Southend. On Saturday last he left his office, which is close to Fenchurch Street station, about one o'clock. He lunched at a restaurant near by, and caught the 2.15 at Fenchurch Street. As this was the train in which his dead body was found, I need hardly detail the inquiries by which I discovered these facts.'

The professor nodded. 'I am prepared to take your word for them,' he said.

'Very well, now let us come to the motive,' continued Hanslet. 'Farquharson was in business with his nephew, a rather wild young fellow named Robert Halliday. It seems that this young man's mother, Farquharson's sister, had a good deal of money in the business, and was very anxious that her son should carry it on after Farquharson's death. She died a couple of years ago, leaving rather a curious will, by which all her money was to remain in her brother's business, and was to revert to her son only at her brother's death.'

The professor rubbed his hands. 'Ah, the indispensable

motive begins to appear!' he exclaimed with a sarcastic smile. 'I am sure that you feel that no further facts are necessary, inspector. It follows, of course, that young Halliday murdered his uncle to secure the money. You described him as a wild young man, I think? Really, the evidence is most damning!'

'It''s all very well for you to laugh at me, professor,' replied Hanslet indignantly. 'I'll admit that you've given me a line on things that I couldn't find for myself, often enough. But in this case there's no possible shadow of doubt about what happened. What would you say if I told you that Halliday actually travelled in the very train in which his uncle's body was found?'

'Speaking without a full knowledge of the facts, I should say that this rather tended to establish his innocence,' said the professor gravely.

Hanslet winked knowingly. 'Ah, but that's by no means all,' he replied. 'Halliday is a Territorial, and he left London on Saturday afternoon in uniform, and carrying a rifle. It seems that, although he's very keen, he's a shocking bad marksman, and a member of a sort of awkward squad which goes down occasionally to Purfleet ranges to practise. Purfleet is a station between London and Tilbury. Halliday got out there, fired a number of rounds, and returned to London in the evening.'

'Dear, dear, I'm sorry for that young man,' remarked the professor. 'First we have a motive, then an opportunity. Of course, he travelled in the same carriage as his uncle, levelled his musket at his head, inflicted a fearful wound, and decamped. Why, there's hardly a weak link in the whole chain.'

'It wasn't quite as simple as that,' replied Hanslet patiently. 'He certainly didn't travel in the same carriage as his uncle, since that very morning they had quarrelled violently. Farquharson, who was rather a strict old boy, didn't approve of his nephew's ways. Not that I can find out much against him, but he's a bit of a young blood, and his uncle didn't like it. He travelled third class, and swears that he didn't know his uncle was on the train.'

'Oh, you have interviewed him already, have you?' said the professor quietly.

'I have,' replied Hanslet. 'His story is that he nearly missed the train, jumped into it at the last moment, in fact. Somewhere after Barking he found himself alone, and that's all he told me. When I asked him what he was doing scrambling along the footboard outside the train between Dagenham and Rainham, he became very confused, and explained that on putting his head out of the window he had seen another member of the awkward squad a few carriages away, and made up his mind to join him. He gave me the man's name, and when I saw him he confirmed Halliday's story.'

'Really, inspector, your methods are masterly,' said the professor. 'How did you know that he had been on the footboard?'

'A man working on the line had seen a soldier in uniform, with a rifle slung over his back, in this position,' replied Hanslet triumphantly.

'And you immediately concluded that this man must be Halliday,' commented the professor. 'Well, guesses must hit the truth sometimes, I suppose. What exactly is your theory of the crime?'

'It seems plain enough,' replied Hanslet. 'Halliday had watched his uncle enter the train, then jumped into a carriage close to his. At a predetermined spot he clambered along with his loaded rifle, shot him through the window, then, to avert suspicion, joined his friend, whom he had also seen enter the train, a little further on. It's as plain as a pikestaff to me.'

'So it appears,' remarked the professor dryly. 'What steps do you propose to take in the matter?'

'I propose to arrest Halliday at the termination of the inquest,' replied Hanslet complacently.

The professor made no reply to this for several seconds. 'I think it would be to everybody's advantage if you consulted me again before doing so,' he said at last.

A cloud passed for an instant over Hanslet's face. 'I will, if you think it would do any good,' he replied. 'But you must see for yourself that I have enough evidence to secure a conviction from any jury.'

'That is just what disquiets me,' returned the professor quickly. 'You cannot expect the average juryman to have an intelligence superior to yours, you know. I have your promise?'

'Certainly, if you wish it,' replied Hanslet rather huffily. He changed the subject abruptly, and a few minutes later he rose and left the house.

In the course of our normal routine I forgot the death of Mr. Farquharson entirely. It was not until the following afternoon, when Mary the parlourmaid entered the study with the announcement that a Miss Farquharson had called and begged that she might see the professor immediately, that the matter recurred to me.

'Miss Farquharson!' I exclaimed. 'Why, that must be the daughter of the fellow who was murdered the other day. Hanslet said he had a daughter, you remember.'

'The balance of probability would appear to favour that theory,' replied the professor acidly. 'Yes, I'll see her. Show Miss Farquharson in, please, Mary.'

Miss Farquharson came in, and the professor greeted her with his usual courtesy. 'To what do I owe the pleasure of this visit?' he inquired.

Miss Farquharson hesitated a moment or two before she replied. She was tall and fair, dressed in deep mourning, with an elusive prettiness which I, at least, found most attractive. And even before she spoke, I guessed something of the truth from the flush which suffused her face at the professor's question.

'I'm afraid you may think this an unpardonable intrusion,' she said at last. 'The truth is that Bob—Mr. Halliday—who is my cousin, has heard of you and begged me to come and see you.'

The professor frowned. He hated his name becoming known in connection with any of the investigations which he undertook, but in spite of all his efforts, many people had come to know of his hobby. Miss Farquharson took his frown for a sign of disapproval, and continued with an irresistible tone of pleading in her voice.

'It was only as a last hope I came to you,' she said. 'It's all so awful that I feel desperate. I expect you know that my father was found dead last Saturday in a train at Tilbury, while he was on his way home?'

The professor nodded. 'I am aware of some of the facts,'

he replied non-committally. 'I need not trouble you to repeat them. But in what way can I be of assistance to you?'

'It's too terrible!' she exclaimed with a sob. 'The police suspect Bob of having murdered him. They haven't said so, but they have been asking him all sorts of dreadful questions. Bob thought perhaps you might be able to do something——'

Her voice tailed away hopelessly under the professor's unwinking gaze.

'My dear young lady, I am not a magician,' he replied. 'I may as well tell you that I have seen Inspector Hanslet, who has what he considers a convincing case against your cousin.'

'But you don't believe it, do you, Doctor Priestley?' interrupted Miss Farquharson eagerly.

'I can only accept the inspector's statements as he gave them to me,' replied the professor. 'I know nothing of the case beyond what he has told me. Perhaps you would allow me to ask you a few questions?'

'Of course!' she exclaimed. 'I'll tell you everything I can.'

The professor inclined his head with a gesture of thanks. 'Was your father in the habit of travelling by the 2.15 train from Fenchurch Street on Saturday afternoons?'

'No,' replied Miss Farquharson with decision. 'Only when he was kept later than usual at the office. His usual custom was to come home to a late lunch.'

'I see. Now, can you tell me the reason for the quarrel between him and your cousin?'

This time Miss Farquharson's reply was not so prompt. She lowered her head so that we could not see her face, and kept silence for a moment. Then, as though she had made up her mind, she spoke suddenly.

'I see no harm in telling you. As a matter of fact, Bob and I have been in love with one another for a long time, and Bob decided to tell my father on Saturday morning. Father was rather old-fashioned, and he didn't altogether approve of Bob. Not that there was any harm in anything he did, but father couldn't understand that a young man liked to amuse himself. There was quite a scene when Bob told him, and father refused to hear anything about it until Bob had reformed, as he put it. But I know that Bob didn't kill him,' she concluded entreatingly. 'It's impossible for anybody who knew him to believe he could. You don't believe it, do you?'

'No, I do not believe it,' replied the professor slowly. 'If it is any consolation to you and Mr. Halliday, I may tell you in confidence that I never have believed it. When is the inquest to be?'

A look of deep thankfulness overspread her features. 'I am more grateful to you than I can say, Doctor Priestley,' she said earnestly. 'The inquest? On Saturday morning. Will you be there?'

The professor shook his head. 'No, I shall not be there,' he replied. 'You see, it is not my business. But I shall take steps before then to make certain inquiries. I do not wish to raise your hopes unduly, but it is possible that I may be able to divert suspicion from Mr. Halliday. More than that I cannot say.'

Tears of thankfulness came to her eyes. 'I can't tell you that this means to Bob and me,' she said. 'He has been terribly distressed. He quite understands that things look very black against him, and he cannot suggest who could have wanted to kill my father. Father hadn't an enemy in the world, poor dear.'

'You are sure of that?' remarked the professor.

'Quite,' she replied positively. 'I knew every detail of his life, he never hid the smallest thing from me.'

And after a further short and unimportant conversation she took her leave of us.

The professor sat silent for some minutes after her departure. 'Poor girl!' he said at last. 'To lose her father so tragically, and then to see the man she loved accused of his murder! We must see what we can do to help her, Harold. Get me the one-inch map of the country between London and Tilbury, and a time-table of the Southend trains.'

I hastened to obey him, and for an hour or more he pored over the map, working upon it with a rule and a protractor. At the end of this period he looked up and spoke abruptly.

'This is remarkably interesting, more so than I imagined at first it would be. Run out and buy me the sheets of the six-inch survey which cover Rainham and Purfleet. I think we shall need them.'

I bought the maps he required and returned with them. For the rest of the day he busied himself with these, and it was not until late in the evening that he spoke to me again.

'Really, my boy, this problem is beginning to interest me,' he said. 'There are many points about it which are distinctly baffling. We must examine the country on the spot. There is a train to Purfleet, I see, at 10.30 to-morrow morning.'

'Have you formed any theory, sir?' I inquired eagerly. The vision of Miss Farquharson, and her conviction of her cousin's innocence, had impressed me in her favour.

The professor scowled at me. 'How often am I to tell you that facts are all that matter?' he replied. 'Our journey to-morrow will be for the purpose of ascertaining facts. Until we know these, it would be waste of time to indulge in conjecture.'

He did not mention the subject again until the next morning, when we were seated in the train to Purfleet. He had chosen an empty first-class carriage, and himself took the right-hand corner facing the engine. He said nothing until the train was travelling at a good speed, and then he addressed me suddenly.

'You are a good shot with a rifle, are you not?' he inquired.

'I used to be pretty fair,' I replied in astonishment. 'But I don't think I've had a rifle in my hand since the war.'

'Well, take my stick, and hold it as you would a rifle. Now go to the far end of the carriage and lean against the door. That's right. Point your stick at my right eye, as though you were going to shoot at it. Stand like that a minute. Thank you, that will do.'

He turned away from me, took a pair of field-glasses from a case he was carrying, and began to survey the country through the window on his side. This he continued to do until the train drew up at Purfleet and we dismounted on to the platform.

'Ah, a lovely day!' he exclaimed. 'Not too warm for a little walking. We will make our first call at Purfleet ranges. This was where young Halliday came to do his shooting, you remember.'

We made our way to the ranges, and were lucky enough to find the warden at home. Dr. Priestley had, when he chose, a most ingratiating way with him, and he and the warden were very shortly engaged in an animated conversation.

'By the way,' inquired the professor earnestly, 'was there any firing going on here between half-past two and three on Saturday last?'

The range-warden scratched his head with a thoughtful expression on his face. 'Let me see, now, last Saturday afternoon? We had a squad of Territorials here on Saturday afternoon, but they didn't arrive till after three. Lord, they was queer hands with a rifle, some of them. Much as they could do to hit the target at all at three hundred. They won't never make marksmen, however hard they try.'

'Isn't it rather dangerous to allow such wild shots to fire at all?' suggested the professor.

'God bless your heart, sir, it's safe enough,' replied the range-warden. 'There's never been an accident the whole time I've been here. They can't very well miss the butts, and even if they did, there's nobody allowed on the marshes when firing's going on.'

'That is comforting, certainly,' said the professor. 'Apart from this squad, you had nobody else?'

The range-warden shook his head. 'No, sir, they was the only people on the range that day.'

'I suppose it is part of your duty to issue ammunition?' inquired the professor.

'As a rule, sir. But, as it happens, this particular squad always brings their own with them.'

The professor continued his conversation for a little longer, then prepared to depart.

'I'm sure I'm very much obliged to you,' he said as he shook hands. 'By the way, I believe there are other ranges about here somewhere?'

'That's right, sir,' replied the range-warden. 'Over yonder, beyond the butts. Rainham ranges, they're called.'

'Is there any objection to my walking across the marshes to them?'

'Not a bit, sir. There's no firing to-day. Just keep straight on past the butts, and you'll come to them.'

The professor and I started on our tramp, the professor pausing every hundred yards or so to look about him through his field-glasses and to verify his position on the map. We reached the Rainham ranges at last, discovered the warden, who fell under the influence of the professor's charm as readily as his colleague at Purfleet had done, and opened the conversation with him in much the same style.

'On Saturday afternoon last, between half-past two and three?' replied the warden to the professor's inquiry. 'Well, sir, not what you might call any shooting. There was a party from Woolwich, with a new sort of light machine-gun, something like a Lewis. But they wasn't shooting, only testing.'

'What is the difference?' asked the professor.

'Well, sir, by testing I mean they had the thing held in a clamp, so that it couldn't move. The idea is to keep it pointing in exactly the same direction, instead of wobbling about as it might if a man was holding it. They use a special target, and measure up the distance between the various bullet-holes on it when they 've finished.'

'I see,' replied the professor. 'I wonder if you would mind showing me where they were firing from?'

'Certainly, sir, it 's close handy.' The range-warden led us to a firing-point near by, and pointed out the spot on which the stand had been erected.

'That 's the place, sir. They were firing at number 10 target over yonder. A thousand yards it is, and wonderful accurate the new gun seemed. Shot the target to pieces, they did.'

The professor made no reply, but took out his map and drew a line upon it from the firing-point to the butts. The line, when extended, led over a tract of desolate marshes until it met the river.

'There is very little danger on these ranges, it appears,' remarked the professor, with a note of annoyance in his voice. 'If a shot missed the butts altogether, it could only fall into the river, far away from any frequented spot.'

'That 's what they were laid out for,' replied the range-warden. 'You see, on the other side there 's a house or two, to say nothing of the road and the railway. It wouldn't do to have any stray rounds falling among them.'

'It certainly would not,' replied the professor absently. 'I see by the map that Rainham station is not far beyond the end of the ranges. Is there any objection to my walking to it past the butts?'

'None at all, sir, it's the best way to get there when there's no firing on. Thank you, sir, it's been no trouble at all.'

We started to walk down the ranges, a puzzled frown on the professor's face. Every few yards he stopped and examined the country through his glasses, or pulled out the map and stared at it with an absorbed expression. We had reached the butts before he said a word, and then it was not until we had climbed to the top of them that he spoke.

'Very puzzling, very!' he muttered. 'There must, of couse, be some explanation. A mathematical deduction from facts can never be false. But I wish I could discover the explanation.'

He was looking through his field-glasses as he spoke, and suddenly his attention became riveted upon an object in front of him. Without waiting for me he hurried down the steep sides of the butts, and almost ran towards a flagstaff standing a couple of hundred yards on the far side of them. When he arrived at the base of it, he drew a couple of lines on the map, walked half round the flagstaff and gazed intently through his glasses. By the time I had caught up with him he had put the glasses back in their case, and was smiling benevolently.

'We can return to town by the next train, my boy,' he said cheerfully. 'I have ascertained everything I wished to know.'

He refused to say a word until our train was running into Fenchurch Street station. Then suddenly he turned to me.

'I am going to the War Office,' he said curtly. 'Will you go to Scotland Yard, see Inspector Hanslet, and ask him to come to Westbourne Terrace as soon as he can?'

I found Hanslet, after some little trouble, and gave him the professor's message.

'Something to do with the Farquharson business, I suppose?' he replied. 'Well, I'll come if the professor wants to see me. But I've got it all fixed up without his help.'

He turned up, true to his promise, and the professor greeted him with a pleasant smile.

'Good evening, inspector, I 'm glad you were able to come. Will you be particularly busy to-morrow morning?'

'I don't think so, professor,' replied Hanslet in a puzzled voice. 'Do you want me to do anything?'

'Well, if you can spare the time, I should like to introduce you to the murderer of Mr. Farquharson,' said the professor casually.

Hanslet lay back in his chair and laughed. 'Thanks very much, professor, but I 've met him already,' he replied. 'It would be a waste of your time, I 'm afraid.'

'Never mind,' said the professor, with a tolerant smile. 'I assure you that it will be worth your while to spend the morning with me. Will you meet me by the bookstall at Charing Cross at half-past ten?'

Hanslet reflected for a moment. The professor had never yet led him on a wild-goose chase, and it might be worth while to humour him.

'All right,' he replied reluctantly. 'I 'll come. But I warn you it 's no good.'

The professor smiled, but said nothing. Hanslet took his leave of us, and the professor appeared to put all thought of the Farquharson case out of his head.

We met again at Charing Cross the next day. The professor had taken tickets to Woolwich, and we got out of the train there and walked to the gates of the arsenal. The professor took an official letter out of his pocket, which he gave to the porter. In a few minutes we were led to an office, where a young officer rose to greet us.

'Good morning, Doctor Priestley,' he said. 'Colonel Conyngham rang me up to say that you were coming. You want to see the stand we use for testing the new automatic rifle? It happens to be in the yard below, being repaired.'

'Being repaired?' repeated the professor quickly. 'May I ask what is the matter with it?'

'Oh, nothing serious. We used it at Rainham the other day, and the clamp broke just as we were finishing a series. We had fired ninety-nine rounds out of a hundred, when the muzzle of the gun slipped up. I don't know what happened to the round. I suppose it went into the river somewhere. Beastly nuisance, we shall have to go down and start all over again.'

'Ah!' exclaimed the professor, in a satisfied tone. 'That explains it. But I wouldn't use number 10 target again, if I were you. Can we see this stand?'

'Certainly,' replied the officer. 'Come along.'

He led us into the yard, where a sort of tripod with a clamp at the head of it was standing. The professor looked at it earnestly for some moments, then turned to Hanslet.

'There you see the murderer of Mr. Farquharson,' he said quietly.

Of course Hanslet, the officer, and myself bombarded him with questions, which he refused to answer until we had returned to London and were seated in his study. Then, fixing his eyes upon the ceiling and putting the tips of his fingers together, he began.

'It was, to any intelligent man, perfectly obvious that there are half a dozen reasons why young Halliday could not have shot his uncle. In the first place, he must have fired at very close range, from one side or other of the carriage, and a rifle bullet fired at such a range, although it very often makes a very extensive wound of entry, does not stay in a man's brain. It travels right through his head, with very slightly diminished velocity. Next, if Halliday fired at his uncle at all, it must have been from the left-hand side of the carriage. Had he fired from the right-hand side, the muzzle of the weapon would have been almost touching his victim, and there would have been signs of burning or blackening round the wound. Do you admit this, inspector?'

'Of course,' replied Hanslet. 'My theory always has been that he fired from the left-hand side.'

'Very well,' said the professor quickly. 'Now Halliday is notoriously a very bad shot, hence his journey to Purfleet. Harold, on the contrary, is a good shot. Yet, during our expedition of yesterday, I asked him to aim at my right eye with a stick while the train was in motion. I found that never for an instant could he point the stick at it. I find it impossible to believe that a bad shot, firing from the footboard and therefore compelled to use one hand at least to retain his hold, could shoot a man on the far side of the carriage exactly on the temple.'

The professor paused, and Hanslet looked at him doubtfully.

'It all sounds very plausible, professor, but until you can produce a better explanation I shall continue to believe that my own is the correct one.'

'Exactly. It was to verify a theory which I had formed that I carried out my investigations. It was perfectly obvious to me, from your description of the wound, that it had been inflicted by a bullet very near the end of its flight, and therefore possessing only enough velocity to penetrate the skull without passing through it. This meant that it had been fired from a considerable distance away. Upon consulting the map, I discovered that there were two rifle ranges near the railway between London and Tilbury. I could not help feeling that the source of the bullet was probably one of these ranges. It was, at all events, a possibility worth investigating.

'But at the outset I was faced with what seemed an insuperable objection. I deduced from the map, a deduction subsequently verified by examination of the ground, that a round fired at any of the targets on either range would take a direction away from the railway. I also discovered that the only rounds fired while the train in which Mr. Farquharson's body was found was passing the ranges were by an experimental party from the arsenal. This party employed a special device which eliminated any inaccuracy due to the human element. At this point it occurred to me that my theory was incapable of proof, although I still adhered to my view that it was correct.'

The professor paused and Hanslet ventured to remark:

'I still do not see how you can prove that the breakage of the clamp could have been responsible,' he said. 'The direction of the bullet remained the same, and only its elevation was affected. By your own showing, the last shot fired from the machine must have landed in the marshes or the river.'

'I knew very well that notwithstanding the apparent impossibility, this must have been the bullet which killed Mr. Farquharson,' replied the professor equably. 'I climbed the butts behind the target at which the arsenal party had been firing, and while there I made an interesting discovery which solved the difficulty at once. Directly in line with number 10 target and some distance behind it was a flagstaff. Further, upon examination of this flagstaff I discovered that it was made of steel.

'Now the map had told me that there was only a short stretch of line upon which a train could be struck by a bullet deflected by this flagstaff. If this had indeed been the case, I knew exactly where to look for traces, and at my first inspection I found them. High up on the staff is a scar where the paint has recently been removed. To my mind the cause of Mr. Farquharson's death is adequately explained.'

Hanslet whistled softly. 'By Jove, there's something in it!' he exclaimed. 'Your theory, I take it, is that Farquharson was struck by a bullet deflected by the flagstaff?'

'Of course,' replied the professor. 'He was sitting on the right-hand side of the carriage, facing the engine. He was struck on the right side of the head, which supports the theory of a bullet coming through the open window. A bullet deflected in this way usually turns over and over for the rest of its flight, which accounts for the size of the wound. Have you any objection to offer?'

'Not at the moment,' said Hanslet cautiously. 'I shall have to verify all these facts, of course. For one thing, I must take the bullet to the arsenal and see if it is one of the same type as the experimental party were using.'

'Verify everything you can, certainly,' replied the professor. 'But remember that facts, not conjecture, are what should guide you.'

Hanslet nodded. 'I'll remember, professor,' he said. And with that he left us.

Two days later Mary announced Miss Farquharson and Mr. Halliday. They entered the room, and Halliday walked straight up to the professor and grasped his hand.

'You have rendered me the greatest service one man can render to another, sir!' he exclaimed. 'Inspector Hanslet tells me that all suspicion that I murdered my uncle has been cleared away, and that this is due entirely to your efforts.'

Before the professor could reply, Miss Farquharson ran up to him and kissed him impulsively. 'Doctor Priestley, you're a darling!' she exclaimed.

The professor beamed at her through his spectacles. 'Really, my dear, you make me feel quite sorry that you are going to marry this young man,' he said.

DOROTHY LEIGH SAYERS

THE IMAGE IN THE MIRROR

THE little man with the cow-lick seemed so absorbed in the book that Wimsey had not the heart to claim his property, but, drawing up the other arm-chair and placing his drink within easy reach, did his best to entertain himself with the Dunlop Book, which graced, as usual, one of the tables in the lounge.

The little man read on, his elbows squared upon the arms of his chair, his ruffled red head bent anxiously over the text. He breathed heavily, and when he came to the turn of the page, he set the thick volume down on his knee and used both hands for his task. Not what is called 'a great reader,' Wimsey decided.

When he reached the end of the story, he turned laboriously back, and read one passage over again with attention. Then he laid the book, still open, upon the table, and in so doing caught Wimsey's eye.

'I beg your pardon, sir,' he said in his rather thin Cockney voice, 'is this your book?'

'It doesn't matter at all,' said Wimsey graciously, 'I know it by heart. I only brought it along with me because it 's handy for reading a few pages when you 're stuck in a place like this for the night. You can always take it up and find something entertaining.'

'This chap Wells,' pursued the red-haired man, 'he 's what you 'd call a very clever writer, isn't he? It 's wonderful how he makes it all so real, and yet some of the things he says, you wouldn't hardly think they could be really possible. Take this story now; would you say, sir, a thing like that could actually happen to a person, as it might be you—or me?'

Wimsey twisted his head round so as to get a view of the page.

'*The Plattner Experiment*,' he said; 'that 's the one about

266

the schoolmaster who was blown into the fourth dimension and came back with his right and left sides reversed. Well, no, I don't suppose such a thing would really occur in real life, though of course it 's very fascinating to play with the idea of a fourth dimension.'

'Well—' He paused and looked up shyly at Wimsey. 'I don't rightly understand about this fourth dimension. I didn't know there was such a place, but he makes it all very clear no doubt to them that know science. But this right-and-left business, now, I know that 's a fact. By experience, if you 'll believe me.'

Wimsey extended his cigarette-case. The little man made an instinctive motion towards it with the left hand and then seemed to check himself and stretched his right across.

'There, you see. I 'm always left-handed when I don't think about it. Same as this Plattner. I fight against it, but it doesn't seem any use. But I wouldn't mind that— it 's a small thing and plenty of people are left-handed and think nothing of it. No. It 's the dretful anxiety of not knowing what I mayn't be doing when I 'm in this fourth dimension or whatever it is.'

He sighed deeply.

'I 'm worried, that 's what I am, worried to death.'

'Suppose you tell me about it,' said Wimsey.

'I don't like telling people about it, because they might think I had a slate loose. But it 's fairly getting on my nerves. Every morning when I wake up I wonder what I 've been doing in the night and whether it 's the day of the month it ought to be. I can't get any peace till I see the morning paper, and even then I can't be sure. . . .

'Well, I 'll tell you, if you won't take it as a bore or a liberty. It all began—' He broke off and glanced nervously about the room. 'There 's nobody to see. If you wouldn't mind, sir, putting your hand just here a minute——'

He unbuttoned his rather regrettable double-breasted waistcoat and laid a hand on the part of his anatomy usually considered to indicate the site of the heart.

'By all means,' said Wimsey, doing as he was requested. 'Do you feel anything?'

'I don't know that I do,' said Wimsey. 'What ought I

to feel? A swelling or anything? If you mean your pulse, the wrist is a better place.'

'Oh, you can feel it *there*, all right,' said the little man. 'Just try the other side of the chest, sir.'

Wimsey obediently moved his hand across.

'I seem to detect a little flutter,' he said after a pause.

'You do? Well, you wouldn't expect to find it that side and not the other, would you? Well, that's where it is. I've got my heart on the right side, that's what I wanted you to feel for yourself.'

'Did it get displaced in an illness?' asked Wimsey sympathetically.

'In a manner of speaking. But that's not all. My liver's got round the wrong side, too, and my organs. I've had a doctor to see it, and he told me I was all reversed. I've got my appendix on my left side—that is, I had till they took it away. If we was private, now, I could show you the scar. It was a great surprise to the surgeon when they told him about me. He said afterwards it made it quite awkward for him, coming left-handed to the operation, as you might say.'

'It's unusual, certainly,' said Wimsey, 'but I believe such cases do occur sometimes.'

'Not the way it occurred to me. It happened in an air-raid.'

'In an air-raid?' said Wimsey aghast.

'Yes—and if that was all it had done to me I'd put up with it and thankful. Eighteen I was then, and I'd just been called up. Previous to that I'd been working in the packing department at Crichton's—you've heard of them, I expect—Crichton's for Admirable Advertising, with offices in Holborn. My mother was living in Brixton, and I'd come up to town on leave from the training-camp. I'd been seeing one or two of my old pals, and I thought I'd finish the evening by going to see a film at the Stoll. It was after supper—I had just time to get in to the last house, so I cut across from Leicester Square through Covent Garden Market. Well, I was getting along when wallop! A bomb came down it seemed to me right under my feet, and everything went black for a bit.'

'That was the raid that blew up Odham's, I suppose.'

'Yes, it was 28th January 1918.   Well, as I say, everything went right out.   Next thing as I knew, I was walking
in some place in broad daylight, with green grass all round
me, and trees, and water to the side of me, and knowing no
more about how I got there than the man in the moon.'

'Good Lord!' said Wimsey.   'And was it the fourth
dimension, do you think?'

'Well, no, it wasn't.   It was Hyde Park, as I come to see
when I had my wits about me.   I was along the bank of the
Serpentine and there was a seat with some women sitting on
it, and children playing about.'

'Had the explosion damaged you?'

'Nothing to see or feel, except that I had a big bruise on
one hip and shoulder as if I'd been chucked up against
something.   I was fairly staggered.   The air-raid had gone
right out of my mind, don't you see, and I couldn't imagine
how I came there, and why I wasn't at Crichton's.   I looked
at my watch, but that had stopped.   I was feeling hungry.
I felt in my pocket and found some money there, but it
wasn't as much as I should have had—not by a long way.
But I felt I must have a bit of something, so I got out of the
Park by the Marble Arch gate, and went into a Lyons.   I
ordered two poached on toast and a pot of tea, and while
I was waiting I took up a paper that somebody had left on
the seat.   Well, that finished me.   The last thing I remembered was starting off to see that film on the 28th—
and here was the date on the paper—30th January!   I'd
lost a whole day and two nights somewhere!'

'Shock,' suggested Wimsey.   The little man took the
suggestion and put his own meaning on it.

'Shock?   I should think it was.   I was scared out of my
life.   The girl who brought my eggs must have thought I
was barmy.   I asked her what day of the week it was, and
she said "Friday."   There wasn't any mistake.

'Well, I don't want to make this bit too long, because
that's not the end by a long chalk.   I got my meal down
somehow, and went to see a doctor.   He asked me what I
remembered doing last, and I told him about the film, and he
asked whether I was out in the air-raid.   Well, then it came
back to me, and I remembered the bomb falling, but nothing
more.   He said I'd had a nervous shock and lost my

memory a bit, and that it often happened and I wasn't to worry. And then he said he 'd look me over to see if I 'd got hurt at all. So he started in with his stethoscope, and all of a sudden he said to me:

'"Why, you keep your heart on the wrong side, my lad!"'

'"Do I?" said I. "That 's the first I 've heard of it."'

'Well, he looked me over pretty thoroughly, and then he told me what I 've told you, that I was all reversed inside, and he asked a lot of questions about my family. I told him I was an only child and my father was dead—killed by a motor lorry, he was, when I was a kid of ten—and I lived with my mother in Brixton and all that. And he said I was an unusual case, but there was nothing to worry about. Bar being wrong side round I was sound as a bell, and he told me to go home and take things quietly for a day or two.

'Well, I did, and I felt all right, and I thought that was the end of it, though I 'd overstayed my leave and had a bit of a job explaining myself to the R.T.O. It wasn't till several months afterwards the draft was called up, and I went along for my farewell leave. I was having a cup of coffee in the Mirror Hall at the Strand Corner House—you know it, down the steps?'

Wimsey nodded.

'All the big looking-glasses all round. I happened to look into the one near me, and I saw a young lady smiling at me as if she knew me. I saw her reflection, that is, if you understand me. Well, I couldn't make it out, for I had never seen her before, and I didn't take any notice, thinking she 'd mistook me for somebody else. Besides, though I wasn't so very old then, I thought I knew her sort, and my mother had always brought me up strict. I looked away and went on with my coffee, and all of a sudden a voice said quite close to me:

'"Hallo, Ginger—aren't you going to say good evening?"'

'I looked up and there she was. Pretty, too, if she hadn't been painted up so much.

'"I 'm afraid," I said, rather stiff, "you have the advantage of me, miss."

'"Oh, Ginger,' says she, "Mr. Duckworthy, and after that Wednesday night!" A kind of mocking way she had of speaking.

'I hadn't thought so much of her calling me Ginger, because that's what any girl would say to a fellow with my sort of hair, but when she got my name off so pat, I tell you it did give me a turn.

'"You seem to think we're acquainted, miss," said I.

'"Well, I should rather say so, shouldn't you?" she said.

'There! I needn't go into it all. From what she said I found out she thought she'd met me one night and taken me home with her. And what frightened me most of all, she said it had happened on the night of the big raid.

'"It *was* you," she said, staring into my face a little puzzled-like. "Of course it was you. I knew you in a minute when I saw your face in the glass."

'Of course, I couldn't say that it hadn't been. I knew no more of what I'd been and done that night than the babe unborn. But it upset me cruelly, because I was an innocent sort of lad in those days and hadn't ever gone with girls, and it seemed to me if I'd done a thing like that I ought to know about it. It seemed to me I'd been doing wrong and not getting full value for my money either.

'I made some excuse to get rid of her, and I wondered what else I'd been doing. She couldn't tell me farther than the morning of the 29th, and it worried me a bit wondering if I'd done any other queer things.'

'It must have,' said Wimsey, and put his finger on the bell. When the waiter arrived, he ordered drinks for two and disposed himself to listen to the rest of Mr. Duckworthy's adventures.

'I didn't think much about it, though,' went on the little man; 'we went abroad, and I saw my first corpse and dodged my first shell and had my first dose of the trenches, and I hadn't much time for what they call introspection.

'The next queer thing that happened was in the C.C.S. at Ypres. I'd got a blighty one near Caudry in September during the advance from Cambrai—half-buried, I was, in a mine explosion and laid out unconscious near twenty-four hours it must have been. When I came to, I was wandering about somewhere behind the lines with a nasty hole in my shoulder. Somebody had bandaged it up for me, but I hadn't any recollection of that. I walked a long way, not knowing where I was, till at last I fetched up in an aid-post. They fixed me up and sent me down the line to a base hospital. I was pretty feverish, and the next thing I knew, I was in bed with a nurse looking after me. The bloke in the next bed to mine was asleep. I got talking to a chap in the next bed beyond him, and he told where I was, when all of a sudden the other man woke up and says:

'"My God," he says, "you dirty ginger-haired swine, it's you, is it? What have you done with them vallables?"

'I tell you, I was struck all of a heap. Never seen the man in my life. But he went on at me and made such a row, the nurse came running in to see what was up. All the men were sitting up in bed listening—you never saw anything like it.

'The upshot was, as soon as I could understand what this fellow was driving at, that he'd been sharing a shell-hole with a chap that he said was me, and that this chap and he had talked together a bit and then, when he was weak and helpless, the chap had looted his money and watch and revolver and what not and gone off with them. A nasty, dirty trick, and I couldn't blame him for making a row about it, if true. But I said and stood to it, it wasn't me, but some other fellow of the same name. He said he recognized me—said he and this other chap had been together a whole day, and he knew every feature in his face and couldn't be mistaken. However, it seemed this bloke had said he belonged to the Blankshires, and I was able to show my papers and prove I belonged to the Buffs, and eventually the bloke apologized and said he must have made a mistake. He died anyhow, a few days after, and we all agreed he must have been wandering a bit. The two divisions were fighting side by side in that dust-up and it was possible for them to get mixed up. I tried afterwards to find out whether by any chance I had a double in the Blankshires, but they sent me back home, and before I was fit again the Armistice was signed, and I didn't take any more trouble.

'I went back to my old job after the war, and things seemed to settle down a bit. I got engaged when I was twenty-one to a regular good girl, and I thought everything in the garden was lovely. And then, one day—up it all went! My mother was dead then, and I was living by myself in lodgings. Well, one day I got a letter from my intended, saying that she had seen me down at Southend on the Sunday, and that was enough for her. All was over between us.

'Now, it was most unfortunate that I 'd had to put off seeing her that week-end, owing to an attack of influenza. It 's a cruel thing to be ill all alone in lodgings, and nobody to look after you. You might die there all on your own and nobody the wiser. Just an unfurnished room I had, you see, and no attendance, and not a soul came near me, though I was pretty bad. But my young lady she said as she had seen me down at Southend with another young woman, and she would take no excuse. Of course, I said, what was *she* doing down at Southend without me, anyhow, and that tore it. She sent me back the ring, and the episode, as they say, was closed.

'But the thing that troubled me was, I was getting that shaky in my mind, how did I know I hadn't been to Southend without knowing it? I thought I 'd been half-sick and half-asleep in my lodgings, but it was misty-like to me. And knowing the things I had done other times—well, there! I hadn't any clear recollection one way or another, except fever-dreams. I had a vague recollection of wandering and walking somewhere for hours together. Delirious, I thought I was, but it might have been sleep-walking for all I knew. I hadn't a leg to stand on by the way of evidence. I felt it very hard, losing my intended like that, but I could have got over that if it hadn't been for the fear of myself and my brain giving way or something.

'You may think this is all foolishness and I was just being mixed up with some other fellow of the same name that happened to be very like me. But now I 'll tell you something.

'Terrible dreams I got to having about that time. There was one thing as always haunted me—a thing that had frightened me as a little chap. My mother, though she was a good, strict woman, liked to go to a cinema now and again. Of course, in those days they weren't like what they are now, and I expect we should think those old pictures pretty crude if we was to see them, but we thought a lot of them at that time.

'When I was about seven or eight I should think, she took me with her to see a thing—I remember the name now —*The Student of Prague*, it was called. I 've forgotten the story, but it was a costume piece, about a young fellow at the university who sold himself to the devil, and one day his reflection came stalking out of the mirror on its own, and went about committing dreadful crimes, so that everybody thought it was him. At least, I think it was that, but I forget the details, it 's so long ago. But what I shan't forget in a hurry is the fright it gave me to see that dretful figure come out of the mirror. It was that ghastly to see it, I cried and yelled, and after a time mother had to take me out.

'For months and years after that I used to dream of it. I 'd dream I was looking in a great long glass, same as the student in the picture, and after a bit I 'd see my reflection smiling at me and I 'd walk up to the mirror holding out my left hand, it might be, and seeing myself walking to meet me with its right hand out. And just as it came up to me, it would suddenly — that was the awful moment — turn its back on me and walk away into the mirror again, grinning over its shoulder, and suddenly I 'd know that *it* was the real person and *I* was only the reflection, and I 'd make a dash after it into the mirror, and then everything would go grey and misty round me and with the horror of it I 'd wake up all of a perspiration.'

'Uncommonly disagreeable,' said Wimsey. 'That legend of the *Doppelgänger*, it 's one of the oldest and the most widespread and never fails to terrify me. When *I* was a kid, my nurse had a trick that frightened me. If we 'd been out, and she was asked if we 'd met anybody, she used to say: "Oh, no—we saw nobody nicer than ourselves." I used to toddle after her in terror of coming round a corner and seeing a horrid and similar pair pouncing out at us. Of course, I 'd have rather died than tell a soul how the thing terrified me. Rum little beasts, kids.'

The little man nodded thoughtfully.

'Well,' he went on, 'about that time the nightmare came back. At first it was only at intervals, you know, but it grew on me. At last it started coming every night. I hadn't closed my eyes before there was the long mirror and the thing coming grinning along, always with its hand out as if it meant to catch hold of me and pull me through the glass. Sometimes I'd wake up with the shock, but sometimes the dream went on, and I'd be stumbling for hours through a queer sort of world—all mist and half-lights, and the walls would be all crooked, like they are in that picture of "Dr. Caligari." Lunatic, that's what it was. Many's the time I've sat up all night for fear of going to sleep. I didn't know, you see. I used to lock the bedroom door and hide the key for fear—you see, I didn't know what I might be doing. But then I read in a book that sleepwalkers can remember the places where they've hidden things when they were awake. So that was no use.'

'Why didn't you get someone to share the room with you?

'Well, I did.' He hesitated. 'I got a woman—she was a good kid. The dream went away then. I had blessed peace for three years. I was fond of that girl. Damned fond of her. Then she died.'

He gulped down the last of his whisky and blinked.

'Influenza, it was. Pneumonia. It kind of broke me up. Pretty she was, too. . . .

'After that, I was alone again. I felt bad about it. I couldn't — I didn't like — but the dreams came back. Worse. I dreamed about doing things — well! That doesn't matter now.

'And one day it came in broad daylight. . . .

'I was going along Holborn at lunch-time. I was still at Crichton's. Head of the packing department I was then, and doing pretty well. It was a wet beast of a day, I remember — dark and drizzling. I wanted a hair-cut. There's a barber's shop on the south side, about half-way along—one of those places where you go down a passage and there's a door at the end with a mirror and the name written across it in gold letters. You know what I mean.

'I went in there. There was a light in the passage, so I could see quite plainly. As I got up to the mirror I could see my reflection coming to meet me, and all of a sudden the awful dream-feeling came over me. I told myself it was all nonsense and put my hand out to the door-handle—my left hand, because the handle was that side and I was still apt to be left-handed when I didn't think about it.

'The reflection, of course, put out its right hand—that was all right, of course—and I saw my own figure in my old squash hat and burberry—but the face—oh, my God! It was grinning at me—and then just like in the dream, it suddenly turned its back and walked away from me, looking over its shoulder——

'I had my hand on the door, and it opened, and I felt myself stumbling and falling over the threshold.

'After that, I don't remember anything more. I woke up in my own bed and there was a doctor with me. He told me I had fainted in the street, and they'd found some letters on me with my address and taken me home.

'I told the doctor all about it, and he said I was in a highly nervous condition and ought to find a change of work and get out in the open air more.

'They were very decent to me at Crichton's. They put me on to inspecting their outdoor publicity. You know. One goes round from town to town inspecting the hoardings and seeing what posters are damaged or badly placed and reporting on them. They gave me a Morgan to run about in. I'm on that job now.

'The dreams are better. But I still have them. Only a few nights ago it came to me. One of the worst I've ever had. Fighting and strangling in a black, misty place. I'd tracked the devil—my other self—and got him down. I can feel my fingers on his throat now—killing myself.

'That was in London. I'm always worse in London. Then I came up here. . . .

'You see why that book interested me. The fourth dimension . . . it's not a thing I ever heard of, but this man Wells seems to know all about it. You're educated now. Dare say you've been to college and all that. What do you think about it, eh?'

'I should think, you know,' said Wimsey, 'it was more likely your doctor was right. Nerves and all that.'

'Yes, but that doesn't account for me having got twisted round the way I am, now, does it? Legends, you talked of. Well, there's some people think those medeeval johnnies knew quite a lot. I don't say I believe in devils and all that. But maybe some of them may have been afflicted, same as me. It stands to reason they wouldn't talk such a lot about it if they hadn't felt it, if you see what I mean. But what I 'd like to know is, can't I get back any way? I tell you, it 's a weight on my mind. I never know, you see.'

'I shouldn't worry too much, if I were you,' said Wimsey. 'I 'd stick to the fresh-air life. And I 'd get married. Then you 'd have a check on your movements, don't you see. And the dreams might go again.'

'Yes. Yes. I 've thought of that. But—did you read about that man the other day? Strangled his wife in his sleep, that 's what he did. Now, supposing I—that would be a terrible thing to happen to a man, wouldn't it? Those dreams. . . .'

He shook his head and stared thoughtfully into the fire. Wimsey, after a short interval of silence, got up and went out into the bar. The landlady and the waiter and the barmaid were there, their heads close together over the evening paper. They were talking animatedly, but stopped abruptly at the sound of Wimsey's footsteps.

Ten minutes later, Wimsey returned to the lounge. The little man had gone. Taking up his motoring coat, which he had flung on a chair, Wimsey went upstairs to his bedroom. He undressed slowly and thoughtfully, put on his pyjamas and dressing-gown, and then, pulling a copy of the *Evening News* from his motoring coat pocket, he studied a front page item attentively for some time. Presently he appeared to come to some decision, for he got up and opened his door cautiously. The passage was empty and dark. Wimsey switched on a torch and walked quietly along, watching the floor. Opposite one of the doors he stopped, contemplating a pair of shoes which stood waiting to be cleaned. Then he softly tried the door. It was locked. He tapped cautiously.

A red head emerged.

'May I come in a moment?' said Wimsey, in a whisper. The little man stepped back, and Wimsey followed him in. 'What 's up?' said Mr. Duckworthy.

'I want to talk to you,' said Wimsey. 'Get back into bed, because it may take some time.'

The little man looked at him, scared, but did as he was told. Wimsey gathered the folds of his dressing-gown closely about him, screwed his monocle more firmly into his eye, and sat down on the edge of the bed. He looked at Mr. Duckworthy a few minutes without speaking, and then said:

'Look here. You've told me a queerish story to-night. For some reason I believe you. Possibly it only shows what a silly ass I am, but I was born like that, so it's past praying for. Nice, trusting nature and so on. Have you seen the paper this evening?'

He pushed the *Evening News* into Mr. Duckworthy's hand and bent the monocle on him more glassily than ever.

On the front was a photograph. Underneath was a panel in bold type, boxed for greater emphasis:

'The police at Scotland Yard are anxious to get into touch with the original of this photograph, which was found in the handbag of Miss Jessie Haynes, whose dead body was found strangled on Barnes Common last Thursday morning. The photograph bears on the back the words "J. H. with love from R. D." Anybody recognizing the photograph is asked to communicate immediately with Scotland Yard or any police station.'

Mr. Duckworthy looked, and grew so white that Wimsey thought he was going to faint.

'Well?' said Wimsey.

'Oh, God, sir! Oh, God! It's come at last.' He whimpered and pushed the paper away, shuddering. 'I've always known something of this sort would happen. But as sure as I'm born I knew nothing about it.'

'It's you all right, I suppose?'

'The photograph's me all right. Though how it came there I *don't* know. I haven't had one taken for donkey's years, on my oath I haven't—except one in a staff group at Crichton's. But I tell you sir, honest-to-God, there's times when I don't know what I'm doing, and that's a fact.'

Wimsey examined the portrait feature by feature.

'Your nose, now—it has a slight twist—if you'll excuse my referring to it—to the right, and so it has in the photograph. The left eyelid droops a little. That's correct, too. The forehead here seems to have a distinct bulge on the left side—unless that's an accident in the printing.'

'No!' Mr. Duckworthy swept his tousled cow-lick aside.

'It's very conspicuous—unsightly, I always think, so I wear the hair over it.'

With the ginger lock pushed back, his resemblance to the photograph was more startling than before.

'My mouth's crooked, too.'

'So it is. Slants up to the left. Very attractive, a one-sided smile, I always think—on a face of your type, that is. I have known such things to look positively sinister.'

Mr. Duckworthy smiled a faint, crooked smile.

'Do you know this girl, Jessie Haynes?'

'Not in my right senses, I don't, sir. Never heard of her —except, of course, that I read about the murder in the papers. Strangled—oh, my God!' He pushed his hands out in front of him and stared woefully at them.

'What can I do? If I was to get away——'

'You can't. They've recognized you down in the bar. The police will probably be here in a few minutes. No—' as Duckworthy made an attempt to get out of bed—'don't do that. It's no good, and it would only get you into worse trouble. Keep quiet and answer one or two questions. First of all, do you know who I am? No, how should you? My name's Wimsey—Lord Peter Wimsey——'

'The detective?'

'If you like to call it that. Now, listen. Where was it you lived at Brixton?'

The little man gave the address.

'Your mother's dead. Any other relatives?'

'There was an aunt. She came from somewhere in Surrey, I think. Aunt Susan, I used to call her. I haven't seen her since I was a kid.'

'Married?'

'Yes—oh, yes—Mrs. Susan Brown.'

'Right. Were you left-handed as a child?'

'Well, yes, I was, at first. But mother broke me of it.'

'And the tendency came back after the air-raid. And were you ever ill as a child? To have the doctor, I mean?'

'I had measles once, when I was about four.'

'Remember the doctor's name?'

'They took me to the hospital.'

'Oh, of course. Do you remember the name of the barber in Holborn?'

This question came so unexpectedly as to stagger the wits of Mr. Duckworthy, but after a while he said he thought it was Biggs or Briggs.

Wimsey sat thoughtfully for a moment, and then said: 'I think that's all. Except—oh, yes! What is your Christian name?'

'Robert.'

'And you assure me that, so far as you know, you had no hand in this business?'

'That,' said the little man, 'that I swear to. As far as I know, you know. Oh, my Lord! If only it was possible to prove an alibi! That's my only chance. But I'm so afraid, you see, that I *may* have done it. Do you think—do you think they would hang me for that?'

'Not if you could prove you knew nothing about it,' said Wimsey. He did not add that, even so, his acquaintance might probably pass the rest of his life at Broadmoor.

'And you know,' said Mr. Duckworthy, 'if I'm to go about all my life killing people without knowing it, it would be much better that they should hang me and done with it. It's a terrible thing to think of.'

'Yes, but you may not have done it, you know.'

'I hope not, I'm sure,' said Mr. Duckworthy. 'I say— what's that?'

'The police, I fancy,' said Wimsey lightly. He stood up as a knock came at the door, and said heartily: 'Come in!'

The landlord, who entered first, seemed rather taken aback by Wimsey's presence.

'Come right in,' said Wimsey hospitably. 'Come in, sergeant; come in, officer. What can we do for you?'

'Don't,' said the landlord, 'don't make a row if you can help it.'

The police sergeant paid no attention to either of them, but stalked across to the bed and confronted the shrinking Mr. Duckworthy.

'It's the man all right,' said he. 'Now Mr. Duckworthy, you'll excuse this late visit, but as you may have seen by the papers, we've been looking for a person answering your description, and there's no time like the present. We want——'

'I didn't do it,' cried Mr. Duckworthy wildly. 'I know nothing about it——'

The officer pulled out his note-book and wrote: 'He said before any question was asked him: "I didn't do it."'

'You seem to know all about it,' said the sergeant.

'Of course he does,' said Wimsey; 'we 've been having a little informal chat about it.'

'You have, have you? And who might you be—sir?' The last word appeared to be screwed out of the sergeant forcibly by the action of the monocle.

'I 'm so sorry,' said Wimsey. 'I haven't a card on me at the moment. I am Lord Peter Wimsey.'

'Oh, indeed,' said the sergeant. 'And may I ask, my lord, what you know about this here?'

'You may, and I may answer if I like, you know. I know nothing at all about the murder. About Mr. Duckworthy I know what he has told me and no more. I dare say he will tell you, too, if you ask him nicely. But no third degree, you know, sergeant. No Savidgery.'

Baulked by this painful reminder, the sergeant said, in a voice of annoyance:

'It 's my duty to ask him what he knows about this.'

'I quite agree,' said Wimsey. 'As a good citizen, it 's his duty to answer you. But it 's a gloomy time of night, don't you think? Why not wait till the morning? Mr. Duckworthy won't run away.'

'I 'm not so sure of that.'

'Oh, but I am. I will undertake to produce him whenever you want him. Won't that do? You 're not charging him with anything, I suppose?'

'Not yet,' said the sergeant.

'Splendid. Then it 's all quite friendly and pleasant, isn't it. How about a drink?'

The sergeant refused this kindly offer with some gruffness in his manner.

'On the wagon?' inquired Wimsey sympathetically. 'Bad luck. Kidneys? Or liver, eh?'

The sergeant made no reply.

'Well, we are charmed to have had the pleasure of seeing you,' pursued Wimsey. 'You 'll look us up in the morning, won't you? I 've got to get back to town fairly early, but

I'll drop in at the police-station on my way. You will find Mr. Duckworthy in the lounge, here. It will be more comfortable for you than at your place. Must you be going? Well, good night, all.'

Later, Wimsey returned to Mr. Duckworthy, after seeing the police off the premises.

'Listen,' he said, 'I'm going up to town to do what I can. I'll send you up a solicitor first thing in the morning. Tell him what you've told me, and tell the police what he tells you to tell them and no more. Remember, they can't force you to say anything or to go down to the police-station unless they charge you. If they do charge you, go quietly and say nothing. And whatever you do, don't run away, because if you do, you're done for.'

Wimsey arrived in town the following afternoon, and walked down Holborn, looking for a barber's shop. He found it without much difficulty. It lay, as Mr. Duckworthy had described it, at the end of a narrow passage, and it had a long mirror in the door, with the name Briggs scrawled across it in gold letters. Wimsey stared at his own reflection distastefully.

'Check number one,' said he, mechanically setting his tie to rights. 'Have I been led up the garden? Or is it a case of fourth dimensional mystery? "The animals went in four by four, *vive la compagnie!* The camel he got stuck in the door." There is something intensely unpleasant about making a camel of oneself. It goes for days without a drink and its table-manners are objectionable. But there is no doubt that this door is made of looking-glass. Was it always so, I wonder? On, Wimsey, on. I cannot bear to be shaved again. Perhaps a haircut might be managed.'

He pushed the door open, keeping a stern eye on his reflection to see that it played him no trick.

Of his conversation with the barber, which was lively and varied, only one passage is deserving of record.

'It's some time since I was in here,' said Wimsey. 'Keep it short behind the ears. Been redecorated, haven't you?'

'Yes, sir. Looks quite smart, doesn't it?'

'The mirror on the outside of the door—that's new, too, isn't it?'

'Oh, no, sir. That's been there ever since we took over.'

'Has it? Then it's longer ago than I thought. Was it there three years ago?'

'Oh, yes, sir. Ten years Mr. Briggs has been here, sir.'

'And the mirror too?'

'Oh, yes, sir.'

'Then it's my memory that's wrong. Senile decay setting in. "All, all are gone, the old familiar landmarks." No, thanks, if I go grey I'll go grey decently. I don't want any hair-tonics to-day, thank you. No, nor even an electric comb. I've had shocks enough.'

It worried him, though. So much so that when he emerged, he walked back a few yards along the street, and was suddenly struck by seeing the glass door of a tea-shop. It also lay at the end of a dark passage and had a gold name written across it. The name was 'The BRIDGET Tea-shop,' but the door was of plain glass. Wimsey looked at it for a few moments and then went in. He did not approach the tea-tables, but accosted the cashier, who sat at a little glass desk inside the door.

Here he went straight to the point and asked whether the young lady remembered the circumstance of a man having fainted in the doorway some years previously.

The cashier could not say; she had only been there three months, but she thought one of the waitresses might remember. The waitress was produced, and after some consideration, thought she did recollect something of the sort. Wimsey thanked her, said he was a journalist— which seemed to be accepted as an excuse for eccentric questions—parted with half a crown, and withdrew.

His next visit was to Carmelite House. Wimsey had friends in every newspaper office in Fleet Street, and made his way without difficulty to the room where photographs are filed for reference. The original of the 'R. D.' portrait was produced for his inspection.

'One of yours?' he sakeed.

'Oh, no. Sent out by Scotland Yard. Why? Anything wrong with it?'

'Nothing. I wanted the name of the original photographer, that's all.'

'Oh! Well, you'll have to ask them there. Nothing more I can do for you?'

'Nothing, thanks.'

Scotland Yard was easy. Chief-Inspector Parker was Wimsey's closest friend. An inquiry of him soon furnished the photographer's name, which was inscribed at the foot of the print. Wimsey voyaged off at once in search of the establishment, where his name readily secured an interview with the proprietor.

As he had expected, Scotland Yard had been there before him. All information at the disposal of the firm had already been given. It amounted to very little. The photograph had been taken a couple of years previously, and nothing particular was remembered about the sitter. It was a small establishment, doing a rapid business in cheap portraits, and with no pretensions to artistic refinements.

Wimsey asked to see the original negative, which, after some search, was produced.

Wimsey looked it over, laid it down, and pulled from his pocket the copy of the *Evening News* in which the print had appeared.

'Look at this,' he said.

The proprietor looked, then looked back at the negative.

'Well, I'm dashed,' he said. 'That's funny.'

'It was done in the enlarging lantern, I take it,' said Wimsey.

'Yes. It must have been put in the wrong way round. Now, fancy that happening. You know, sir, we often have to work against time, and I suppose—but it's very careless. I shall have to inquire into it.'

'Get me a print of it right way round,' said Wimsey.

'Yes, sir, certainly, sir. At once.'

'And send one to Scotland Yard.'

'Yes, sir. Queer it should have been just this particular one, isn't it, sir? I wonder the party didn't notice. But we generally take three or four positions, and he might not remember, you know.'

'You'd better see if you've got any other positions and let me have them too.'

'I 've done that already, sir, but there are none. No doubt this one was selected and the others destroyed. We don't keep all the rejected negatives, you know, sir. We haven't the space to file them. But I 'll get three prints off at once.'

'Do.' said Wimsey. 'The sooner the better. Quick-dry them. And don't do any work on the prints.'

'No, sir. You shall have them in an hour or two, sir. But it 's astonishing to me that the party didn't complain.'

'It 's not astonishing,' said Wimsey. 'He probably thought it the best likeness of the lot. And so it would be—to him. Don't you see—that 's the only view he could ever take of his own face. That photograph, with the left and right sides reversed, is the face he sees in the mirror every day—the only face he can really recognize as his. "Wad the gods the giftie gie us," and all that.'

'Well, that 's quite true, sir. And I 'm much obliged to you for pointing the mistake out.'

Wimsey reiterated the need for haste, and departed. A brief visit to Somerset House followed; after which he called it a day and went home.

Inquiry in Brixton, in and about the address mentioned by Mr. Duckworthy, eventually put Wimsey on to the track of persons who had known him and his mother. An aged lady who had kept a small greengrocery in the same street for the last forty years remembered all about them. She had the encyclopaedic memory of the almost illiterate, and was positive as to the date of their arrival.

'Thirty-two years ago, if we lives another month,' she said. 'Michaelmas it was they come. She was a nice-looking young woman, too, and my daughter, as was ex-pecting her first, took a lot of interest in the sweet little boy.'

'The boy was not born here?'

'Why, no, sir. Born somewheres on the south side, he was, but I remember she never rightly said where—only that it was round about the New Cut. She was one of the quiet sort and kep' herself to herself. Never one to talk, she wasn't. Why, even to my daughter, as might 'ave good reason for bein' interested, she wouldn't say much about 'ow she got through 'er bad time. Chlorryform she said she 'ad, I know, and she disremembered about it, but it 's my belief it 'ad gone 'ard with 'er and she didn't care to think overmuch about it. 'Er 'usband—a nice man 'e was, too—'e says to me: "Don't remind 'er of it, Mrs. 'Arbottle, don't remind 'er of it." Whether she was frightened or whether she was 'urt by it I don't know, but she didn't 'ave no more children. "Lor!" I says to 'er time and again, "you 'll get used to it, my dear, when you 've 'ad nine of 'em same as me," and she smiled, but she never 'ad no more, none the more for that.'

'I suppose it does take some getting used to,' said Wimsey, 'but nine of them don't seem to have hurt *you*, Mrs. Harbottle, if I may so. You look extremely flourishing.'

'I keeps my 'ealth, sir, I am glad to say, though stouter than I used to be. Nine of them does 'ave a kind of spreading action on the figure. You wouldn't believe, sir, to look at me now, as I 'ad a eighteen-inch waist when I was a girl. Many 's the time me pore mother broke the laces on me, with 'er knee in me back and me 'olding on to the bed-post.'

'One must suffer to be beautiful,' said Wimsey politely. 'How old was the baby, then, when Mrs. Duckworthy came to live in Brixton?'

'Three weeks old, 'e was, sir—a darling dear—and a lot of 'air on 'is 'ead. Black 'air it was then, but it turned into the brightest red you ever see—like them carrots there. It wasn't so pretty as 'is ma's, though much the same colour. He didn't favour 'er in the face, neither, nor yet 'is dad. She said 'e took after some of 'er side of the family.'

'Did you ever see any of the rest of the family?'

'Only 'er sister, Mrs. Susan Brown. A big, stern, 'ard-faced woman she was—not like 'er sister. Lived at Evesham she did, as well I remembers, for I was gettin' my grass from there at the time. I never sees a bunch o' grass now but what I think of Mrs. Susan Brown. Stiff, she was, with a small 'ead, very like a stick o' grass.'

Wimsey thanked Mrs. Harbottle in a suitable manner and took the next train to Evesham. He was beginning to wonder where the chase might lead him, but discovered, much to his relief, that Mrs. Susan Brown was well known in the town, being a pillar of the Methodist Chapel and a person well respected.

She was upright still, with smooth, dark hair parted in the middle and drawn tightly back—a woman broad in the base and narrow in the shoulder—not, indeed, unlike the stick of asparagus to which Mrs. Harbottle had compared her. She received Wimsey with stern civility, but disclaimed all knowledge of her nephew's movements. The hint that he was in a position of some embarrassment, and even danger, did not appear to surprise her.

'There was bad blood in him,' she said. 'My sister Hetty was softer by half than she ought to have been.'

'Ah!' said Wimsey. 'Well, we can't all be people of strong character, though it must be a source of great satisfaction to those that are. I don't want to be a trouble to you, madam, and I know I'm given to twaddling rather, being a trifle on the soft side myself—so I'll get to the point. I see by the register at Somerset House that your nephew, Robert Duckworthy, was born in Southwark, the son of Alfred and Hester Duckworthy. Wonderful system they have there. But of course—being only human—it breaks down now and again—doesn't it?'

She folded her wrinkled hands over one another on the edge of the table, and he saw a kind of shadow flicker over her sharp dark eyes.

'If I'm not bothering you too much—in what name was the other registered?'

The hands trembled a little, but she said steadily:

'I do not understand you.'

'I'm frightfully sorry. Never was good at explaining myself. There were twin boys born, weren't there? Under what name did they register the other? I'm so sorry to be a nuisance, but it's really rather important.'

'What makes you suppose that there were twins?'

'Oh, I don't suppose it. I wouldn't have bothered you for a supposition. I know there was a twin brother. What became—at least, I do know more or less what became of him——'

'It died,' she said hurriedly.

'I hate to seem contradictory,' said Wimsey. 'Most unattractive behaviour. But it didn't die, you know. In fact, it 's alive now. It 's only the name I want to know, you know.'

'And why should I tell you anything, young man?'

'Because,' said Wimsey, 'if you will pardon the mention of anything so disagreeable to a refined taste, there 's been a murder committed and your nephew Robert is suspected. As a matter of fact, I happen to know that the murder was done by the brother. That 's why I want to get hold of him, don't you see. It would be such a relief to my mind— I am naturally nice-minded—if you would help me to find him. Because, if not, I shall have to go to the police, and then you might be subpoena'd as a witness, and I shouldn't like—I really shouldn't like—to see you in the witness-box at a murder trial. So much unpleasant publicity, don't you know. Whereas if we can lay hands on the brother quickly, you and Robert need never come into it all.'

Mrs. Brown sat in grim thought for a few minutes.

'Very well,' she said, 'I will tell you.'

'Of course,' said Wimsey to Chief-Inspector Parker a few days later, 'the whole thing was quite obvious when one had heard about the reversal of friend Duckworthy's interior economy.'

'No doubt, no doubt,' said Parker. 'Nothing could be simpler. But all the same, you are aching to tell me how you deduced it and I am willing to be instructed. Are all twins wrong-sided? And are all wrong-sided people twins?'

'Yes. No. Or rather, no, yes. Dissimilar twins and some kinds of similar twins may both be quite normal. But the kind of similar twins that result from the splitting of a single cell *may* come out as looking-glass twins. It depends on the line of fission in the original cell. You can do it artificially with tadpoles and a bit of horsehair.'

'I will make a note to do it at once,' said Parker gravely.

'In fact, I 've read somewhere that a person with a reversed inside practically always turns out to be one of t pair of similar twins. So you see, while poor old R. D. was burbling on about the *Student of Prague* and the fourth dimension, I was expecting the twin-brother.'

'Apparently what happened was this. There were three sisters of the name of Dart—Susan, Hester and Emily.

Susan married a man called Brown; Hester married a man called Duckworthy; Emily was unmarried. By one of those cheery little ironies of which life is so full, the only sister who had a baby, or who was apparently capable of having babies, was the unmarried Emily. By way of compensation, she overdid it and had twins.

'When this catastrophe was about to occur, Emily (deserted, of course, by the father) confided in her sisters, the parents being dead. Susan was a tartar—besides, she had married above her station and was climbing steadily on a ladder of good works. She delivered herself of a few texts and washed her hands of the business. Hester was a kind-hearted soul. She offered to adopt the infant, when produced, and bring it up as her own. Well, the baby came, and, as I said before, it was twins.

'That was a bit too much for Duckworthy. He had agreed to one baby, but twins were more than he had bargained for. Hester was allowed to pick her twin, and, being a kindly soul, she picked the weaklier-looking one, which was our Robert—the mirror-image twin. Emily had to keep the other, and, as soon as she was strong enough, decamped with him to Australia, after which she was no more heard of.

'Emily's twin was registered in her own name of Dart and baptized Richard. Robert and Richard were two pretty men. Robert was registered as Hester Duckworthy's own child—there were no tiresome rules in those days requiring notification of births by doctors and midwives, so one could do as one liked about these matters. The Duckworthys, complete with baby, moved to Brixton, where Robert was looked upon as being a perfectly genuine little Duckworthy.

'Apparently Emily died in Australia, and Richard, then a boy of fifteen, worked his passage home to London. He does not seem to have been a nice little boy. Two years afterwards, his path crossed that of Brother Robert and produced the episode of the air-raid night.

'Hester may have known about the wrong-sidedness of Robert, or she may not. Anyway, he wasn't told. I imagine that the shock of the explosion caused him to revert more strongly to his natural left-handed tendency. It also seems to have induced a new tendency to amnesia under similar shock-conditions. The whole thing preyed on his mind, and he became more and more vague and somnambulant.

'I rather think that Richard may have discovered the existence of his double and turned it to account. That explains the central incident of the mirror. I think Robert must have mistaken the glass door of the tea-shop for the door of the barber's shop. It really was Richard who came to meet him, and who retired again so hurriedly for fear of being seen and noted. Circumstances played into his hands, of course—but these meetings do take place, and the fact that they were both wearing soft hats and burberrys is not astonishing on a dark, wet day.

'And then there is the photograph. No doubt the original mistake was the photographer's, but I shouldn't be surprised if Richard welcomed it and chose that particular print on that account. Though that would mean, of course, that he knew about the wrong-sidedness of Robert. I don't know how he could have done that, but he may have had opportunities for inquiry. It was known in the army, and rumours may have got round. But I won't press that point.

'There's one rather queer thing, and that is that Robert should have had that dream about strangling, on the very night, as far as one could make out, that Richard was engaged in doing away with Jessie Haynes. They say that similar twins are always in close sympathy with one another —that each knows what the other is thinking about, for instance, and contracts the same illness on the same day and all that. Richard was the stronger twin of the two, and perhaps he dominated Robert more than Robert did him. I'm sure I don't know. Dare say it's all bosh. The point is that you've found him all right.'

'Yes. Once we'd got the clue there was no difficulty.'

'Well, let's toddle round to the Cri and have one.'

Wimsey got up and set his tie to rights before the glass.

'All the same,' he said, 'there's something queer about mirrors. Uncanny, a bit, don't you think so?'

HENRY WADE

A MATTER OF LUCK

IN the small, plainly furnished office which he occupied
in Jermyn Street, Mr. Isidore Cohen sat entering the day's
business in a flat ledger. Mr. Cohen was a small, sturdily
built man, with greying hair and small, neat hands. The
handwriting in the ledger was small and neat like the
hands, and the book as clean and well-kept as its owner's
person.

It was nearly 9 p.m., but Mr. Cohen never stopped work
until there was no more work to be done, and as he employed
no clerks, nobody was the worse for the long hours he kept.
Now, having completed his ledger, he remembered a letter
that had still to be written. Pulling out a piece of plainly-
stamped stationery, he began:

'DEAR SIR,

'With reference to your suggestion of a further
advance . . .'

A bell over the door whirred faintly. Mr. Cohen paused;
a slight frown on his brow. It was late; still, it was known
that he worked late and some clients thought odd hours
avoided publicity. He went down and opened the front
door. On the step stood a tall man wearing a dark overcoat and a soft hat.

'Good evening, Mr. Cohen. May I come in and have a
word with you?'

Recognizing a client, Cohen drew back, and, closing the
street door behind his visitor, led the way up to his office.

'Come in, Dr. Enterfield,' he said. 'Will you take a
chair, and a cigar?' He pushed a box across the table,
but his visitor shook his head and sank into the proffered
chair. By the brighter light of the room he could be seen
to be a strong, erect man of about forty, with crisp, dark

hair, grey eyes, and perfect teeth. His hands were lean
and muscular, with long, sensitive fingers.

'And to what may I attribute the pleasure of this
visit?' asked the Jew, dropping into his professional
formula.

Dr. Enterfield shifted in his chair.

'You remember, Mr. Cohen, that I spoke to you once
or twice about a patient of mine, a lady, who had asked me
about raising some money? People—especially women—
do ask their doctors curious things. Well, she 's definitely
asked me now to get you to come and see her and arrange
a loan.'

Cohen tapped his fingers on the blotter in front of him.

'I had hoped, doctor,' he said, 'that you had come to
make a repayment on your own loan. It hath been
running thome time, you know.'

'I know, I know. But you can't get blood out of a
stone. The practice is doing quite nicely as far as work 's
concerned, but I can't get my money in. These rich
people never think it necessary to pay their doctor.'

'You 've told me that before, doctor, and I 've given you
more time than I ought to. It can't go on; the end of this
month is the utmotht limit of time I can give you.'

Dr. Enterfield shrugged his shoulders.

'Yes, you 've told me that,' he said, 'and I 've told you
that you 're throwing your own money away if you fore-
close. I 've got a big future in front of me if I can make
a start. Still, you know your own business best, and anyway that 's not what I came to see you about. This Mrs.
Vaccont, of whom I 've been telling you, wants me to take
you out to see her to-night. She can't come here; she 's
bedridden—one of my best patients,' he added with a
grim smile.

Mr. Cohen showed some signs of uneasiness.

'But what doth she want?' he asked. 'I cannot go
with you to thome unknown place, with a lot of money
for thomeone I do not know.'

Enterfield laughed.

'Oh, you needn't be afraid,' he said. 'You 're not being
decoyed somewhere to be robbed and murdered. She
doesn't want any money at once, but she wants to see you

and discuss terms. And she wants you just this very
night. She's one of those hot-headed women who must
have what they want, when they want it—or they probably
won't have it at all. If you want this job, Cohen, I advise
you to come with me or it may drop. From the look of
her house, I should say there was plenty of security.'

'And why, doctor, are you tho keen that I should make
the little buthneth?'

'Because I want a commission. It'll act as some
instalment of my loan.'

'How much do you want?'

'Don't know. Don't know what money's in it. I'll
leave it to you to give me a fair commission. You're a
hard man, Cohen; I suppose in your business you've got
to be; but I think you're fair.'

The Jew smiled.

'Very well, I will come,' he said. 'Must just finish
thith letter. To thave time, look up in the directory the
address of Gordon, Kitchener & Co., thomewhere off
Regent Street.'

Cohen continued his interrupted letter and Enterfield
flicked over the pages of the telephone directory.

'This it?' he asked. 'Gordon, Kitchener & Co., Financial
Agents, 37 East Brook Street? Good old patriotic firm.'

Cohen smiled.

'They think it good for buthneth,' he said. 'I am a
Jew and a moneylender, and I call myself what I am:
Isidore Cohen, Moneylender. I think my clients trust me.
But others like to be deceived, so—Gordon, Kitchener.'

He sealed his letter and, picking the other letters from
his basket, put on his coat, scarf, and hat.

'You have a car?'

'Yes, on the park.'

Outside the door, Cohen slipped his letters into a pillar
box, then followed his guide down the hill towards St.
James's Square. As they came within sight of the close-
packed ring of cars that surrounded the railed-off grass,
Enterfield looked quickly to right and left. Away to the
right, the car attendant was superintending the backing of
a large car into a vacant space. Enterfield turned to the
left and, walking along the line of cars, stopped beside a

large Corland Eight coupé.   Turning the handle, he opened
the door, slipped into the driver's seat and pressed down
the self-starter.   The engine whirred into life.   Enterfield
pushed open the left-hand door and called to his companion, who was standing by the near front mudguard
with a look of astonishment on his face.

'Jump in.'

Mr. Cohen got in, and the car crept out of its place and
turned right-handed towards Lower Regent Street.   There
was a distant shout.

'Thomeone calling you, I think,' said Cohen.

'That's the car attendant who wants a shilling for not
watching my car,' replied his companion.   'Why, any one
might have driven off in it.'

Cohen chuckled.

'Quite right, my boy.   Don't throw your money away.
But thith car; she is *de luxe*—a rich man's car.   How ith it
that you, with your little difficulties, have a car like thith?'

'Not a bad little bus, is she?   Have to keep up appearances.   I got her second-hand for the price of a new
cheap model.'

Silently the Corland threaded its way up Lower Regent
Street, slipped across Piccadilly Circus, and was soon
rushing smoothly up a half-empty Regent Street.   Within
a few minutes it was into and out of Regent's Park and,
turning into one of the quiet side streets of St. John's
Wood, pulled up in front of a big, silent house, half-hidden
by intervening trees and shrubs.

'Here we are,' said Enterfield.   'I'll open the door
for you.'

He leant across his companion and the next moment
Mr. Cohen felt a searing pain, followed by a sharp blow in
his chest.   He gasped, heaved his body, and then his head
dropped forward on his breast.   Opening the dead man's
clothes, the doctor put his handkerchief against the wound,
then carefully withdrew the weapon (a small amputating
knife) and pressed together the edges of the wound.   It
would not bleed much anyhow—a heart wound—but he
did not want one drop upon himself or the car.   For a
minute or two he sat, holding the wound, then restarted
the car and drove on.

Regaining the main road at Swiss Cottage, the Corland swept up the Finchley Road and, turning into the new Hendon Way, leapt forward to the touch of its driver's foot, past Mill Hill and on to the Watford By-pass, where the speedometer crept quickly to eighty. There were wisps of fog about, and at the St. Albans cross-roads a freak of visibility caused Enterfield to miss seeing a crossing car till it was almost on him. The Corland's magnificent brakes saved a smash, but the other car rocked and groaned in agony. An A.A. man appeared from nowhere—he had not been controlling traffic—but again the quick pick-up of the Corland enabled Enterfield to slip off before the man reached the car. He switched off his lights for a second, so that his number couldn't be taken. Within a couple of minutes he turned off into a side road, and from that into what was little more than a grassy track, ending at a gate into a wood. Enterfield stopped the car and switched off the lights.

Ever since he had started reading detective stories at school, Enterfield had been intrigued by the problem of the disposal of the body—one of the vital problems of successful murder. After buying—with Cohen's money—his expensive practice in St. John's Wood, the doctor had got into the habit of keeping himself fit by long walks in the country on Sunday afternoons, and it was during the course of one of these that he had come across what seemed to him the ideal solution. In a small wood on the top of the high ground near Leavesden Green he had come across a brick funnel, about fifteen feet high. The smell of stale soot and a reference to his ordnance survey map showed him that it was an air-shaft to the tunnel of the disused branch line to Abbot's Langley which had been closed in the war. Further investigations had shown him that the two entrances to the tunnel had been closed.

When Mr. Cohen's pressure for repayment of his loan had reached a stage that indicated elimination as the only solution, Dr. Enterfield made the necessary preparations for making full use of his find. He now carried the body to the foot of the shaft, and, laying it carefully on the ground, began to poke about among the undergrowth. Almost at once he found and pulled out a roughly made

ladder of the necessary height—evidently knocked up on
the spot—and erected it against the brick shaft. Up it
he climbed, and with some difficulty removed the rusty
iron grating from the top, dropping it to the ground with
an unwelcome clatter. Then he climbed down, hoisted the
body carefully on to his shoulder and, mounting slowly
to the top, let the body fall down the shaft. After an
appreciable pause, there was a dull thud; Isidore Cohen's
body had reached a hiding-place where it might never
be found.

Replacing the grating and hiding the ladder, Enterfield
brushed his clothes, re-entered the car, and backed slowly
down the lane. In a minute he was racing back to London.
On the empty roads and through the empty streets he
was back in Regent Street in an incredibly short time.
Turning the car into the slip of roadway between Swan
& Edgar's and the Piccadilly Hotel, he pulled up, looked
quickly about him, slipped out of the car and, crossing
Piccadilly, was a minute later inserting Mr. Cohen's latch-
key into Mr. Cohen's door in Jermyn Street. All was quiet
in the house, but Enterfield tiptoed up the old stairs and,
opening the door of the office, closed it quietly behind him.

Drawing a torch from his pocket, Enterfield knelt down
in front of the safe in which he had only an hour ago seen
Cohen lock his ledger. His gloved hands sorted out the
obvious key and the safe swung open. There was the
ledger; a quick glance showed him his own name mentioned
in more than one place; it would be hopeless to try and
erase it—dangerously obvious. The whole book must go.
But it was the promissory note that he wanted, and it did
not take him long to find it, neatly docketed with scores
of others. He extracted it, and then a thought struck
him: was it safe, wise, to take only his own? Might it not
be better to take them all? Especially as the ledger had
got to go anyhow. What settled him was the thought
of the unexpected joy that his action would bring to a
hundred harassed men and women. It would make rather
a parcel, but he had got to carry the ledger anyhow, and
done up in brown paper—which he quickly found—he
could probably carry it under his coat without its being
noticed. A careful search in the safe revealed nothing else

likely to be of any danger. Personal accounts of Cohen's, bills, receipts, and a small ledger marked 'A. LEVI,' containing a list of names and amounts in no way corresponding with Cohen's own ledger.

Soon after 11 p.m. Dr. Enterfield let himself out again into Jermyn Street. Slipping down behind the Plaza Cinema, he emerged into Lower Regent Street just as the audience was beginning to pour from the picture-house. Forcing his way against the stream, he entered the cinema by the lower exit and, walking down the broad, soft-carpeted foyer, made his way out by the main entrance, where he stopped to say good night to the chief commissionaire, making some complimentary remarks on the show.

Out in Regent Street again, he strode quickly down to Waterloo Place, and, approaching the car park, began to roll up the muff of a modest Morris-Cowley. The attendant approached and Enterfield showed him his ticket.

'You've been over yer two hours, guv'nor,' said the man, pointing at the '8.40' scribbled on the ticket. 'I was afride the police 'd get yer.'

'Did you stave them off? Good fellow,' said Enterfield, slipping half a crown into the willing palm. Ten minutes later, the doctor was back in St. John's Wood, in a very modest side street. Locking his car into his small wooden garage, he let himself into his house, fetched a few papers from his study, drank a stiff whisky and water, and made his way down to the furnace room in the basement.

At 11.10 p.m. the same evening, No. 4354 P.C. Gellot strolled quietly into Vine Street Police Station and addressed the inspector in charge.

'There's been a car left standing in Air Street these last ten minutes at least, sir; no one in charge. I've waited for the owner, but no one's turned up. Shall I ring the Yard garage to send for it?'

'Give it another ten minutes and get the chap's name if he comes; if not by then, it must be fetched.'

P.C. Gellot gave the name and make of the car, and left. The inspector, entering the description in the Station Register, stopped.

'Isn't that the car reported missing from St. James's Square? Yes, I thought so.'

Taking his cap, he called to Sergeant Odlam to take charge and walked round to Air Street, a few yards away. P.C. Gellot, in the shadows, was awaiting the delinquent owner.

'This car's been pinched,' said Inspector Blatt. 'Bit of nerve leaving it at our back door. Lucky for you you found it, Gellot. I'm taking it round to the station.'

Slipping into the driver's seat, Inspector Blatt, with the silent efficiency of his profession, drove the big Corland round to the quiet alley in front of Vine Street Station. Fetching a powerful torch, he swept it over the inside of the car, but could find nothing illuminating. He had given up the search and had closed the near-side door, which was next the pavement, when he noticed a small spot on the running-board that showed a glint of red. Fetching an envelope, he carefully scraped off the spot and dropped it into the receptacle.

'Nothing in that—but you never know,' was his comment.

Eleven hours later, an elderly clerk with a harassed expression entered Vine Street and addressed the superintendent who was now in charge.

'My guv'nor's very worried about his partner, Mr. Isidore Cohen,' he said.

'Who are you and who's your guv'nor?' asked Superintendent Oliver, reaching for a pen.

'Gordon, Kitchener & Co., Financial Agents, we are, sir. My guv'nor's Mr. Samuel Samuels and I'm Sterson, chief clerk. Mr. Cohen's a partner in the business, but he's got another business in his own name in Jermyn Street. We had a most extraordinary letter from him this morning, posted in Jermyn Street at midnight last night. Addressed to the firm, but beginning as if it was meant for someone else and then going on in the most odd way. But here it is, sir.'

Mr. Sterson laid before the superintendent the letter which Mr. Cohen had been writing when he had been interrupted on the previous night and which he had finished and posted before going down to the car in St.

James's Square.   The envelope was addressed and stamped
as Sterson had stated.   The letter ran as follows:

'DEAR SIR,

 'With reference to your suggestion of a further
advance . . .

 'Sam. Wash out the above, it's the beginning of
another letter I was writing and I don't want to seem to
start a new one. Dr. Enterfield of 26 York Street,
St. John's Wood, a client of mine, has called to fetch
me out to what seems like a new bit of business in
St. John's Wood—a Mrs. Vaccont. It's probably all
right, but in case I don't come back you know who
I went with.

                                     'ISIDORE.'

 'And he's not come back?' queried the superintendent
calmly.

 'No, sir. Mr. Samuels sent me round at once and he's
not there, and the woman who comes to do for him at
seven says his bed's not been slept in.'

 The superintendent closed his note-book, placing the
letter in a pocket.

 'Right,' he said. 'I'll call on your guv'nor presently.'

 An hour later, Superintendent Oliver sat in Dr. Enterfield's consulting room in St. John's Wood. His official
card lay upon the doctor's table.

 'A Mr. Isidore Cohen, of 101A Jermyn Street, has disappeared. I came to ask you, doctor, when you last
saw him.'

 Enterfield felt an icy shudder course down his spine.
In a flash the thoughts passed through his brain: 'If I
acknowledge I know him, all point in destroying the papers
will be gone and even dangerous; if I deny it and he *knows*
I know him, it's even worse.' He took the risk.

 'I don't know who you're talking about,' he said quietly.

 'Come, sir,' said Oliver. 'You were seen leaving his
house with him late last night by the caretaker.'

 'The caretaker! There's . . .' Enterfield pulled himself up short.

Superintendent Oliver concealed a grim smile.

'You deny all knowledge of Mr. Cohen? I advise you to think carefully before you answer, sir.'

'There's nothing to think about, I tell you; I've never heard of the man.'

'Very well, sir; then I'm afraid I must ask you to come to Vine Street with me for further interrogation. I should say that we have definite proof that you knew Isidore Cohen.'

'But I've a string of patients waiting to see me.'

'Tell 'em you've got an urgent call. You might be back in an hour or so, if they like to wait. Mind, I say "might,"' added the superintendent significantly.

Five minutes after Dr. Enterfield and Superintendent Oliver had left the house, Detective-Sergeant Gray of C Division rang the bell.

'Dr. Enterfield in?'

'He's just been called away, sir; something urgent.'

'Oh, dear! Any idea when he'll be back?'

'Might be back in an hour, he said. There's a lot waiting to see him. You'd have to take your turn.'

'Oh, but it's most urgent. My wife. . . . I must see him as soon as he gets back. Look here, couldn't you put me straight into his surgery? Then I should short-circuit the others.'

A ten-shilling note fluttered and the parlourmaid fell.

Once in the doctor's consulting-room, and having assured himself that the maid was not listening, Gray set to work upon the hardest of all a detective's jobs—the quick, silent search through a mass of papers for something significant —a search, too, that must leave no trace of itself. For half an hour he worked, satisfied himself that what he was looking for did not any longer exist—at any rate in that room—rang the bell and explained that he must seek another doctor.

Returning to Vine Street, the detective found Inspector Blatt, back on duty, engaged in conversation with an angry gentleman.

'Yes, I know you've found the car! Hardly help finding it when they dropped it on your doorstep. But what I want to know is: Who 's the —— that pinched it? What all you policemen are up to, I can't think. You force us to park our cars in the most inconvenient places and then you let any Tom, Dick, or Harry come along and pinch 'em. Coolest thing I ever saw! Right under my nose. I was coming along from King Street and I saw a fellow standing in the roadway near where I had left my car—about a hundred yards away from me. Then he disappeared among the cars, and the next moment my car was driven out of the line and turned away right-handed. I shouted, but, of course, they paid no attention. The car attendant was half a mile away and, of course, there was no policeman. All busy taking bribes from——'

'Better not say that, sir,' cut in Inspector Blatt sharply. 'What did this chap you saw look like?'

'Short, stumpy fellow in a heavy overcoat—looked as as if it might have a fur collar; soft hat.'

'Doesn't sound much like the typical car-jumper, sir.'

'Well, he jumped mine all right. At least, I 'm not sure that he drove it. I have an idea that there were two chaps in the car when it went off.'

The irate owner having been shepherded out into the open air, Detective-Sergeant Gray, who had listened to the conversation, approached Inspector Blatt.

'That description of the car-jumper, sir; that was pretty well the description the Super gave me of Cohen. Short, stout, might be wearing a fur coat and soft hat.'

'Good Lord!' Inspector Blatt became thoughtful.

'Look here, Gray,' he said. 'I found a spot of blood on the near-side running-board of that stolen car. Didn't think anything of it at the time, but here it is.'

He drew the envelope from a drawer and showed the little cake of dried blood to the detective.

'And St. James's Square 's only a step from Jermyn Street,' said the latter. 'I must get on to this. Have you done anything about tracing the car, sir?'

'Nothing beyond a general information. After all, the car 's back, undamaged—it looked like a joke. We could waste a lot of time hunting for its movements. Still, of course, I agree that now it 's got to be traced.'

'I 'll do it, sir. If you 'll do the routine part—stiffen

up the information call?—I 'll try the odds and ends.
The car 's pretty sure to have started towards St. John's
Wood anyhow, to keep old Cohen from suspecting any-
thing.'

The detective walked across to the telephone and put a
call through to the A.A. Within a few minutes he had
struck oil. The traffic-control man at the St. Albans cross-
roads on the Watford By-pass reported a Corland Eight
coupé in a narrow escape from a collision just after 10 p.m.
as he was going off duty. There was no damage and the
driver of the Corland didn't seem to want to be stopped.
He had slipped off quick and doused his lights so that his
back number couldn't be seen. All the scout could give
was the make and body of the car and he thought there
were two men in it.

This was good going. Gray put through calls to the
police at Watford, King's Langley, Hemel Hempstead,
Berkhamsted, and St. Albans, to see if the car could be
traced going through any of those places after 10 p.m.
He doubted if it had, because of the time factor—it was
back in London by eleven. Then he took the tube to
Watford and, interviewing the local superintendent,
organized a search of the district over a radius of twenty
miles. Within an hour the tracks of the distinctive Corland
balloon tyres had been found in the lane near Leavesden
Green, and within another half-hour the body of Isidore
Cohen had been hoisted up from its brief resting-place.

Not a great deal was learnt from the body, when it was
found, though the neatness of the wound certainly pointed
to the work of an expert in anatomy. Sergeant Gray
realized that he had been extraordinarily lucky in getting
the evidence of the A.A. man, which had led him almost
directly to the body, but he also realized that it was by
such fortuitous and incalculable bits of luck—or bad luck
—that almost all murderers were convicted. The job was
now to *prove* Enterfield's connection with the dead man;
apart from Cohen's letter, there was so far no proof. The
complete disappearance of all papers connected with the
clientele of Cohen's business made it rather a difficult
matter. But Superintendent Oliver was no doubt attending
to that.

Superintendent Oliver, having got his man to Vine Street, produced Cohen's letter to Gordon, Kitchener & Co. Dr. Enterfield read it, shrugged his shoulders, and handed it back.

'Man must be daft,' he said.

'It 'll take some explaining, doctor,' said Oliver grimly. 'If you persist in denying any knowledge of Cohen, or of having been with him last night, don't you think you 'd better tell me what you *were* doing between, say, nine and eleven?'

'No difficulty about that; I was at the Plaza.'

'Oh, quite close by; what a coincidence! And when were you there?'

'I got there, I suppose, at about a quarter to nine, and left at the end of the show—soon after eleven, I should think.'

'How did you get there and back? Tube? Taxi?'

'No; I came in my own car; parked it in Waterloo Place.'

Superintendent Oliver's eyebrows rose slightly.

'Could you prove that?'

'Dunno. There 's a car attendant might remember me.'

'We 'll check it; do it now. We 'll have a taxi; I don't want to keep you longer than I can help.'

Rather to Enterfield's surprise, the same attendant was on duty—long hours, he thought, but profitable. The attendant at once recognized Enterfield.

'Ho, yus,' he said. 'I recollecks 'im well. Told 'im 'e was lucky not to get pinched for leavin' 'is car over two hours—the reg'lations. 'E come about a quarter afore nine and wasn't back 'ere till arter eleven. Well over 'is two hours 'e was.'

'What do you call well after eleven—half-past?'

'Ow, now; ow, now. Ten past at the ahtside. Just after the crowd come aht o' the Plaza. I can see 'em from 'ere, and it 's gener'ly five past eleven near as no matter. 'E might a' come aht with 'em, judging from the time 'e got 'ere.'

'He didn't tell you he had?'

'Now; I was just guessin'.'

The superintendent turned to Enterfield:

'You don't happen to have kept your parking ticket?'

The doctor thrust his hands into his overcoat pockets. ''Fraid not,' he said. 'Never occurred to me it might be wanted. Wait a minute, though; what's this?' His fingers were in his ticket pocket and he drew out a crumpled yellow form, opened it, and handed it to the superintendent, who glanced at it and put it calmly away in his note-book.

'Right,' he said. 'Now we'll just go and have a talk to the manager of the Plaza. We might walk that, I think.'

'Look here, superintendent,' said Enterfield, when the car attendant was out of earshot. 'I'm not sure that you're quite playing the game with me. Are you charging me with this murder, or not?'

'Not at the moment, sir. I'm just checking up your story. You can refuse if you like; perhaps you'd like to consult your solicitor?'

'Good Lord, no! I've nothing to consult about. But I can't afford to be away from my practice all day long, you know.'

'No, sir. I won't keep you much longer. Here we are.'

Within two minutes they were in the manager's office and Oliver was explaining what he wanted.

'This gentleman tells me that he was at your performance last night and I want to check up on that statement. I'd like to ask him to give an account of the film that he saw here and I want you, sir, to tell me whether it's correct.'

Enterfield laughed.

'Good Lord,' he said, 'that's a pretty stiff test! I'm not such a film fan that I listen to every word of stuff that's put across in a couple of hours.'

'No, sir, but if you were here you can give us an outline.'

'All right; I'll have a shot at it. There were two films and some odds and ends. The first film was New York Underworld. Young fellow up from the West gets drawn into a bootlegging fight between two rival gangs. He saves one of the leaders, gets him to his quarters and helps his girl to nurse him back to life. He falls in love with the girl, who apparently can't make up her mind which she likes best. The boss recovers, organizes an attack on his rival—good show that was, too, really exciting—and this time does get it in the neck for good. Happy ending for boy and girl.'

Oliver glanced at the manager, who nodded. 'A very neat précis,' he said.

'Then were were topicals,' went on Enterfield. 'Queen in a crèche in Whitechapel, England and France Rugger match, Lloyd George shaking hands with Betty Nuthall at a Charity Bazaar. I can't remember the rest. The last thing I couldn't make head or tail of. *Blazing Love* I think it was called. All legs and chorus girls taken from odd angles, and old gentlemen behind the scenes and a young fellow who got the sack for stamping on the leading man's toe when he was trying to be familiar with the last recruit to the chorus. Rather rot, I thought.'

The manager laughed.

'I 'm not surprised,' he said. 'It 's a wonder to me what the public like—but they do like it. There 's no doubt the gentleman was here, sir.'

'How many nights has the same show been on?'

'Last night was the fourth.'

'So, if he 'd been here one of the other nights he could have told the same story.'

'That is so.'

'Oh, come, superintendent,' broke in Enterfield, 'what 's the good of my proving anything to you? As a matter of fact I can prove I was here last night. I know the chief commissionaire; I had a chat to him as I came in.'

'Is he here? Can I see him?' asked Oliver sharply.

The manager rang a bell. Within a minute a tall, brilliantly-uniformed figure appeared, saluted the manager, and recognizing Enterfield with surprise, saluted him too. In answer to Superintendent Oliver's inquiries, he confirmed that he had seen and spoken to Dr. Enterfield when the latter bought a ticket and entered the cinema last night. As to time, he could not say exactly, but he thought about twenty minutes after the beginning of the last house—say, 8.45 to 8.50. He had also seen him leave at the end, soon after eleven. The commissionaire saluted and left. A thought struck Oliver.

'If Dr. Enterfield only came in twenty minutes after

the beginning of the last sequence of films, how could he describe the whole programme? He must have missed a large part of the New York film.'

Both men turned to Enterfield, who shrugged his shoulders. 'I missed the beginning of it, certainly, but there's no difficulty in reconstructing the early part; all these stories are alike.'

The manager acquiesced; it was quite possible for an intelligent frequenter of the films to make such a reconstruction of the beginning.

'Funny thing you didn't think of telling us you had at the time,' snarled the superintendent. 'I take it, manager, that there's nothing to have stopped him buying his seat, occupying it for five minutes and then going out on the other side?'

The manager, whose sympathy was now entirely with Enterfield, shrugged his shoulders.

'It is conceivable,' he said. 'You are hard to satisfy.'

'I know he wasn't here; that's why.'

Superintendent Oliver stumped out of the cinema.

'I shan't want you any more, Dr. Enterfield,' he said—'at present.'

'Thank you—for your courtesy,' replied the doctor.

Baffled, but dissatisfied, Superintendent Oliver made his way down Jermyn Street and, letting himself into Cohen's house with the caretaker's key, he made a thorough search of the dead man's rooms. He found nothing to interest him, unless it was a small ledger marked 'A. LEVI,' containing a long list of names, mostly Jewish, with notes as to amounts loaned and dates of repayment. The name of Enterfield did not appear in it. He slipped it in his pocket and returned to Vine Street. Here he found Detective-Sergeant Gray and received his report of the finding of the body.

'Still nothing to connect him with Enterfield,' he said, 'nothing except that letter, and I doubt if that'll be enough for a jury. He's got a good alibi; nothing like bullet-proof, but it sounds hellish convincing to an unsuspecting mind.'

'Anything more I can do, sir?' asked the eager Gray.

Oliver thought, then drew the 'A. LEVI' ledger from his pocket. 'Find out about that,' he said.

The detective took it, glanced through it, and retired to the telephone. Within ten minutes he had discovered that a moneylender of that name had a small office in Aldersgate. With a word of explanation to the superintendent, he disappeared.

For an hour or more Superintendent Oliver and Inspector Blatt continued to discuss the case in all its bearings.

'He's done it well, you know. Alibi carefully prepared —no doubt he saw that film a day or two ago. Stole a car so that his own couldn't be identified. Hid the body in a place where it was only found by a stroke of luck. Destroyed all evidence against himself in Cohen's office. Kept his head well to-day. But he's had bad luck. Cohen tricked him cleverly—wrote that letter under his nose, from the look of it. Then that collision and the A.A. man spotting the make of the car—sheer bad luck. It's those unforeseeable clues that give a clever murderer away every time.'

'Still, sir, he's not done yet,' said Inspector Blatt. 'There's nothing to confirm Cohen's letter in connecting him to Enterfield.'

'Something 'll turn up,' said Oliver.

Detective-Sergeant Gray walked quietly into the office.

'Mr. Cohen was a busy man, sir,' he said.

'How d' you mean?'

'He's not only "Isidore Cohen, Moneylender," but a partner in "Gordon, Kitchener & Co., Financial Agents."'

'Good Lord, man, I know that!'

'And two afternoons a week he's "Abraham Levi, Loans Arranged," in Aldersgate.'

Superintendent Oliver whistled.

'And he was a cautious gentleman, too, was Mr. Cohen. In his two businesses where there were no partners or clerks, he kept a duplicate register of the other business. In Isidore Cohen's office there was an outline register of Abe Levi's business.'

Superintendent Oliver leant forward eagerly.

'And in Abe Levi's office there was an outline register of Isidore Cohen's business.'

Detective-Sergeant Gray quietly laid a small ledger before his superior.

Oliver flicked over the pages.

'Ah! 18th January 1929. Dr. Richard Enterfield, £3,000. April. Dr. Enterfield, £500 due, not paid. July. £1,100 due. £300 paid. Oct. £1,300 due. £200 paid. Jan. 1930. £1,600 due. Nothing paid. Warning sent. February. Second warning sent. March. Final warning sent.'

Superintendent Oliver reached out his hand.

'Warrant form,' he said.

MILWARD KENNEDY

SUPERFLUOUS MURDER

As the train came to a standstill and he alighted from his carriage, John Mansbridge was amazed at the steadiness of his nerves. It was long since he had felt so calm and serene. Perhaps it was because he had reached a definite decision, after weeks of agonized doubt and fear. And yet his decision was not absolutely definite. He did not intend his visit to end in his cousin's murder if there was any hitch, however slight, in his careful yet simple plan.

In accordance with the plan, he engaged the ticket-collector in conversation about a mythical parcel which he pretended to have left on the platform on the occasion of his last visit, nearly a month ago. Naturally, he could get no news of it, but time enough was occupied to make him leave the station a clear five minutes after the few other passengers who had left the train at Gorse Hill had departed into the night.

'By Jove!' he said to the ticket-collector, looking up at the station clock, 'is it as late as that? My cousin, Mr. Felix Mansbridge, will be wondering what has become of me, and it will take me a good three-quarters of an hour to walk to his house.'

'All of that, sir, on a night like this,' said the ticket-collector, and bade him a good night which was the more cordial for the shilling which was slipped into his hand.

John Mansbridge stepped briskly out of the station and down the country road towards the village. So far, so good. He had clearly established two facts: to wit, the time when he had left the station, and his intention to make his way on foot to his cousin's house.

He walked rapidly to the village and stopped at the 'Four Feathers' to repeat his inquiry about his parcel—there was just a chance, he suggested, that he had left it there. Again he was at pains to establish the time of his visit; it was just on closing time, so he made his drink a short one. To himself he reflected that the whisky would put just the right edge on his judgment.

Then he went on his way, and at the far end of the village called a cheerful good night to the policeman on duty there. He smiled in the darkness to reflect that the police system was an integral part of his plan. In something under an hour's time the constable would be relieved, and his relief came down the lonely hill past Felix's house.

He walked on steadily, treading rather heavily to ensure that the policeman heard him, until he had turned the next corner. Then he took to his heels along the grass at the edge of the road, climbed a gate on the left, and doubled along a cart-track which led back to the other side of the village. He did not follow it to its end, but turned off across a smooth meadow and found his way without difficulty to a tumble-down shed. He pulled the door open and, drawing an electric torch from his pocket, flashed it on the interior before entering. He gave an involuntary sigh of satisfaction—the dust was undisturbed since his last visit; it seemed safe to assume that the presence of the bicycle had not been noticed.

He had taken great pains with that bicycle—bought it second-hand, and yet in good condition, with tyres well worn (so that they left no distinctive tracks) and yet with plenty of life in them. The dealer in the far-away Gloucestershire town who had sold it to him had taken no particular interest in the deal, and its transport to Gorse Hill had been effected by slow and unobtrusive stages—the last of them, to the abandoned shed, under the cover of darkness. The heap of loose sand inside the shed afforded an admirable means of covering up all signs of the use to which its shelter had been put.

He repeated his precautions, steeling himself against a tendency to hustle. The bicycle was carefully lifted out of the shed and leant against the wall; the heap of sand was used to conceal the marks of his feet; the heap itself was artistically arranged. Then he carried the bicycle to the footpath beyond the shed and mounted it.

Dark as the night was, he found it easy to follow the

track. Thanks to the drought, it was hard and firm and he made good speed. Not only that, he was confident that there would be few, if any, traces of his passage. The wind at his back also helped him on his course.

Nor did he hear or see a soul; the dogs, even, at the one farm-house which he passed at some distance on his right, failed, apparently, to detect him. Almost before he realized it, a dark shimmer told him he had reached his first objective, the pond. He dismounted and, wheeling the bicycle, made his way cautiously to the spot which he had previously marked down as suitable to his purpose—where the bank was covered with short, dry stubble and where, he knew, the water was nearly four feet deep up to the very edge.

He knelt and lowered the bicycle silently into the pond. It was a little more difficult than he had expected, but still, his plan worked smoothly. The bicycle certainly had disappeared; it would be invisible in the dirty water and soon would sink deep into the soft mud and slime. So far as he could judge, the surface weeds would not look as though they had been wilfully and rather drastically disturbed. Deliberately he did what he could to improve this impression.

But he could not afford to linger; on the second stage of his journey time was of vital importance. He left the footpath, skirted the far end of the pond, climbed another gate, and ran across the field beyond it. From the far side he came in sight of his cousin's house. A soft light shone from the windows of the study, but otherwise there was no sign of life. That was as it should be; the married couple who 'did' for Felix were away on holiday and he was being ministered to by a woman from the village who 'came in by the day.'

John Mansbridge hurried on till he reached the gate at the bottom of the garden. Here he forced himself to pause in order to recover his breath. His heart was pounding against his ribs—this he firmly ascribed to his physical efforts and not to excitement.

Very cautiously he pulled out his watch and flashed his torch on its face. Again he sighed, this time not so much in contentment as because Fate seemed to have committed

him to the deed. He had 'gained' a good twenty minutes
—in other words, he had reached the house some twenty-
two minutes before, on the evidence which he had created,
it was possible for him to have done so. He was satisfied
that he had arrived in entire secrecy, and it had taken him
two minutes less than he had allowed.

He opened the gate and closed it behind him so carefully
that the latch did not make a sound. He walked swiftly
up the path—or rather the grass border—until he came
to the lawn. He tiptoed across it towards the windows.
They were closed, and the thin red curtains drawn. He
leant close to the glass, though careful not to touch it, and
with a shock detected the sound of a voice which seemed
strange to him. Had all his plan split upon a single rock?

He crept round to the window at the other side. It was
open, and though this side was sheltered from the breeze,
the curtain had blown sufficiently aside to give him a
clear view of most of the room. Simultaneously his lips
smiled and his heart gave a fierce thump. The 'strange
voice' was that of the loudspeaker, delivering a lecture on
Babylonian pottery. Apparently it had had the effect of
sending Felix to sleep.

He was sitting in an arm-chair of the 'grandmother'
variety; its back was towards the door, so that it was
sideways to the window through which John Mansbridge
was peering. His bald head was lodged comfortably on a
cushion, and his eyes were closed. His thin hands clasped
the arms of the chair. He looked ill and tired, and his
cousin felt almost sorry for him, till he noticed also the
smug little smile on his lips. On the table beside him were
a tumbler and a reading-lamp and a paper or two. On a
table in the middle of the room stood a tray containing a
small whisky decanter, a siphon, and a couple more glasses.

Anger welled up in John Mansbridge. How infernally
comfortable and smug Felix was! Always so full of advice
and patronage, and at the same time as mean as sin.

All very well to 'advise you, my dear John, to settle
down to a steady job; give up the night club and melo-
drama existence.' As if he didn't know perfectly well that
if Felix wasn't so infernally afraid of hurting himself and
that heart which he pretended was so weak (as a matter of

fact, he probably hadn't got such a thing), he'd have been painting the world red himself. Except that he was so mean. Positively hurt him to spend a halfpenny. Always whining about having no money. Damn it, hadn't he, John, seen the old man's will? He knew damned well that Felix had inherited a fat fortune. And when his only living relative asked him for a hundred or two, to help things along, he said he couldn't do it. Paying off debts of his father's.

Damned lie, that's what it was. Enough to make any one—well—sign the wrong name on a cheque. It ought to teach Felix a lesson, but the chances were that it would lead him to suppose that a lecture on morality was called for. All very fine to be honest when you've got more money than you want, and hate spending any of it. Canting hypocrite, that's all Felix was; piously swearing he was a poor man. 'All I can do, John, is to carry a large insurance on my life. And I had to pay a stiff price for that—it was all I could do to get the company to accept me at all. My heart, you know. Still, I wanted to do what I could for you, and I'm not likely to live long.'

No, he was not likely to live long, but it wouldn't be his heart that finished him off. And when he wrote that note asking his cousin to come and see him one day next week about a 'cheque which he didn't quite understand,' he finally settled his own fate. If the shock of what his cousin said didn't polish him off then and there (which wasn't likely; nothing wrong with his heart at all), then something else would. And John Mansbridge felt almost grateful to his cousin for being so feeble and flabby; he wouldn't put up much of a fight even for his life.

These thoughts, of a kind which had haunted him for weeks, flashed through John Mansbridge's mind in the second or two which he spent at the window. They served to give him fresh strength and determination.

A new thought suddenly struck him. There was Felix, to all appearances fast alseep. If he crept in noiselessly enough, he might be able to finish him off there, in the chair. It would be easy to fake signs of a struggle afterwards. That Indian club hanging in the hall. But suppose Felix woke up and saw him? Well, it would only curtail the interview. True, he would be sorry not to fire off the speech he had rehearsed, but that was a small point. Damn it, he'd have a shot at it.

He crouched on the lawn and cautiously took off his shoes; he tied the laces together for ease in carrying. He slipped on the gloves which were in his pocket and drew out from his ticket-pocket the 'spare' latch-key which he had so successfully purloined when last he was down at Gorse Hill. He crept round to the front door, deposited his shoes on the doorstep and, with infinite precaution, slipped the key into the Yale lock. To his satisfaction the door opened silently. He dared not turn on the hall light, but there was sufficient illumination from the half-open door of the study to show him all that he needed to see.

There was a faint scrape as he withdrew the key. He paused, but no sound came from the study. A second later the front door was safely and securely closed again. He took down an Indian club (not the first, but the one by the door of the dining-room), and tried its weight with a savage grin. Slipping the door-key back into his pocket, he advanced silently into the study.

Felix had not stirred—a nice way to welcome your only cousin! There was his bald head temptingly visible above the back of the chair. John stepped forward and swung the club. . . .

That was that. All old scores wiped out. No need to make sure of the result—and no need to look at it. One had done things of the same kind in the war and felt none the worse. Funny what a difference there was, all the same. Still, no time to lose. No use getting sentimental. Find the cheque, that was the first thing. That ought not to be difficult—Felix would be sure to have it at hand, all ready for the interview; probably in the top drawer of the writing-desk. He jumped as he suddenly became conscious that the voice of the Babylonian expert filled the room, and with an oath he switched off the wireless. Now for the cheque.

But there was no forged cheque in the top drawer, and none in any other drawer of the desk. He began to tear envelopes open feverishly; pulled open the cupboard below the bookshelves; even ran up to Felix's bedroom. Where the hell could it be? He looked at his watch and a sick despair seized him. He had only seven minutes left before he must leave the house, and a lot had still to be done.

Good heavens, perhaps it was in Felix's pocket. What a fool not to think of it! Actually he *had* thought of it, but had thrust the idea aside; he didn't want to touch the body. Well, there was no help for it.

In the breast pocket was nothing but a pocket-book. Well, the notes would be useful, anyway. He took them, and thrust the pocket-book roughly back again. Then in the right hand side-pocket of the dinner-jacket his fingers detected an envelope. He pulled it out, and involuntarily gave a whistle of surprise. The envelope was addressed to himself, and the flap stuck down. He ripped it open. The cheque was inside, enclosed, apparently, in a letter. He heaved a sigh of relief, and thrust the envelope into his own pocket. He had meant to destroy the cheque then and there, but his programme must be slightly modified. The change involved only a very small risk.

He put the spare key back in the top drawer of the writing-table, from which he had originally purloined it; pushed it well to the back amongst some papers in case its loss had been discovered, and in order to suggest that it had been hidden in the drawer all the time. You could not be too careful of details. Then he went to the front door and wedged it carefully open with the door-mat. He went outside and with a stick from the hall smashed a pane of glass in the dining-room window. He thrust in his hand, unlatched the window, and opened it at the bottom. He returned to the house and again shut the front door. This time he brought his shoes in with him.

Hastily he pulled open the sideboard cupboard in the dining-room, seized some spoons and forks, rolled them roughly in a strip of green baize which was in the cupboard, and tossed the package on the table. That was good enough, he thought.

Then back into the study for the last and most unpleasant job.

He lifted his cousin's arm with a reluctant shudder, and turned back the hand of his wrist-watch until it pointed to about five minutes after the time when he, John, had left the pub in the village. He heaved his cousin's body out of the arm-chair and arranged it as well as he could to suggest that he had been standing by the fire-place when he was struck. He laid the body on its right side; the left arm he stretched roughly across the fender, and made sure that the blow had stopped the watch. He stood up again and surveyed the room. He knocked over a small chair, but decided that otherwise his own search had produced an excellent representation of a struggle. The club he left lying by the fire-place.

He looked at his watch. All was well. He was within his scheduled time again. He put on his shoes, tying the bows neatly, despite the involuntary trembling of his hands, and made his exit from the silent house by way of the open window in the dining-room. His jump carried him clear of the narrow flower-bed below the window, on to the flagged path leading from the gate to the front door. Then he ran round the house, back to the garden gate, across the paddock to the left, and so through a well-worn gap in the hedge, into the lane from the village. At this point it dipped between two hills. He took off and pocketed his gloves and then walked quickly on for about thirty yards up the hill in the direction of the village, keeping to the grass by the roadside. He stopped and drew from his pocket a pipe, tobacco-pouch, and a silver match-box. He filled his pipe and struck one of the wax vestas. The wind blew it out at once and he threw it aside. He used three others before his pipe was fairly alight, and then he began to walk slowly back, down the hill towards the house. He walked at the side of the road, and made a point of kicking his shoes on the loose stones. He ought to arrive with dusty shoes, and he was by no means anxious for his second approach to be as silent as his first.

He reached the gate and paused in some anxiety. The relieving constable was due to pass at any moment now. The direction of the wind for the first time became a slight disadvantage. However, he must take no risks. He walked to the front door, rang the bell, waited, and rang again. Then he knocked. After a further interval he walked back towards the gate and listened intently. To his joy, he caught the sound of footsteps. He ran back to the house and shouted, 'Felix! Felix!' in tones of increasing excitement. He heard the footsteps reach the gate and pause. 'Felix! Felix!' he shouted. 'Are you there?'

The gravel scrunched under a pair of heavy boots.

'Anything the matter?' asked a deep, comfortable voice.

'What? Who's that?' John Mansbridge hoped that he had sounded startled.

'Police, sir. What's the trouble?'

John Mansbridge hastily explained his identity.

'This is my cousin's house. Mr. Felix Mansbridge.'

'That's right, sir.'

'He asked me to come and see him and stay the night—I do from time to time. Keep a pair of pyjamas here, don't you know, and I've just walked up from the station and, well—I can't make him hear—or any one else. I know he's expecting me. And—look at that!' The constable had reached the door and, urged by the excited cousin, peered at the open window.

'Half a minute,' he said. 'I'll just have a look——'

'Here, I've got a torch,' said John and produced his from his pocket. The constable took it with a word of thanks. He flashed it on the window and gave a grunt of surprise. He seemed uncertain what to do next.

Mansbridge thumped on the knocker again; then the two men strained their ears—or one of them did.

'I wonder if one of the other windows . . .' suggested Mansbridge. The constable leapt at the idea and led the way rapidly round the house until he reached the window through which his companion had peered—oh, years ago, it seemed

'Looks bad, sir,' said the constable. 'We'd best get round to the front again.' Indeed, the study window was too narrow to admit of entrance.

The constable became a man of action. He bade Mansbridge wait by the door while he climbed in by the window, and Mansbridge again reflected with satisfaction that if he had left any traces by either window, the burly constable would have eliminated them pretty completely.

A moment later the door was opened.

'Come in, sir,' the constable whispered hoarsely, 'and wait outside the room where the light is, if you don't mind. I just want to have a look first.'

He walked to the study and half-closed the door behind him. John Mansbridge waited for what seemed an eternity, but in fact was only a few seconds. The constable sized up the situation and returned, switching on the light in the hall. The other man had been fighting to retain control of his nerves, but he was conscious that sweat was pouring down his face. The constable glanced at him with respectful sympathy and muttering, 'Afraid this will be a shock to you, sir,' led the way to the study.

John Mansbridge followed; his return to the horrible scene which he had left only a few minutes before seemed somehow to act as a stimulant to his nerves. His performance of horror and shock was a convincing one, and all the time his inner consciousness was gleefully congratulating him upon it.

'How—how did it happen?' he gasped.

'Ah, queer business,' the constable answered. 'Can't make out what's happened to the room.'

'Yes, but Felix—my cousin?'

'Well, that will have to be seen to,' was the ponderous reply. 'Maybe he smashed himself on the fender there. But it's queer. You see, sir'—he hesitated and then went on—'it's a case of suicide, seemingly. I found this on the table there, with the glass on it.'

And he held out a sheet of paper, covered with Felix's writing. John stared at it; how in the devil's name had he overlooked the little table? Of course he found the forged cheque before he got as far, but . . .

Through the daze which beset him read the opening words:

'I, Felix Edward Mansbridge, being of sound mind, solemnly declare that I am dying by my own act. I have taken poison . . .'

The room and the paper whirled before his eyes. From a distance he heard the constable say, 'I'll just ring up the station.' Then a 'Hallo,' but addressed, it seemed, not to the Exchange but to himself, and a strong arm lowered him into the very chair where Felix had sat, his bald head just visible. . . .

There was a clink of glass.

'Drink this, sir,' said the constable, holding a tumbler to his lips.

'Now let's see where we are,' the superintendent addressed the sergeant and the constable; the latter was manifestly uneasy at the prominence into which his part in the affair had thrust him.

'First, let's fix the known facts about this man, John Mansbridge's, movements. We know the train he came by and the time he left the station; we know he was in the "Four Feathers" just before closing time, and we know he left it and walked past Robson, who was still on duty, in the direction of his cousin's house. There is no turning off the lane, and it's pretty deserted at night. In fact, I doubt if any one uses it except you, Longden. And about forty minutes or three-quarters of an hour after John Mansbridge left the village, you see two or three matches struck as you come down the hill towards the house. And when you get to the house, you find the man hammering at the door. That correct?'

The sergeant and the constable agreed.

'Right. And I may add that we're pretty sure it *was* Mr. John Mansbridge who lit his pipe, because he carried a box of wax vestas—not so common these days in country villages—and we found no less than four used matches of the same kind just about the spot where Longden here indicated.'

The constable perked up a little, as if detecting a word of praise for himself.

'All very well and good,' the superintendent continued. 'It certainly looks as if the man walked from the station as he said he was going to. Took just the normal time, and his shoes bear out his story. And I don't see how else he could have got there. We may, of course, find someone who met him in the lane, but I should think that unlikely. So much for that.'

He paused for a moment, as if to arrange his thoughts in order, and then resumed his lecture (as it seemed to be).

'Now let's consider this Felix Mansbridge. It seems a pretty clear case of suicide to me'—the sergeant made as if to interrupt—'but I admit that isn't what we're supposed to think. What we are supposed to think is this; that someone or other broke into the house, began to steal the silver, was disturbed, caught up that club from the hall, knocked the dead man on the head, after a struggle, and decamped. And the broken watch is to suggest that this happened about five minutes after Mr. John Mansbridge left the "Four Feathers" and when, consequently, he couldn't be at his cousin's house. I 'm afraid I can't swallow that story.'

'You 're sure he was poisoned, then, sir?' asked the sergeant.

'Perfectly. And that 's not all. In the first place, though, it 's not impossible that he was killed in a struggle, it 's surprising—considering that the blow was delivered from behind and from above. Then, secondly, there 's his confession of suicide. You see, it pretty well fixes the time.'

'How 's that, sir?'

'Why, he talked about taking his departure from the world to Wagner's accompaniment.'

'Crazy,' said the sergeant.

'Not in the way you mean. I 've no doubt he was thinking of the wireless. You look up last night's programmes and you 'll find a Wagner item, and you 'll see why, in my opinion, he only took the poison ten minutes after the time shown by the broken watch. And, finally, there 's the wound on the head. You take my word, the doctors will find that it was delivered after the man was dead.'

'But why in the name of——?'

'Sheer accident, sergeant, in my opinion. Result of sticking to a prearranged plan too closely. Whoever used the club believed that Felix Mansbridge was alive—and that means premeditated murder. Why, in the name of whatever you were going to say, should a burglar suddenly stop his burgling to go into the next room and bash in the head of the owner of the house, and then take to his heels, leaving the swag behind? It stands to reason there never was a burglar at all.'

'Then who 'd you reckon it was, sir?'

The superintendent shrugged his shoulders.

'Strictly speaking, I suppose we ought to lay hands on a suspicious fugitive, an unknown visitor,' he said, 'but I fancy it would be sheer waste of time. There was only one visitor—the cousin, John Mansbridge.'

'But his alibi, sir.'

'I know. And I don't see how we're to break it. All I can say is that *somehow* he got there long before he met you, Longden. And as we can *prove* that he got there some minutes at least before Longden found him at the door, I don't think his alibi holds water after all. I admit I don't see how he rigged it, but I'm satisfied that it's a fake.'

'You can *prove* it, sir?' the sergeant interposed, in a tone which suggested respectful doubt.

'Certainly. For here's a letter which was found in his pocket. It's addressed to him and dated yesterday. The woman who looked after Mr. Felix Mansbridge said he wrote a letter before she left, but as he hadn't got a stamp he said it could wait till next day. I haven't a doubt this is the letter—no letter was found in the house ready for post, and you can see that this envelope was addressed *and* gummed down. And the woman says he put the letter in the side pocket of his dinner-jacket—the right side. You'll observe here that if it really was in the right side-pocket it would have been a job to take it out as the body lay, on its right side, in front of the fire-place—in other words, it was taken out before the body lay there. That's a small point, perhaps.

'The main thing is the letter itself—addressed to John Mansbridge Esq., and found in John Mansbridge Esquire's pocket. I suggest that he found it after the writer was dead, and probably before his body lay on the hearth-rug. For we know that he didn't take the letter while he was in the house with Longden—and therefore he must have done so a good five minutes sooner, and pretty certainly more than that.'

'What's in the letter, sir?' the sergeant inquired.

'A hint of a motive, to put it mildly. It's long; here's the gist of it. Felix says that he has had no answer to his note, and supposes that the cousin cannot face him; in other words, he cannot deny the forging of the cheque. Felix says it is hopeless. His cousin will never be convinced

that he, Felix, is indeed and in truth a poor man
—the large sums mentioned in his father's will were
swallowed up by the unpaid debts. Nor, apparently, does
the cousin believe that Felix is indeed a sick man. So
sick, that though he isn't likely to die next month, the
doctors say that he can't live more than a year at the
outside. The forgery is the last straw; he's to have no
peace in this world, so he'll go to the next, and leave his
cousin to inherit his life insurance and what little else
there is. And he is not to worry; he will make it quite
clear to the police that it was a case of suicide—which,
thanks to a special clause, will not invalidate the insurance
policy. Oh, yes, he encloses the forged cheque in question,
which, he says, he has told the bank is in order. Points
to a motive, eh? And makes John Mansbridge's character
pretty clear. Thorough wrong 'un.'

There was another pause.

'I see, sir,' the sergeant said slowly. 'And you don't
think that John Mansbridge got in quite innocently and
found that letter—say, five minutes before Longden saw
him light his pipe?'

The superintendent shook his head.

'No, that meeting with Longden, like those calls at the
"Four Feathers" and the station, were all part of the man's
plan. The pipe-lighting was deliberate—he must have
been at pains to observe the exact hour at which Longden
walked down that lane. He never thought that out on
the spur of the moment.'

Police-constable Longden cleared his throat.

'If I may be so bold, sir, do you mean to say Mr. Felix
was dead before this Mr. John came, and that Mr. John
smashed his head in, not knowing he was dead already?'

'That's it, in a nutshell, constable. How he got to the
house in time, and how he got in, I don't know. Perhaps
he had a duplicate key, and chucked it away in the grass
somewhere. But in my opinion, however he did it he
came down to murder his cousin, and to the best of his
belief till you stuck that confession in his hands he *had*
murdered his cousin.'

'Thank you, sir. Then to all intents and purposes he
was a murderer?'

'I haven't a doubt of it.'

'Well, sir,' and the constable wiped his brow, 'that kind of makes things easier. I don't rightly know what you'll do about it, officially like, but I feel easier in me own mind. I can tell you, sir, when I finished with telephoning and found this Mr. John Mansbridge dead in the arm-chair—well, I didn't know whether I was alive or dead meself. Fancy me trying to help him over the shock of seeing his cousin's corpse by giving him a stiff dose of the very same whisky as his cousin had put the poison in. Act of God like, wasn't it, sir?'

He spoke hopefully, with no intention of irreverence.

HENRY CHRISTOPHER BAILEY

THE YELLOW SLUGS

THE big car closed up behind a florid funeral procession which held the middle of the road. On either side was a noisy congestion of lorries. Mr. Fortune sighed and closed his eyes.

When he looked out again he was passing the first carriage of another funeral, and saw beneath the driver's seat the white coffin of a baby. For the road served the popular cemetery of Blaney.

Two slow miles of dingy tall houses and cheap shops slid by, with vistas of meaner streets opening on either side. The car gathered speed across Blaney Common, an expanse of yellow turf and bare sand, turbid pond and scrubwood, and stopped at the brown pile of an old poor law hospital.

Entering its carbolic odour, Mr. Fortune was met by Superintendent Bell. 'Here I am,' he moaned. 'Why am I?'

'Well, she's still alive, sir,' said Bell. 'They both are.'

Mr. Fortune was taken to a ward in which, secluded by a screen, a little girl lay asleep.

Her face had a babyish fatness, but in its pallor looked bloated and unhealthy. Though the close July air was oppressive and she was covered with heavy bed-clothes, her skin showed no sign of heat and she slept still as death.

Reggie sat down beside her. His hands moved gently within the bed. . . . He listened . . . he looked . . .

A nurse followed him to the door. 'How old, do you think?' he murmured.

'That was puzzling me, sir. She's big enough for seven or eight, but all flabby. And when she came to, she was talking almost baby talk. I suppose she may be only about five.'

Reggie nodded. 'Quite good, yes. All right. Carry on.'

From the ward he passed to a small room where a nurse and a doctor stood together watching the one bed.

A boy lay in it, restless and making noises—inarticulate words mixed with moaning and whimpering.

The doctor lifted his eyebrows at Reggie. 'Get that?' he whispered. 'Still talking about hell. He came absolutely unstuck. I had to risk a shot of morphia. I——' He broke off in apprehension as Reggie's round face hardened to a cold severity. But Reggie nodded and moved to the bed. . . .

The boy tossed into stertorous sleep, one thin arm flung up above a tousled head. His sunken cheeks were flushed, and drips of sweat stood on the upper lip and the brow. Not a bad brow—not an uncomely face but for its look of hungry misery—not the face of a child—a face which had been the prey of emotions and thwarted desires. . . .

Reggie's careful hands worked over him . . . bits of the frail body were laid bare. . . . Reggie stood up, and still his face was set in ruthless, passionless determination.

Outside the door the doctor spoke nervously. 'I hope you don't——'

'Morphia's all right,' Reggie interrupted. 'What do you make of him?'

'Well, Mr. Fortune, I wish you'd seen him at first.' The doctor was uncomfortable beneath the cold insistence of a questioning stare. 'He was right out of hand—a sort of hysterical fury. I should say he's quite abnormal. Neurotic lad, badly nourished—you can't tell what they won't do, that type.'

'I can't. No. What age do you give him?'

'Now you've got me. To hear him raving, you'd think he was grown up, such a flow of language. Bible phrases and preaching. I'd say he was a twelve-year-old, but he might only be eight or ten. His development is all out of balance. He's unhealthy right through.'

'Yes, that is so,' Reggie murmured. 'However. You ought to save him.'

'Poor little devil,' said the doctor.

In a bare, grim waiting-room Reggie sat down with Superintendent Bell, and Bell looked anxiety. 'Well, sir?'

'Possible. Probable,' Reggie told him. 'On the evidence.'

'Ah. Cruel, isn't it? I hate these child cases.'

'Any more evidence?' Reggie drawled.

Bell stared at his hard calm gloomily. 'I have. Plenty.'

The story began with a small boy on the bank of one of the ponds on Blaney Common. That was some time ago. That was the first time anybody in authority had been aware of the existence of Eddie Hill. One of the keepers of the common made the discovery. The pond was that one which children used for the sailing of toy boats. Eddie Hill had no boat, but he loitered round all the morning, watching the boats of other children. There was little wind, and one boat lay becalmed in the middle of the pond when the children had to go home to dinner.

An hour later the keeper saw Eddie Hill wade into the pond and run away. When the children came back from dinner there was no boat to be seen. Its small owner made weeping complaint to the keeper, who promised to keep his eyes open, and some days later found Eddie Hill and his little sister Bessie lurking among the gorse of the common with the stolen boat.

It was taken from them and their sin reported to their mother, who promised vengeance.

Their mother kept a little general shop. She had been there a dozen years—ever since she married her first husband. She was well liked and looked up to; a religious woman, regular chapel - goer and all that. Her second husband, Brightman, was the same sort—hard-working, respectable man; been at the chapel longer than she had.

The day-school teachers had nothing against Eddie or the little girl. Eddie was rather more than usually bright, but dreamy and careless; the girl a bit stodgy. Both of 'em rather less naughty than most.

'Know a lot, don't you?' Reggie murmured. 'Got all this to-day?'

'No, this was all on record,' Bell said. 'Worked out for another business.'

'Oh. Small boy and small girl already old offenders. Go on.'

The other business was at the chapel Sunday school.

Eddie Hill, as the most regular of its pupils, was allowed the privilege of tidying up at the end of the afternoon. On a Sunday in the spring the superintendent came in unexpectedly upon the process and found Eddie holding the money-box in which had been collected the contributions of the school to the chapel missionary society.

Eddie had no need nor right to handle the money-box. Moreover, on the bench beside him were pennies and a sixpence. Such wealth could not be his own. Only the teachers ever put in silver. Moreover, he confessed that he had extracted the money by rattling the box upside down, and his small sister wept for the sin.

The superintendent took him to the police-station and charged him with theft.

'Virtuous man,' Reggie murmured.

'It does seem a bit harsh,' Bell said. 'But they'd had suspicions about the money-box before. They'd been watching for something like this. Well, the boy's mother came and tried to beg him off, but of course the case had to go on. The boy came up in the Juvenile Court—you know the way, Mr. Fortune; no sort of criminal atmosphere, magistrate talking like a father. He let the kid off with a lecture.'

'Oh, yes. What did he say? Bringin' down mother's grey hairs in sorrow to the grave—wicked boy—goin' to the bad in this world and the next—anything about hell?'

'I couldn't tell you.' Bell was shocked. 'I heard he gave the boy a rare old talking to. I don't wonder. Pretty bad, wasn't it, the Sunday-school money-box? What makes you bring hell into it?'

'I didn't. The boy did. He was raving about hell to-day. Part of the evidence. I was only tracin' the origin.'

'Ah. I don't like these children's cases,' Bell said gloomily. 'They don't seem really human sometimes. You get a twisted kind of child and he'll talk the most frightful stuff—and do it too. We can only go by acts, can we?'

'Yes. That's the way I'm goin'. Get on.'

The sharp impatience of the tone made Bell look at him with some reproach. 'All right, sir. The next thing is this morning's business. I gave you the outline of that on the phone. I 've got the full details now. This is what it comes to. Eddie and his little sister were seen on the common; the keepers have got to keeping an eye on him. He wandered about with her—he has a casual, drifting sort of way, like some of these queer kids do have—and they came to the big pond. That 's not a children's place at all; it 's too deep; only dog bathing and fishing. There was nobody near; it was pretty early. Eddie and Bessie went along the bank, and a labourer who was scything thistles says the little girl was crying, and Eddie seemed to be scolding her, and then he fair chucked her in and went in with her. That 's what it looked like to the keeper who was watchin' 'em. Him and the other chap, they nipped down and chucked the lifebuoy; got it right near, but Eddie didn't take hold of it; he was clutching the girl and sinking and coming up again. So the keeper went in to 'em and had trouble getting 'em out. The little girl was unconscious, and Eddie sort of fought him.' Bell stopped and gave a look of inquiry, but Reggie said nothing, and his face showed neither opinion nor feeling. 'Well, you know how it is with these rescues from the water,' Bell went on. 'People often seem to be fighting to drown themselves and it don't mean anything except fright. And about the boy throwing the girl in—that might have been just a bit of a row or play—it 's happened often—not meant vicious at all; and then he 'd panic, likely enough.' Again Bell looked an anxious question at the cold, passionless face. 'I mean to say, I wouldn't have bothered you with it, Mr. Fortune, but for the way the boy carried on when they got him out. There he was with his little sister unconscious, and the keeper doing artificial respiration, and he called out: 'Don't do it. Bessie 's dead. She must be dead.' And the keeper asked him: 'Do you want her dead, you little devil?' And he said: 'Yes, I do. I had to.' Then the labourer chap came back with help and they got hold of Eddie; he was raving, flinging himself about and screaming if she lived she 'd only get like him and go to hell, so she must be dead. While they brought him along here he was sort of preaching to 'em bits of the Bible, and mad stuff about the wicked being sent to hell and tortures for 'em.'

'Curious and interestin',' Reggie drawled. 'Any particular torture?'

'I don't know. The whole thing pretty well gave these chaps the horrors. They didn't get all the boy's talk. I don't wonder. There was something about worms not dying, they told me. That almost turned 'em up. Well—there you are, Mr. Fortune. What do you make of it?'

'I should say it happened,' Reggie said. 'All of it. As stated.'

'You feel sure he could have thrown that fat little girl in? He seemed to me such a weed.'

'Yes. Quite a sound point. I took that point. Development of both children unhealthy. Girl wrongly nourished. Boy inadequately nourished. Boy's physique frail. However. He could have done it. Lots of nervous energy. Triumph of mind over matter.'

Bell drew in his breath. 'You take it cool.'

'Only way to take it,' Reggie murmured,' and Bell shifted uncomfortably. He has remarked since that he had seen Mr. Fortune look like that once or twice before—sort of inhuman, heartless, and inquisitive; but there it seemed all wrong, it didn't seem his way at all.

Reggie settled himself in his chair and spoke—so Bell has reported, and this is the only criticism which annoys Mr. Fortune—like a lecturer. 'Several possibilities to be considered. The boy may be merely a precocious rascal. Having committed some iniquity which the little girl knew about, he tried to drown her to stop her giving him away. Common type of crime, committed by children as well as their elders.'

'I know it is,' Bell admitted. 'But what could he have done that was worth murdering his sister?'

'I haven't the slightest idea. However. He did steal. Proved twice by independent evidence. Don't blame if you don't want. "There, but for the grace of God, go I." I agree. Quite rational to admit that consideration. We shall certainly want it. But he knew he was a thief; he knew it got him into trouble—that's fundamental.'

'All right,' said Bell gloomily. 'We have to take it like that.'

'Yes. No help. Attempt to murder sister may be

connected with consciousness of sin. I should say it was. However. Other possibilities. He's a poor little mess of nerves; he's unsound, physically, mentally, spiritually. He may not have meant to murder her at all; may have got in a passion and not known what he was doing.'

'Ah. That's more likely.' Bell was relieved.

'You think so? Then why did he tell everybody he did mean to murder her?'

'Well, he was off his head, as you were saying. That's the best explanation of the whole thing. It's really the only explanation. Look at your first idea: he wanted to kill her so she couldn't tell about some crime he'd done. You get just the same question, why did he say he meant murder? He must know killing is worse than stealing. However you take the thing, you work back to his being off his head.'

Reggie's eyelids drooped. 'I was brought here to say he's mad. Yes. I gather that. You're a merciful man, Bell. Sorry not to satisfy your gentle nature. I could swear he's mentally abnormal. If that would do any good. I couldn't say he's mad. I don't know. I can find you mental experts who would give evidence either way.'

'I know which a jury would believe,' Bell grunted.

'Yes. So do I. Merciful people, juries. Like you. Not my job. I'm lookin' for the truth. One more possibility. The boy's motive was just what he said it was—to kill his little sister so she shouldn't get wicked and go to hell. That fits the other facts. He'd got into the way of stealing; it had been rubbed into him that he was doomed to hell. So, if he found her goin' the same way, he might think it best she should die while she was still clean.'

'Well, if that isn't mad!' Bell exclaimed.

'Abnormal, yes. Mad—I wonder,' Reggie murmured.

'But it's sheer crazy, sir. If he believed he was so wicked, the thing for him to do was to pull up and go straight, and see that she did too.'

'Yes. That's common sense, isn't it?' A small, contemptuous smile lingered a moment on Reggie's stern face. 'What's the use of common sense here? If he was like this—sure he was going to hell; sure she was bein' driven

there too—kind of virtuous for him to kill her to save her.
Kind of rational. Desperately rational. Ever know any
children, Bell? Some of 'em do believe what they're
taught. Some of 'em take it seriously. Abnormal, as you
say. Eddie Hill is abnormal.' He turned and looked full
at Bell, his blue eyes dark in the failing light. 'Aged twelve
or so—too bad to live—or too good. Pleasant case.'

Bell moved uneasily. 'These things do make you feel
queer,' he grunted. 'What it all comes to, though—we
mean much the same—the boy ought to be in a home.
That can be worked.'

'A home!' Reggie's voice went up, and he laughed.
'Yes. Official home for mentally defective. Yes. We
can do that. I dare say we shall.' He stood up and
walked to the window and looked out at the dusk. 'These
children had a home of their own. And a mother. What's
she doing about 'em?'

'She's been here, half off her head, poor thing,' said
Bell. 'She wouldn't believe the boy meant any harm.
She told me he couldn't, he was so fond of his sister. She
said it must have been accident.'

'Quite natural and motherly. Yes. But not adequate.
Because it wasn't accident, whatever it was. We'd better
go and see mother.'

'If you like,' Bell grunted reluctantly.

'I don't like,' Reggie mumbled. 'I don't like anything.
I'm not here to do what I like.' And they went.

People were drifting home from the common. The mean
streets of Blaney had already grown quiet in the sultry
gloom.

Shutters were up at the little shop which was the home
of Eddie Hill, and still bore in faded paint his father's
name. No light showed in the windows above. Bell
rapped on the door, and they waited in vain. He moved
to a house door close beside the shop. 'Try this. This
may be theirs too,' he said, and knocked and rang.

After a minute it was opened by a woman who said
nothing, but stared at them. From somewhere inside
came the sound of a man's voice, talking fervently.

The light of the street lamp showed her of full figure, in
neat black, and a face which was still pretty but distressed.

'You remember me, Mrs. Brightman,' said Bell. 'I'm Superintendent Bell.'

'I know.' She was breathless. 'What's the matter? Are they—is Eddie—what's happened?'

'They're doing all right. I just want a little talk with you.'

'Oh, they're all right. Praise God!' She turned; she called out: 'Matthew, Matthew dear, they're all right.'

The man's voice went on talking with the same fervour, but not in answer.

'I'll come in, please,' said Bell.

'Yes, do. Thank you kindly. Mr. Brightman would like to see you. We were just asking mercy.'

She led the way along a passage, shining clean, to a room behind the shop. There a man was on his knees praying, and most of the prayer was texts: 'And we shall sing of mercy in the morning. Amen. Amen.' He made an end.

He stood up before them, tall and gaunt, a bearded man with melancholy eyes. He turned to his wife. 'What is it, my dear? What do the gentlemen want?'

'It's about the children, Matthew.' His wife came and took his arm. 'It's the police superintendent, I told you. He was so kind.'

The man sucked in his breath. 'Ay, ay. Please sit down. They must sit down, Florrie.' There was a fluster of setting chairs. 'This is kind, sir. What can you tell us to-night?'

'Doin' well. Both of 'em,' Reggie said.

'There's our answer, Florrie,' the man said, and smiled, and his sombre eyes glowed. 'There's our prayers answered.'

'Yes. I think they're going to live,' said Reggie. 'But that's not the only thing that matters. We have to ask how it was they were nearly drowned.'

'It was an accident. It must have been,' the woman cried. 'I'm sure Eddie wouldn't—he never would, would he, Matthew?'

'I won't believe it,' Brightman answered quickly.

'Quite natural you should feel like that,' Reggie nodded. 'However. We have to deal with the facts.'

'You must do what you think right, sir, as it is shown you.' Brightman bent his head.

'Yes, I will. Yes. Been rather a naughty boy, hasn't he?' Brightman looked at his wife's miserable face and turned to them again. 'The police know,' he said. 'He has been a thief—twice he has been a thief—but little things. There is mercy, surely there is mercy for repentance. If his life is spared, he should not be lost; we must believe that.'

'I do,' Reggie murmured. 'Any special reason why he should have been a thief?'

Brightman shook his head. 'He's always had a good home, I'm sure,' the woman moaned. She looked round her room, which was ugly and shabby, but all in the cleanest order.

'What can I say?' Brightman shook his head. 'We've always done our best for him. There's no telling how temptation comes, sir, and it's strong and the little ones are weak.'

'That is so. Yes. How much pocket-money did they have?'

'Eddie has had his twopence a week since he was ten,' Brightman answered proudly. 'And Bessie has her penny.'

'I see. And was there anything happened this morning which upset Bessie or Eddie?'

'Nothing at all, sir. Nothing that I know.' Brightman turned to his wife. 'They went off quite happy, didn't they?'

'Yes, of course they did,' she said eagerly. 'They always loved to have a day on the common. They took their lunch, and they went running as happy as happy—and then this,' she sobbed.

'My dearie.' Brightman patted her.

'Well, well.' Reggie stood up. 'Oh. By the way. Has Eddie—or Bessie—ever stolen anything at home here—money or what not?'

Brightman started and stared at him. 'That's not fair, sir. That's not a right thing to ask. There isn't stealing between little ones and their mother and father.'

'No. As you say. No,' Reggie murmured. 'Good night. You'll hear how they go on. Good night.'

'Thank you, sir. We shall be anxious to hear. Good

night, sir,' said Brightman, and Mrs. Brightman showed
them out with tearful gratitude. As the door was opened,
Brightman called: 'Florrie! Don't bolt it. Mrs. Wiven
hasn't come back.'

'I know. I know,' she answered, and bade them good
night and shut the door.

A few paces away, Reggie stopped and looked back at
the shuttered shop and the dark windows. 'Well, well.
What does the professional mind make of all that?'

'Just what you'd expect, wasn't it?' Bell grunted.

'Yes. Absolutely. Poor struggling shopkeepers, earnestly
religious, keeping the old house like a new pin. All in
accordance with the evidence.' He sniffed the night air.
'Dank old house.'

'General shop smell. All sorts of things mixed up.'

'As you say. There were. And there would be. Nothing
you couldn't have guessed before we went. Except that
Mrs. Wiven is expected—whoever Mrs. Wiven is.'

'I don't know. Sounds like a lodger.'

'Yes, that is so. Which would make another resident in
the home of Eddie and Bessie. However. She's not come
back yet. So we can go home. The end of a beastly day.
And to-morrow's another one. I'll be out to see the
children in the morning. Oh, my Lord! Those children.'
His hand gripped Bell's arm. . . .

By eight o'clock in the morning he was at the bedside
of Bessie Hill—an achievement of stupendous but useless
energy, for she did not wake till half-past.

Then he took charge. A responsible position, which he
interpreted as administering to her cups of warm milk
and bread and butter. She consumed them eagerly; she
took his service as a matter of course.

'Good girl.' Reggie wiped her mouth. 'Feelin' better?'

She sighed and snuggled down, and gazed at him with
large eyes. 'Umm. Who are you?'

'They call me Mr. Fortune. Is it nice here?'

'Umm. Comfy.' The big eyes were puzzled and
wondering. 'Where is it?'

'Blaney Hospital. People brought you here after you
were in the pond. Do you remember?'

She shook her head. 'Is Eddie here?'

'Oh, yes. Eddie's asleep. He's all right. Were you cross with Eddie?'

Tears came into the brown eyes. 'Eddie was cross wiv me,' the child whimpered. 'I wasn't. I wasn't. Eddie said must go into ve water. I didn't want. But Eddie was so cross. Love Eddie.'

'Yes. Little girl.' Reggie stroked her hair. 'Eddie shouldn't have been cross. Just a little girl. But Eddie isn't often cross, is he?'

'No. Love Eddie. Eddie's dear.'

'Why was he cross yesterday?'

The brown eyes opened wider. 'I was naughty. It was Mrs. Wiven. Old Mrs. Wiven. I did go up to her room. I didn't fink she was there. Sometimes is sweeties. But she was vere. She scolded me. She said I was little fief. We was all fiefs. And Eddie took me away and oh, he was so cross; he said I would be wicked and must not be. But I aren't. I aren't. Eddie was all funny and angry, and said not to be like him and go to hell, and then he did take me into pond wiv him. I didn't want! I didn't want!'

'No. Of course not. No. Poor little girl. Eddie didn't understand. But it's all right now.'

'Is Eddie still cross wiv me?' she whimpered.

'Oh, no. No. Eddie won't be cross any more. Nobody's cross, little girl.' Reggie bent over her. 'Everybody's going to be kind now. You only have to be quiet and happy. That's all.'

'Oooh.' She gazed up at him. 'Tell Eddie I'm sorry.'

'Yes. I'll tell him.' Reggie kissed her hand and turned away.

The nurse met him at the door. 'Did she wake in the night?' he whispered.

'Yes, sir, asking for Eddie. She's a darling, isn't she? She makes me cry, talking like that of him.'

'That won't do any harm,' Reggie said, and his face hardened. 'But you mustn't talk about him.'

He went to the room where Eddie lay. The doctor was there, and turned from the bedside to confer with him. 'Not too bad. We've put in a long sleep. Quite quiet since we waked. Very thirsty. Taken milk with a dash of coffee nicely. But we're rather flat.'

Reggie sat down by the bed. The boy lay very still. His thin face was white. Only his eyes moved to look at Reggie, so little open, their pupils so small that they seemed all greenish-grey. He gave no sign of recognition, or feeling, or intelligence. Reggie put a hand under the clothes and found him cold and damp, and felt for his pulse.

'Well, young man, does anything hurt you now?'

'I 'm tired. I 'm awful tired,' the boy said.

'Yes. I know. But that 's going away.'

'No, it isn't; it 's worse. I didn't ought to have waked up.' The faint voice was drearily peevish. 'I didn't want to. It 's no good. I thought I was dead. And it was good being dead.'

'Was it?' Reggie said sharply.

The boy gave a quivering cry. 'Yes, it was!' His face was distorted with fear and wonder. 'I thought it would be so dreadful and it was all quiet and nice, and then I wasn't dead, I was alive and everything 's awful again. I 've got to go on still.'

'What 's awful in going on?' said Reggie. 'Bessie wants you. Bessie sent you her love. She 's gettin' well quick.'

'Bessie? Bessie 's here in bed like I am?' The unnatural greenish eyes stared.

'Of course she is. Only much happier than you are.'

The boy began to sob.

'Why do you cry about that?' Reggie said. 'She 's got to be happy. Boys and girls have to be happy. That 's what they 're for. You didn't want Bessie to die.'

'I did. You know I did,' the boy sobbed.

'I know you jumped in the pond with her. That was silly. But you 'd got rather excited, hadn't you? What was it all about?'

'They 'll tell you,' the boy muttered.

'Who will?'

'The keepers, the p'lice, the m-magistrate, everybody. I 'm wicked. I 'm a thief. I can't help it. And I didn't want Bessie to be wicked too.'

'Of course you didn't. And she isn't. What ever made you think she was?'

'But she was.' The boy's voice was shrill. 'She went to Mrs. Wiven's room. She was looking for pennies.

I know she was. She'd seen me. And Mrs. Wiven said we were all thieves. So I had to.'

'Oh, no, you hadn't. And you didn't. You see? Things don't happen like that.'

'Yes, they do. There's hell. Where their worms don't die.'

The doctor made a muttered exclamation.

Reggie's hand held firm at the boy's as he moved and writhed. 'There's God too,' he murmured. 'God's kind. Bessie's not going to be wicked. You don't have to be wicked. That's what's come of it all. Somebody's holding you up now.' His hand pressed. 'Feel?' The boy's lips parted; he looked up in awe. 'Yes. Like that. You'll see me again and again. Now good-bye. Think about me. I'm thinking about you.' . . . He stayed a while longer before he said another 'Good-bye.'

Outside, in the corridor, the doctor spoke: 'I say, Mr. Fortune, you got him then. That was the stuff. I thought you were driving hard before. Sorry I spoke.'

'I was.' Reggie frowned. His round face was again of a ruthless severity. '"Difficult matter to play with souls,"' he mumbled. 'We've got to.' He looked under drooping eyelids. 'Know the name of the keeper who saw the attempted drowning? Fawkes? Thanks.'

He left the hospital and walked across the common.

The turf was parched and yellow, worn away on either side of paths loosened by the summer drought. Reggie descried the brown coat of a keeper, made for him, and was directed to where Fawkes would be.

Fawkes was a slow-speaking, slow-thinking old soldier, but he knew his own mind.

There was no doubt in it that Eddie had tried to kill Bessie, no indignation, no surprise. Chewing his words, he gave judgment. He had known Eddie's sort, lots of 'em. 'Igh strung, wanting the earth, kicking up behind and before 'cause they couldn't get it. He didn't mind 'em. Rather 'ave 'em than young 'uns like sheep. But you 'ad to dress 'em down proper. They was devils else. Young Eddie would 'ave to be for it.

That business of the boat? Yes, Eddie pinched that all right. Smart kid; you'd got to 'and him that. And yet not so smart. Silly, lying up with it on the common; just the way to get nabbed. Ought to 'ave took it 'ome and sailed it over at Wymond Park. Never been spotted then. But 'im and 'is sister, they made a reg'lar den up in the gorse. Always knew where to look for 'em. Silly. Why, they was up there yesterday, loafing round, before 'e did 'is drowning act.'

'Take you there? I can, if you like.'

Reggie did like. They went up the brown slopes of the common to a tangle of gorse and bramble over small sand-hills.

'There you are.' The keeper pointed his stick to a patch of loose sand in a hollow. 'That's young Eddie's funk-'ole. That's where we spotted 'em with the blinking boat.'

Reggie came to the place. The sand had been scooped up by small hands into a low wall round a space which was decked out with pebbles, yellow petals of gorse, and white petals of bramble.

'Ain't that just like 'em!' The keeper was angrily triumphant. 'They know they didn't ought to pick the flowers. As well as you and me they do, and they go and do it.'

Reggie did not answer. He surveyed the pretence of a garden and looked beyond. 'Oh, my Lord!' he muttered. On the ground lay a woman's bag.

''Allo, 'allo.' The keeper snorted. 'They've been pinching something else.'

Reggie took out his handkerchief, put his hand in it, and thus picked up the bag. He looked about him; he wandered to and fro, going delicately, examining the confusion of small footmarks, further and further away.

'Been all round, ain't they?' the keeper greeted him on his return.

'That is so. Yes.' Reggie mumbled and looked at him with searching eyes. 'Had any notice of a bag lost or stolen?'

'Not as I've 'eard. Better ask the 'ead keeper. 'E'll be up at the top wood about now.'

The wood was a thicket of birch and crab-apple and thorn. As they came near, they saw on its verge the head keeper and two other men who were not in the brown coats of authority. One of these was Superintendent Bell. He came down the slope in a hurry.

'I tried to catch you at the hospital, Mr. Fortune,' he said. 'But I suppose you 've heard about Mrs. Wiven?'

'Oh. The Mrs. Wiven who hadn't come back,' Reggie said slowly. 'No. I haven't heard anything.'

'I thought you must have, by your being out here on the common. Well, she didn't come back at all. This morning Brightman turned up at the station very fussy and rattled to ask if they had any news of his lodger, Mrs. Wiven. She never came in last night, and he thought she must have had an accident or something. She 'd been lodging with them for years. Old lady, fixed in her habits. Never went anywhere, that he knew of, except to chapel and for a cup o' tea with some of her chapel friends, and none of them had seen her. These fine summer days she 'd take her food out and sit on the common here all day long. She went off yesterday morning with sandwiches and a vacuum flask of tea and her knitting. Often she wouldn't come home till it was getting dark. They didn't think much of her being late; sometimes she went in and had a bit o' supper with a friend. She had her key, and they left the door unbolted, like we heard, and went to bed, being worn out with the worry of the kids. But when Mrs. Brightman took up her cup of tea this morning and found she wasn't in her room, Brightman came running round to the station. Queer business, eh?'

'Yes. Nasty business. Further you go the nastier.'

Bell looked at him curiously and walked him away from the keeper. 'You feel it that way? So do I. Could you tell me what you were looking for out here—as you didn't know she was missing?'

'Oh, yes. I came to verify the reports of Eddie's performances.'

'Ah! Have you found any error?'

'No. I should say everything happened as stated.'

'The boy 's going to get well, isn't he?'

'It could be. If he gets the chance.'

'Poor little beggar,' Bell grunted. 'What do you really think about him, Mr. Fortune?'

'Clever child, ambitious child, imaginative child. What children ought to be—twisted askew.'

'Kind of perverted, you mean.'

'That is so. Yes. However. Question now is, not what I think of the chances of Eddie's soul, but what's been happening. Evidence inadequate, curious, and nasty. I went up to the private lair of Eddie and Bessie. Same where he was caught with the stolen boat. I found this.' He showed Bell the woman's bag.

'My oath!' Bell muttered, and took it from him gingerly. 'You wrapped it up! Thinkin' there might be finger-prints.'

'Yes. Probably are. They might even be useful.'

'And you went looking for this—not knowing the woman was missing?'

'Wasn't lookin' for it,' Reggie snapped. 'I was lookin' for anything there might be. Found a little pretence of a garden they'd played at—and this.'

'Ah, but you heard last night about Mrs. Wiven, and this morning you go up where Eddie hides what he's stolen. Don't that mean you made sure there was something fishy? You see when we're blind, Mr. Fortune.'

'Oh, no. I don't see. I knew more than you did. Little Bessie told me this morning she was in Mrs. Wiven's room yesterday, privily and by stealth, and Mrs. Wiven caught her and called her a thief, and said they were all thieves. I should think little Bessie may have meant to be a thief. Which would agree with Eddie's effort to drown her so she should die good and honest. But I don't see my way.'

'All crazy, isn't it?' Bell grunted.

'Yes. The effort of Eddie is an incalculable factor. However. You'd better look at the bag.'

Bell opened it with cautious fingers. A smell of pepper-mint came out. Within was a paper bag of peppermint lozenges, two unclean handkerchiefs marked E. W., an empty envelope addressed to Mrs. Wiven, a bottle of soda-mint tablets, and some keys.

'Evidence that it is the bag of the missing Mrs. Wiven strong,' Reggie murmured. He peered into it. 'But no money. Not a penny.' He looked up at Bell with that cold, ruthless curiosity which Bell always talks about in discussing the case. 'Stealin' is the recurrin' motive. You notice that?'

'I do.' Bell stared at him. 'You take it cool, Mr. Fortune. I've got to own it makes me feel queer.'

'No use feelin' feelings,' Reggie drawled. 'We have to go on. We want the truth, whatever it is.'

'Well, all right, I know,' Bell said gloomily. 'They're searching the common for her. That's why I came out here. They knew her. She did sit about here in summer.' He went back to the head keeper and conferred again. . . .

Reggie purveyed himself a deck-chair, and therein sat extended and lit a pipe and closed his eyes. . . .

'Mr. Fortune!' Bell stood over him. His lips emitted a stream of smoke. No other part of him moved. 'They've found her. I suppose you expected that.'

'Yes. Obvious possibility. Probable possibility.' It has been remarked that Mr. Fortune has a singular capacity for becoming erect from a supine position. A professor of animal morphology once delivered a lecture upon him—after a hospital dinner—as the highest type of the invertebrates. He stood up from the deck-chair in one undulating motion. 'Well, well. Where is the new fact?' he moaned.

Bell took him into the wood. No grass grew in it. Where the sandy soil was not bare, dead leaves made a carpet. Under the crab-apple trees, between the thornbrakes, were nooks obviously much used by pairs of lovers. By one of these, not far from the whale-back edge of rising ground which was the wood's end, some men stood together.

On the grey sand there lay a woman's body. She was small; she was dressed in a coat and skirt of dark grey cloth and a black and white blouse. The hat on her grey hair was pulled to one side, giving her a look of absurd frivolity in ghastly contrast to the distortion of her pallid face. Her lips were closely compressed and almost white. The dead eyes stared up at the trees with dilated pupils.

Reggie walked round the body, going delicately, rather like a dog in doubt how to deal with another dog.

Beside the body was a raffia bag which held some knitting, a vacuum flask, and an opened packet of sandwiches.

Reggie's discursive eyes looked at them and looked again at the dead face, but not for long. He was more interested in the woman's skirt. He bent over that, examined it from side to side, and turned away and went on prowling further and further away, and as he went he scraped at the dry sand here and there.

When he came back to the body, his lips were curved in a grim, mirthless smile. He looked at Bell. 'Photographer,' he mumbled.

'Sent a man to phone, sir,' Bell grunted.

Reggie continued to look at him. 'Have you? Why have you?'

'Just routine.' Bell was startled.

'Oh. Only that. Well, well.' Reggie knelt down by the body. His hands went to the woman's mouth. . . . He took something from his pocket and forced the mouth open and looked in. . . . He closed the mouth again, and sat down on his heels and contemplated the dead woman with dreamy curiosity. . . . He opened her blouse. Upon the underclothes was a dark stain. He bent over that and smelt it; he drew the clothes from her chest.

'No wound, is there?' Bell muttered.

'Oh, no. No.' Reggie put back the clothes and stood up and went to the flask and the sandwiches. He pulled the bread of an unfinished sandwich apart, looked at it, and put it down. He took the flask and shook it. It was not full. He poured some of the contents into its cup.

'Tea, eh?' said Bell. 'Strong tea.'

'Yes. It would be,' Reggie murmured. He tasted it and spat, and poured what was in the cup back into the flask and corked it again and gave it to Bell.

'There you are. Cause of death, poisoning by oxalic acid or binoxalate of potassium—probably the latter—commonly called salts of lemon. And we shall find some in that awful tea. We shall also find it in the body. Tongue and mouth, white, contracted, eroded. Time of death, probably round about twenty-four hours ago. No certainty.'

'My oath! It's too near certainty for my liking,' Bell muttered.

'Is it?' Reggie's eyelids drooped. 'Wasn't thinkin' about what you'd like. Other interestin' facts converge.'

'They do!' Bell glowered at him. 'One of the commonest kinds of poisoning, isn't it?'

'Oh, yes. Salts of lemon very popular.'

'Anybody can get it.'

'As you say. Removes stains, cleans brass and what not. Also quickly fatal, with luck. Unfortunate chemical properties.'

'This boy Eddie could have got some easy.'

'That is so. Yes. Lethal dose for a penny or two anywhere.'

'Well, then—look at it!'

'I have,' Reggie murmured. 'Weird case. Ghastly case.'

'Gives me the horrors,' said Bell. 'The old lady comes out here to spend the day as usual, and somebody's put a spot of poison in her drop o' tea and she dies; and her bag's stolen, and found without a farthing where the boy Eddie hides his loot. And, about the time the old lady's dying, Eddie tries to drown his sister. What are you going to make of that? What can you make of it? It was a poison any kid could get hold of. One of 'em must have poisoned her to steal her little bit o' money. But the girl's not much more than a baby. It must have been Eddie that did it—and that goes with the rest of his doings. He's got the habit of stealing. But his little sister saw something of it, knew too much, so he put up this drowning to stop her tongue—and then, when she was saved, made up this tale about killing her to keep her honest. Devilish, isn't it? And when you find a child playing the devil—my oath! But it is devilish clever—his tale would put the stealing and all the rest on the baby. And we can't prove anything else. She's too little to be able to get it clear, and he's made himself out driven wild by her goings on. If a child's really wicked, he beats you.'

'Yes, that is so,' Reggie drawled. 'Rather excited, aren't you? Emotions are not useful in investigation. Prejudice the mind into exaggeratin' facts and ignorin' other facts. Both fallacies exhibited in your argument. You mustn't ignore what Bessie did say—that she went into Mrs. Wiven's room yesterday morning and Mrs. Wiven caught her. I shouldn't wonder if you found Bessie's fingerprints on that bag.'

'My Lord!' Bell stared at him. 'It's the nastiest case I ever had. When it comes to babies in murder——'

'Not nice, no. Discoverin' the possibilities of corruption of the soul. However. We haven't finished yet. Other interestin' facts have been ignored by Superintendent Bell. Hallo!' Several men were approaching briskly. 'Is this your photographer and other experts?'

'That's right. Photographer and fingerprint men.'

'Very swift and efficient.' Reggie went to meet them. 'Where did you spring from?'

'By car, sir.' The photographer was surprised. 'On the road up there. We had the location by phone.'

'Splendid. Now then. Give your attention to the lady's skirt. Look.' He indicated a shining streak across the dark stuff. 'Bring that out.'

'Can do, sir,' the photographer said, and fell to work.

Reggie turned to Bell. 'Then they'll go over the whole of her for fingerprints, what? And the sandwich paper. And the flask. Not forgettin' the bag. That's all. I've finished here. She can be taken to the mortuary for me.'

'Very good,' Bell said, and turned away to give the orders, but, having given them, stood still to stare at the thin glistening streak on the skirt.

Reggie came quietly to his elbow. 'You do notice that? Well, well.' Bell looked at him with a puzzled frown and was met for the first time in this case by a small, satisfied smile which further bewildered him. He bent again to pore over the streak. 'It's all right.' Reggie's voice was soothing. 'That's on record now. Come on.' Linking arms, he drew Bell away from the photographers and the fingerprint men. 'Well? What does the higher intelligence make of the line on the skirt?'

'I don't know. I can't make out why you think so much of it.'

'My dear chap! Oh, my dear chap!' Reggie moaned. 'Crucial fact. Decisive fact.' He led Bell on out of the

wood and across the common, and at a respectful distance
Bell's two personal satellites followed.

'Decisive, eh?' Bell frowned. 'It was just a smear
of something to me. You mean salts of lemon would
leave a shiny stain?'

'Oh, no. No. Wouldn't shine at all.'

'Had she been sick on her skirt?'

'Not there. No. Smear wasn't human material.'

'Well, I thought it wasn't. What are you thinking of?'

'I did think of what Eddie said—where their worm
dieth not.'

'My God!' Bell muttered. 'Worms?' He gave a
shudder. 'I don't get you at all, sir. It sounds mad.'

'No. Connection is sort of desperate rational. I told
you Eddie was like that. However. Speakin' scientifi-
cally, not a worm, but a slug. That streak was a slug's
trail.'

'Oh. I see.' Bell was much relieved. 'Now you say
so, it did look like that. The sort o' slime a slug leaves
behind. It does dry shiny, of course.'

'You have noticed that?' Reggie admired him.
'Splendid!'

Bell was not pleased. 'I have seen slugs before,' he
grunted. 'But what is there to make a fuss about?
I grant you, it's nasty to think of a slug crawling over
the woman as she lay there dead. That don't mean
anything, though. Just what you'd expect, with the
body being all night in the wood. Slugs come out when
it gets dark.'

'My dear chap! Oh, my dear chap!' Reggie moaned.
'You mustn't talk like that. Shakes confidence in the
police force. Distressin' mixture of inadequate observation
and fallacious reasonin'.'

'Thank you. I don't know what's wrong with it.'
Bell was irritated.

'Oh, my Bell! You shock me. Think again. Your
general principle's all right. Slugs do come out at night.
Slugs like the dark. That's a general truth which has its
particular application. But you fail to observe the conditions. The body was in a wood with no herbage on the
ground: and the ground was a light dry sand. These are

not conditions which attract the slug. I should have been much surprised if I 'd found any slugs there, or their tracks. But I looked for 'em—which you didn't, Bell. I 'm always careful. And there wasn't a trace. No. I can't let you off. A slug had crawled over her skirt, leavin' his slime from side to side. And yet his slime didn't go beyond her skirt on to the ground anywhere. How do you suppose he managed that? Miracle—by a slug. I don't believe in miracles if I can help it. I object to your simple faith in the miraculous gasteropod. It 's lazy.'

'You go beyond me,' said Bell uneasily. 'You grasp the whole thing while I 'm only getting bits. What do you make of it all?'

'Oh, my Bell!' Reggie reproached him. 'Quite clear. When the slug walked over her, she wasn't lying where she was found.'

'Is that all?' Bell grunted. 'I dare say. She might have had her dose, and felt queer and lay down, and then moved on to die where we found her. Nothing queer in that, is there?'

'Yes. Several things very queer. It could be. Oxalic poisoning might lay her out and still let her drag herself somewhere else to die. Not likely she 'd take care to bring her flask and her sandwiches with her. Still less likely she 'd lie long enough for a slug to walk over her and then recover enough to move somewhere else—and choose to move into the wood, where she wouldn't be seen. Why should she? She 'd try for help if she could try for anything. And, finally, most unlikely she 'd find any place here with slugs about. Look at it; it 's all arid and sandy and burnt up by the summer. No. Quite unconvincin' explanation. The useful slug got on to her somewhere else. The slug is decisive.'

'Then you mean to say she was poisoned some other place, and brought here dead?' Bell frowned. 'It 's all very well. You make it sound reasonable. But would you like to try this slug argument on a jury? They 'd never stand for it, if you ask me. It 's all too clever.'

'You think so?' Reggie murmured. 'Well, well. Then it does give variety to the case. We haven't been very

clever so far. However. Study to improve. There is
further evidence. She'd been sick. Common symptom
of oxalic poisoning. But she'd been sick on her underclothes and not on her outside clothes. That's very difficult. Think about it. Even juries can be made to think
sometimes. Even coroners, which is very hard. Even
judges. I've done it in my time, simple as I am. I might
do it again. Yes, I might. With the aid of the active
and intelligent police force. Come on.'

'What do you want to do?'

'Oh, my Bell! I want to call on Mr. and Mrs. Brightman. We need their collaboration. We can't get on
without it.'

'All right. I don't mind trying 'em,' Bell agreed
gloomily. 'We've got to find out all about the old woman
somehow. We don't really know anything yet.'

'I wouldn't say that. No,' Reggie mumbled. 'However. One moment.'

They had come to the edge of the common by the
hospital, where his car waited. He went across to it and
spoke to his chauffeur.

'Just calmin' Sam,' he apologized on his return. 'He
gets peevish when forgotten. Come on.'

They arrived again at the little general shop. Its un-
shuttered window now enticed the public with a meagre
array of canned goods and cartons which had been there
some time. The door was shut but not fastened. Opening
it rang a bell. They went in, and found the shop empty,
and for a minute or two stood in a mixture of smells
through which soap was dominant.

Mrs. Brightman came from the room behind, wiping red
arms and hands on her apron. Her plump face, which
was tired and sweating, quivered alarm at the sight of
them. 'Oh, it's you!' she cried. 'What is it? Is there
anything?'

'Your children are doing well,' said Reggie. 'Thought
I'd better let you know that.'

She stared at him, and tears came into her eyes. 'Praise
God!' she gasped. 'Thank you, sir, you're very kind.'

'No. You don't have to thank me. I'm just doin'
my job.'

But again she thanked him, and went on nervously: 'Have you heard anything of Mrs. Wiven?'

'I want to have a little talk about her. Is Mr. Brightman in?'

'No, he isn't, not just now. Have you got any news of her, sir?'

'Yes. There is some news. Sorry Mr. Brightman's out. Where's he gone?'

'Down to the yard, sir.'

'Out at the back here?'

'No. No. Down at his own yard.'

'Oh. He has a business of his own?'

'Yes, sir, a little business. Furniture dealing it is. Second-hand furniture.'

'I see. Well, well. We could get one of the neighbours to run down and fetch him, what?' Reggie turned to Bell.

'That's the way,' Bell nodded. 'What's the address, ma'am?'

She swallowed. 'It's just round the corner. Smith's Buildings. Anybody would tell you. But he might be out on a job, you know; I couldn't say.'

Bell strode out, and the messenger he sent was one of his satellites.

'Well, while we're waitin', we might come into your nice little room,' Reggie suggested. 'There's one or two things you can tell me.'

'Yes, sir, I'm sure, anything as I can, I'll be glad. Will you come through, please?' She lifted the flap of the counter for him, she opened the curtained glass door of the room behind. It was still in exact order, but she had to apologize for it. 'I'm sorry we're all in a mess. I'm behindhand with my cleaning, having this dreadful trouble with the children and being so worried I can't get on. I don't half know what I'm doing, and then poor Mrs. Wiven being lost——' She stopped, breathless. 'What is it about Mrs. Wiven, sir? What have you heard?'

'Not good news,' Reggie said. 'Nobody will see Mrs. Wiven alive again.'

The full face grew pale beneath its sweat, the eyes stood

out. 'She's dead! Oh, the poor soul! But how do you know? How was it?'

'She's been found dead on the common.'

Mrs. Brightman stared at him: her mouth came open and shook: she flung her apron over her head and bent and was convulsed with hysterical sobbing.

'Fond of her, were you?' Reggie sympathized.

A muffled voice informed him that she was a dear old lady—and so good to everybody.

'Was she? Yes. But I wanted to ask you about the children. What time did they go out yesterday?' Still sobbing under her apron, Mrs. Brightman seemed not to hear. 'Yesterday morning,' Reggie insisted. 'You must remember. What time was it when Eddie and Bessie went out?'

After a moment the apron was pulled down from a swollen, tearful face. 'What time?' she repeated looking at her lap and wiping her eyes. 'I don't know exactly, sir. Just after breakfast. Might be somewheres about nine o'clock.'

'Yes, it might be,' Reggie murmured. 'They were pulled out of the pond about then.'

'I suppose so,' she whimpered. 'What's it got to do with Mrs. Wiven?'

'You don't see any connection?'

She stared at him. 'How could there be?'

The shop-door bell rang, and she started up to answer it. She found Bell in the shop. 'Oh, have you found Mr. Brightman?' she cried.

'No, not yet. Where's Mr. Fortune?'

Reggie called to him, 'Come on, Bell,' and she brought him into the back room and stood looking from one to the other. 'So Mr. Brightman wasn't in his yard?'

'No, sir. Nobody there. At least, they couldn't make anybody hear.'

'Well, well,' Reggie murmured.

'But I told you he might have gone off on a job. He often has to go to price some stuff or make an offer or something.'

'You did say so. Yes,' Reggie murmured. 'However. I was asking about the children. Before they went out yesterday—Bessie got into trouble with Mrs. Wiven, didn't she?'

The woman looked down and plucked at her apron.

'You didn't tell us that last night,' Reggie said.

'I didn't want to. I didn't see as it mattered. And I didn't want to say anything against Bessie. She's my baby.' Her eyes were streaming. 'Don't you see?'

'Bessie told me,' said Reggie.

'Bessie confessed! Oh, it's all too dreadful. The baby! I don't know why this was to come on us. I brought 'em up to be good, I have. And she was such a darling baby. But it's God's will.'

'Yes. What did happen?' said Reggie.

'Mrs. Wiven was always hard on the children. She never had a child herself, poor thing. Bessie got into her room, and Mrs. Wiven caught her and said she was prying and stealing like Eddie. I don't know what Bessie was doing there. Children will do such, whatever you do. And there was Bessie crying and Eddie all wild. He does get so out of himself. I packed 'em off, and I told Mrs. Wiven it wasn't nothing to be so cross about, and she got quite nice again. She was always a dear with me and Brightman. A good woman at heart, sir, she was.'

'And when did Mrs. Wiven go out?' said Reggie.

'It must have been soon after. She liked her days on the common in summer, she did.'

'Oh, yes. That's clear.' Reggie stood up and looked out at the yard, where some washing was hung out to dry. 'What was Mrs. Wiven wearing yesterday?'

'Let me see——' Mrs. Brightman was surprised by the turn in the conversation. 'I don't rightly remember—she had on her dark coat and skirt. She always liked to be nicely dressed when she went out.' Under the frown of this mental effort swollen eyes blinked at him. 'But you said she'd been found. You know what she had on.'

'Yes. When she was on the common. Before she got there—what was she wearing?'

Mrs. Brightman's mouth opened and shut.

'I mean, when she caught Bessie in her room. What was she wearing then?'

'The same—she wouldn't have her coat on—I don't

know as I remember—but the same—she knew she was going out—she'd dress for it—she wouldn't ever dress twice in a morning.'

'Wouldn't she? She didn't have that overall on?' Reggie pointed to a dark garment hanging on the line in the yard which stretched from house to shed.

'No, she didn't, I'm sure. That was in the dirty clothes.'

'But you had to wash it to-day. Well, well. Now we want to have a look at Mrs. Wiven's room.'

'If you like. Of course, nothing's been done. It's all untidy.' She led the way upstairs, lamenting that the house was all anyhow, she'd been so put about.

But Mrs. Wiven's room was primly neat and as clean as the shining passage and stairs. The paint had been worn thin by much washing, the paper was so faded that its rosebud pattern merged into a uniform pinkish grey. An old fur rug by the bedside, a square of threadbare carpet under the rickety round table in the middle of the room, were the only coverings of the scoured floor. The table had one cane chair beside it, and there was a small basket chair by the empty grate—nothing else in the room but the iron bedstead and a combination of chest of drawers, dressing-table, and washstand, with its mirror all brown spots.

Mrs. Brightman passed round the room, pulling this and pushing that. 'I haven't even dusted,' she lamented.

'Is this her own furniture?' Reggie asked.

'No, sir, she hadn't anything. We had to furnish it for her.'

'Quite poor, was she?'

'I don't really know how she managed. And, of course, we didn't ever press her; you couldn't. She had her savings, I suppose. She'd been in good service, by what she used to say.'

'No relations?'

'No, sir. She was left quite alone. That was really why she came to us, she was that lonely. She'd say to me she did so want a home, till we took her. When she was feeling down, she used to cry and tell me she didn't know what would become of her. Of course, we wouldn't ever have let her want, poor dear. But it's my belief her bit of money was running out.'

Reggie gazed about the room. On the walls were many cards with texts.

'Mr. Brightman put up the good words for her,' Mrs. Brightman explained, and gazed at one of the texts and cried.

'"In My Father's house are many mansions."' Reggie read it out slowly, and again looked round the bare little room.

Mrs. Brightman sobbed. 'Ah, she's gone there now. She's happy.'

Bell was moving from one to other of the cupboards beside the grate. Nothing was in them but clothes. He went on to the dressing-table. 'She don't seem to have any papers. Only this.' He lifted a cash-box, and money rattled in it.

'I couldn't say, I'm sure,' Mrs. Brightman whimpered.

Reggie stood by the table. 'Did she have her meals up here?' he asked.

Mrs. Brightman thought about that. 'Mostly she didn't. She liked to sit down with us. She used to say it was more homely.'

Reggie fingered the table-cloth, pulled it off, and looked at the cracked veneer beneath. He stooped, felt the strip of old carpet under the table, drew it back. On the boards beneath was a patch of damp.

Mrs. Brightman came nearer. 'Well there!' she said. 'That comes of my not doing out the room. She must have had a accident with her slops and never told me. She always would do things for herself.'

Reggie did not answer. He wandered round the room, stopped by the window a moment, and turned to the door.

'I'm taking this cash-box, ma'am,' said Bell.

'If you think right——' Mrs. Brightman drew back. 'It's not for me to say—I don't mind, myself.' She looked from one to the other. 'Will that be all, then?'

'Nothing more here.' Reggie opened the door.

As they went downstairs, the shop bell rang again, and she hurried on to answer it. The two men returned to the room behind the shop.

'Poor old woman,' Bell grunted. 'You can see what sort of life she was having—that mingy room and her money running out—I wouldn't wonder if she committed suicide.'

'Wouldn't be wonderful. No,' Reggie murmured. 'Shut up.'

From the shop came a man's voice, lazy and genial. 'Good afternoon, mum. I want a bit o' salts o' lemon. About two penn'orth would do me. 'Ow do you sell it?'

There was a mutter from Mrs. Brightman. 'We don't keep it.'

'What? They told me I'd be sure to get it 'ere. Run out of it, 'ave you? Ain't that too bad!'

'We never did keep it,' Mrs. Brightman said. 'Whoever told you we did?'

'All right, all right. Keep your hair on, missis. Where can I get it?'

'How should I know? I don't rightly know what it is.'

'Don't you? Sorry I spoke. Used for cleaning, you know.'

Bell glowered at Reggie, for the humorous cockney voice was the voice of his chauffeur. But the cold severity of Reggie's round face gave no sign.

'We don't use it, nor we don't keep it, nor any chemist's stuff,' Mrs. Brightman was answering.

'Oh, good day!' The bell rang again as the shop door closed.

Mrs. Brightman came back. 'Running in and out of the shop all day with silly people,' she panted. She looked from one to the other, questioning, afraid.

'I was wonderin',' Reggie murmured. 'Did Mrs. Wiven have her meals with you yesterday—or in her room?'

'Down here.' The swollen eyes looked at him and looked away. 'She did usual, I told you. She liked to.'

'And which was the last meal she ever had?'

Mrs. Brightman suppressed a cry. 'You do say things! Breakfast was the last she had here. She took out a bit o' lunch and tea.'

'Yes. When was that put ready?'

'I had it done first thing, knowing she meant to get out—and she always liked to start early. It was there on the sideboard waiting at breakfast.'

'Then it was ready before the children went out? Before she had her quarrel with Bessie?'

Mrs. Brightman swallowed. 'So it was.'

'Oh. Thank you. Rather strong, the tea in her flask,' Reggie mumbled.

'She always had it fairly strong. Couldn't be too strong for her. I'm just the same myself.'

'Convenient,' Reggie said. 'Now you'll take me down into the cellar, Mrs. Brightman.'

'What?' She drew back so hastily that she was brought up by the wall. 'The cellar?' Her eyes seemed to stand out more than ever, so they stared at him, the whites of them more widely bloodshot. With an unsteady hand she thrust back the hair from her sweating brow. 'The cellar? Why ever do you want to go there? There's nothing in the cellar.'

'You think not?' Reggie smiled. 'Come down and see.'

She gave a moaning cry; she stumbled away to the door at the back, and opened it, and stood holding by the door-post, looking out to the paved yard.

From the shed in it appeared Brightman's bearded face. 'Were you looking for me, dearie?' he asked, and brought his lank shape into sight, brushing it as it came.

She made a gesture to him; she went to meet him and muttered: 'Matthew! They're asking me to take 'em down to the cellar.'

'Well, to be sure!' Brightman gave Reggie and Bell a glance of melancholy, pitying surprise. 'I don't see any reason in that.' He held her up, he stroked her and gently remonstrated. 'But there's no reason they shouldn't go to the cellar if they want to, Florrie. We ain't to stand in the way of anything as the police think right. We ain't got anything to hide, have we? Come along, dearie.'

An inarticulate quavering sound came from her.

'That's all right, my dearie, that's all right,' Brightman soothed her.

'Is it?' Bell growled. 'So you've been here all the time, Mr. Brightman. While she sent us to look for you down at your own place. Why didn't you show up before?'

'I've only just come in, sir,' Brightman said quietly.

'I came in by the back. I was just putting things to rights in the wash-house. The wife's been so pushed. I didn't know you gentlemen were here. You're searching all the premises, are you? I'm agreeable. I'm sure it's in order, if you say so. But I don't know what you're looking for.'

'Mrs. Brightman will show us,' said Reggie, and grasped her arm.

'Don't, don't,' she wailed.

'You mustn't be foolish, dearie,' said Brightman. 'You know there's nothing in the cellar. Show the gentlemen if they want. It's all right. I'll go with you.'

'Got a torch, Bell?' said Reggie.

'I have.' Bell went back into the room. 'And here's a lamp, too.' He lit it.

Reggie drew the shaking woman through the room into the passage. 'That's the door to your cellar. Open it. Come on.'

Bell held the lamp overhead behind them. Reggie led her stumbling down the stairs, and Brightman followed close.

A musty, dank smell came about them. The lamp-light showed a large cellar of brick walls and an earth floor. There was in it a small heap of coal, some sacks and packing-cases and barrels, but most of the dim space was empty. The light glistened on damp.

'Clay soil,' Reggie murmured, and smiled at Brightman. 'Yes. That was indicated.'

'I don't understand you, sir,' said Brightman.

'No. You don't. Torch, Bell.' He took it and flashed its beam about the cellar. 'Oh, yes.' He turned to Bell. With a finger he indicated the shining tracks of slugs. 'You see?'

'I do,' Bell muttered.

Mrs. Brightman gave a choked, hysterical laugh.

Reggie moved to and fro. He stooped. He took out his pocket-book and from it a piece of paper, and with that scraped something from a barrel side, something from the clay floor, and sighed satisfaction.

Standing up, he moved the ray of the torch from place to place, held it steady at last to make a circle of light on the ground beneath the steps. 'There,' he said, and Mrs. Brightman screamed. 'Yes. I know. That's where you put her. Look, Bell.' His finger pointed to a slug's trail which came into the circle of light, stopped, and went on again at another part of the circle. 'It didn't jump. They don't.'

He swung round upon Mrs. Brightman. He held out to her the piece of paper cupped in his hand. On it lay two yellow slugs.

She flung herself back, crying loathing and fear.

'Really, gentlemen, really now,' Brightman stammered. 'This isn't right. This isn't proper. You've no call to frighten a poor woman so. Come away now, Florrie, dearie.' He pulled at her.

'Where are you going?' Reggie murmured. She did not go. Her eyes were set on the two yellow slugs. '"Where their worm dieth not,"' Reggie said slowly.

She broke out in screams of hysterical laughter; she tore herself from Brightman, and reeled and fell down writhing and yelling.

'So that is that, Mr. Brightman.' Reggie turned to him.

'You're a wicked soul!' Brightman whined. 'My poor dearie!' He fell on his knees by her; he began to pray forgiveness for her sins.

'My oath!' Bell muttered, and ran up the steps shouting to his men. . . .

Some time afterwards the detective left to keep the little shop ushered Reggie out.

On the other side of the street, aloof from the gaping, gossiping crowd, superior and placid, his chauffeur smoked a cigarette. It was thrown away; the chauffeur followed him, fell into step beside him. 'Did I manage all right, sir?' The chauffeur invited praise.

'You did. Very neat. Very effective. As you know. Side, Sam, side. We are good at destruction. Efficient incinerators. Humble function. Other justification for existence, doubtful. However. Study to improve. What we want now is a toyshop.'

'Sir?' Sam was puzzled.

'I said a toyshop,' Reggie complained. 'A good toy-shop. Quick.' . . .

The light of the sunlight was shining into the little room at the hospital where Eddie Hill lay. Upon his bed stood part of a bridge built of strips of metal bolted together, a bridge of grand design. He and Reggie were working on the central span.

There was a tap at the door, a murmur from Reggie, and the nurse brought in Bell. He stood looking at Reggie with reproachful surprise. 'So that's what you're doing,' he protested.

'Yes. Something useful at last.' Reggie sighed. 'Well, well. We'll have to call this a day, young man. You've done enough. Mustn't get yourself tired.'

'I'm not tired,' the boy protested eagerly. 'I'm not really.'

'No. Of course not. Ever so much better. But there's another day to-morrow. And you have a big job. Must keep fit to go on with it.'

'All right.' The boy lay back, looked at his bridge, looked wistfully at Reggie. 'I can keep this here, can I, sir?'

'Rather. On the table by the bed. So it'll be there when you wake. Nice, making things, isn't it? Yes. You're going to make a lot now. Good-bye. Jolly, to-morrow, what? Good-bye.' He went out with Bell. 'Now what's the matter with you?' he complained.

'Well, I had to have a word with you, sir. This isn't going to be so easy. I thought I'd get you at the mortuary doing the post-mortem.'

'Minor matter. Simple matter. Only the dead buryin' their dead. The boy was urgent. Matter of savin' life there.'

'I'm not saying you're not right,' said Bell wearily. 'But it is a tangle of a case. The divisional surgeon reports Mrs. Brightman's mad. Clean off her head.'

'Yes. I agree. What about it?'

'Seemed to me you pretty well drove her to it. Those slugs—oh, my Lord!'

'Got you, did it? It rather got me. I'd heard Eddie talk of "the worm that dieth not." I should say he'd seen that cellar. Dreamed of it. However. I didn't drive the woman mad. She'd been mad some time. Not medically mad. Not legally mad. But morally. That was the work of our Mr. Brightman. I only clarified the situation. He almost sent the boy the same way. That's been stopped. That isn't going to happen now. That's the main issue. And we win on it. Not too bad. But rather a grim day. Virtue has gone out of me. My dear chap!' He took Bell's arm affectionately. 'You're tucked up too.'

'I don't mind owning I've had enough,' said Bell. 'This sort of thing tells me I'm not as young as I was. And it's all a tangle yet.'

'My dear chap! Oh, my dear chap!' Reggie murmured. 'Empty, aren't we? Come on. Come home with me.'

While Sam drove them back, he declined to talk. He stretched in the corner of the car and closed his eyes, and bade Bell do the same. While they ate a devilled sole and an entrecôte Elise, he discussed the qualities of Elise, his cook, and of the Romanée which they drank, and argued bitterly (though he shared it) that the cheese offered in deference to Bell's taste, a bland Stilton, was an insult to the raspberries, the dish of which he emptied.

But when they were established in big chairs in his library, with brandy for Bell and seltzer for himself, and both pipes were lit, 'Did you say a tangle?' he murmured. 'Oh, no. Not now. The rest is only routine for your young men and the lawyers. It 'll work out quite easy. You can see it all. When Mrs. Brightman was left a widow with her little shop, the pious Brightman pounced on her and mastered her. The little shop was only a little living. Brightman wanted more. Children were kept very short —they might fade out, they might go to the bad—either way the devout Brightman would be relieved of their keep; and meanwhile it was pleasant making 'em believe they were wicked. Old Mrs. Wiven was brought in as a lodger—not out of charity, as the wretched Mrs. Brightman was trained to say; she must have had a bit of money. Your young men will be able to trace that. And they 'll find Brightman got it out of her and used it to set up his second-hand furniture business. Heard of that sort of thing before, what?'

'I should say I have,' Bell grunted. 'My Lord, how often! The widow that falls for a pious brute—the old woman lodger with a bit of money.'

'Oh, yes. Dreary old game. And then the abnormal variations began. Pious bullyin' and starvin' didn't turn the boy into a criminal idiot. He has a mind. He has an imagination, poor child. Mrs. Wiven didn't give herself up to Brightman like his miserable wife. She had a temper. So the old game went wrong. Mrs. Wiven took to fussin' about her money. As indicated by Bessie. Mrs. Wiven was going to be very awkward. Your young men will have to look about and get evidence she'd been grumbling. Quite easy. Lots of gossip will be goin'. Some of it true. Most of it useful at the trial. Givin' the atmosphere.'

Bell frowned. 'Fighting with the gloves off, aren't you?'

'Oh, no. No. Quite fair. We have to fight the case without the children. I'm not going to have Eddie put in the witness-box, to be tortured about his mad mother helpin' murder. That might break him up for ever. And he's been tortured enough. The brute Brightman isn't going to hurt him any more. The children won't be givin' evidence. I'll get half the College of Physicians to certify they're not fit, if they're asked for. But that's not goin' to leave Mr. Brightman any way out. Now then. Things bein' thus, Brightman had his motive to murder Mrs. Wiven. If he didn't stop her mouth she'd have him in jail. Being a clever fellow, he saw that Eddie's record of stealin' would be very useful. By the way—notice that queer little incident, Bessie bein' caught pilferin' by Mrs. Wiven yesterday morning? Brightman may have fixed that up for another black mark against the children. I wonder. But it didn't go right. He must have had a jolt when Mrs. Wiven called out they were all thieves. Kind of compellin' immediate action. His plan would have been all ready, of course—salts of lemon in her favourite strong tea; a man don't think of an efficient way of poisonin' all of a sudden. And then the incalculable Eddie intervened. Reaction of Mrs. Wiven's explosion on him, a sort of divine command to save his sister from hell by seeing she died innocent. When

Brightman had the news of that effort at drowning, he took it as a godsend. Hear him thanking heaven? Boy who was wicked enough to kill a little sister was wicked enough for anything. Mr. Brightman read his title clear to mansions in the skies. And Mrs. Wiven was promptly given her cup o' tea. She was sick in her room, sick on her overall and on her underclothes. Evidence for all that conclusive. Remember the damp floor. I should say Mrs. Brightman had another swab at that to-day. She has a craze about cleaning. We saw that. Feels she never can get clean, poor wretch. Well. Mrs. Wiven died. Oxalic poisoning generally kills quick. I hope it did. They hid the body in the cellar. Plan was clever. Take the body out in the quiet of the night and dump it on the common with a flask of poisoned tea—put her bag in Eddie's den. All clear for the intelligent police. Devil of a boy poisoned the old lady to steal her money, and was drownin' his little sister so she shouldn't tell on him. That's what you thought, wasn't it? Yes. Well-made plan. It stood up against us last night.'

'You did think there was something queer,' Bell said.

'I did,' Reggie sighed. 'Physical smell. Damp musty smell. Probably the cellar. And the Brightmans didn't smell nice spiritually. However. Lack of confidence in myself. And I have no imagination. I ought to have waited and watched. My error. My grave error. Well. It was a clever plan. But Brightman was rather bustled. That may account for his errors. Fatal errors. Omission to remove the soiled underclothes when the messed-up overall was taken off. Failure to allow for the habits of *Limax flavus*.'

'What's that?' said Bell.

'Official name of yellow slug—cellar slug. The final, damning evidence. I never found any reason for the existence of slugs before. However. To round it off— when you look into Mr. Brightman's furniture business, you'll find that he has a van, or the use of one. You must prove it was used last night. That's all. Quite simple now. But a wearin' case.' He gazed at Bell with large, solemn eyes. 'His wife! He'd schooled her thorough. Ever hear anything more miserably appealing than her on

her dear babies and poor old Mrs. Wiven? Not often?
No. Took a lot of breakin' down.'

'Ah. You were fierce,' Bell muttered.

'Oh, no. No.' Reggie sighed. 'I was bein' merciful.
She couldn't be saved. My job was to save the children.
And she—if that brute hadn't twisted her, she'd have done
anything to save 'em too. She'd been a decent soul once.
No. She won't be giving evidence against me.'

'Why, how should she?' Bell gaped.

'I was thinkin' of the day of judgment,' Reggie murmured. 'Well, well. Post-mortem in the morning. Simple
straight job. Then I'll be at the hospital if you want
me. Have to finish Eddie's bridge. And then we're
going to build a ship. He's keen on ships.'

C. DALY KING

THE EPISODE OF THE NAIL AND THE REQUIEM

Characters of the Episode

JERRY PHELAN, the narrator
GLEEB, manager of Tarrant's apartment house
WICKS, apartment house electrician
BARBARA BREBANT, wealthy débutante of bohemian tastes
MICHAEL SALTI, an artist in oils
MULLINS, a lieutenant of police; large and loud
PEAKE, deputy inspector; tall, thin, soft voiced
WEBER, patrolman; a regular cop
TREVIS TARRANT, interested in sealed rooms
KATOH, his butler-valet

THE episode of the nail and the requiem was one of the most characteristic of all those in which, over a relatively brief period, I was privileged to watch Trevis Tarrant at work. Characteristic, in that it brought out so well the unusual aptitude of the man to see clearly, to welcome *all* the facts, no matter how apparently contradictory, and to think his way through to the only possible solution by sheer logic, while every one else boggled at impossibilities and sought to forget them. From the gruesome beginning that November morning, when he was confronted by the puzzle of the sealed studio, to the equally gruesome denouement that occurred despite his own grave warning twenty-four hours later, his brain clicked successively and infallibly along the rails of reason to the inevitable, true goal.

Tarrant had been good enough to meet us at the boat when Valerie and I had returned from our wedding trip; and a week later I had been delighted with the opportunity of spending the night at his apartment, telling him of the trip and our plans and hearing of his own activities during the interval. After all, he was largely responsible for my having won Valerie when I did; our friendship had grown to intimacy during those few days when the three of us, and Katoh too, had struggled with the thickening horror in Valerie's modernistic house.

It was that most splendid time of year when the suburban air is tinged with the smoke of leaves, when the country beyond flaunts beauty along the roads, when the high windows of the city look out every evening through violet dusk past myriad twinkling lights at the gorgeous painting of sunset. We had been to a private address at the Metropolitan Museum by a returning Egyptologist; we had come back to the apartment and talked late into the night. Now, at eight-thirty the next morning, we sat at breakfast in Tarrant's lounge while the steam hissed comfortably in the wall radiators and the brisk, bright sky poured light through the big window beside us.

I remember that we had nearly finished eating and that Tarrant was saying: 'Cause and effect rule this world; they may be a mirage but they are a consistent mirage; everywhere, except possibly in subatomic physics, there is a cause for each effect, and that cause can be found,' when the manager came in. He wore a fashionable morning coat and looked quite handsome; he was introduced to me as Mr. Gleeb. Apparently he had merely dropped in, as was his custom, to assure himself that all was satisfactory with a valued tenant, but the greetings were scarcely over when the phone rang and Katoh indicated that he was being called. His monosyllabic answers gave no indication of the conversation from the other end; he finished with 'All right; I'll be up in a minute.'

He turned back to us. 'I'm sorry,' he said, 'but there is some trouble at the penthouse. Or else my electrician has lost his mind. He says there is a horrible kind of music being played there and that he can get no response to his ringing at the door. I shall have to go up and see what it is all about.'

The statement was a peculiar one and Tarrant's eyes, I thought, held an immediate gleam of curiosity. He got out of his seat in a leisurely fashion, however, and declared: 'You know, Gleeb, I'd like a breath of fresh air after breakfast. Mind if we come up with you? There's a terrace,

I believe, where we can take a step or so while you're untangling the matter.'

'Not at all, Mr. Tarrant. Come right along. I hardly imagine it's of any importance, but I can guarantee plenty of air.'

There was, in fact a considerable wind blowing across the open terrace that, guarded by a three-foot parapet, surrounded the penthouse on all sides except the north, where its wall was flush with that of the building. The penthouse itself was rather small, containing as I later found, besides the studio which comprised its whole northern end, only a sleeping room with a kitchenette and a lavatory off its east and west sides respectively. The entrance was on the west side of the studio and here stood the electrician who had come to the roof to repair the radio antennae of the apartment house and had been arrested by the strange sounds from within. As we strolled about the terrace, we observed the penthouse itself as well as the wide view below. Its southern portion possessed the usual window but the studio part had only blank brick walls; a skylight was just visible above it and there was, indeed, a very large window, covering most of the northern wall, but this, of course, was invisible and inaccessible from the terrace.

Presently the manager beckoned us over to the entrance door and, motioning us to be silent, asked: 'What do you make of that, Mr. Tarrant?'

In the silence the sound of doleful music was more than audible. It appeared to emanate from within the studio; slow, sad, and mournful, it was obviously a dirge and its full-throated quality suggested that it was being rendered by a large orchestra. After a few moments' listening Tarrant said: 'That is the rendition of a requiem mass and very competently done, too. Unless I'm mistaken, it is the requiem of Palestrina. . . . There; there's the end of it. . . . Now it's beginning again.'

'Sure, it goes on like that all the time,' contributed Wicks, the electrician. 'There must be someone in there, but I can't get no answer.' He banged on the door with his fist, but obviously without hope of response.

'Have you looked in at the windows?'

'Sure.'

We, too, stepped to the available windows and peered in, but beyond a bedroom that had not been used, nothing was visible. The door from the bedroom to the studio was closed. The windows were all locked.

'I suggest,' said Tarrant, 'that we break in.'

The manager hesitated. 'I don't know. After all, he has a right to play any music he likes, and if he doesn't want to answer the door——'

'Who has the penthouse, anyhow?'

'A man named Michael Salti. An eccentric fellow, like many of these artists. I don't know much about him, to tell the truth; we can't insist on as many references as we used to, nowadays. He paid a year's rent in advance and he hasn't bothered any one in the bulding, that's about all I can tell you.'

'Well,' Tarrant considered, 'this performance *is* a little peculiar. How does he know we may not be trying to deliver an important message? How about his phone?'

'Tried it,' Wicks answered. 'The operator says there isn't any answer.'

'I'm in favour of taking a peek. Look here, Gleeb, if you don't want to take the responsibility of breaking in, let us procure a ladder and have a look through the skylight. Ten to one that will pass unobserved; and if everything seems all right we can simply sneak away.'

To this proposal the manager consented, although it seemed to me that he did so most reluctantly. Possibly the eerie sounds that continued to issue through the closed door finally swayed him, for their quality, though difficult to convey, was certainly upsetting. In any event the ladder was brought and Tarrant himself mounted it, once it had been set in place. I saw him looking through the skylight, then leaning closer, peering intently through cupped hands about his eyes. Presently he straightened and came down the ladder in some haste.

His face, when he stood beside us, was strained. 'I think you should call the police,' he grated. 'At once. And wait till they get here before you go in.'

'The police? But—what is it?'

'It's not pleasant,' Tarrant said slowly. 'I think it's murder.'

Nor would he say anything further until the police, in the person of a traffic patrolman from Park Avenue, arrived. Then we all went in together, Gleeb's pass-key having failed and the door being broken open.

The studio was a large, square room, and high, and the light, sweeping in through the north wall and the skylight, illuminated it almost garishly. It was sparsely furnished; a couch, a chair, a stool, an easel and a cabinet for paints and supplies stood on a hardwood floor which two rugs scarcely covered. The question of the music was soon settled; in one corner was an electric victrola with an automatic arrangement for turning the record and starting it off again when it had reached its end. The record was of Palestrina's Requiem Mass, played by a well-known orchestra. Someone, I think it was Tarrant, crossed the room and turned it off, while we stood huddled near the door, gazing stupidly at the twisted, bloody figure on the couch.

It was that of a girl, altogether naked; although she was young—not older than twenty-two certainly—her body was precociously voluptuous. One of her legs was contorted into a bent position, her mouth was awry, her right hand held a portion of the couch covering in an agonized clutch. Just beneath her left breast the hilt of a knife protruded shockingly. The bleeding had been copious.

It was Tarrant again who extinguished the four tall candles, set on the floor and burning at the corners of the couch. As he did so he murmured: 'You will remember that the candles were burning at eight-forty-seven, officer. I dislike mockery.'

Then I was out on the terrace again, leaning heavily against the western parapet. In the far distance the Orange mountains stood against the bright horizon; somewhat nearer, across the river, huddled the building masses that marked Newark; overhead a plane droned south-westward. I gagged and forced my thoughts determinedly toward that plane. It was a transport plane, it was going to Newark Airport; probably it was an early plane from Boston. On it were people, prosaic people, thank God. One of them was perhaps a button salesman; presently he would enter the offices of Messrs. Simon and Morgetz and display his buttons on a card for the benefit of Mr. Simon. . . . Now my insides were behaving less drastically. I could gasp; and I did gasp, deep intakes of clear, cold air.

When I came back into the studio, a merciful blanket covered the girl's body. And for the first time I noticed the easel. It stood in the south-east corner of the room, diagonally opposite the couch and across the studio from the entrance doorway. It should have faced north-west, to receive the light from the big north window, and in fact the stool to its right indicated that position. But the easel had been partly turned, so that it faced south-west, toward the bedroom door; and one must walk almost to that door to observe its canvas.

This, stretched tightly on its frame, bore a painting in oil of the murdered girl. She was portrayed in a nude, half-crouching pose, her arms extended, and her features held a revoltingly lascivious leer. The portrait was entitled 'La Séduction.' In the identical place where the knife had pierced her actual body, a large nail had been driven through the web of the canvas. It was half-way through, the head protruding two inches on the obverse side of the picture; and a red gush of blood had been painted down the torso from the point where the nail entered.

Tarrant stood with his hands in his pockets, surveying this work of art. His gaze seemed focused upon the nail, incongruous in its strange position and destined to play so large a part in the tragedy. He was murmuring to himself and his voice was so low that I scarcely caught his words.

'Madman's work. . . . But why is the easel turned away from the room? . . . Why is that? . . .'

It was late afternoon in Tarrant's apartment and much activity had gone forward. The Homicide Squad in charge of Lieutenant Mullins had arrived and unceremoniously ejected every one else from the penthouse, Tarrant included. Thereupon he had called a friend at headquarters and been assured of a visit from Deputy Inspector Peake, who would be in command of the case, a visit which had not yet eventuated.

I had gone about my business in the city somewhat dazedly. But I had met Valerie for luncheon downtown and her presence was like a fragrant, reviving draught of pure ozone. She had left again for Norrisville, after insisting that I stay with Tarrant another night when she saw how excited I had become over the occurrences of the morning. Back in the apartment Katoh, who, for all that he was a man of our own class in Japan, was certainly an excellent butler in New York, had immediately provided me with a fine bottle of Irish whisky (Bushmills, bottled in 1919). I was sipping my second highball and Tarrant was quietly reading across the room, when Inspector Peake rang the bell.

He advanced into the room with hand outstretched. 'Mr. Tarrant, I believe? . . . Ah. Glad to know you, Mr. Phelan.' He was a tall, thin man in mufti, with a voice unexpectedly soft. I don't know why, but I was also surprised that a policeman should wear so well-cut a suit of tweeds. As he sank into a chair, he continued; 'I understand you were among the first to enter the penthouse, Mr. Tarrant. But I'm afraid there isn't much to add now. The case is cut and dried.'

'You have the murderer?'

'Not yet. But the drag-net is out. We shall have him, if not to-day, then to-morrow or the next day.'

'The artist, I suppose?'

'Michael Salti, yes. An eccentric man, quite mad. . . . By the way, I must thank you for that point about the candles. In conjunction with the medical examiner's evidence it checked the murder definitely at between one and two a.m.'

'There is no doubt, then, I take it, about the identity of the criminal.'

'No,' Peake asserted, 'none at all. He was seen alone with his model at 10.50 p.m. by one of the apartment house staff and the elevator operators are certain no one was taken to the penthouse during the evening or night. His fingerprints were all over the knife, the candlesticks, the victrola record. There was a lot more corroboration, too.'

'And was he seen to leave the building after the crime?'

'No, he wasn't. That's the one missing link. But since he isn't here, he must have left. Perhaps by the firestairs; we've checked it and it's possible. . . . The girl is Barbara Brebant—a wealthy family.' The inspector shook his head. 'A wild one, though; typical Prohibition product. She has played around with dubious artistics from the Village and elsewhere for some years; gave most of 'em more than they could take, by all accounts. Young, too; made her debut only about a year ago. Apparently she has made something of a name for herself in the matter of viciousness; three of our men brought in the very same description—a vicious beauty.'

'The old Roman type,' Tarrant surmised. 'Not so anachronistic in this town, at that. . . . Living with Salti?'

'No. She lived at home. When she bothered to go home. No one doubts, though, that she was Salti's mistress. And from what I've learned, when she was any man's mistress he was pretty certain to be dragged through the mire. Salti, being mad, finally killed her.'

'Yes, that clicks,' Tarrant agreed. 'The lascivious picture and the nail driven through it. Madmen, of course, act perfectly logically. He was probably a loose liver himself, but she showed him depths he had not suspected. Then remorse. His insanity taking the form of an absence of the usual values, he made her into a symbol of his own vice, through the painting, and then killed her, just as he mutilated the painting with the nail. . . . Yes, Salti is your man all right.'

Peake ground out a cigarette. 'A nasty affair. But not especially mysterious. I wish all our cases were as simple.' He was preparing to take his leave.

Tarrant also got up. He said: 'Just a moment. There were one or two things——'

'Yes?'

'I wonder if I could impose upon you a little more, Inspector. Just to check some things I noticed this morning. Can I be admitted to the penthouse now?'

Peake shrugged, as if the request were a useless one, but took it with a certain good grace. 'Yes, I'll take you up. All our men have left now, except a patrolman who will guard the premises until we make the arrest. I still have an hour to spare.'

It was two hours, however, before they returned. The inspector didn't come in, but I caught Tarrant's parting words at the entrance. 'You will surely assign another man to the duty to-night, won't you?' The policeman's reply sounded like a grunt of acquiescence.

I looked at my friend in amazement when he came into the lounge. His clothes, even his face, were covered with dirt; his nose was a long, black smudge. By the time he had bathed and changed and we sat down to one of Katoh's dinners, it was nearly half-past nine.

During dinner Tarrant was unaccustomedly silent. Even after we had finished and Katoh had brought our coffee and liqueurs, he sat at a modernistic tabouret stirring the black liquid reflectively, and in the light of the standing lamp behind him I thought his face wore a slight frown.

Presently he gave that peculiar whistle that summoned his man, and the butler-valet appeared almost immediately from the passage to the kitchen. 'Sit down, doctor,' he spoke without looking up.

Doubtless a small shift in my posture expressed my surprise, for he continued, for my benefit: 'I've told you that Katoh is a doctor in his own country, a well-educated man who is over here really on account of this absurd spy custom. Because of that nonsense I am privileged to hire him as a servant, but when I wish his advice as a friend, I call him doctor—a title to which he is fully entitled—and institute a social truce. Usually I do it when I'm worried . . . I'm worried now.'

Katoh, meantime, had hoisted himself on to the divan, where he sat smiling and helping himself to one of Tarrant's Dimitrinoes. 'Sozhial custom matter of convenience,' he acknowledged. 'Conference about what?'

'About this penthouse murder,' said Tarrant without further ado. 'You know the facts related by Inspector Peake. You heard them?'

'I listen. Part my job.'

'Yes, well, that portion is all right. Salti's the man. There's no mystery about that, not even interesting, in fact. But there's something else, something that isn't right. It stares you in the face, but the police don't care. Their business is to arrest the murderer; they know who he is and they're out looking for him. That's enough for them. But there *is* a mystery up above, a real one. I 'm not concerned with chasing crooks, but their own case won't hold unless this curious fact fits in. It is as strange as anything I 've ever met.'

Katoh's grin had faded; his face was entirely serious. 'What this mystery?'

'It 's the most perfect sealed room, or rather sealed house, problem ever reported. There was no way out and yet the man isn't there. No possibility of suicide; the fingerprints on the knife are only one element that rules that out. No, he was present all right. But where did he go, and how? . . . Listen carefully. I 've checked this from my own observation, from the police investigations, and from my later search with Peake.

'When we entered the penthouse this morning, Gleeb's pass-key didn't suffice; we had to break the entrance door in because it was bolted on the inside by a strong bar. The walls of the studio are of brick and they had no windows except on the northern side where there is a sheer drop to the ground. The window there was fastened on the inside and the skylight was similarly fastened. The only other exit from the studio is the door to the bedroom. This was closed and the key turned in the lock; the key was on the studio side of the door.

'Yes, I know,' Tarrant went on, apparently forestalling an interruption; 'it is sometimes possible to turn a key in a a lock from the wrong side, by means of pincers or some similar contrivance. That makes the bedroom, the lavatory and the kitchenette adjoining it, possibilities. There is no exit from any of them except by the windows. They were all secured from the inside and I am satisfied that they cannot be so secured by any one already out of the penthouse.'

He paused and looked over at Katoh, whose head nodded up and down as he made the successive points. 'Two persons in penthouse when murder committed. One is victim, other is Salti man. After murder only victim is visible. One door, windows and skylight are only exits and they are all secured on inside. Cannot be secured from outside. Therefore, Salti man still in penthouse when you enter.'

'But he wasn't there when we entered. The place was thoroughly searched. I was there then myself.'

'Maybe trap-door. Maybe space under floor or entrance to floor below.'

'Yes,' said Tarrant, 'well, now get this. There are no trap-doors in the flooring of the penthouse, there are none in the walls and there are not even any in the roof. I have satisfied myself of that with Peake. Gleeb, the manager, who was on the spot when the penthouse was built, further assures me of it.'

'Only place is floor,' Katoh insisted. 'Salti man could make this himself.'

'He couldn't make a trap-door without leaving at least a minute crack,' was Tarrant's counter. 'At least I don't see how he could. The flooring of the studio is hardwood, the planks closely fitted together, and I have been over every inch of it. Naturally there are cracks between the planks, lengthwise; but there are no transverse cracks anywhere. Gleeb has shown me the specifications of that floor. The planks are grooved together and it is impossible to raise any plank without splintering the grooving. From my own examination I am sure none of the planks has been, or can be, lifted.

'All this was necessary because there *is* a space of something like two and a half feet between the floor of the penthouse and the roof of the apartment building proper. One has to mount a couple of steps at the entrance of the penthouse. Furthermore, I have been in part of this space. Let me make it perfectly clear how I got there.

'The bedroom adjoins the studio on the south, and the lavatory occupies the north-west corner of the bedroom. It is walled off, of course. Along the northern wall of the lavatory (which is part of the southern wall of the studio) is the bath-tub; and the part of the flooring under the bath-tub has been cut away, leaving an aperture to the space beneath.'

I made my first contribution. 'But how can that be? Wouldn't the bath-tub fall through?'

'No. The bath-tub is an old-fashioned one, installed by Salti himself only a few weeks ago. It is not flush with the floor, as they make them now, but stands on four legs.

The flooring has only been cut away in the middle of the tub, say two or three planks, and the opening extended only to the outer edge of the tub. Not quite that far, in fact.'

'There is Salti man's trap-door,' grinned Katoh. 'Not even door; just trap.'

'So I thought,' Tarrant agreed grimly. 'But it isn't. Or if it is he didn't use it. As no one could get through the opening without moving the tub—which hadn't been done, by the way—Peake and I pulled up some more of the cut plank by main force and I squeezed myself into the space beneath the lavatory and bedroom. There was nothing there but dirt; I got plenty of that.'

'How about space below studio?'

'Nothing doing. The penthouse is built on a foundation, as I said, about two and a half feet high, of concrete building blocks. A line of these blocks runs underneath the penthouse, directly below the wall between the studio and bedroom. As the aperture in the floor is on the southern side of that wall, it is likewise to the south of the transverse line of building blocks in the foundation. The space beneath the studio is to the north of these blocks, and they form a solid wall that is impassable. I spent a good twenty minutes scrummaging along the entire length of it.'

'Most likely place,' Katoh confided, 'just where hole in lavatory floor.'

'Yes, I should think so too. I examined it carefully. I could see the ends of the planks that form the studio floor partway over the beam above the building blocks. But there isn't a trace of a loose block at that point, any more than there is anywhere else. . . . To make everything certain, we also examined the other three sides of the foundation of the bedroom portion of the penthouse. They are solid and haven't been touched since it was constructed. So the whole thing is just a cul-de-sac; there is no possibility of exit from the penthouse even through the aperture beneath the bath-tub.'

'You examine also foundations under studio part?'

'Yes, we did that, too. No result. It didn't mean much, though, for there is no entrance to the space beneath the studio from the studio itself, nor is there such an entrance from the other space beneath the bedroom portion.

That opening under the bath-tub must mean something, especially in view of the recent installation of the tub. But what does it mean?'

He looked at Katoh long and searchingly and the other, after a pause, replied slowly: 'Can only see this. Salti man construct this trap, probably for present use. Then he do not use. Must go some other way.'

'But there *is* no other way.'

'Then Salti man still there.'

'He isn't there.'

'Harumph,' said Katoh reflectively. It was evident that he felt the same respect for a syllogism that animated Tarrant, and was stopped, for the time being at any rate. He went off on a new tack. 'What else specially strange about setting?'

'There are two other things that strike me as peculiar,' Tarrant answered, and his eyes narrowed. 'On the floor, about one foot from the northern window, there is a fairly deep indentation in the floor of the studio. It is a small impression and is almost certainly made by a nail partly driven through the planking and then pulled up again.'

I thought of the nail through the picture. 'Could he have put the picture down on that part of the floor in order to drive the nail through it? But what if he did?'

'I can see no necessity for it, in any case. The nail would go through the canvas easily enough just as it stood on the easel.'

Katoh said: 'With nail in plank, perhaps plank could be pulled up. You say no?'

'I tried it. Even driving the nail in sideways, instead of vertically, as the original indentation was made, the plank can't be lifted at all.'

'O.K. You say some other thing strange, also.'

'Yes. The position of the easel that holds the painting of the dead girl. When we broke in this morning, it was turned away from the room, toward the bedroom door, so that the picture was scarcely visible even from the studio entrance, let alone the rest of the room. I don't believe that was the murderer's intention. He had set the rest of the stage too carefully. The requiem; the candles. It doesn't fit; I'm sure he meant the first person who entered to be confronted by the whole scene, and especially by that symbolic portrait. It doesn't accord even with the position of the stool, which agrees with the intended position of the easel. It doesn't fit at all with the mentality of the murderer. It seems a small thing but I 'm sure it 's important. I 'm certain the position of the easel is an important clue.'

'To mystery of disappearance?'

'Yes. To the mystery of the murderer's escape from that sealed room.'

'Not see how,' Katoh declared after some thought. As for me, I couldn't even appreciate the suggestion of any connection.

'Neither do I,' grated Tarrant. He had risen and began to pace the floor. 'Well, there you have it all. A little hole in the floor near the north window, an easel turned out of position and a sealed room without an occupant who certainly ought to be there. . . . There 's an answer to this; damn it, there must be an answer.'

Suddenly he glanced at an electric clock on the table he was passing and stopped abruptly. 'My word,' he exclaimed, 'it 's nearly three o'clock. Didn't mean to keep you up like this, Jerry. You either, doctor. Well, the conference is over. We 've got nowhere.'

Katoh was on his feet, in an instant once more the butler. 'Sorry could not help. You wish night-cap, Mister Tarrant?'

'No. Bring the Scotch, Katoh. And a siphon. And ice. I 'm not turning in.'

I had been puzzling my wits without intermission ever since dinner over the problem above, and the break found me more tired than I realized. I yawned prodigiously. I made a half-hearted attempt to persuade Tarrant to come to bed, but it was plain that he would have none of it.

I said, 'Good night, Katoh. I 'm no good for anything until I get a little sleep. . . .' Night, Tarrant.'

I left him once more pacing the floor; his face, in the last glimpse I had of it, was set in the stern lines of thought.

It seemed no more than ten seconds after I got into bed that I felt my shoulder being shaken and, through the fog of sleep, heard Katoh's hissing accents. '——Misster Tarrant just come from penthouse. He excited. Maybe you wish wake up.' As I rolled out and shook myself free from slumber, I noticed that my wrist watch pointed to six-thirty.

When I had thrown on some clothes and come into the living-room, I found Tarrant standing with the telephone instrument to his head, his whole posture one of grimness. Although I did not realize it at once, he had been endeavouring for some time to reach Deputy Inspector Peake. He accomplished this finally a moment or so after I reached the room.

'Hallo, Peake? Inspector Peake? This is Tarrant. How many men did you leave to guard that penthouse last night ? . . . What, only one ? But I said two, man. Damn it all, I don't make suggestions like that for amusement! . . . All right, there 's nothing to be accomplished arguing about it. You 'd better get here, and get here pronto. . . . That 's *all* I 'll say.' He slammed down the receiver viciously.

I had never before seen Tarrant upset; my surprise was a measure of his own disturbance, which resembled consternation. He paced the floor, muttering below his breath, his long legs carrying him swiftly up and down the apartment. . . . 'Damned fools . . . everything must fit. . . . Or else . . .' For once I had sense enough to keep my questions to myself for the time being.

Fortunately I had not long to wait. Hardly had Katoh had opportunity to brew some coffee, with which he appeared somewhat in the manner of a dog wagging its tail deprecatingly, than Peake's ring sounded at the entrance. He came in hurriedly, but his smile, as well as his words, indicated his opinion that he had been roused by a false alarm.

'Well, well, Mr. Tarrant, what *is* this trouble over?'

Tarrant snapped: 'Your man 's gone. Disappeared. How do you like that?'

'The patrolman on guard?' The policeman's expression was incredulous.

'The *single* patrolman you left on guard.'

Peake stepped over to the telephone, called headquarters.

After a few brief words he turned back to us, his incredulity at Tarrant's statement apparently confirmed.

'You must be mistaken, sir,' he asserted. 'There have been no reports from Officer Weber. He would never leave the premises without reporting such an occasion.'

Tarrant's answer was purely practical. 'Come and see.'

And when we reached the terrace on the building's roof, there was, in fact, no sign of the patrolman who should have been at his station. We entered the penthouse and, the lights having been turned on, Peake himself made a complete search of the premises. While Tarrant watched the proceedings in a grim silence, I walked over to the north window of the studio, grey in the early morning light, and sought for the nail hole he had mentioned as being in the floor. There it was, a small clean indentation, about an inch or an inch and a half deep, in one of the hardwood planks. This, and everything else about the place, appeared just as Tarrant had described it to us some hours before, previous to my turning in. I was just in time to see Peake emerge from the enlarged opening in the lavatory floor, dusty and sorely puzzled.

'Our man is certainly not here,' the inspector acknowledged. 'I cannot understand it. This is a serious breach of discipline.'

'Hell,' said Tarrant sharply, speaking for the first time since we had come to the roof. 'This is a serious breach of intelligence, not discipline.'

'I shall broadcast an immediate order for the detention of Patrolman Weber.' Peake stepped into the bedroom and approached the phone to carry out his intention.

'You needn't broadcast it. I have already spoken to the night operator in the lobby on the ground floor. He told me a policeman left the building in great haste about 3.30 this morning. If you will have the local precinct check up on the all-night lunch-rooms along Lexington Avenue in this vicinity, you will soon pick up the first step of the trail that man left. . . . You will probably take my advice, now that it is too late.'

Peake did so, putting the call through at once; but his bewilderment was no whit lessened. Nor was mine. As he put down the instrument, he said: 'All right. But it doesn't make sense.   Why should he leave his post without notifying us?   And why should he go to a lunch-room?'

'Because he was hungry.'

'But there has been a crazy murderer here already.   And now Weber, an ordinary cop, if ever I saw one.   Does this place make everybody mad?'

'Not as mad as you 're going to be in a minute.   But perhaps you weren't using the word in that sense?'

Peake let it pass.   'Everything,' he commented slowly, 'is just as we left it yesterday evening.   Except for Weber's disappearance.'

'Is that so?' Tarrant led us to the entrance from the roof to the studio and pointed downwards.   The light was now bright enough to disclose an unmistakable spattering of blood on one of the steps before the door.   'That blood wasn't there when we left last night. I came up here about five-thirty, the moment I got on to this thing,' he continued bitterly.   'Of course I was too late. . . . Damnation, let us make an end to this farce.   I 'll show you some more things that have altered during the night.'

We followed him into the studio again as he strode over to the easel with its lewd picture, opposite the entrance. He pointed to the nail still protruding through the canvas. 'I don't know how closely you observed the hole made in this painting by the nail yesterday.   But it 's a little larger now and the edges are more frayed.   In other words the nail has been removed and once more inserted.'

I turned about to find that Gleeb, somehow apprised of the excitement, had entered the penthouse and now stood a little behind us.   Tarrant acknowledged his presence with a curt nod; and in the air of tension that his tenant was building up the manager ventured no questions.

'Now,' Tarrant continued, pointing out the locations as he spoke, 'possibly they have dried, but when I first got here this morning there was a trail of moist spots still leading from the entrance door-way to the vicinity of the north window.   You will find that they were places where a trail of blood had been wiped away with a wet cloth.'

He turned to the picture beside him and withdrew the nail, pulling himself up as if for a repugnant job.   He walked over to the north window and motioned us to take our places on either side of him. Then he bent down and inserted the nail, point first, into the indentation in the plank, as firmly as he could. He braced himself and apparently strove to pull the nail towards the south, away from the window.

I was struggling with an obvious doubt. I said: 'But you told us the planks could not be lifted.'

'Can't,' Tarrant grunted. 'But they can be *slid*.'

Under his efforts the plank was, in fact, sliding. Its end appeared from under the footboard at the base of the north wall below the window and continued to move over a space of several feet. When this had been accomplished, he grasped the edges of the planks on both sides of the one already moved and slid them back also. An opening quite large enough to squeeze through was revealed.

But that was not all. The huddled body of a man lay just beneath; the man was clad only in underwear and was obviously dead from the beating in of his head.

As we bent over, gasping at the unexpectedly gory sight, Gleeb suddenly cried: 'But that is not Michael Salti! What is this, a murder farm? I don't know this man.'

Inspector Peake's voice was ominous with anger. 'I do. That is the body of Officer Weber. But how could he——'

Tarrant had straightened up and was regarding us with a look that said plainly he was anxious to get an unpleasant piece of work finished. 'It was simple enough,' he ground out. 'Salti cut out the planks beneath the bath-tub in the lavatory so that *these* planks in the studio could be slid back over the beam along the foundation under the south wall; their farther ends in this position will now be covering the hole in the lavatory floor. The floor here is well fitted and the planks are grooved, thus making the sliding possible. They can be moved back into their original position by someone in the space below here; doubtless we shall find a small block nailed to the under portion of all three planks for that purpose.

'He murdered his model, set the scene and started his phonograph, which will run interminably on the electric current. Then he crawled into his hiding-place. The discovery of the crime could not be put off any later than the chambermaid's visit in the morning, and I have no doubt he took a sadistic pleasure in anticipating her hysterics when she entered. By chance your radio man, Gleeb, caused us to enter first.

'When the place was searched and the murderer not discovered, his pursuit passed elsewhere, while he himself lay concealed here all day. It was even better than doubling back upon his tracks, for he had never left the starting post. Eventually, of course, he had to get out, but by that time the vicinity of this building would be the last place in which he was being searched for.

'Early this morning he pushed back the planks from underneath and came forth. I don't know whether he had expected any one to be left on guard, but that helped rather than hindered him. Creeping up upon the unsuspecting guard, he knocked him out—doubtless with that mallet I can just see beside the body—and beat him to death. Then he put his second victim in the hiding-place, returning the instrument that closes it from above, the nail, to its position in the painting. He had already stripped off his own clothes, which you will find down in that hole, and in the officer's uniform and coat he found no difficult in leaving the building. His first action was to hurry to a lunch-room, naturally, since after a day and a night without food under the floor here, he must have been famished. I have no doubt that your men will get a report of him along Lexington Avenue, Peake; but, even so, he now has some hours' start on you.'

'We 'll get him,' Peake assured us. 'But if you knew all this, why in Heaven's name didn't you have this place opened up last night, before he had any chance to commit a second murder? We should have taken him red-handed.'

'Yes, but I didn't know it last night,' Tarrant reminded him. 'It was not until late yesterday afternoon that I had any proper opportunity to examine the penthouse. What I found was a sealed room and a sealed house. There was no exit that had not been blocked nor, after our search, could I understand how the man could still be in the penthouse. On the other hand, I could not understand how it was possible that he had left. As a precaution, in case he were still here in some manner I had not fathomed, I urged you to leave at least two men on guard, and it was my understanding that you agreed. I think it obvious, although I was unable then to justify myself, that the precaution was called for.'

Peake said: 'It was.'

'I have been up all night working this out. What puzzled me completely was the absence of any trap-doors. Certainly we looked for them thoroughly. But it was there right in front of us all the time; we even investigated a portion of it, the aperture in the lavatory floor, which we supposed to be a trap-door itself, although actually it was only a part of the real arrangement. As usual the trick was based upon taking advantage of habits of thought, of our habitized notion of a trap-door as something that is lifted or swung back. I have never heard before of a trap-door that slides back. Nevertheless, that was the simple answer, and it took me until five-thirty to reach it.'

Katoh, whom for the moment I had forgotten completely, stirred uneasily and spoke up. 'I not see, Mister Tarrant, how you reach answer then.'

'Four things,' was the reply. 'First of all, the logical assumption that, since there was no way out, the man was still here. As to the mechanism by which he managed to remain undiscovered, three things. We mentioned them last night. First, the nail hole in the plank; second, the position of the easel; third, the hole in the lavatory floor. I tried many ways to make them fit together, for I felt sure they must *all* fit.

'It was the position of the easel that finally gave me the truth. You remember we agreed that it was wrong, that murderer had never intended to leave it facing away from the room. But if the murderer had left it as he intended, if no one had entered until we did, and still its position was wrong, what could have moved it in the meantime? Except for the phonograph, which could scarcely be responsible, the room held nothing but motionless objects. *But if the floor under one of its legs had moved, the easel would have been slid around.* That fitted with the other two items, the nail hole in the plank, the opening under the bath-tub.

'The moment it clicked, I got an automatic and ran up here. I was too late. As I said, I've been up all night. I'm tired; and I'm going to bed.'

He walked off without another word, scarcely with a parting nod. Tarrant, as I know now, did not often fail. He was a man who offered few excuses for himself, and he was humiliated.

It was a week or so later when I had an opportunity to ask him if Salti had been captured. I had seen nothing of it in the newspapers, and the case had now passed to the back pages with the usual celerity of sensations.

Tarrant said: 'I don't know.'

'But haven't you followed it up with that man, Peake?'

'I'm not interested. It's nothing but a straight police chase now. This part of it might make a good film for a Hollywood audience, but there isn't the slightest intellectual interest left.'

He stopped and added after an appreciable pause: 'Damn it, Jerry, I don't like to think of it even now. I've blamed the stupidity of the police all I can; their throwing me out when I might have made a real investigation in the morning, that delay; then the negligence in overlooking my suggestion for a pair of guards, which I made as emphatic as I could. But it's no use. I should have solved it in time, even so. There could only be that one answer and I took too long to find it.

'The human brain works too slowly, Jerry, even when it works straight. . . . It works too slowly.'